The characters and events portrayed in this book are fictitious. Any similarity to real persons, living or dead, is coincidental and not intended by the author.

Printed in the United States of America.

Published by Thomas & Mercer, Seattle

www.apub.com

ISBN-13: 9781612181950
ISBN-10: 1612181953
LCCN: 2013906098

THE BARKEEP

A Novel of Zenspense

WILLIAM LASHNER

ALSO BY WILLIAM LASHNER

The Accounting
Blood and Bone

THE VICTOR CARL NOVELS:

A Killer's Kiss
Marked Man
Falls the Shadow
Past Due
Fatal Flaw
Bitter Truth (Veritas)
Hostile Witness

WRITING AS TYLER KNOX:

Kockroach

For My Big Brother Bret

IF YOU WANT A DOG TO STOP KISSING YOU,
turn your head away silently
like another dog.

—Jack Kerouac
Some of the Dharma

1.

MOJITO

The old man climbed onto a stool and knuckled the wood to snag the barkeep's attention.

From behind the bar, the bartender nodded his head in acknowledgment. Just then he was in the middle of something because, even at the slowest of times, the barkeep made sure he was in the middle of something. No one wants a bartender looming over the bar, daring you to interrupt his leisure. No one wants a bartender lurching into action to pour you a drink. The barkeep was always busy enough so that when he took your order it felt like a favor. But not a favor from a friend, because this bartender was never your friend. If you wanted a friend, you bought a pet fish; you bellied up to his bar for a drink.

"A Mojito, doctor, if you please," said the old man in a voice ripened by unspeakable vice, "but only if you know how to whip one up with a little pizzazz."

It was a bit of a dig, but the barkeep didn't take it personally. He was twenty-nine years old, thin and hard and handsome as a blade, and he didn't take anything personally. He gave the old man the same look he gave the regulars and the first-timers, the cops and the politicians, the prostitutes and the corporate lawyers who rented the prostitutes by the hour, the same look that he would give to you if you took a seat across from him. He looked at the old man levelly but not intently—a bartender never probes beneath the surface—and he smiled as if he approved not only of the old man's drink choice but of his life choices, of everything that led him to this one moment, where he stepped into this bar and ordered this drink. The whole expression was as crucial a part of the job as a Boston shaker. But truth was, the barkeep never cared what you were drinking, or where you came from, or the evils that were plaguing your soul. And he knew his Mojito rocked, so he didn't need your approval either. You were a customer, that's all there was to it, and behind the bar he existed solely to mix you a drink.

The Mojito man was lean and weathered and sickly pale. His shave wasn't close enough, his greased white hair was a little yellow and a little long. He had one of those raw faces that bespoke long hard years on the road, and too-bright teeth too big for his mouth that bespoke a cheap set of dentures. There was something about him that the barkeep didn't like on the spot, some arrogant sense of his own damn self that pushed at the barkeep's buttons in a way no one had in years. But the barkeep recognized his dislike as weakness and took a moment to let it pour out of him. You know the voice that's always barking, the one in your head that goes on and on and never shuts the hell up? For the past few years the barkeep had been training himself to turn off that voice like one turns off a spigot.

"You look like you're doing all right," said the old man.

"I've done this before."

"That's not what I meant."

The barkeep was in the middle of preparing the old man's drink, so he didn't quite catch the full drift of the comment. He took his craft seriously, selecting the brightest mint leaves from the batch he had picked fresh that afternoon, pouring a precise measurement of the simple syrup he had prepped in the kitchen at the start of his shift. He brought to the mixing of a drink all the tranquility and generosity of a formal tea ceremony. He was in the process of gently muddling the leaves into the syrup right in the highball glass, concentrating on the gentle part because anything more and the mint ripped apart, leaving the drink with the general consistency of pond scum.

"You look like you're doing okay for yourself, I mean," said the old man. "Like things, they worked out all for the best."

"I love my job." That was the extent of what the barkeep ever said about himself to a customer. "How you doing tonight?" said the regulars at Zenzibar when they climbed onto their stools and asked for their usual drinks. "I love my job," he'd say.

"That's a good thing, to love your work," said the old man. "I loved my work, too. It was a hard job, harder than you can imagine. It took more out of me than I even knew I had. But it was what I did, what I was. Excepting it's pretty much over."

The barkeep sliced a lime in half, squeezed the juice from each half into a jigger, dropped one of the emptied hulls into the glass along with a shot of the juice.

"I guess you could say I'm retired now," said the old man. "Didn't have no choice about it. My health couldn't keep up with the demands of the profession. And then my health, bad as it was, it took a turn for the worse. There's not much left of me anymore but the sickness. My last kidney is shot, my liver, my throat riddled with something. That's why I'm on this little tour."

The old man wanted to talk, needed to talk. The barkeep didn't want to listen, but as he measured in two shots of white rum, he affected a mild interest. That was part of the job, to pretend to listen, to feign concern. There are three professions who play at that game; barkeeps are the ones who do it on their feet.

"You ever hear of a fellow named Walter J. Freeman," said the old man, "a doctor of sorts?"

"No, never did," said the barkeep as he opened a bottle of sparkling water and poured it into the glass. He used San Pellegrino in his Mojitos because the bubbles were so fine they gave the drink an admirable tightness. He filled the glass to the top with crushed ice and stirred with a straw.

"Quite an interesting man. He invented an operation that scrambled the front part of the brain like an egg. Lobotomy, he called it. He'd go right through the bone above the eyeballs to do it, with nothing more than a hammer and an ice pick. The man performed thousands of the operations all over the country. Claimed his lobotomy calmed the mind and aided digestion. Dr. Walter J. Freeman."

When the drink was chilled and the glass frosty, the barkeep twisted off a sprig of mint, smacked it between his palms to activate the scent, and dropped it on top of the drink. He placed the glass atop a coaster and slid it before the old man. The old man looked at the drink as if it were a lover slipping her legs beneath his sheets. He rolled up his sleeves, lifted the glass, closed his eyes and pursed his lips daintily as he took a sip. His eyelids fluttered with pleasure.

"That works, boy," he said. "That's just jimmy. Simple and pure. I feel like I'm back in that whorehouse in Cuba where I tasted my first."

"Twelve fifty," said the barkeep.

"That's damn stiff for a drink."

"It's a stiff drink."

"You mind if I run a tab, doctor?"

The barkeep glanced over at Marson, sitting like a sentry at the other end of the bar, before sizing up the chances of the old man being a runner. Marson would take it out of the barkeep's check if the bill went unpaid. On the old man's newly bared forearms were two matching tattoos, monochromatically blue but intricately wrought. On the left forearm was the head of Jesus; on the right forearm was the head of the Devil. Both were staring up at the barkeep.

"Suit yourself," he said. He set up the tab as the customer rambled on.

"So this lobotomy doctor, this Dr. Freeman, late in life he was cast out by all them fancy-pants doctors who claimed his operation did more harm than good, which is always the way of it. And so Dr. Freeman, he drove all over the country, visiting his old patients, trying to see for himself how it all turned out. Sort of a farewell tour. And to him, his handiwork looked pretty damn sweet. Gave him a bit of satisfaction as the end approached."

"I suppose it would."

It was still quiet at the bar, early afternoon, before the happy-hour crowd arrived with their after-work bonhomie, and even as the barkeep kept himself busy wiping bottles and slicing limes, he had no choice but to nod and listen. He liked it busy at the bar, he liked it when the crowd was three deep and the calls for drinks came from all sides like a rising tide of feverish chants, when there wasn't time to take in the stories and the gripes and he was able to lose himself in the work. That was the quest in everything he did: the work, the meditation, the exercise, the sex. To lose himself. And as the barkeep would be the first to tell you, it was not without reason.

"That's what I'm doing now," said the old man. "That's why I'm here. I'm taking my farewell tour. Before the sickness closes me down for good. To see how things, they worked out, to see the results of my handiwork." He picked up what was left of his drink, examined it as if he were appraising an uncut diamond. "And from where I'm sitting now, things look like they didn't work out half-bad."

The barkeep stared while the old man guzzled the rest of his drink. Truth is, a bartender is only ever a sounding board. You don't care about his opinion when you are spilling your guts, and why should you? But the barkeep still would stand there like he cared, nodding now and then, never reacting with more than a casual raise of the eyebrow. And you would see in his affect what you wanted to see in his affect rather than the truth, that he didn't give a damn. But there was something about this old man and the buttons he pushed that seemed to make what he was saying personal to the barkeep. The barkeep watched as the old man greedily drank the dregs of his drink, like a vampire trying to suck every last ounce from a pale stretch of neck.

"The name's Grackle," said the old man after he thumped down his glass. "Birdie Grackle."

"Birdie?"

"You know Gene Vincent?"

"'Bird Doggin'.'"

"There you go. Not so dumb as you look. I'd be hunting still if anything worked. But now it all just sets there like an old hound sleeping 'neath a cottonwood in the midday heat."

"Another Mojito, Birdie?"

"Not at those prices," he said, trying to laugh but ending up with a sputtering cough that turned his raw face red and brought tears to his eyes. "Why don't you pour me up a gut puncher, just for the kick of it?"

The barkeep turned and grabbed a bottle of whiskey from the bottom shelf, something more suitable for stripping paint than drinking. As he poured, Birdie Grackle stared at the rising brown liquor as if it were some golden elixir that could transform body and soul.

"How much is that?" said Grackle.

"Four dollars."

"That's a crime."

"I'll put it on your tab."

"You do that," said Grackle, picking up the shot glass. "And put two more on while you're at it." He downed the shot with a snatch of his wrist, let out a small slurp as his mouth and throat absorbed the alcohol, and slammed the glass onto the bar. "Another one for me and one for you to boot."

"Thank you all the same," said the barkeep, "but I never drink with customers."

"Pour them both out, doctor. You'll do me the honor before we're through here."

"And why's that?" said the barkeep as he laid out a second shot glass next to the first and filled them both.

"Because, Justin boy, on this stop of my farewell tour, you're the old patient I came to see."

"You know my name."

"I know more than that, doctor." Grackle took hold of one of the glasses. "Here's to blood in your eye."

"What are we drinking to?"

"Your mother."

The barkeep stared at him for a long moment, took in the old man's alky eyes, his pale, ruined cheeks, the peculiarly self-satisfied twist of his lips. He glanced again at the tattoos of Jesus and the Devil on the old man's forearms and realized, with a start, that despite the differing hair and expressions, the features on each were the same, they were the old man's features, those of Birdie Grackle himself, both savior and Satan. The barkeep took the second glass of whiskey and downed it quickly, let the cheap rotgut burn his throat until something close to pain slipped out.

"Good for you," said the old man before he drank his own.

"You knew my mother?"

"Not really. I only met her that once."

"When was that, Birdie?"

Birdie Grackle sucked his dentures for a moment and then said, "The night I done killed her."

2.

FUZZY NAVEL

Justin was filled with the sudden urge to punch this Birdie Grackle in his filthy mouth. It came upon him so unexpectedly that he actually savored the bitter teeth-grinding pleasure of it. He didn't feel much these days—he worked hard not to feel much—and so it was almost a novelty, this bitter anger that soaked through his flesh and into his gut. But it was a disappointing failure too, and so he bit his lip and stifled the urge. The barkeep had learned to stifle most of his urges, which is what happens to sons who stumble upon their mothers' murdered bodies, or to bartenders when the customer is always right. Back to apparent calm, he stared evenly at Birdie Grackle, the rheumy eyes, the uneasy lips working hard to keep the dentures from falling onto the bar.

Justin figured the old man for a liar, and with good reason. First, Grackle had made his confession in a bar. Justin had learned long ago that looking for truth in a bar is like looking for sex in a convent, you might eventually find something worth all the trouble, but the search will be long and full of the deepest frustrations. And second, Justin knew enough about life to know that your mother's murderer didn't just happen to walk into your bar and introduce himself to you over a Mojito.

But Justin's emotional response to the old man and what he had said was so unusual that he felt compelled to explore it. It was like, liar or no, the old man was a test that Justin needed to pass.

Justin leaned forward and poured another shot into Birdie Grackle's glass. With an especially laconic voice he said, "Are you hungry, Birdie?"

"I must admit to being a mite bit peckish," said the old man.

"With all your infirmities, can you still chew yourself a prime piece of beef?"

Grackle's smile was revolting enough to force Justin to pull back. "So long as I cut them pieces small enough."

"Capital Grille on Broad Street, then. Let's say half past eight?"

"Let's say," said Birdie Grackle, "so long as you're treating."

"I wouldn't have it any other way," said Justin. "And forget about your tab here. I'll take care of that, too."

"That's mighty neighborly, considering," said Birdie. "And seeing as you're being so generous to an old man on death's door, what say we have usselves another Mojito."

Marson bitched about the change in plans, but Justin had become the beating heart of Zenzibar's evening trade, and so there wasn't much the boss could do about it. The on-call sub showed up at seven to take over Justin's shift, which left Justin enough time to prepare himself for another dose of Birdie Grackle, as pleasant a prospect as another dose of clap.

Justin Chase lived in a nineteenth-century "trinity" he rented on the cheap. The real estate agent, before she showed

Justin the little tiny town house, described it as cozy. What he discovered when he toured the place was that each of the three floors was about the size of a prison cell. But the agent needn't have worried her perfectly coiffed head of hair about it; Justin thought the place perfect. The first level now held a couch, a small dining table, and a galley kitchen. The second level was taken up by a futon on the floor, a bureau, and the bathroom. The third level was completely empty, the floor covered with light-green tatami mats Justin had picked up off Craigslist.

He showered on the second floor to get the stench of the bar off his skin and then, with his long dark hair loose about his shoulders and clad only in a blue silk robe, he slowly climbed the stairs. Without haste he took his position on one of the tatami mats.

A Zen master was once visited by an acclaimed scholar who intended to make a study of the master's religious practices. As they sat for the tea ceremony, the master poured tea into the scholar's cup until it overflowed and then kept on pouring. "Stop," said the scholar. "No more will go in." "Like this cup, you are full of your own opinions and emotions," said the master as he kept pouring. "How can I teach you anything until you first empty your cup?"

In the wake of his mother's murder six years before, Justin had zipped through the first three stages of grief—shock, denial and bargaining—got hung up a bit on the guilt and the anger, and then crashed headfirst into depression, where he moldered without relief, as if locked within a dark, damp cage. It was in the midst of this breakdown that he stumbled onto an answer for how to get out of his prison. He found it in a book, of all places, pressed upon him by the shaking hands of a fellow patient at the mental hospital where his brother had sent him. The volume was small, black, bound in frayed, moth-eaten cloth, old and musty, Eastern and mystical. The first time he opened it, he found it filled with the most ridiculous of gibberish. It fit his mood perfectly.

The book was a methodology for allowing his mind, as the text described, to rest undistractedly in the nothing-to-do, nothing-to-hold condition of the primordial void state. Easier said than done, and not so easily said. But Justin, at the time, intuitively saw in it a route out of his pain. Whatever horrors he faced in this world, whatever demons approached, the answer was not to flee in terror. Instead the book taught him to face the horror of the world with a calm courage. *Fear it not,* read the book. *Be not terrified. Be not awed. Know it to be the embodiment of thine own intellect.*

There was a rational side to our thinking, and there was an emotional side, and the book gave him a clue how to separate one from the other. He gave the book's methods a try and, shockingly, they seemed to work. He saw clearly the futility of trying to leave a mark on the shifting planes of reality, like trying to write his name in the foam of an ocean wave. He learned to discard his dreams of worldly success and let his entire existence float on the winds of chance. As he quieted his hopes, his emotions dimmed; as he made fewer and fewer choices, he became more and more content to let his life come to him. And slowly, from the words of the book and through his practice, he found for himself an equilibrium outside his pain. That was how he finally left the cage of his depression, and then left the institution, and then flitted across the surface of the country with the perfect mindlessness of a moth. That was how he ended in this house, in this life, that was how he became a barkeep.

But now that old bastard Birdie Grackle had done the one impermissible thing: he had threatened to breach the floodgates of Justin's emotions. Justin had no doubts where that would lead if he let it continue: with Justin lying curled on the floor, unable to stand, unable to breathe, unable to see anything but the darkness. That way led to the asylum. He had been there and back already, he wouldn't go again. But by hard experience Justin had learned how to deal with rogue emotions that pierced his placid surface. He sat cross-legged on the tatami mat, closed his eyes, evened out his breathing, and began to empty his cup.

Slowly and carefully, he called forth his emotions and let them rise within him. He didn't now try to stifle them or dim their force. Instead he thought of his mother and her lovely face. And he remembered lugging the great fusty bundle of his laundry, like the great burden of his youthful ambitions, along the dark path from the street to the large stone house with bold white pillars. And he remembered slipping on something and almost losing his balance, figuring it to be a smear of mud left over from the rain. And he remembered reaching the front door, which was slightly ajar. And the wedge of light that leaked out of the narrow opening. And the slick of red he could now see on the sole of his running shoe. And, even as the inkling that something was deadly wrong blossomed monstrous in his heart, the way he called out "Mom?" as he pushed the door open. "Mom?"

And as he remembered, he let the emotions flow, as if he were an urn being filled with a never-ending stream. They poured into him, dark and roiling, and he tasted each of them, the silvery bitterness, the shock and the hurt, the pain of betrayal, the despair, the fury, the sadness, such sadness, the sense of loss, the sense of being lost, loneliness, anger, fury, guilt. Yes, guilt. Despite his even breaths and quiet body, his heart raced as the emotions rose to choke him. They filled him with their trial and turmoil, and for a moment he had the panicky sensation that he was drowning.

He wanted to escape, to flee, to swim to the surface and cast everything aside, but he maintained his posture. The emotions kept rising, one pushing up the next, each pushing out the other. He became a deep pool of these dark and swirling emotions, the bottom unfathomable, the emotions themselves rising so quickly a stream fell out of one low edge of the pool and plunged down a craggy slope until emptying into some great sea. And each of these emotions, after they filled him with their power and pain, followed one after the other down that fall and away.

After a long period of turmoil, Justin's heart slowed, and the pool cleared, and he felt overcome with calm. A perfect stillness, a moment of absolute tranquility. It wasn't an easy place to get to, and he struggled to stay there once he found it, but it felt like home when he was there. And he was there now.

Have you ever seen the road shimmer before you on a hot summer's day, the way it looks more like a dream than a hard piece of reality? When Justin's mind was clean of cant and emotion, when both past and future fell away, the whole world shimmered like that for him.

Shimmered like the harmless illusion that it was. And what kind of barkeep would he be if he could be spooked by an illusion?

3.

SOMETHING HARD

There are two types of the mentally deficient in this world. The first type mistake their lack of understanding for bold perception. This type of deficiency is often found in urologists and presidential candidates and is as dangerous as the plague. The second type are acutely aware of their own limitations and embrace the narrow range of their capacities. Think of the idiot savant with a rare genius, who gives the world a great artistic gift that can be both stunning and transformative.

Derek belongs to this second class, being himself a bit of an idiot and a bit of a savant.

Derek knows all that he does not know. Plots and plans fly in the air about him, conspiracies flourish. He can sense the purposes and cross-purposes battling around him, but he is unable to appreciate their true import and so he has left off trying to understand. Schemes are hatched and thrive and die ugly deaths while Derek goes about his business blissfully unaware.

He lets Vern take care of the plotting now. He trusts Vern because he has no choice but to trust Vern. He cannot find the jobs, negotiate the fees, avoid the double cross, count the money. He knows how hard it is to keep the business end of things straight because Vern constantly tells him how hard it is to keep the business end of things straight. And after that job went sour with Tree, and Derek was left holding the bag in Harrisburg, he is grateful that Vern has stepped into the void. Vern counseled him on how to make his mark in prison so that everyone would leave him alone. Vern counseled him on how to play the parole board when his time was up. Vern counseled him on how to get back into the business. Vern stepped up when Derek needed someone to step up for him.

And so now he trusts Vern. As he had trusted Tree before Vern. And had trusted Rodney before Tree. And had trusted Sammy D before Rodney. They were the smart guys, they were the ones who understood the world. And that they all are dead, except for Vern, only reinforces Derek's satisfaction with his place in the world. Let the others scheme their way through life, using him as a tool; Derek just goes about his business. Coolly, efficiently, brutally. He might not be an artistic savant, but he is not without talents. And in their strange way, his abilities put a song in his heart.

It is still light when Derek slips along the alleyway to the back door of the Kensington row house north of Center City Philadelphia. He examines the lock, a simple Yale with a rusted cylinder, before taking the proper torque wrench and a half-diamond pick from the vinyl envelope he always keeps in his pocket. A lock like this Derek can scrub open as quick as a breath.

Sammy D taught Derek how to open locks. Sammy D knew everything about lock-picking, but by the time Derek was through with his lessons he was better at it than Sammy D. Rodney could do locks too, but he was a squirrelly little guy, always worried about who was coming up behind him or what was waiting for him inside or how long the job was taking or how much noise was being made. It was the powder that made him nervous. Sometimes Rodney, under pressure, would fail repeatedly, throwing all the timing out of whack. But Derek never has such problems. He trusts his handler to worry about everything else but the step-by-step of the job. So when he is working a lock, all he cares about is raising the pins and manipulating the cylinder. It is just him and the lock and after a moment—*click, plock, click*—the pins align as if on their own.

Once inside the row house, with the door closed behind him, Derek takes out his flashlight and begins to navigate his way. He knows he has enough time to get in position because Vern has told him he has enough time. The rear door opens into a basement filled with boxes and junk and smelling slightly of crap. A cockroach scurries away from the light, and Derek follows it with his beam until it slips beneath a sagging carton. Derek leans down and sees the slight antennae wave at him. He waves back.

Derek is fascinated with animals of all kinds—bugs, rabbits, muscular mastiffs—and they all seem just as fascinated with him. But of all the animals, Derek is most fascinated with horses. He loves their coats, their smell, the way they lift their front hooves, the way they feel between his legs when he rides them. And Vernon has promised Derek his own horse if all works out right. He has always wanted his own horse and has been promised one many times before, but as of yet he is still waiting. Derek is tired of waiting. Derek is going to hold Vern to that promise.

A set of rough wooden stairs climbs to a doorway that leads into a large eat-in kitchen, with bare counters, an old rusted stove, yellow linoleum flooring. Derek passes through the kitchen like a shadow, through an arched passageway to a dining alcove, and then to a living room with the front door on its far wall. A sagging sofa, an old television, a telephone set by a greasy green easy chair in the corner. The room smells of mold and body odor.

Derek walks over to the phone and picks up the handset. He dials the number Vern told him to dial. He has instructions for what to do if the phone is answered and what to do if it is not answered. There is no answer now, so he waits for the voice-mail message and then stays on the line, humming to keep it from shutting off. Vern told him to hum something, but Derek needed more specific instructions, so Vern told Derek to just hum his favorite song. Derek had to choose between "God Bless America" and "Mary Had a Little Lamb" and he worried about that decision for the longest time until he decided to sort of mix them together. When he is done humming, he hangs up the phone, sits in the green chair, and waits.

And here is another advantage of Derek's mental deficiency in his unique line of work. This could be a difficult moment, the waiting, when doubts start sprouting like weeds. Rodney could never bear these moments. He could not stop himself from nervously talking when they were in it together. Yap-yap-yammering about plans and angles and things that Derek never could follow. Rodney had never learned the trick that seems to come naturally to Derek. As the outside darkens into night, Derek's mind goes just as dark; in the quiet of the room, Derek's mind is just as quiet. His pulse remains low, his breathing even. And it stays that way, until he hears the scuffing at the front door.

When the front door finally opens, a man slouches in, shuts the door behind him, and flicks the light switch by the door. The room is bathed with a dull yellow from an overhead fixture, but the man is so preoccupied with emptying his pockets onto a side table and examining the contents, including a small packet with white powder inside, that it takes a moment for him to realize that someone else is in the room.

"What the hell—" says the man. He is old and skinny, wearing a pair of dirty jeans and a long-sleeved T-shirt. His shoulder-length gray hair is stringy with grease, his face is bathed in sweat, and he smells bad, as if he has not showered in weeks. When he opens his mouth, Derek can see a set of rotting teeth behind his thin, scabby lips.

"Are you Flynn?" says Derek. His voice is slow and deliberate, and every syllable is equally accented.

The old man examines Derek for a moment, and then a smile emerges. He is calmed by Derek's voice. Everyone seems to be calmed by Derek's voice. "Yeah," says the old man. "I'm Flynn. What, did Mac send you?"

"Who did you talk to?" says Derek, only asking what he has been instructed to ask.

"No one. Why?"

"The DA?"

"She called. No biggie. I just repeated what was in the thing I signed. She insisted that I come to the office to talk to her. I'm going tomorrow. If I had a choice, I'd say no. But, you know, I'm still on probation and so—"

"Who else did you talk to?"

"No one."

"The son?" says Derek.

"Frank? No, of course not. The son of a bitch almost killed me last time I saw him."

"And the other son?"

"Who, the kid? No, jeez, I told Mac I'd seen him in the street, but he passed me by like he didn't know me. I haven't talked to him since the whole thing happened." Flynn bounces his weight nervously from one leg to the other. "You tell Mac it's all clean. I knows I owe him. I was jammed up before, but this I can handle. Tell him he can count on me."

"Where were you?" says Derek.

"Out. Getting some provisions."

"Drugs?"

"Food and stuff."

"Drugs?"

"Okay, yeah, if you can call them that," says the old man with a derisive snort. "There's so much talcum in each bag, it would be more worthwhile to dust my dick with it than to put it in my arm. But it's tough staying here, waiting, like I'm supposed to, and I got this thing tomorrow. I just needed something to take the edge off, that's all. You tell Mac not to worry."

"I have something for you," says Derek. He rises from the chair, walks over to the table where the old man has dumped the contents from his pocket, and drops a small box on top of the pile.

It is covered with a bright-blue paper, a red ribbon wrapped around it and tied into a bow. It is pretty.

"What's that?" says the old man.

"A present," says Derek. He backs away and sits again in the chair.

Flynn looks at the box, raises his head to look at Derek in the corner, and turns his attention back to the box. He waits for a moment before attacking the box like a kid on Christmas morning with a real family to take care of him, sliding off the ribbon, ripping the paper, opening the lid. He pulls out a small plastic bag filled with a few large chunks of dark-red powder.

"What's this?" says Flynn.

"A present."

"From Mac? I don't understand."

"Go ahead."

Flynn opens the bag, takes a sniff. His eyes flutter.

"Go ahead," says Derek.

"Oh, I see. Something to keep me busy, to make sure I play my part and don't talk to anybody. I told you he doesn't have to worry, but you tell him I appreciate the gesture. You want a taste?"

Derek simply shakes his head. He tried heroin once, Derek has tried everything once, including sex, but like sex, heroin did not take. Derek does not need drug-fueled flights of fantasy or an escape from the hard truths of reality. Because Derek does not pretend to understand the hard truths of reality. He lives in the simplicity of the moment, and there is beauty there, even in this crumbling Kensington row house. So, content in the limitations of his own mind, he watches as the old man sits down on the couch by the table and makes his preparations.

Sammy D, Derek's first partner, was an addict. Derek watched Sammy D shoot up hundreds of times in the worst kinds of shooting galleries in Baltimore, watched Sammy D follow the step-by-step path to nowhere, with the spoon and the candle and the cotton and the needle. Sammy D was the first to promise Derek a horse, when Derek was just starting out in the business and Sammy was hustling for jobs. "Horse" was also what Sammy D called the powder he threw away their money on, and so Derek watched the horse slip needleful by needleful up Sammy's arm. When Sammy finally expired, all Derek could think was that if he had gotten the animal, they both would have been better off.

Now Flynn has the needle prepared. Derek watches as he rolls up his sleeve and ties the rubber strap around his biceps, grabbing it with his teeth. The old man flicks his forearm, like Sammy used to flick his forearm, and then sticks the needle in, drawing blood into the syringe before releasing the dark-brown fluid. The last thing Derek sees is a dreamy smile before the old man nods off.

Derek sits in the chair and waits for the old man to wake up. Vern told him what to do. Derek likes his instructions simple, and that is what these are. If the old man wakes up, Derek is supposed to slice his throat. But from the way the old man's breathing catches, stops, and starts again more weakly, Derek knows the old man is not going to wake up. The way Sammy D did not wake up when Derek prepared a second batch and gave it to him while he was still nodding off to the first. "What are you doing?" Sammy said dreamily as Derek gently pressed the plunger.

When the old man's breath catches for a second time and stops again, Derek does nothing. He sits and waits, and waits some more. When he is sure, he stands and goes over to the table, picking up the wrapping paper, the ribbon, the box, the plastic bag. He does not know why the old man had to die, does not know who wanted him dead, does not know how much Vern has been paid for the job.

All he knows is that he has done exactly what he was supposed to do. And that Vern better get him a horse.

4.

JOHNNIE WALKER RED

The Capital Grille was one of the big-bellied, flushed-faced steak joints that had taken over Broad Street. Old guys like Birdie Grackle fervently believed the height of living was a hunk of grilled cow, hold the veggies, which was why Justin had suggested the place. Steak as bait.

They were at a white-tableclothed table in the corner of the restaurant, set away from other diners at Justin's request. The porterhouse on Birdie's plate was the size of his head, and his dentures danced as he chewed. Between bites he slurped his Scotch like it was mother's milk. A few intrepid drops escaped his greasy maw and slid down the side of his stubbled chin. It was altogether a lovely sight, and Justin was paying for every disgusting inch of it. But Justin figured it was worth the price, because even as Grackle chewed with his mouth foully open, he was talking all the while.

"I like a good cut of meat now and then," said Birdie Grackle, grease glossing his lips. "Have you ever noticed how a fine piece of strip has the faint taste of pussy in it? Meaty and plump. That's why men eat steak. And why Marges all love their tuna fish, because ain't nothing faint about that. But you get a taste of something, it can be hard to get it out your mouth.

Like killing. What's that green gunk you're eating?"

"It's spinach," said Justin. "Creamed."

"You don't take to steak?"

"I don't eat meat anymore."

"What, are you a fruit?"

"No."

"Then you're like a veterinarian or something."

"Something like that, yes."

"Well, that's a cause of concern right there. I haven't met too many veterinarians that wasn't something wrong with they heads. So what is it, you trying to live forever? Or are you forgoing meat out of empathy with the cow? Because if that's it, I got to tell you from long experience that your basic cow is as dumb an animal as exists on this good earth."

"I work in a bar, so you'll be hard-pressed to convince me of that."

"You might have a point," said Grackle with a wink as he sliced off a slab of beef and held it in the air with his fork so that it dripped red onto his plate. "So tell me, doctor. What turned you off to one of the great pleasures in this life?"

"Let's just say when you come home and find your mother in the hallway, facedown on the floor, her head smashed open and her blood and urine pooling on the marble tile, the sight and the smell, it steals away your taste for meat."

Birdie Grackle looked at Justin for a moment, stared right into his eyes, and then, still staring, he shoved the bleeding piece of steak between his false teeth. "That might do it," he said as he chewed, "for some. But I never let the dead stop me from living. I learned that piece of wisdom in the war along with my technique."

"Technique? What kind of technique does it take to bash a defenseless woman in the head?"

"You don't want to go into the details, son, trust me."

"You're wrong, Birdie. Into the details is exactly where I want to go."

"Suit yourself."

Grackle picked his napkin off the table, wiped his greasy lips, laid the napkin neatly on his lap. Before Justin could react, Birdie's arms leaped at Justin with the quickness of two cobras. One hand grabbed hold of the right side of Justin's skull and pulled him close, the other stuck something sharp into the skin behind Justin's left earlobe.

"What the—"

"Right now I got an ice pick pointed at your brain stem. A quick punch and that will be all she wrote about your pathetic little story."

As the sharp tip of the pick pressed against his flesh, Justin felt no fear, just a placid stillness and the faint glimmerings of a strange and unreadable hope. "Is that what you claim you did to my mother?" he said calmly.

Grackle pressed the sharp thing deeper into Justin's flesh and then suddenly let go. Justin caught a glimpse of something dully metallic in the old man's right hand as his arms dropped beneath the table.

"It's just a technique of mine is all," said Grackle. "One of them. I learned me a bunch, all courtesy of Uncle Sam. But the most important was, it don't matter how many bullets you put in a fellow's chest, if you want him dead, you better ice-pick his brain. You want to order me another drink?"

Justin raised his arm for the waiter.

"I wasn't a young man when I found myself in the middle of the killing," said Birdie Grackle after the liquor came. "A judge in Odessa gave me a choice, prison or the army, and I chose wrong. But one night in the jungle, a fat-faced lieutenant asked me if I wanted to volunteer for some sort of counterinsurgency unit. He said I'd be sent to Saigon for training and then would work primarily behind our own lines. Fresh sheets at night, hot and cold running bar girls, a chance to shack with a piece of hooch. Counterinsurgency? Count me in. But I'll tell you this, in a lot of ways it was more than I bargained for."

"What were you, in an intelligence unit?"

"Don't be a fool. I ain't exactly dumb, but no one in his right mind woulda hired me for something to do with intelligence. No, we was only about elimination. We'd get our orders, go out and take care of it. Small villages within our sector, spies working in Saigon itself. When we showed up, they all shit because we never left nothing breathing behind, not even the pigs, that was our way. It was hard at first, coming to grips with what we was doing, but I managed, and it sure as hell beat crawling through the jungles at night, pissing my pants in fear. It's funny what kind of hell you can get used to. And the things I learned, boy, you couldn't get them things on your own in a hundred years. When I came back, what I fell into just seemed like a continuation of my war. I was in a slaughterhouse in Texas for a bit, killing those dumb pieces of beef with a bolt gun at that same spot in the head I showed you, pulling out the stinking stomachs full of acid. And then I got an opportunity to raise it up a notch."

"By becoming a contract killer, Birdie? Is that what you're saying?"

"I was what I was, is all. Was a man named Preacher who gave me my running orders. Never knew who was running him and never cared. He gave me a name, an address, any sundry instructions for the job, and a do-by date. That was all I needed. It doesn't take long to shadow a name enough to figure all the angles, as long as you know how to finish it off."

"And you were hired to kill my mother."

"It wasn't much of a job, truth be told. She was too nice a lady to make it hard. I put on a brown uniform, told her through the door I had a package to deliver. At one point she turned her back to me, and that was it."

"Who hired you?"

"That's the question, isn't it? But Preacher, he never told me that. Ever. It was just a name, an address, special instructions and a do-by date."

"That's a hell of a story."

"You don't believe me," said Grackle. "I can tell. But it don't much matter either way. Was a whore in Lubbock named Stella who used to scream out like a gut-shot bear in the middle of the action. I never believed a bit of it, but it still felt good. You'll carry this with you a long time. And I want you to know, I did a clean job before I messed it up for them police. Your momma, she didn't feel nothing. She went peaceful as a piece of veal."

"Fuck you," blurted out Justin, surprising himself at the vehemence of his words.

"Maybe, yeah. But in time you'll be thanking me. It just needs some curing is all."

Justin stared for a moment and tried to gauge his own emotions. They were pretty damn raw, as raw as if he actually were face-to-face with his mother's killer. Something in the old man was drawing the worst out of Justin, had been drawing it out from the first, and he couldn't quite figure out what. It was more than just his false claim about Justin's mother, it was something in the old man's smell, maybe, or in the old man's very being. Justin took a moment to let his emotions rise within him, rise and burn and wash through him until he was left with nothing but the placid stillness.

"Okay," said Justin. "I think I've heard enough of your story, and seen you chew enough burnt muscle to keep me nauseous for a week. So what is it you want here, Birdie? What's your angle?"

"No angle. This is my farewell tour, like I said. A chance to offer a confession and to ease my soul. An opportunity to meet face-to-face the son of one of my victims and see that my life hasn't been all that ruinous. And a chance, maybe, to make some sort of amends."

Justin stared at the old man, saw the devious glint in his wet eyes, tried to fight a smile and lost.

"Amends?"

"Well, most of my jobs you could see the reason behind. Miserable sons of bitches, fat slobs and corporate types. You know, nothing to get all misty about. I even laughed when I drowned a banker in his own marble tub. But your momma, that was something different. Couldn't see no reason why she got what she got. And she was nice enough to let me use her bathroom."

"You crapped in our bathroom?"

"I pinched a loaf there, yes I did. A two-flusher for sure. That was why I always felt a bit bad about that job there."

"You have a kind and gentle heart."

"So I thought, maybe, as a final gesture, I'd do one more piece of work, just for your mom. I'd take care of whoever it was what set her up in the first place."

"But you don't know who it is. You said so yourself."

"Well, maybe I have myself some clues."

"Maybe I do too," said Justin. "And since the killer is already in jail for the rest of his miserable life, maybe I don't need your amends."

"If he's the right one."

There was something in Birdie Grackle's smile that hooked Justin's gaze like a barb hooking skin. "Oh, he's the right one, all right."

"Don't be so sure," said Birdie. "'Cause Preacher, when he hired me, he let slip with something that says he ain't."

"And you can't wait to tell me."

"For a price."

And in that moment a knot in Justin's gut loosened. He wasn't facing the fiend who had murdered his mother. All he was facing was a pathetic old man lying through his false teeth. He had figured the old man was lying about the killing from the start, but Justin couldn't quite figure out why. All the lies ever told in a bar could be distilled into three: I'm not a drunk; I'm not trying to pick your pocket; I'm not looking for meaningless impersonal sex. Justin already knew the old man was a stew, and he hoped to God he wasn't after sex. Which left Birdie Grackle trying to pick Justin's pocket, and Justin was curious as hell as to how the old man intended to use his mother's murder to do that. Maybe he had done it already, what with the drinks and the meal, but Justin sensed someone like Birdie was after more than a meal. And now here it came.

"You want me to hire you to tell me who hired you to kill my mom."

"That's part of it."

"And the other part?"

"To take care of it, like I said."

"By take care of it you mean..."

"That's right."

"And how much will this cost me?"

"Being as I'm half-dead and feeling sentimental, I'm going to give you a discount. Ten thousand flat, plus expenses."

"Up front?"

"Half now, half on completion."

"That all?"

"A bargain."

"I mean you did all this, learned all you had to learn, sought me out for a mere five thousand dollars. It hardly seems worth it, Birdie."

"Ten thousand."

"Let's just talk about the half you want now."

"Even half ain't no chicken feed."

"But still."

"Well, you know, it's more the spirit of the thing than the money."

And that's when Justin burst out laughing. This whole hit-man act, played by a soused Texas con man with an old-time baseball name, was comical enough. But then to top it off with his self-satisfied mien as he tried to pawn off his moneygrubbing as charity was just too damn rich. The whole show had been worth the price of dinner, and Justin was almost sorry to have to piss on the old man's well-laid plans.

"What's so funny?" said Grackle.

"You, Birdie. You've worked this up pretty well, I must say, this whole I-killed-your-momma thing. You've been digging through the old newspaper accounts, no doubt. But there were a couple of parts you didn't think out. First, I don't want to kill anyone."

"Even the person who killed your mom?"

"Based on what you said, that would be you."

"I'm just the instrument, like a gun. And you know what they say about guns."

"Whatever you might be, I'm not a killer. It's hard enough to live with myself as it is. The karma would be all wrong. And besides, I don't have any money. I don't sling drinks for my health. End of the month I'm strapped like everyone else. There's nothing to tap, here, Birdie. Sorry."

"You could raise it if you wanted."

"No I couldn't."

"What about your daddy? He sure got it somewheres. You could ask him."

With the swiftness of an arctic wind, Birdie Grackle became suddenly less amusing. "I don't talk to my father," said Justin.

"Maybe it's time to start."

"Maybe it's time for you to go to hell."

"Don't you worry, boy. At the rate things is closing down on me, that won't be too long."

"And the third reason your little scheme isn't going to work is that I know very well who killed my mom. And he is currently in jail for the rest of his natural-born life. So I have no need for your services. We're done. Your scam isn't going to work, but I have to admit it is a first."

"Is that how it's going to be?"

"That's how it's going to be."

"Suit yourself," said Birdie. He picked up his drink, slurped the rest of it down, pulled a piece of paper out of his pocket with a number scrawled on it. "You reconsider, you give me a call. I'll be in town for a few days, catch a ball game maybe, but then I'm gone." He stood and looked down. "Don't take too long."

"Don't hold your breath."

Grackle smiled at Justin as if he knew something that Justin didn't, before turning, hitching up his pants, and heading out of the restaurant. Then he stopped, like he had suddenly remembered he left his teeth beneath the napkin, and came back to the table.

"You know, that job, the instructions Preacher gave me, it was supposed to look like a robbery. And whatever I took, I was supposed to hand over to Preacher for him to give the client as proof. But I didn't hand over everything. I used to take souvenirs from my jobs. Little things, knickknacks to remind me of what I was. But I don't need them trophies no more, so I thought you might like this." He pulled from his jacket pocket an old, worn envelope and tossed it onto the table. It landed with a thunk.

Justin picked up the envelope. There was something small inside, small but heavy. He tore the end of the envelope and dumped the object onto the tablecloth.

A turtle.

He looked up to see Birdie Grackle's back retreating from him, looked down again at the turtle. Not a real one, a pin, a women's brooch, made of green enamel with rhinestone eyes. It was a cute little thing, something that would appeal to a kid's sensibilities. Justin knew this because he had bought the enamel turtle for his mother for Mother's Day when he was the tender age of twelve.

5.

LIME RIKKI

The doubts came at night for Mia Dalton, and they came with teeth bared.

During the daytime, Mia Dalton lived in a world of certainties. The sky was blue, the ocean was salty, guilt was a condition of the soul merely ratified in court by a jury of the defendant's peers. And the most important certainty of all was that when Mia Dalton was prosecuting homicides with a ferocity that made hers a cursed name in penitentiaries all across the state, she was always acting as a crusading instrument of justice.

Mia Dalton had convicted some of the most notorious murderers in Philadelphia's history, including a famous sixties icon who decades ago had decapitated his girlfriend, stuffed her body into a trunk, and then gone on the lam in France until being found and extradited. Now chief of the Homicide Division, Mia was much in demand as an after-dinner speaker, peppering her popular talk with the lurid details of her most lurid cases. And after each of these talks, during the Q-and-A, there seemed always to be the same type of questioner: young, a bit scruffy, a law student usually, with an eye on a job with the public defender.

"Have any of your convictions been reversed?" would ask the questioner.

"I work especially hard to keep my trial records spotless," she would say, standing proudly behind the lectern. "I take no shortcuts and follow the letter of the law. I'm proud that none of my convictions have ever been overturned on appeal."

"Has any new scientific evidence ever shown one of your convictions to be unjust?"

"No, never," she would reply. "In fact, in the few cases where new DNA tests were requested and allowed, the tests only confirmed the rightness of each conviction."

"So you have no doubts about the guilt of any of the defendants you've convicted of murder?"

"Let's just say I sleep well at night. Very well."

But this last response was a lie. Because Mia Dalton did not sleep well at all.

Late at night, lying beside the hard body of Rikki, she would sleep uneasily, fitfully, waiting for the doubts to descend. And descend they would, with a marauding relentlessness, teeth of doubt within a huge gaping maw that would swallow her whole and leave her twisting with anxiety in the darkness. Doubts about life, about love, about her uneasy place in the world, about her mother's cancer and her father's clumsy hands, about Rikki's fidelity, about any good she had ever tried to do. And worst of all, doubts about her stellar career. The strategies, the tactics and tricks, the closing arguments structured with telling bits of humor and outrage. And all the men and women sitting behind bars as their lives rotted away because of her. What if her self-righteous certainties were only a tattered curtain to hide unthinkable truths? What if one of her defendants was really a victim himself, whose life was rent by her ability in court? What if her electric ambition was not a servant of justice but instead just another instrument of injustice in a soiled world? And for Mia, these last, most serious of doubts had a name.

Mackenzie Chase.

She had already been the star of the Homicide Division, up for promotion to deputy chief, when she had been assigned the Eleanor Chase murder. It was a hot case for an ambitious prosecutor, and the press was all over it. The Chestnut Hill mansion, the well-loved poet and teacher, the body tragically found by the youngest son, a scruffy law student at the time. The husband, a prosperous businessman, had an airtight alibi: he was at a meeting at the time of the killing. The marriage by all accounts was strong. The victim, by all accounts, had no enemies. And there was clear evidence of a theft, making the crime seem like a targeted robbery gone horribly wrong. The case was going nowhere, and Mia Dalton was at a loss, when the son who found the body, a boy named Justin Chase, had paid her an unscheduled visit.

He was sallow, soft and a little heavy, wary, his clothes unkempt and eyes red, as if he had been getting stoned nonstop in the weeks since he had found his mother's body. If so, she couldn't blame the kid. "I know how hard this must be for you," she had said.

"Do you?"

She ignored the comment because she didn't, she couldn't. "I just want to assure you that our office and the police department are doing everything we can."

"Do you have any leads?"

"Absolutely."

"Suspects?"

"Of course we do, and we're looking at each of them quite carefully. Unfortunately, there is nothing we can talk about now, but please be assured, Justin, that the investigation is moving forward. You know, we've asked you to come to the office and speak with us, but you never responded."

"I made a statement the night I found her."

"Yes, and it was quite detailed. But sometimes we like to go over things a second or third time."

"They kept me at the Roundhouse for twelve hours."

"And I assume you told them everything."

"Pretty much."

She thought she was being perceptive, noting the tone and flavor, and then pouncing with the predatory instinct of a career prosecutor. But she could see now that those words were like a lure for a hungry trout, something to flit across the water, to reflect light and entice, before the fish leaped for the bait. And she had come to believe, now, that all the time this Justin Chase had known she was that fish.

"Pretty much?" she had asked.

He didn't say anything.

"Justin?"

"Would it matter," he had said finally, as if she had squeezed it out of him, "if you found out my father was having an affair?"

Would it matter? Of course it would matter.

And once she had the hook in her mouth, there was no stopping her run. The husband who had lied to the police. The mistress, a luscious tomato named Annie Overmeyer who had much to say. The friend in custody who testified against the defendant to shorten his own sentence. The circumstances of the alibi that had always seemed so peculiar. It all came so easily, so naturally, and her performance at the trial was so brutally inspired that the conviction seemed like an inevitability.

It was only later, after Mackenzie Chase had been sent off to rot his life away in jail, that she began to see how loose it all was, how weak and circumstantial was the case, and how brilliantly, in the face of that weakness, she had brought it all together for the jury and drove the conviction home. It was only later, as the doubts began to descend in the middle of her nights, that she saw how maybe she had been cunningly manipulated by the young Justin Chase in some perverse oedipal drama of his own.

So you have no doubts about the guilt of any of the defendants you've convicted of murder?

If she were a stronger person, she would have taken hold of the Chase file on her own initiative and reviewed everything to make sure the result was just. If she were a stronger person, she would have welcomed the questions and doggedly followed their twisting paths to some firm resolution. But in the dark of the night when the doubts came, she simply hoped, prayed, that if she ignored them long enough, maybe they would simply disappear. Or maybe no one would notice. Or maybe something would come along and make everything moot, like maybe a car accident, or a heart attack.

But she needn't have bothered with all that hoping, for all the good it did. Life is unbearably perverse; that which we most seek to avoid always becomes unavoidable. How inevitable then that the Mackenzie Chase file would once again sit open upon her desk.

"He's late," said Mia.

"He's an addict," said Detective Scott. "Of course he's late."

"And you're sure there's nothing here?"

"I told you already, Mia, I never laid a glove on him."

From behind her desk, she looked over her reading glasses at the detective. Scott was a large hunch of a man with rounded shoulders and a thick, ugly tie. At the time of the Chase murder he had been one of the old bulls in Homicide, but since then he had been farmed out to Missing Persons as the department eased his path to retirement. He was strictly a desk jockey now, and apparently quite content with his reduced duties, which allowed him to comfortably drink his coffee and do the Jumble every morning. He wasn't pleased that Mia had jerked him away from his desk and up to the DA's office for today's interview.

"That's not what he says." Mia looked down at the file and traced her finger across a page. "He says you put a knee in his gut, grabbed him by the hair, and hit him so hard in the jaw you loosened a tooth."

"I don't doubt his tooth was loose. Guys under as long as he was, their mouths look like ruined cemeteries. But I never popped him, never needed to. The guy was facing serious time for a burglary. He needed to deal, he made the claim, they brought me in. All I did was sit there with a stenographer while he spilled."

"So why is he recanting? And why now?"

"He's an addict. All you need to know is that if he's an addict, he's lying."

"He was an addict then, too."

"True."

"So?"

"So, what do you want me to say? Was he lying then? Who the hell knows? C'mon, Mia, you more than anyone know what the deal is here. He made his statement, we went soft on his sentencing, and we put everything on the record. They cross-examined him. They cross-examined me. You gave a hell of an argument, and the jury convicted. You got your stat. I closed a case. It all sounds good to me."

"And you're ready to testify about what went on in that room?"

"If you need me to."

"Oh, we'll need you to, if we're going to keep that bastard behind bars."

Mackenzie Chase had killed his wife because of love. At least that was the theory. He had been in love with his mistress, Annie Overmeyer, with her alluring lines and pouting lips. And Annie Overmeyer herself was ready to testify about his repeated promises to her that they would be married, and soon, just as soon as he could do something about his wife. And then, of course, the wife had been brutally murdered. But there had been no apparent opportunity for Chase to have done the deed himself. He had been in a late meeting in his factory at the time of his wife's murder. And though the meeting had been hastily called, and the matters discussed were in no way pressing, and the other participants had been puzzled as to why the meeting had been called so late at night, there was no doubt that the meeting had taken place. So Mia Dalton somehow had to link Mackenzie Chase with a murder he couldn't have committed himself, and this had proved exceedingly difficult. It was why no indictment had been issued for weeks, even after Justin's unannounced visit to Mia's office.

And then Detective Scott had come up with the answer. And his name was Timmy Flynn.

Timmy Flynn was a high-school classmate of Mackenzie Chase's at Overbrook High. Everyone has one old friend who turns into a burnout, who loses himself in drugs and crime and lives a life you find almost unimaginable, one friend you keep up with even though you shouldn't. You keep up out of loyalty, out of fascination, out of acknowledgment of the fact that the two of you are not so different as it might seem. That was Timmy Flynn for Mackenzie Chase. They spun in different circles, but every now and then they met in a bar or at a ball game and caught up on the different trajectories of their lives. Flynn was like a visitor from Mackenzie's own dark side. And for Flynn, Mackenzie was living the life Flynn could have lived if only he had made different choices. They both seemed to need each other. And then, during one of their meetings, out of the blue, Chase asked Flynn if he knew anyone who could do a certain job.

"What kind of job?" had asked Flynn, according to the statement he gave to Detective Scott.

"Maybe I need someone taken care of," said Mackenzie.

"What are you talking about? You looking for a nurse?"

"Don't be an idiot, Timmy."

"Are you asking what I think you're asking?"

"I'm just asking."

"Well, don't."

"So you don't know anyone?"

"What I'm saying is, you don't want to be asking that question."

"Maybe I do."

"What the hell is going on with you? Someone causing you problems?"

"Do you have any idea, Timmy," had said Mackenzie Chase, according to Timmy Flynn's statement, "how much a divorce costs?"

Mia Dalton put Timmy Flynn on the stand, and she still wondered whether she had done the right thing. He was so undeniably unreliable, his statement was so self-serving, that she herself didn't really believe a word he said. But there wasn't enough of a case without him, and Justin Chase had somehow put the bit in her mouth, and her certainty about

Mackenzie Chase's guilt was so secure that she decided to leave it up to the jury. She put that skeevy old addict on the stand, and the jury bought it. Even after Chase's lawyer sliced and diced Timmy Flynn like a Genoa salami, the jury bought it. And the maw of doubt bared its teeth.

Now, five years after his conviction, and after all appeals had been exhausted, Mackenzie Chase was petitioning the court for a new trial. And the basis for that petition was the recantation of Timmy Flynn. So this interview was going to be quite difficult for Mia. She wasn't just after some sense of why Flynn was changing his story, and why now. She was also hoping to encounter maybe something close to the truth. Because if she saw even a glimpse of the truth, perhaps the doubts would subside, finally, and she could get a full night's sleep.

"Where the hell is he?" said Mia.

"You want I should pick him up?" said Scott.

"You know where he lives?"

"Probation has him down in Kensington."

"Go get him."

Detective Scott slapped his legs and breathed heavily as he stood.

"And Scott," said Mia Dalton, "do me a favor."

"What's that?"

"Don't go alone."

Detective Scott stared at Mia for a moment and then smiled. "I get the feeling, Mia, that you don't trust me."

"You know what I've always admired about you, Detective?"

"What's that?"

"Your perspicacity."

"I'll take it as a compliment," said the detective, "whatever the hell it means."

An hour later the call came in.
"Dalton," she said into the phone.
"It's Scott."
"You find him?"
"I think you better get down here."
"Did you find him?"
"Unfortunately, yes."

6.

BLUE STAR

The body sprawled on the sofa smelled god-awful.

Mia knew well the sickly smell of putrefied flesh and fat, but this stink was different. There were no signs of rampant decomposition here, no greening of the skin or bloating of the flesh, which meant that, except for the tang of fecal stench that slid through everything, Flynn had probably smelled this bad while still alive. It never failed to amaze her how low the high could send you spinning.

She stood with Scott in front of a green easy chair across the room from the dead man, while two detectives and a CSI unit worked the scene. As chief of Homicide, she would be supervising any prosecution that came out of this death, so she had apparent authority here, but still she knew her most important job at any crime scene was to keep the hell out of the way.

"Any idea when he died?" said Mia quietly to Scott.

"It's hard to say without an official report from the coroner."

"How long were you in Homicide?"

"Twelve years."

"In that time you developed some skills, I assume."

"I like to think I did."

"Then quit with the pitter-patter and give me an estimate."

"Based on the stiffness of the joints, the color of the skin, and the noticeable livor mortis, he died sometime last night."

"How did you get inside?"

"Back door."

"Did you break in?"

"That wouldn't be legal, now, would it?"

"Answer the question."

"Officer Blitner and I knocked on the front door. No response. We saw something that looked like a man on the sofa through the window. We knocked on the front door again and yelled out 'Police.' No response. I grew worried for the man's safety, so we went around and checked the basement door at the rear of the house. It was open."

"Unlocked or open?"

"Open, slightly. Fearing exigent circumstances, the officer and I went in, climbed the stairs, saw the body. Once I determined that the man was dead, I called Homicide, and then I called you. How's that?"

"It'll do. So what do you think?"

"It's easy enough to figure, isn't it?"

"Could it be anything else?"

"You mean could he have been murdered?"

"Yes."

"Why?"

"Just tell me what you see."

"There are no evident injuries to the body, no awkward limb positions or signs or rebuttoning or rezippering, so the man wasn't moved or dressed after he died. His watch and a ring haven't been taken, so there wasn't a robbery. Everything points to him putting the fix in himself. What's going on, Mia? You act like you're disappointed that this pain in our collective asses took a hit too many."

"It just seems damn convenient, doesn't it?"

"You bet," said Scott. "And it couldn't have happened to a nicer guy. Will this keep us out of court?"

"Most likely."

"Then cheer up, it's all good."

One of the detectives on the scene, a tall, lugubrious man named Kingstree, came over to the two of them. "You really don't have to stay, Ms. Dalton. The way we see it, this isn't anything more than a simple shot-in-the-arm gone wrong. Nothing to prosecute here, unless we find the knucklehead who sold him the drugs."

"You sure?" said Mia.

"Take a look. The strap is still around his biceps."

"I want you to run the tourniquet for fingerprints," said Mia. "The rubber should pick up a nice impression. And the rest of this room, too."

"Whatever you say. But this is all pretty cut-and-dried. There was a nickel bag along with the dead man's kit, a glassine envelope with a blue star printed on it."

"Blue star?" said Mia.

"It's a neighborhood brand."

"Good stuff?"

"Narcotics tells us it's pretty weak, actually. Low-grade, but plentiful and cheap."

"Not quite overdose material for a lifetime pro like Flynn."

"Sometimes the heart just gives out."

"And sometimes the giving out is helped along. Is the envelope completely empty?"

"No, actually. Come to think of it, it's still pretty full."

"Then he must have used something else. Did you find a second envelope?"

"Not yet."

"Then you better keep looking, huh, Kingstree? I'll want an autopsy."

"It's an overdose."

"Do it."

"Yes, ma'am."

"And I want the stuff in the envelope tested too."

"Fine."

"And until you get notification from me directly, I want you to treat this as a crime scene and this death as an active homicide."

"Anything else?"

"Just do your job."

Kingstree glared a bit and then turned to walk back to his partner, shaking his head.

"That's why you're such a popular gal among the rank and file," said Scott.

"Popularity is for prom queens," said Mia. "Do you see a tiara on my head? They do what I tell them and we all get a stat. That's the way it's been from the beginning."

"Seeing you in action makes me so happy they transferred my ass to Missing Persons."

"I didn't know you liked your new post so much," said Mia.

"It's grand."

"Too bad, then. I'm getting you assigned to me for the next couple of weeks."

"Shit," said Scott slowly.

"It's about time you saddled up again, you old fraud."

"What the hell's flown up your butt, anyway?"

"I think this guy was axed."

"You're hallucinating."

"You're probably right," said Mia Dalton as she stared at the dead body of Timmy Flynn. But even as she said it, she didn't believe it for a second. Flynn was murdered in the coldest of blood, and it had everything to do with Mackenzie Chase. This was the moment, this was a gift. One way or the other, this time, now, she was going to put all those doubts about the Chase case to rest. And sadly, she already sensed where it all would lead.

Justin, Justin, Justin, she said to herself. What the hell have you done?

7.

LA BOMBA

Zenzibar was an austere, windowless room on the bottom floor of a brownstone office building. You stepped down a half flight from street level, pulled open the solid black door, and entered a classic *izakaya,* or Japanese pub, with a low wooden ceiling and a mural of koi on the scuffed walls. But when Marson bought the place, he added burgers and wings to the menu, Guinness on draft, a jukebox of classic rock, Monday Quizzo and Wednesday karaoke. With its original theme completely muddled, it had turned into your basic neighborhood dive, only with cleaner lines and backlit liquor shelves that made the bottles glow in all their unreal colors.

Like every bar in the city, Zenzibar had waxed and waned in popularity over the years, but the latest wane had been long and deep. Zenzibar became known as overpriced and undersexed, the perfect lounge in which to be alone with your cocktail and your thoughts, and Marson spent nights rechecking the receipts and deciding which bills to pay. But then Justin Chase, attracted by the bar's name more than anything else, had drifted in off the street and asked for a job. Zenzibar was still a neighborhood joint, but now it was a busy one. A few mentions in the papers, some choice reviews on a handful of popular blogs, and Justin behind the bar had brought in the hordes. Marson, barely cracking a smile, had immediately upped the drink prices. Each night he stationed himself at the far end of the bar, running checks and filling the waitstaff's orders, while Justin worked the wood, serving a diverse crowd of hipsters and suits, posh girls, and college kids, and his own crop of regulars.

"Where were you last night?" said Lee, sitting on her usual stool in the middle of the bar.

"Something came up," said Justin as he washed a stack of pints one by one.

"We missed you," she said. Lee, who drank Cosmos, was tall and way too glamorous for Zenzibar. Tonight the top of her dress dipped well below the start of her cleavage, which meant she had changed out of her business attire before stopping at the bar. She was either dolling up for her night of drinking or for Justin, and either way she was headed for regret. "Still, I hoped you might call. I waited up all night."

"You weren't staying up for me, you have insomnia."

"True, but that doesn't mean you couldn't have called."

"And then what?" said Justin.

"Yes," she said. "You're right. What was I thinking?"

"Lee?"

"I'm sorry," she said. "It's just that I've been so tired lately."

"You should go home and try to get some sleep."

"It's the trying that's making me so tired."

"I think it's finally over," said Larry, from the stool next to Lee. Larry, who drank draught Yuengling by the pint, was huge and bald, with tattoos up and down both arms and on his neck. He worked as a trainer at a gym on Twelfth Street, and would often frighten his clients into that extra rep, but his heart was as tender as his body was ripped. As far as Justin could tell, that was his problem right there, which meant that Justin had spent untold hours pretending to listen to Larry's romantic predicaments. "The long distance finally killed it," said Larry. "I mean, I'm kidding myself here, aren't I?"

Justin didn't answer because Larry didn't want an answer.

"Why would I even want another chance to have my heart ripped out? I'm ready to move on, finally. I mean it's been six months without a word."

"That is a long time," said Justin, trying to be helpful and realizing his mistake right away.

"You think so?" said Larry, his face suddenly suffused with hope. "Really? Because Quentin said he needed a break. Do you think six months is a long enough break? Should I give him a call?"

"Hey, Justin," said a kid stepping up to the wood with a book-sized package wrapped in brown paper, "could you hold this behind the bar for me?"

"No," said Justin.

"Dude, come on. I don't want to have to be lugging it around while I mingle, know what I mean?"

"The coatrack's next to the men's room."

"But then I'd have to keep my eye on it."

"You care if you lose it?"

"Uh, yeah."

"Well, I don't. But if I take it from you, suddenly I'm the one who has to keep his eye on it. What's in it anyway?"

"Nothing much."

"Then it will be safe enough on the rack."

"Dude."

"It's a rule. Nothing behind the bar. So what are you having?"

"A bottle of Rock."

"Coming up."

"What do you recommend to put me to sleep?" said Lee.

"Warm milk?" said Justin.

"How about another Cosmo instead?"

"But I know he's thinking about me," said Larry. "Because I'm thinking about him. Pittsburgh might be three hundred miles away, but the emotions are flying back and forth through the ether."

"Is that the way it works?" said Lee.

"Sure, why not?"

"Because it seems to me that the more I think about them, the less they think about me."

"That's because you're too good-looking," said Larry.

"What does that have to do with it?"

"The most beautiful are the most forgettable, that's just the way it is. Now Quentin is just ugly enough to be memorable. And I know he still cares, because I can feel it. I know he still loves me, he just doesn't know how to tell me."

"Buy him a fucking cell phone," said Lee.

"Hey guys, what's shaking?" said Cody, bellying up to the bar in a loose bowling shirt. He was short and wiry, with an unkempt Afro and the nervous face of a ferret, always glancing side to side, whether for predators or prey it was hard to tell. A manila envelope in his hand, he took the stool on the other side of Larry. Cody, who liked his drinks sweet, was an operator of sorts, although of exactly what sort was hard to tell. He was on a first-name basis with staid corporate lawyers and gold-toothed North Philly bookies, and it wasn't clear if he flirted with the line or just ignored it completely. The only certain thing was that he was a very bad gambler.

"You look cheery," said Lee.

"I caught a piece of information today that I intend to

parlay into mucho dinero, my amigos. When I stepped out the door this morning, I was wondering how I was going to pay the rent, and now I'm thinking of booking a cruise."

"Where to?" said Lee.

"I don't know. I've been thinking Paraguay. Don't know anything about the place, but I like the sound of it. Paraguay."

"That would be a hell of a cruise," said Justin. "What are you having, Cody?"

"Surprise me. Something new and cruisy, fresh and fruity."

"Have you met Larry?" said Lee.

"Hold this back there, would you?" said Cody, sliding the envelope to Justin.

Without saying a word, Justin smoothly snatched the envelope and dropped it into a drawer. Then he started preparing Cody his drink.

Justin's following as a barkeep was surprisingly loyal. Whenever Justin changed jobs, and he changed jobs often, applying his philosophy of drift to all facets of his life, his following followed. There wouldn't be any announcement on the Internet or a flyer posted on a tree. One day Justin would be there behind the bar, mixing drinks and raising his eyebrow in feigned interest while the pub owner smiled contentedly at his suddenly burgeoning business, and the next night he'd be gone. And then, a few weeks later, word would get out that Justin had reappeared, and slowly much of the crowd from the first bar would slip over to the second.

It wasn't that Justin prepared brilliant drinks that no one else could match. His drinks were solid, yes, and his repertoire wide—Justin could whip up a Sazerac or a New-Fashioned as tasty as any in the city—but there were dozens of inventive mixologists plying their trade in the city who used artisanal spirits, house-made bitters, and complex recipes to craft exquisite jewellike drinks that Justin didn't care to try to match. And it wasn't that Justin was a brilliant conversationalist who befriended his customers. Justin made it clear to all that as a professional bartender he was decidedly not your friend. Instead there was a core group that followed him from place to place, almost as a sport. And once this group switched, so did many others, a popular pub crawl taking place in slow motion. And at the head of Justin's core group were Cody and Larry and Lee.

"So what about tonight?" said Lee.

Justin thought about it as he rubbed the rim of a cocktail glass with a lime before dipping the rim onto a small plate of sugar, leaving a narrow white band.

He had spent much of the morning on the tatami mats, recovering from the trauma of Birdie Grackle, with his mantra and his book. *Be not terrified. Be not awed. Know it to be the embodiment of thine own intellect.* After a day of meditation, he had reduced Birdie Grackle to a meaningless mote floating in the depths of his consciousness. And Justin had come up with a simple explanation for the turtle: it was a fake. The missing piece of turtle jewelry had been mentioned in the media reports of the murder. It wasn't much of a trick to get such a brooch made and aged especially for Birdie's little con. Hell if Justin could tell if it was the original; he hadn't really looked at the thing in the fifteen years after he bought it in that antique store on Pine Street. For his own venal reasons, Birdie Grackle had been trying to rope Justin into stepping into the past, but Justin was going to have none of it. He wasn't seeking remembrance and reconciliation, he wasn't seeking to revisit the traumas of his youth when he was still ruled by the illusion of ambition. Instead he was taking the only true path this world allowed, to lose himself and his petty troubles in the enormity of the void. And he had found that one of the best places to lose himself was in Lee's bed.

"Tonight sounds good," he said to her as he sliced into the back of another wedge of lime and perched it on the tip of the glass like a half-moon.

When he looked up and saw the brightness of Lee's smile and the expectation in her eyes, he had doubts. There was an inequality to their relationship that he didn't like, but still, it wasn't like he hadn't been clear about where they stood.

"So where were you last night, Justin?" said Larry. "Hot date?"

Lee looked at Larry and then back at Justin.

"Sort of," said Justin as he took out his tin, added two long splashes of juice, first orange and then pineapple. "If a geriatric basket case with false teeth counts."

Into the shaker went a hot shot of tequila and a splash of Cointreau. Justin dumped in some ice, capped the lid, lifted the tin to a precise angle, and went at it. He didn't dance when he shook his drinks, or spin the shaker like a six-shooter, or in any way make a spectacle of himself. Plenty of bartenders tried to put on a show; Justin was simply preparing a drink. After enough time had passed to mix and cool and create the perfect light froth, he unscrewed the top and, using it as a strainer for the ice, filled the glass with the pale-orange cocktail.

"That almost looks good enough to drink," said Cody.

"It's not done," said Justin as he grabbed a bottle of grenadine he had made in his kitchen and put in two quick dashes that wound their way like bright red scarves down to the bottom of the glass.

"Psychedelic," said Larry as Justin slid it forward.

"La Bomba," said Justin.

Cody picked up the glass by the stem, his pinky out for effect, and took a sip. "Not half-bad."

"Maybe I'll have one, too, instead of the Cosmo," said Lee. "It looks so festive and it suddenly fits my mood."

"Coming right up," said Justin.

As he was finishing Lee's drink, he caught sight of a ghost entering the front door. He blinked at the ghost until it resolved into the figure of a middle-aged man with a blond flattop, and Justin's throat closed in on him with panic. The panic was a surprise, and a disappointment, seeing as it was the second time in two nights that his emotions had risen unbidden to throttle his neck. But you couldn't say that the panic was unwarranted, seeing that the last time Justin had seen this selfsame man, four and a half years ago, the man had threatened to shoot a hole through Justin's forehead. And he'd had a gun in his hand to back up the threat.

"Here you go," said Justin distractedly, watching the man step up to the bar even as Justin pushed the drink toward Lee. "Enjoy."

Lee followed Justin's worried gaze. "Do you know him?"

"Not really," said Justin. "He's just my brother."

8.

BLOODY URINE

Frank was older than Justin remembered, and heavier, jowlier, but that might have said more about the remembering than about any deterioration on Frank's part. In Justin's mind, his older brother remained the high-school hero who seemed to know the secrets to everything—to life, love, scoring touchdowns, scoring the best marijuana, everything important—rather than the tired middle-aged man who was now leaning on the bar.

Justin wondered if Frank had maybe unwittingly stumbled in simply for a drink, but no, he turned to Justin and stared without a smile.

Justin grabbed the bar rag for protection and headed over, wiping the bar as if wiping out the past.

"So you've returned," said Frank, his voice surprisingly soft. In Justin's memory, there was always a load of bluster in Frank, inherited directly from their father, like the blue of Frank's eyes and the pug of his nose.

"I'm like the herpes virus, I always come back," said Justin. "What can I get you to drink?"

Frank surveyed the bottles behind Justin as if he were choosing a new car. "Wine maybe?"

"Wine? Such a sophisticate you've become."

"Cindy took me out to Napa last year."

"I told you that woman would ruin you. We have a shitty red, a shitty white, or a shitty rosé, although you would think the vineyard would come up with better names. Maybe something like Cheap and Nasty, or Bloody Urine."

"Bloody Urine sounds good."

"Coming right up." As he poured the blush into a long-stemmed glass, he said, "How did you find me?"

"Jarmusch saw you in here a couple weeks ago."

"I thought that was him, but the son of a bitch didn't say hello and then he stiffed me on the tip."

"Jarmusch always was an asshole. When did you get back in town?"

"About half a year ago. I tried a few other places, the desert, the coast, but it all seemed the same. I've been working at staring down my demons, and this seemed to be the place to do it."

"And now here I am. So how'd you end up tending bar?"

Justin rubbed a spill of condensation off the counter. "I picked it up in Reno."

"I wasn't asking about your STD."

"That I picked up in Big Sur."

Frank leaned both elbows on the bar, took a sip of the wine, winced. "Bloody Urine fits." He took a bigger gulp. "You are such an asshole."

"I know."

"You should have called."

"The last time we got together you threatened to shoot me."

"That was just a little misunderstanding."

"You were pointing a revolver at my face."

"Okay, maybe I was. But I've been working through my anger, working through the way I've always felt about you. Did you know that when Mom told me she was having another baby, I broke out into tears?"

"If she had told me I was being born, I would have broken out into tears myself."

"I guess I resented you from the first, and that colored everything after. And it didn't help that you were the perfect little boy, the honor-roll kid, Mom's favorite. And then there you were banging that Carla Jane, who I had a crush on."

"Carla Jane DeAngelo. I wonder what happened to her. Maybe I should give her a call."

"She married Jarmusch."

"Son of a bitch."

"But I've realized now that most of the problems with us were my fault. Not all of them, of course—you were an insufferable little bastard—but still. And, believe it or not, I've missed you."

"You must have a hell of a therapist."

"It's not a therapist," said Frank. "It's Dad."

The reference to Justin's father hit Justin like a mud ball to the jaw. He turned his head away from his brother as if from the blow.

"I visit him every week," said Frank. "We talk. He's been really helpful. And he wants you to know he forgives you."

"I don't need his forgiveness."

"And yet he still has given it to you as a gift."

"Tell the bastard he can have it back."

Justin took his rag and went to the far end of the bar and let the orders wash over him. He poured a beer with too much head, made a Belvedere Dry Martini that was supposed to be a Grey Goose Dirty, and botched a Long Island Tea when he grabbed all the wrong bottles and topped it off with tonic. When he broke a glass in the ice well, he stopped himself, took a step back, took a deep breath. Usually the work was like a cleansing stream, but somehow having his brother at the other end of the bar mucked everything.

"What do you want, Frank?" said Justin, after he had made his way, order by order, back to his brother.

"More wine?"

As Justin filled the glass, he said, "What are you really doing here?"

"I came to say hello to my little brother."

"Consider it done."

"Dad says you need to see him."

"I don't want to see him."

"It doesn't matter. He put you on his visitor list. He thinks you need to come."

"If he wanted to see me again, maybe he shouldn't have killed my mother."

"She was my mother, too, and he didn't do it."

"A jury said he did, and that's good enough for me."

"Really? The jury convinced you? Because it looked like you made up your mind long before a jury ever heard a stick of evidence. And considering Dad had an alibi and they never found the real killer, it seems really—"

"I'm not going over it again. I'm so far beyond it now that if I turn around, all I see is a single speck on the clean line of the horizon."

"Must be nice," said Frank as he stared into the pale, ruddy wine. "Uncle Timmy died last night."

"Oh."

"Of a drug overdose."

"Shit."

"I'm springing for his funeral. At Mulligan's. Thursday morning at ten. He never really had any family except for us."

"Frank, I hate to break it to you, but he wasn't our real uncle."

"Still, Dad asked me to make the funeral. I thought you might want to come."

"Maybe, I don't know." Justin thought of the strange, skinny man on his motorcycle in his blue-jean jacket, looking so unlike Justin's straightlaced father it was almost comical to see them together. "I'm surprised Dad still cared after what Uncle Timmy did at the trial."

"He had changed his testimony," said Frank.

"Who?"

"Uncle Timmy. He changed his testimony and claimed that Dad never asked for help in killing Mom and that the police forced him to lie. He signed an affidavit and was ready to testify. Dad was trying to get a new trial based on Uncle Timmy's changed testimony. And then he has to go and die of a fucking overdose."

Justin thought about this, didn't understand what it might mean, didn't want to understand. "Thursday?"

"Yeah."

"Can't make it."

"Justin."

"Look, I have to go. I have other customers." Justin tried to smile, grimacing like he had an attack of gas. "The wine's on the house."

"Cindy says hello."

"Give her my regards. I always liked Cindy."

"No, you didn't. And what about Dad?"

"What about him?"

"You need to see him."

"I think I very much need not to see him. He's found his place in the world: prison. I'm still looking for mine, and frankly, Frank, I don't think he can help."

"You know," said Frank, calmly staring at his brother, "when I found out you were back and tending bar, I thought you might have changed. I thought maybe life had knocked the breathtaking arrogance out of you. But I was wrong."

"Change is a mirage," said Justin. "Like everything else in this fucked-up world."

Frank opened his wallet and dug out a ten. "For the wine," he said as he dropped the bill beside the wineglass.

9.

SLIPPERY NIPPLE

Lee was inspiringly beautiful, especially when she was naked and lying beneath Justin with her legs hitched around his waist and her hands grabbing at his hair like it was a mane. Her cheekbones were sharp and high, her lips glossed, her teeth pearly, her tongue moist and pink, her breasts soft mounds of perfection, her stomach lean, her legs long, her knees dimpled. If the Buddha was right, and all suffering derives from desire, then Justin, as he moved slowly atop her and gently pulled at her lower lip with his teeth, was suffering greatly.

There were times, especially in the middle of his suffering, when Justin desired more than raw sex with Lee. In those moments he longed for some deeper attachment than their pale friendship-with-benefits. Part of him wanted to hold her, to hold on to her, to love her and commit to her, to add a level of possession to their relationship, to create for themselves and all their progeny a sun-dappled future. The craving became almost unbearable, and he felt his heart break with the wanting.

And then he would come. To his senses.

For who knew better than Justin Chase where all of that emotional attachment would lead. The holding would devolve into a jealous clench, the loving would become a bitter chain around both their necks, the possession would turn into soul-killing ownership, the sun-dappled future would darken, the spawn would die, and there would be nothing left but the misery and the pain.

"That was so nice," said Lee.

"That's what I aspire to," said Justin, lying on his back now, his hands clasped behind his head, "a genial niceness."

"You know what I mean."

Lee leaned over and kissed him, and Justin sort of kissed back.

"It was strange seeing your brother at the bar," she said.

"You're telling me."

"You never mentioned your brother before," she said. "And whatever you guys were talking about, it sure as hell got you upset. I had never seen you like that before."

"A momentary lapse."

"I liked it, it showed you were human."

"More like an adolescent turkey, squawking away. Family can do that to you."

"Do you see him much?"

"I hadn't seen him for years actually."

"He doesn't look like you at all."

"He takes after my father."

"Oh," said Lee, the exclamation filled with all manner of understanding, just to remind Justin that she knew, along with everyone else, his sordid history. He closed his eyes for a moment and tasted the emotions before they slipped away. It wasn't embarrassment he was feeling, it was more a bitterness at the note of pity that had slipped into the "Oh." *Oh, you poor boy. Oh, I understand your tragedy. Oh, if there is anything I can do...* Part of him wanted to spit all the bitterness back into her pretty face, but that would be just another sad crack in the wall he had built around his emotions over the years, and two in two days was enough. So instead he did what he always did when things grew uncomfortable with Lee, he acted like a dog.

He rolled over, sat up, fetched his underwear.

"What's wrong?" she said.

"I need to go."

"Oh," she said, another of her "Ohs." This one was just as clear. *Oh, it's going to be like that, again, is it?* "I could go in late tomorrow if you wanted to stay," she said as Justin buttoned his shirt. "We could play in the morning."

"I don't think so."

"I bought some new shoes."

Justin's head whipped toward her.

"Stilettos," she said.

"The plot thickens."

"Black patent leather with red soles."

"They sound dangerous."

"You don't know the half of it."

He thought for a moment, the image of those shoes slicing at the sheets before they slowly rose into the air working at his resolve. But then he'd have to go through this again, the buttoning of the shirt, the mute entreaties to stay. "I can't. And you look tired, Lee. You've looked tired for a while. You need your sleep."

"I'd sleep better with you here."

"I doubt it. Have you ever heard me snore?"

"No."

He looked at her, at the way she looked at him. "It's getting late."

"Sure. I get it. Thanks."

"For what?"

She gave a rueful little laugh. "Hey, Justin, just go fuck yourself, all right."

"Lee?"

She looked at him for a moment and then rolled away from him, showing him her lovely back, her clavicles spreading her smooth pale flesh. "Sorry," she said. "It just slipped out."

"We talked about this before. The rare beauty of nonattachment."

"And it is so rarely beautiful. But everything's good, everything's perfect. I have too much going on anyway for anything more. It's just that it's hard to tell what we are. What are we, Justin? Lovers? Friends? Am I your whore? Because that I can deal with, I just want to know."

"No, you're not that."

"Then what? Cousins."

"That would be pretty hot."

"It would just help if I had a name. Hi, this is Justin, he's my—"

"Bartender," said Justin. "I'm your bartender."

"Is it as sad as it sounds?"

A Zen master was deciding who would be named abbot for a monastery. He put a pitcher on the floor and asked a number of monks what it was, adding, "Don't say it's a pitcher." The monks in the room were very clever, and they each came up with a clever answer to his question. Then the cook, untrained in Zen, stepped up and kicked the pitcher over, shattering it into tiny pieces. "This man," said the master, "is our new abbot."

"We are what we are," said Justin. "Everything else is just words."

"Of course you're right. Don't mind me, I just haven't been sleeping. I need to drink more. Or less. Or something. Good night, Justin. We'll save the shoes for next time."

"Promise? Because I love that new-shoe smell."

"I promise." She turned to him and smiled weakly. "God, you are filthy."

He tried leering, but his heart wasn't in it. Whatever they had together, it was collapsing under its own weight. He could see the signs. Her dissatisfaction was showing, like a slip beneath the hem of a crisply pleated skirt, and it ruined the whole effect. When he was fully dressed, he sat on the bed and leaned over her. "I'll see you at the bar."

"Sure," she said, putting her hand on his cheek. "Good night, my barkeep."

"You should sleep in anyway. It would do you good."

"This does me good," she said, and then she grabbed his cheek with her fist, gripping the flesh tight like an insistent aunt, and pulled him close. "And next time it's going to hurt."

He leaned in and kissed her. And even as he was kissing, even as he felt her mouth soften and open to him and her tongue reach for his, he knew it was time to kick the pitcher. Which meant he'd have to find a new bar soon. Which was a shame, because he liked Zenzibar. But Lee was letting him know he had already been there too long. And with his brother back in the equation, and with the likes of Birdie Grackle trying to scam him back into his past, maybe this whole back-home thing wasn't working like he had hoped. Maybe it was time to move on, not just to another bar, but to another city. He'd heard good things about Louisville. Or Kansas City. And there were some amazing sunsets in Sedona.

Sedona, that was the ticket. He'd head out as soon as he could. But not before he got a whiff of those shoes. Because what was life but suffering?

10.

BLACK MAGIC

Mia Dalton was mired in the paperwork that had defined her job ever since her promotion when Detective Scott entered her office with a big old smile on his face. She stared at him balefully over her reading glasses. In Mia's experience, cops didn't smile like that unless they had just opened a box of doughnuts or closed a case. The lack of powdered sugar dusted on Scott's jacket indicated the latter.

"I've been babysitting Kingstree on the Flynn investigation like you told me," said Scott. "The forensics just came in."

"And you're smiling like a customer walking out of a whorehouse because I was wrong, and the case is going to be closed as an accidental overdose, and now you get to go back to your quiet little desk."

"No, Mia, I'm smiling because every time I step into this office and see the sign that reads CHIEF, HOMICIDE DIVISION, I remember when you first showed up in court. You were so green the sap was still dripping from your elbows. You couldn't stop your knees from shaking. I never thought you'd last."

"I grew up quick."

"Yes, you did. And I'd almost be proud as a papa if you weren't such a pain in the ass."

"Are you going to make me wait?"

"They found a load of different prints around the house, and they've logged them. Most are unknown. A few match some known drug users, and Kingstree is running them down. The place was just a step up from a shooting gallery, so there was probably loads of traffic. Kingstree doesn't expect the prints will lead anywhere."

"Anything indicate Flynn had help getting his last high?"

"The only partial print they found on the rubber tourniquet belonged to the victim. The autopsy showed no fresh bruising, no signs of a struggle of any kind. Flynn strapped himself up, slipped in the needle, injected himself, and then stopped breathing."

"So I was wrong."

"It's hard to take, isn't it?"

"Is that all you've got?"

"Well, there is something else. They tested the heroin our boy had bought, the Blue Star. Just as narcotics had told us, it had been cut over and again. The coroner said even something at that strength could be enough to kill—things happen to users, and all their organs weaken over time—but even so, this was a pretty mild brew."

"What about toxicology?"

"More interesting. They found a level of heroin inconsistent with the quality of the Blue Star. He would have had to inject a suitcaseful of the crap he bought to get that level of intensity. But it wasn't just that. They found something else in the blood. Fentanyl."

"Fentanyl?"

"You remember a couple years back when addicts started dying all over the city and they blamed it on this new superheroin that was coming in from Mexico. They called it 'Magic.'"

"I remember. It was a bloodbath."

"A decade before, the same crap devastated the addict population of New York under the name 'Tango and Cash.' It comes in waves, this stuff, heroin with a synthetic additive that makes it way more powerful and way more dangerous."

"And the additive is fentanyl?"

"That's it. At first I wondered if someone gave him a second shot while he was nodding off from the first, so I had the coroner go over the whole body again. He squawked, but he did it, and said there was only one fresh injection site. Flynn shot this supercrap into himself."

"Something pure and deadly, which would be irresistible to a goner like Flynn."

"Except," said Scott, "the guys in the drug lab told me there hasn't been anything with fentanyl in the city for a couple of years."

"So how did Flynn get hold of it?"

Scott tossed the file onto Mia's desk and slumped into a chair. "That's the question, isn't it?"

"What do you think?"

Scott leaned back. "I don't know what the hell to think. I guess either the son of a bitch got lucky and somehow got his hands on this killer stuff, an addict's dream, or he got a gift designed to kill him."

"Anything going on with him?"

"Other than the Chase case? I sent Kingstree out to interview known associates. He's grumbling, but he's afraid of you, so he's doing it."

Mia smiled.

"But he's not finding anything," continued Scott, "and I don't think he will. The timing is too perfect for it to be anything other than connected with Chase. Maybe it's not just cops that you frighten. Maybe you frightened Timmy Flynn enough that he offed himself so he didn't have to come down and talk to you."

"You don't believe that, do you?"

"You have Kingstree shaking in his loafers. But no, not a hard case like Flynn. But why would someone care enough about his changed testimony in the Chase case to give him a gift this deadly?"

"That's what we're going to find out, Detective," said Mia. "I hate to interrupt the hours of leisure available to you in your declining years, but I have a job for you."

"I bet you do."

"Remember Chase's youngest son? The law student who told us about his father's affair with that Overmeyer woman when we still had nothing?"

"Sure. The defense made some argument the jury never bought, like the son was setting up the father for some twisted personal revenge."

"His name is Justin, Justin Chase. Last I heard he had checked out of some insane asylum and left the city. See if he's back, and if he is, find him and bring him in. Let's see if maybe the defense had a point after all."

11.

SOMETHING NEAT

There is something untidy about the job Vern has given to Derek that Derek does not like.

Derek does not like untidiness of any kind. He makes his bed every morning when he has a bed, launders his pants in the sink every evening. Sammy D taught him that cleanliness is important in this line of work. Sammy D was neat for an addict. Usually addicts had the worst teeth, like that guy in the row house that Vern sent Derek to a couple nights back, but Sammy D's teeth gleamed. And there was always a pleat in his pants. Grooming is the sign of a professional, Sammy taught him.

Rodney, on the other hand, was a slob. He was too nervous to keep anything clean. Wherever he went, he shed like a Labrador retriever: tissues, papers, coins, hair. Sammy taught Derek that anything left at the scene is like a map from the deed to the doer, but Rodney never cared. His method was to keep moving, always stay one step ahead. "They can't catch you if they can't find you" was his motto. This untidy job would have been perfect for Rodney. After this job Rodney would have been headed right out of the city, to Altoona or Ypsilanti. Derek traveled halfway across the country with Rodney, washing his pants in motel sinks from Maine to New Mexico as Rodney stuffed the powder up his nose and made fun of Derek's habits.

Derek is now inside the little house where Vern has sent him, sitting on the couch on the first floor. The lock on the back door had not been much of a challenge, and there is no alarm, which did not surprise Derek once he got inside. There is not anything in the house worth stealing. It is a nice little neighborhood off a nice little square, and the house, tiny as it is, should have been crammed full with nice stuff. But there is an emptiness here that Derek likes. The top floor has nothing but these greenish mats; the second, a bed on the floor; the first, just the couch and a table. And there is no television.

Rodney loved television. Every night in their cheap motels, he would watch whatever was on, anything that blared and snorted. Derek would wake up in the middle of the night from some noise or other, and the television would be on even though Rodney was asleep and snoring. And whenever Derek turned it off, Rodney would snap awake. "What is it? What happened?" And then it would go back on as some late-night infomercial tried to sell something to clean the house that Rodney would never dream of buying.

Derek likes this little house more than anyplace he has seen since he left home. As he sits on the couch set beside the front door, he can imagine living here with a dog and a bird, maybe a horse out back, sleeping in the quiet of the second floor, washing his pants in the kitchen sink, practicing the Korean-style violence that Tree taught him on the mats on the top floor. And no television to blare at him through the night. The house is very tidy. He likes the house as much as he hates the untidiness of the job he has been given.

Vern told him the man would go out sometime in the day to run, like he did every day. So Derek waited until the man left. Vern also told him the man would come back within an hour or so to get ready for work. That was when the job would take place. Vern went over it again and again, as if Derek had not heard him the first time. Lately Vern has been acting as if Derek is deaf. Derek does not like when people act like he is deaf.

Derek thought Vern was a cool customer, but lately Vern has been losing it, acting almost as nervous as Rodney. Derek can tell that things are coming to a boil, even though he has no idea what those things might be or what the boil might consist of, other than that he will be a big part of it, like always. And then Vern gave him this untidy job and loudly repeated the details again and again. Derek does not know what to think about it, so he does not. Think, that is. He just sits and waits and rehearses the lines that Vern has given him to say. But he is not as calm as usual before a job. It is the untidiness that is getting to him, especially in a house as empty and clean as this. He wants to go to the top floor and stick his foot through a knee. He wants to slam open a skull with his elbow. He wants to kill. That always calms him down. There is nothing as tidy as death.

That was what Rodney discovered, finally, in Baltimore. The job was a woman. Rodney was a wreck as they waited in the second-floor apartment for her to come home. Rodney was worried that she might not be alone when she came home. He was worried that if she brought a man with her, the man would have a gun. He was worried that the man would start shooting before Derek could do anything about him. Rodney paced around the apartment, spitting and snorting, touching everything, eating from the fridge and putting the half-eaten pieces of meat back inside. He even made a call from the phone to make sure everything was still on. When Derek told him he ought to be more careful, Rodney told him to go wash his damn pants and shut up.

The woman in Baltimore came home alone. By the time she realized anything was wrong, Derek already had an arm around her neck. And then Rodney insisted on playing with her a bit, like he liked to. He said it was part of the job, to throw the cops off as to the reason, but Derek could tell that Rodney did it just because he liked to. The powder made the inside of Rodney's head as untidy as his clothes. When it was over, Rodney decided they should leave by the window that led to the alley instead of by the door. He was worried that someone would see them leaving from the front. Derek just shrugged and followed along. That was what he always did in his jobs with Rodney, shrug and follow along and pick up on all the mistakes Rodney made. Derek went out first, hung onto the sill, and jumped down. It was not a long drop, it was not a big deal. But when Rodney tried it, something slipped and he fell, hard. He grabbed his broken leg and screamed louder than the woman when Rodney had diddled her.

And in that moment Derek decided that Rodney needed some tidying up.

Footsteps. Derek stops remembering about Rodney and starts remembering about the job. Footsteps echoing on the narrow street outside. Derek waits for them to pass, but they do not pass. They stop at the front door of the house. Derek stands and silently slips into a darkened corner of the room. A jangle from outside. The turn of the lock. The opening of the door. When the man steps inside, his back is to Derek.

Derek waits motionless, breathless, until the door closes.

12.

SNAKEBITE

The blow on the back of Justin's head was so sudden and sharp it barely registered before a thick fog cloaked every sensation. As he found himself inexplicably falling, he had no idea what had happened. The crack of his cheek upon the floor jerked him out of the mist and gave him a pretty good idea.

"What the hell—"

Something hard and ferocious kicked into his side, knocking out his breath and the words at the same time, but when a crushing pressure slammed his face into the floor, he knew the answer just the same. He was being mugged, brutally, he was being robbed. Which was a joke, really, because he owned nothing worth caring about and he cared about nothing he owned.

"Take anything...everything," he gasped out. "There's some money...in a drawer...in the kitchen...Take it...Go ahead. I won't stop you."

"There is no TV," came a voice close to his ear. The voice was strange, a little slurry, with every syllable evenly stressed.

"I don't...There isn't one...I don't have one."

"Good."

"What?...Why?"

A slap across the top of his head forced an explosion of air into his ear. Through the ringing, he could just make out the strange voice saying, "Rodney watched too much TV."

"Rodney?" said Justin, sucking in breaths as fast as he could manage. "Who's Rodney?...I don't know a Rodney."

Justin struggled to rise from the floor, but he felt a huge presence, inhuman almost, spidery yet strong, pressing him down. When he fought to raise his cheek off the floor, his head was grabbed by the hair and smashed back down.

The pain birthed an anger in him, dark, growing exponentially, welling up inside like a huge, fetid bubble. He closed his eyes and tensed the muscles in his arms, in his back, in his legs, tensed each of his muscles as if to somehow explode the attacker off his back, whatever the cost. It was futile, he knew it, the attacker had the weight and the leverage, he knew it, but still, damn it, he wasn't going to take this. He was going to do something. He was going to kill this bastard, to throw him off his back and stick a foot in his neck and kill him, kill him, kill—

In the midst of his struggle, he saw words as if writ in Sanskrit within the lids of his closed eyes. *Be not terrified. Be not awed. Know it to be the embodiment of thine own intellect.* It was all part of the same thing, this attack, at one with all that had happened and would happen, his mother's murder, the sex he'd had the night before with Lee, his job as a barkeep, his brother, his father, his face, the floor, it was all part of the same thing, the same illusion. He felt his anger anew, felt it burn like acid, and then he let it flow out of him, pour out of him as from a broken jug. And as the anger flowed away, the tension in his muscles lessened, slowly. The tightness pulling at his bones loosened, slowly. His whole body slowly melted as the floor enveloped him, softly, lovingly, like a pillow. Everything in him eased, his bones were made of Jell-O, the pain in his body diminished. Until the pain was focused only on his cheek. And there it blossomed, brightly. Like a flower. Like a gift.

"What do you want?" said Justin with a new calm.

"You need to stay away," said the voice.

"From where?"

"What happened to your mother is over," said his attacker as Justin's face was pressed hard into the floor, and the flower in his cheek grew wild and lovely. The words were said in those evenly accented syllables, slurred and without inflection, as if they were being read off a paper without being understood. "Your father is where he belongs. If you turn over any dirt, you'll only be digging your grave. Stay out of it, or else."

"Out of what?" said Justin.

"You want it repeated?"

"Yes. Please."

"You need to stay away," said the attacker in that same strange voice. "What happened to your mother is over. Your father is where—"

A knock at the door. And again. Loud knocks. Bang. Bang.

"Who is that?" said the attacker.

"I don't know," said Justin.

"Say 'Go away.'"

"Go away," Justin shouted.

Bang. Bang. "Mr. Chase?" came a man's voice through the door. "This is the police."

In an instant, the attacker was off Justin's back and charging toward the rear doorway that led to the small fenced backyard and then to Panama Street. Justin didn't have any desire to run after his attacker like he would have just a few moments before, when he was twisted dark by his anger. Instead he lifted up his head and turned his neck so he could catch sight of the man just as he reached the back of the house—a darkly clothed figure with short legs and broad shoulders, his wide back hunched and powerful, running quite quickly despite a slight limp, ripping open the door with massive arms, tearing out into the light, glancing back with a quick twist of his huge neck before jumping like a cheetah over the fence.

Bang. Bang. "Mr. Chase? Justin Chase?"

Justin, still on the floor, rolled over, put a hand on his bruised cheek, and said, "Come on in."

The door opened and the police officer stood in the doorway. He was an older African American, grizzled, squat of figure, with big hands and a curious tilt to his mouth. And curiously familiar. He stepped up to Justin and stared down at him on the floor for a long moment, as if trying to figure out what he was seeing.

"Yoga?" said the cop finally.

"Not quite," said Justin.

13.

ZOMBIE

Mia's worst fears about Justin Chase were confirmed with a single glance. If she hadn't known who he was, she would never have recognized him.

The nervous law student with his pale skin and worried eyes, his soft face and body, his uneasy stammer, had been replaced by something far harder. It was the kind of physical transformation she had seen sometimes in meth addicts. His body fat had been reduced enough so that his cheekbones were sharp as scythes. With his dark flat eyes and long hair and aggressive sort of calm, he indeed looked more like a drug dealer or a motorcycle madman than the anxious, ambitious kid he had been. And the dark-red bruise on his cheek, speckled with fresh blood, made him seem all the more dangerous.

Dangerous enough to have killed Timmy Flynn to keep his father in jail?

"What happened to your face, Justin?" said Mia.

"I fell."

"Detective Scott said that what he heard on the other side of the door sounded like a confrontation of some sort. Like there was a fight going on."

"I was mad at myself for falling," he said evenly.

"And then I heard footfalls," said Scott. "Like someone running away from the police."

"Who was running away, Justin?" said Mia.

"That was just me, pounding the floor in frustration," he lied. And he lied with such a perfect calm that Mia felt a shiver roll down her spine. Was he as accomplished a liar even before this sad transformation—like, say, when he came into her office that first time to point the finger at his father? "What is this all about?" said Justin.

"Timmy Flynn."

"Uncle Timmy? He just died. So?"

"How did you know Mr. Flynn died, Justin?"

"My brother told me."

"Frank?" she said, surprised. She remembered how bitter the feelings had been between the two brothers at the time of the trial. Frank fully supported his father, while Justin was convinced of his father's guilt. The scenes in the courthouse between the two were brutally tense, once almost coming to blows. "Do you see Frank often?"

"Not really. But he found me the other night and told me about Uncle Timmy. The funeral is tomorrow."

"Are you planning on attending?"

"I haven't seen the guy in years, and he was sort of a loser."

She looked at Justin and said nothing, trying to pull out more with her silence.

"The drugs, I mean," he said.

"What about your drug use?"

"I don't," said Justin.

"You've lost some weight since I last saw you."

"I run."

"Had you been in touch with Mr. Flynn since the trial?"

"No."

"Had he been in touch with you? Did he call you or ask you for anything?"

"No."

"Did he tell you he was changing his testimony about your father? Did he tell you that his whole story about your father asking him to help him find someone to kill your mother was made up because of police pressure?"

"How could he have told me that," said Justin evenly, "if we hadn't been in touch?"

"I just told you a major witness against your father had changed his testimony and you don't look shocked, or angry, or even like you need time to process the information. You look like you knew it already and had known it for a while."

"My brother told me that, too."

"The same night he told you Mr. Flynn was dead."

"That's right."

"Busy night," said Mia, looking at Scott. He nodded at her in indication that he would check things out with the brother right after the interview. She looked down at the file on the desk and softened her voice as if the next question were a throwaway while she figured out what she really wanted to ask. "How's your father doing?"

"He's in jail."

"Yes, I know, I put him there. But some inmates deal with incarceration better than others. Some even flourish. How's your dad doing?"

"I don't know. I don't see him."

"When was the last time you talked to your father?"

"Before he was arrested."

Mia lifted her head and stared at Justin. "And not since then?"

"He killed my mother, Ms. Dalton."

"So you haven't forgiven him."

"Is something like that forgivable? And truthfully, I don't expect he gives a damn whether I forgive him or not."

She recalled the old Justin Chase, how hurt and bewildered he had been, and she softened. "I seem to remember seeing your name on a list of graduating law students."

"Yeah, how do you like that? They let anybody graduate law school these days."

"Not from Penn they don't. Where did you pass the bar?"

"I didn't."

She just stared at him.

"I never took the test. I only finished law school because it was easier going through the motions than actually quitting and finding something else to do. But after my mother, I didn't want to do the lawyer thing anymore."

"So what thing do you do now?"

"I tend bar."

Mia stared and waited for some sort of explanation.

"The public has a thirst and I'm the man to quench it."

"Nothing wrong with the job, but it's a bit of a shame. You would have been a damn good lawyer."

"Do you think?"

"Yes, I think. Part of the law is about convincing a group of jurors to see the world the way you see it. Being persuasive might be your special skill. It sure worked with me."

"What worked?"

"You convinced me that your father killed your mother."

"I thought the evidence convinced you."

Mia saw something working on Justin's hard new features just then, something she hadn't seen yet in the interview, and it took her a moment to figure out what it was. Fear, that was it. You would think a kid brought in by a cop to the

DA's office would be scared, even a bit, but not this kid. He had been strangely nonplussed by the whole thing, until now. She glanced at Scott to see if he had noticed it too, but he was too busy looking at her. As if she had said something wrong or revealed too much.

"Yes, of course," said Mia, turning back to Justin. "It was mostly the evidence. Including Mr. Flynn's testimony. But you were a part of convincing me, too. We can't deny that, can we, Justin?"

"I assumed you had more to go on than me. I noticed your new title on the door, Ms. Dalton. Chief of the Homicide Division. That's a nice promotion. Convicting my father didn't hurt your prospects."

"Your father is asking for a new trial. Did Frank tell you that, too?"

"Yes."

"How does that make you feel?"

"I try not to feel too much now. But I suppose I would prefer he just sit back in his cell and rot."

"You sound like some prosecutors I know," Mia said with a slight smile. "So what did you and Mr. Flynn talk about?"

"Talk?"

"When he called you. The night he died. And you two chatted."

"I told you I hadn't talked to him in years."

"He called your phone," said Detective Scott. "We have the records from Verizon. They're quite detailed. The two of you talked for three minutes and forty-three seconds, according to the records."

"Three minutes and forty-three seconds," said Mia. "That's enough time to catch up a bit, don't you think?"

"I told you we didn't talk."

"Okay, Justin, you have your story and you're sticking to it. Just like there was no one inside your apartment beating the hell out of you just before Detective Scott showed up. That's all for now. Thank you so much for being so forthcoming. Do you need a ride home?"

"I can manage," he said as he stood up to leave. "I have to say though, that I feel like I was just interrogated about something. I thought Uncle Timmy died of an overdose."

He stared at her with such an impassive expression that she was a bit terrified of him at that moment, like he was cold enough to be capable of anything. She turned to Scott and nodded to him.

"Flynn did die of an overdose," said Scott. "But there are details of the death we can't square, and there is some suspicion of foul play. We have concerns that if there was foul play, it might involve your father's case, since Mr. Flynn was scheduled to meet with us to talk about his changed testimony the day after his death."

"And so you naturally called me in for questioning," said Justin with the same impassivity, no fear now, no resentment, just something cold.

"Naturally," said Mia.

"Merely wanted to get that straight. Seeing as I'm a suspect in a murder case, I guess I should watch my step."

"Where were you thinking of stepping?" said Mia.

"It was an interesting experience seeing you both again."

"Don't leave town."

"Don't worry."

After Justin closed the door behind him, it took a moment for Mia to catch her breath. It wasn't often she was taken by surprise in her job anymore, but this whole interview with Justin Chase had swept her off her bearings. What the hell had happened to the kid she had known, and what was going on behind the flat, dark eyes of the cold man he had become?

"He's changed a bit, hasn't he?" she said to Scott.

"He toughened up," said Scott, with a touch of admiration in his voice. "You said he was in an asylum after he left law school. That will change anybody."

"He was lying."

"About what happened just before I showed? Of course he was. But there could have been a lot of things going on. If it was something personal, maybe a fight with a pal, it would make sense that he wouldn't want the cops involved. And it's not as if he made a good show of it. It was like he was telling us that what was going on in there was none of our damn business."

"What about the rest? What about the phone call?"

"All he said was that he hadn't talked to Flynn. Just because Flynn called him didn't mean they spoke."

"The conversation was over three minutes long."

"Maybe someone else answered. Maybe it went to voice mail."

"He didn't say he got a voice mail."

"You didn't ask."

"How did he get so cold?"

"He found his murdered mother's body," said Scott. "That will do it."

"He scared me."

"You're getting jumpy. He just seemed a little mixed-up is all."

"He seemed more than that," said Mia.

"You got something against the kid?"

"Maybe I do," she said, wondering if it was something personal and then dismissing the notion. "Or maybe I'm just suspicious by nature. Check with the brother and then find out what you can about our Justin. I want to know who he hangs with, who he sleeps with, where he spends his money. He's into something, I'd bet you that, and whatever it is, it's rotten to the core."

14.

THE LORD OF DEATH

Now what?

Justin had been so whipsawed by the events of the past few hours that he hadn't really had a chance to think them through. He had moved without respite from Birdie Grackle to the surprise visit of his brother at the bar—where all Justin's Zen cool had devolved into adolescent brattiness—to the warning that had been violently administered in his house by the strange assailant, to his interrogation in Mia Dalton's office, where he learned that Timmy Flynn had probably been murdered and he, Justin, was a prime suspect.

It had required all Justin's control to hold onto whatever semblance of calm he still retained through Mia Dalton's questioning. But as soon as he was down the elevator and out of that building, he felt it, the past rising terrifyingly high, like a rogue wave coming from behind, about to crash down and obliterate him. And that was when he decided, with a rush of jittery panic, that the only thing to do was to run. Fast. To get the hell out of Dodge.

It wasn't a fear for his physical safety, and it surely wasn't a fear that he'd end up in jail. Instead it was the fear of dealing with it all again, the pain, the loss, the blood and guilt, dealing with the whole murderous mess that had slammed upon his head six years before. He feared he would break apart again if he had to revisit any of it. Which was why he had lied to the police about the beating, and why he hadn't told them about Birdie Grackle. It all needed just to go away, and that wasn't going to happen if he set the police onto Grackle's trail.

Something dark was going on, something full of twists and lies, and it would take some heavy digging to figure out exactly what it was. But Justin simply wasn't going to dig. Let them all play their little games—Frank, Mia Dalton, Detective Scott, Birdie Fucking Grackle—let them all dance around the maypole of his mother's murder. He was after something deeper and more meaningful than the mere solution to an earthly puzzle. He wasn't going to allow himself to get distracted. It was saner just to up and get on the road to someplace far away where he could find the peace he needed to perfect his life. Mia Dalton had told him to stick around, but she could simply stick it.

Justin didn't have a car, but he did have a motorcycle, a Harley he had bought for two months' worth of tip money from a guy he worked with a couple of spots before he worked at Zenzibar. The bike was old and loud and smelled like something was burning when he rode it, but it was also loaded with chrome, its tank was a sweet cobalt blue, and with the detachable windshield and leather saddlebags that came with it, it was in shape enough to carry him out onto the road all over again. Throw some shirts, underwear, and the proverbial towel into the saddlebags and head west, ever west, until he reached Sedona and found a spot in the desert where he could meditate his past into submission beneath a moon-drenched sky stretched over canyons and red mesas.

It was a plan—not much of a plan, but enough to capture his imagination. He liked the simplicity of the solution. Just go, get out, hit the open open road. And it wasn't like the idea hadn't risen within him over and again the past few months. It was why he bought the Harley in the first place, along with the tent and the compression sleeping bag that he could tie onto the seat. It was his route out, that Harley, his escape pod. And a run west would fit his philosophy of drift perfectly. Everything was pushing him away. And if everything was pushing him away, it only made sense to go with the flow.

He was already rifling his drawers for the essential clothes to toss into his saddlebag when he came upon the small black book, and he stopped, suddenly, as if someone had smacked him in the head and told him to get a grip.

Be not terrified. Be not awed.

He sat down on his bed and opened the book. He had read the volume so often that the words, familiar as a favorite old song, had begun to lose their sense. But the words now shivered with meaning in front of his eyes. And as he read, he realized why Birdie Grackle had gotten under his skin, and why he had reacted like an adolescent to his brother, and why the thug had bashed his face into the floor, and why Mia Dalton had called him in for an interrogation. They were tests, all of them, and he was failing.

The book prophesized that he would be so tested, that a series of fiends would come to him, one after the other, the so-called blood-drinking wrathful deities, one after the other, brandishing grotesque weapons and licking at skulls full of blood, and he would be tempted to run away in terror. But to run would show only how far he still was from any kind of enlightenment. The thing to do was to hold his ground, to look closely at the demons arising against him and see the truth behind their horrifying visages.

Be not terrified. Be not awed.

And in that moment he saw not the truth behind the wrathful deities sent his way, but instead the truth of his own pathetic failures. For the past years, he had been blind and awestruck, running away as fast as he could, running from his past, his truth, himself. He had read the book over and again and still he hadn't understood a word of it. His detachment was a trick, nothing more. If he was running, as he had been running for the past six years, it meant he was still in thrall to what he had been, in thrall to what had happened to his mother, to what had happened to his life. Still chained to the rock-hard lies of the physical world.

He had failed at every step of his journey, he had failed at every test that had been thrown his way. But according to the book, there was one last test, one last demon to face in order to prove his worthiness. And this demon was described with utter clarity in the book. His eyes glassy, his hair knotted on top of his head, big-bellied, narrow-waisted, shouting out "Strike! Slay!," licking human brain, drinking human blood, tearing the heads from corpses, tearing out the hearts, filling worlds with blood. He was the final and most fearsome of all the demons the book predicted Justin would have to face, the Dharma-Rāja, Yama, the Lord of Death, holding in his hand the karmic register of Justin's own life, having come into the world to drag Justin down into the pit of hell.

Which, all in all, was a pretty fair description of Justin's father.

15.

BRASS MONKEY

Justin was wholly unprepared for what he felt in the visiting room of the State Correctional Institution at Graterford.

He wasn't surprised at the interminable wait, at the rudeness of the guards behind the visiting desk when he showed his ID and signed in both his motorcycle and himself, or at the kindness the other visitors showed a first-timer. He wasn't surprised at the way he was required to empty his pockets before he went through the detectors and put everything, along with his helmet, into a locker. And he wasn't surprised at the shabbiness of the visiting area, like the stale-smelling cafeteria of a decrepit grade school in the Soviet archipelago, or at the crap that was sold in the vending machines. He had never been in a prison before, but still, none of it was unexpected. It was as if the good folks at Graterford were trying hard to live down to all his foulest expectations.

No, what surprised him were the emotions he felt as he waited for his name to be called—the fear and nervousness, the bitterness, the anger, the hatred—emotions he had thought had been bled from him long ago. But even more surprising was the keen expectation that cut through those emotions like a shining blade slicing through a dark curtain. Suddenly, trumping all the hard truths was the simple fact that he was a young man waiting to see his father, and whatever the reality of their relationship and their pasts, just the generic notion of a generic young man waiting to see his generic father for the first time in half a decade couldn't help but send the generic parts of his heart aflutter.

And then Justin stood as if ordered to attention when the inmate door opened and Mackenzie Chase, in his brown prison uniform, stepped into the room. His father's gray hair was pulled back neatly, his face had the hard, tight quality of an executive just off the golf course, and he held himself with the same haughtiness with which he had tromped through life before his conviction. He looked at the now-standing Justin with an achingly familiar air of authority and disappointment. Nothing had changed, absolutely nothing.

It was all enough to lodge a stone in Justin's heart.

His father stared at him for a moment longer and Justin stared back, speechless in the truest sense of the word, not just decidedly quiet but actually numb and dumb, as if the speech had been knocked out of him by the very sight of this man, who haunted his life and his dreams. The Lord of Death indeed.

"So, you've come finally to visit your father, yes?" said Mackenzie Chase in his soft, precise voice, every perfectly pronounced syllable a rebuke. "Come to poke the animal in his cage."

"Frank said you wanted to see me," said Justin, softly and not without a stammer.

"If that is what Frank told you, then he was mistaken. I said it was you who needed to see me."

"I needed to see you?"

"A boy needs his father, don't you think?"

"A boy needs his mother," said Justin.

"A whelp, maybe. But after the nursing is through, it is the father who straightens his boy's spine." Justin's father eyed Justin's long hair, his earring. "And it seems to me your spine needs some straightening. We're only allowed contact at the beginning and end of the visits. But I think we can forgo the obligatory hug, don't you?"

Justin's father took a seat at the table, gesturing to a chair on the other side. And Justin felt a strange sense of deflation, as if deep in the unexplored tunnels of his heart lived the hope that his father, when he saw him for the first time in years, would have rushed over and hugged Justin hard, and buried his tear-wetted face into Justin's neck. Justin took a moment to flood those tunnels with a fierce detachment before sitting down.

"Frank says you're pouring drinks in some lowlife bar," said his father.

"It's actually a high-life bar, since we serve Miller."

"Is this why I sent you to law school, to serve liquor to weak-mouthed drunks?"

"It's against the law to serve them if they're drunk."

"I remember when I tried to convince you to spend a summer clerking at Talbott, Kittredge, the firm your great-grandfather started, and you went to the public defender instead. You said you wanted to be Clarence Darrow, Thurgood Marshall. I don't remember Thurgood Marshall making Margaritas."

"How do you think he won *Brown*?"

"What the hell happened to you?"

"Someone killed my mother," said Justin, with a dose of bitterness that surprised him, "and my priorities changed."

"So you ended up in a bar. She would have been so proud."

"I ended up where I ended up. It's a job, it pays the rent. It has nothing to do with who I am, and that's the way I like it."

"That's what failures always try to tell themselves, but it is self-deception. You are what you do in this world, and what you do, Justin, is crap."

"What about you, Dad? What do you do now?"

"I seethe."

And Justin could see it, in the hunch of his shoulders, the tightness of his jaw. His father's fists clenched so stiffly the knuckles were white. Justin's throat tightened at the sight of it, as if his father's anger were reaching across the table to throttle him. For a moment, Justin had to look away to catch his breath.

"Frank told me about Uncle Timmy," said Justin.

"It was inevitable."

"I'm sorry. I know you were close."

"Timmy was always troubled. Even when we were boys, you could see it. He couldn't control his weakness, so he decided to feed it instead. He thought the junk would keep it at bay, but all it did was make the weakness stronger. It is no surprise that it overwhelmed him in the end."

"Frank said you asked him to pay for the funeral."

"It seemed the thing to do."

"I was surprised you would do that for him even after he testified against you."

"Timmy had an excuse," said Justin's father, a note of accusation ringing in his bitter voice before he looked away from Justin, as if for the moment he couldn't bear the sight of his own spawn. "The police used his weakness to twist him around. I understood. In the end, weakness was all he had left. Without it, he would have been nothing but bones."

"The funeral was this morning."

"Did you attend?"

"No."

"Came to visit me instead. Penance?"

"Not penance," said Justin. "In fact, I actually wasn't sure why I was coming, until I saw you walk in the door."

"And the grand revelation?"

"You're my father, it's as simple as that."

Mackenzie Chase stared at his son, and for the briefest moment something soft slipped through his expression, like a darting fish. What was it Justin saw there in that instant? Regret? About what? About their failed relationship? About Justin's dead mother? About all they had lost together? It was there and then it was gone and his father had changed the subject, but the effect lingered, like a hope.

"I heard about your motion," said Justin.

"I'll never stop fighting to clear my name."

"Is that what it's all about, your name?"

"It's your name, too."

"Don't remind me."

"You came to me, Justin. Obviously you're looking for something."

"I think I want you to admit what happened. I think I want you to tell me the truth for once. No transcript, no tapes, nothing to prejudice your precious motion. I just want to hear the truth."

"You don't want the truth, you just want some pabulum to fill your tummy."

"Try me."

"The truth is I didn't kill her."

"I don't believe you."

"And there we are." Justin's father took a deep breath. "I didn't kill her, Justin. I loved her. I've been trying to prove that from the first. I still am. And I was close to proving it, because Timmy was going to come clean and tell the truth for once."

"Why did Timmy change his story?"

"Maybe the guilt had been wearing on him. It can do that, you know. It can corrode like an acid until it turns your insides to mush. But for whatever reason, he came to me, out of the blue, and he apologized for the lie. And it was a lie. The very idea that I would say to him what he said I said. I mean, who knew better than me how unreliable he was? In this visit he said he would do anything to make it right. I had met a lawyer while in here who offered to take up my case. I sent Timmy to the lawyer and we filed our motion for a new trial."

"And then he died."

"He was chasing death his whole life, like a dog chasing the same car day after day. Finally, he caught the bumper in his teeth. Damn inconvenient—the timing, I mean. But accidents are always damn inconvenient."

"Except the cops think it wasn't an accident."

"What else could it be?"

"They think it might have been murder. And they think I did it."

"You?" His father smiled—or was it a smirk—to think Justin capable of something so hard as that.

"They suspect I killed Uncle Timmy because he had changed his story and was trying to get you out."

"Aren't they clever. Always trying to pin the tail on whatever donkey they see in front of them."

"I was hauled into Mia Dalton's office and told to watch my step."

"Sweet girl, that, like a lemon drop without the sugar. Watch out for her, before she does to you what she did to me."

"So who would want to kill him? Who would still care enough?"

"Other than you?"

"It's not funny."

"Don't tell me, tell that Dalton woman. I don't know who would have wanted Timmy dead. You make a lot of enemies in that life. Are they sure it was murder?"

"They seem to be."

"Maybe it was a dealer he owed money to. Or maybe it was someone who wants to keep me in here to protect himself. I don't know. Maybe the real killer is afraid I'll get out and find the son of a bitch."

"Just like O. J."

"That's who you see when you see me?"

"What else should I see?"

The old man leaned forward, lowered his voice. "Look around. I'm not sitting on a beach somewhere, I'm not pounding Piña Coladas and dating models. I'm in this hellhole with a life sentence around my neck. And unless something dramatic happens, I'll be stuck in this pit for the rest of my life. You don't need to keep punishing me. Mia Dalton did a good enough job of that herself."

"What kind of relationship can we have if you won't admit what I know to be the truth?"

"I envy you."

"Why?"

"With all the world's uncertainties and injustices, with all the doubt that piles around us like dead leaves in an autumn storm, you remain so sure of your truths. It must be comforting to be so sure." Justin's father tapped a couple of times on the table and then rose from his chair.

He stood there a moment and stared at Justin as if expecting something. Justin stayed seated and watched as his father's expression veered from sour amusement to something pained. And he looked old suddenly, stooped and beaten, far older than he had seemed before.

"It's nice to have something to hold on to," said Justin's father, "even if it is just your hate. No one knows that better than I."

Justin watched as the bent old man shuffled toward the inmate door. His father had aged three decades in the course of the visit. And as his father was let out of the room, Justin felt a strange longing. Not a longing for this man, who Justin still firmly believed was a murderous son of a bitch, but a longing for that generic emotion he had felt a hint of before, the generic caring of a generic son for his generic father. He wanted a father who hadn't killed his mother, a father who meant the things he said, a father who truly sought a relationship with his son. It was gone, that possibility, gone forever, for Mackenzie Chase hadn't just taken away Justin's mother, he had taken away Justin's father too. And for a moment he felt the longing and the loss so strongly that it cracked his heart.

Right in that room he did what he had to do to banish the emotion. He closed his eyes and concentrated, let the longing rise like a dark, foul fluid in the clear pool of his consciousness, let it rise until it nearly choked him with its poison, and then he let it flow out again, all the hope and need, all the longing.

He felt a tapping on his shoulder and he looked up into the face of a guard telling him it was time to go. But Justin put up a finger and asked for a moment, and the guard, seeing something in Justin's face, backed away. And Justin closed his eyes again and let the emotions flow out and away and disappear so that they could do him no harm.

Until he was left with nothing but the clearest, purest water.

In that moment he peered into the clear pool he had now become and saw something in the depths, something bright, iridescent. He reached in with an arm, stretched until he could just get his fingers around the object, green and sparkly and shaped like a turtle. And he clutched it tight in his fist, as if it were his final, brightest hope in a world of tragic illusions.

16.

LOW AND SLOW

Detective Scott was leaning on the hood of a car parked next to Justin's motorcycle in the prison parking lot. He was wearing a blue sport coat so tight the seams stretched as he crossed his arms. Justin walked up to his bike and plopped the helmet on the seat.

"Checking up on old friends?" said Justin.

"I have my share inside," said Detective Scott. "Most everyone I put in there knows I play the game square."

"My father would beg to differ."

"I didn't say all were fans," said Scott, "but all got the same square deal, your father included. You weren't at Timmy Flynn's funeral."

"I was busy."

"So you visited your father instead. I thought you told us you didn't see him anymore."

"What I said was true when I said it. I'd suggest you check the visitor log, but I assume you already have."

"Maybe I did at that. So why now?"

"After you hauled me in, told me that Uncle Timmy had been murdered, and accused me of doing it, I thought I ought to let my father know what was going on."

"What did he say?"

"He said I should watch my ass before you and Ms. Dalton railroad me like you railroaded him. Are you going to railroad me, Detective?"

Scott smiled. "Not me."

"How about Ms. Dalton?"

"She has it out for you for some reason. So when word was passed that you were here visiting your father, I thought I'd show and give you a heads-up. You don't want to be getting too involved in this case right now, son. Play it slow and lay low, that's always been my motto. It's kept me out of trouble."

"Low and slow. Is that how you play basketball, too?"

"Not when I was young and a terror on the court."

"I would have liked to have seen that. Okay, warning received and appreciated."

"Good. So now that we're alone, why don't you tell me, off the record, who was beating the hell out of you in your apartment when I showed up."

"I thought we dealt with that already."

"No," said Detective Scott. "You lied and we let it go, but it hasn't been dealt with. At first I assumed it was unrelated to your father's case, a drug buy gone bad maybe, not a good thing for you but nothing for me to get all sassed about. But it turns out you don't use drugs. You don't even drink, which is a funny thing for a bartender. And you don't care about money. And you don't have any friends. And you don't have anything to steal. Not even a television. How do you get by without a television?"

"I stare at the wall."

"So it was a puzzle, until I got word that you showed up here. And then I got to wondering if maybe the beating wasn't somehow related to your father's case after all. Am I wrong?"

"No."

"Who was it?"

"I don't know. He jumped me from behind and told me that what happened to my mother was over, and my father was where he belonged. And he said if I turned over any dirt, I'd be digging my own grave."

"Jesus. Why didn't you tell us all this at the meeting?"

"Isn't it obvious?"

"No...Unless...Oh, I get it. It seems to indicate that your father might have been framed, and you don't believe that. You still believe he did it."

"Don't you?"

"Sure I do. But that warning and Flynn's murder might be enough to get me asking questions."

"If I told you, Detective, that a geezer named Birdie Grackle came into my bar and told me he was an old hit man who had been hired by some unknown party to kill my mother, would you believe me?"

"You maybe, him no."

"That's what I thought."

"And even if something happened to my common sense and I did believe him, it wouldn't mean that your father wasn't the one who did the hiring."

"Point."

"Look, Justin. If Flynn really was murdered, then somebody had to do it. And that somebody could be dangerous as hell to anyone involved. Maybe you ought to listen to that warning, mind your own business, and let us worry about all this."

"I'll think about it."

"Is that your way of saying 'Go to hell'?"

"I guess you're not a detective for nothing," said Justin.

Because he absolutely was going to look into it, he had no choice. If there was a possibility that his father was telling the truth and hadn't killed Justin's mother, then there was a possibility that Justin could satisfy that strange yearning he had felt in the visiting room. He could never get his mother back, her voice was stilled forever, but maybe he could still get back his father.

"I have a hard time figuring a kid like you," said Scott. "Giving up the law to be a bartender I can understand. I met enough lawyers in my day to see how miserable they are. But no television? That's flat-out weird. Word is you're some sort of Zen guy. What does that mean, anyway?"

"When you find out, tell me."

"Does it help a sore back, this Zen thing of yours? Because I have this sore back that just kills me."

"You want my advice on that?"

"Absolutely."

"Lose some weight.

"Don't I know that. But how?"

"Get rid of the TV for starters. And then give up meat."

"No TV, no meat. Can I still have sex?"

"I don't know, can you?"

Scott laughed. "Dalton wants me to keep an eye on you, so that's what I'm going to do. But I'm on your side more than you know. I'm giving you heartfelt advice here to just stay out of this." Scott reached into his pocket and pulled out a card. "But if you got anything to say, I'll be glad to hear it. And if there's anything I can do for you, just let me know."

"Anything?"

"Sure."

Justin took the card and stared at it for a moment as he thought about the turtle he saw in the middle of his meditation. "Well, there is one thing," he said. "I'd like to see some pictures of my mother."

"Don't you have enough?"

"Not of her corpse," said Justin.

17.

JOHNNIE WALKER BLUE

Birdie Grackle fidgeted and hitched his way to the bar, moving through Zenzibar's lively evening crowd as smoothly as a dented old pickup, throwing rods every which way, trying to parallel park in a spot two feet too short. As Justin stood off to the side and checked the IDs of two very young women away from the sorority house for the evening, Birdie sidled up to the mahogany, leaned an elbow on the bar, stuck out his stomach, rubbed a finger over his big fake teeth. Standing at the bar, he held himself like the world owed him a favor that he was born to collect.

"Do you know how to make a Long Beach Tea?" shouted one of the young women, a sprite with bright-red lipstick.

"Do you know how to drink one?" said Justin.

"Sure I do," she said. "Fast."

Justin wanted to put his hand on her shoulder and go all avuncular, but that wasn't his role. He wasn't a caring uncle, he was a bartender, he mixed drinks. "Coming right up," he said.

"And a Cosmo," said the other woman.

"You bet."

The Long Beach Tea was simple enough—fill a pint glass with ice, grab bottles of rum and gin with one hand, vodka and triple sec with the other, and fill most of the glass. Top it with sour and a healthy splash of cranberry, pretty it up with a lemon slice, give it a quick stir with a straw. It was the kind of drink college girls ordered, because it tasted like fruit juice but stung like a bee. The Cosmo took a little more work, but it was sweet as candy and went down easily too. And all the while he poured and stirred and shook and strained, he had his eye on Birdie Grackle. The old man wanted money; Justin didn't have any. So the question of the night was how to get the old man to spill without spilling a check.

When he cashed out the two college girls, Justin headed over to the old man at the bar. "Thanks for coming, Birdie," said Justin with a spic-and-span politeness.

"I knew you'd make that call. Didn't have no doubts. But I bet it choked your heart a bit to do it."

"I had the opportunity to review my mother's autopsy and some of the photographs taken at the scene of her murder." Justin reached over and tapped Birdie on the spot behind his ear. "There seemed to be a mark right there."

"And so you called."

"And so I called."

Birdie surveyed the glowing bottles arrayed like little soldiers in their ranks on the shelves behind Justin. "How is it working tonight, doctor? Same arrangement?"

"You mean am I still treating?"

"That's what I mean."

Justin looked at the old man for a long moment. If he was telling the truth, a definite if, then this bastard had killed his mother. How to handle such a thing? How not to rip his throat right out of his neck? *Be not terrified. Be not awed.* "Sure, Birdie. Same arrangement."

"Then let's say I have another of those Mojitos you whipped

up for me. Make it an extra extra. And since it's on the house, make one for her, too," said Birdie, jerking a thick thumb at the pretty college girl who had ordered the Long Beach Tea. "She looks just young enough."

"Young enough to watch *Sesame Street* maybe."

"A girl like that, with only a little help she can get so cock-eyed she won't notice how old I am. Just because I can't no more get it up don't mean I don't still like a taste of fresh now and then." He leered and winked at the same time, a quite attractive duo. "And she don't even need to be awake for me to get it."

"One Mojito coming up."

"You getting judgmental on me, boy?"

"I have no judgments," said Justin, as he started building the drink. "I'm just a barkeep."

"So you got me my money?"

"Money?"

Grackle's face screwed tight, like he was sucking something sour. "The money what we talked about. You know, for the job. Half up front."

"Oh, that money."

"And here all along I thought you was supposed to be such a smart cracker."

"If I was so smart, Birdie," said Justin, his work with the muddler maybe a bit too vigorous, "would I be mixing drinks? But no, there won't be any money. There won't be any job."

"No job?"

"No job."

"You're letting a killer go free, boy."

"Karma covers all," said Justin. "I'm no caped avenger, I'm just a barkeep. And to tell you the truth, Birdie, I don't think you really exist. I think you're simply a figment of my imagination."

"What the hell's going on in that head of yours?"

"Nothing."

"You don't need tell me that."

"So how about one more drink, and then you go and leave me alone."

"That's what you called me for? You don't want to never know the truth of the thing?"

"Whatever truth there is, I don't think you have it."

"I gave you the turtle with them diamonds, didn't I?"

"Rhinestones. And the description of the pin was in all the papers. You could have had it made up just for the occasion, scraped it to make it look old, popped it in my lap to fool my eye."

"I ain't that clever."

"That might be the first thing you've said all night that I believe."

"So you don't want to know the one behind it all. The one what hired Preacher to hire me."

"You told me you didn't know who it was."

"That's about what I said, paraphrased and without the whoop-de-doo, though it's the whoop-de-doo what makes it all worthwhile. But even if I don't know who it was specifically, I can help you find out."

"And for that you want money."

"That's the deal."

Justin smacked a sprig of mint between his palms, and maybe he smacked it a little too hard. He made an effort to be slow in placing the drink before the old man. "Well, how about this, Birdie. You help me find out who it was that hired you, and if it pans out, then we'll talk money."

Grackle looked at the drink, longingly, looked at Justin suspiciously, looked back at the drink and lifted it. He sipped it daintily at first, and then greedily. When he plopped the half-empty drink on the counter, he said, "Keep them coming, boy."

"In a sec," said Justin. "I need to take care of some people over there."

Justin let Birdie stew in his Mojito as he served the other side of the bar. A couple of beers, a Dirty Martini, a Scotch neat, two shots of Tully. He poured Larry a fresh Yuengling. Lee asked for a Cosmo of her own, and Cody, who had just come in, asked for a Sazerac, which was rye sweetened with sugar and bitters, finished with a kiss of absinthe and lemon zest.

From the corner of his eye, Justin could see Birdie raise his empty glass to show he needed a refill, and Justin pretended not to notice. Have you ever been to a bar and found it impossible to get the bartender's attention? This wasn't an accident. She knew you were there, she saw you waving to catch her eye—she sees everything that happens at her bar top—and yet still she went on, seemingly oblivious to you and your thirst as she worked the other side of the bar. It's all part of the bartender's creed: make them fresh, make them cold, but most of all, if they're a little overeager, make them wait. And just then, Justin wanted to make that son of a bitch wait.

"Hey, boy," Grackle called out in his desiccated voice. "I'm still thirsty."

Justin gave Birdie a glance to let him know he'd heard the baying of the wolf, and then went back to ignoring him. Grackle wanted alcohol, Justin would make him wait. Grackle wanted money, Justin would make him wait.

"A couple guys came in a little earlier looking for you," said Justin to Cody as he built the Sazerac.

"Friends?" said Cody, looking around like a ferret in a trap.

"They didn't look so friendly, and they were big enough to back it up. Said something about a Solly something."

"What did you tell them?"

"Cody who?"

"Exactly. Christ, I stepped in it now."

"I guess the 'sure thing' wasn't so sure."

"Kobe missed two free throws just before the buzzer. When's he ever do that? *Ever*?"

"Never."

"Exactly."

Justin twisted a strip of lemon rind over the Sazerac, releasing the oils into the drink, before dropping the rind to the bottom of the glass. He slid the drink in front of Cody, and then leaned close enough so Lee or Larry couldn't hear their conversation. "I might have an opportunity for you to make some of it back. You see that old guy making the fuss over there?"

"Yellow hair?" said Cody, without turning his head. "Tats on his forearms?"

"That's the one. I'll cover you here for the next few weeks if after he leaves, you find out where he heads off to."

"You care if he spots me following?"

"It's better if he doesn't. And I'll pay twenty bucks an hour for you to find out what you can about him."

"A little detective work."

"Exactly."

"Anything I should be worried about?"

"A man that old and a guy tough as you?"

"Nah, you're right." Cody looked at Justin for a moment more and then smiled slyly. "Thirty-five."

"Thirty."

"Deal."

Without so much as a nod, Justin moved along the bar and filled more orders. When enough time had passed for Grackle to get seriously pissed—and one thing bartenders know is how to get someone waiting for a drink seriously pissed—Justin ambled over.

"Sorry, Birdie, but it's a busy night."

"I told you to keep them coming," said Birdie. "I'm a paying customer."

"You're half-right."

"You called me, sonny, not the other way around. Let me have a couple shots to take the edge off. And then we'll talk again about my money."

Justin turned around and checked the selection. At the Capital Grille, Birdie had ordered Johnnie Walker Red, a cheaper blended malt. Red was all right for mixing, but if you were drinking your blended Scotch straight, you wanted something with a bit more character. There was Black, which was better, and Gold which was better still. And then, on the very top shelf, glowing like a shiny doubloon, was a rare bit of luxury, a bottle so cherished each was individually numbered. Justin reached up and pulled the bottle from the shelf.

"You ever have any Johnnie Walker Blue, Birdie?" said Justin.

"Is it better than Black?"

"It makes Black taste like kerosene."

"Oh my. I might have heard something about it. More like a rumor than anything else. Is that it?"

"That's it. But it's expensive."

Someone called out for a beer from the far end of the bar. Justin ignored him, his eyes flat on Birdie.

"Let's not let expense get in the way of a friendship," said the old man.

"Let's not," said Justin, before opening the bottle, waving it beneath his own nose, and rising on tiptoes like he was smelling youth itself. He slammed a rocks glass on the bar and poured, slowly, as carefully as if the amber liquid were as precious as gold. He poured, and he kept pouring, the level rising generously until the six-ounce glass was more than three-quarters full. A feast of smooth oblivion.

Birdie licked his lips involuntarily and reached for the liquor. Before he got hold, Justin pulled it away.

"After," said Justin.

"After what?"

"You said you were handled by a man named Preacher. You said Preacher let slip something that told you it wasn't my father that had hired you."

"That's what I said, all right."

"What did he let slip, Birdie?"

Birdie eyed the glass and the Scotch whiskey inside. His fake teeth chattered. "You're not playing fair, boy."

"My mother played fair every damn day of her life."

"No need bringing her into it. What about my money?"

"Are you drinking, or am I throwing this away?"

"You ain't that cruel."

Justin snatched the glass and dashed the contents into the sink.

He ignored the appalled gasp from behind as he lifted the precious bottle back to the top shelf and, making a point not to look at the old man, went off to satisfy the orders that had been piling all around him. Birdie Grackle was playing him, had been playing him from the start, and it was time he played back. Sure, the geezer could just pick up and leave, but Justin had read Birdie as a battered old alky from the first, and one thing Justin had learned as a barkeep was that an alky never lets go of his drink. Even more so when it is something from the top shelf. Old drunks have an unholy reverence for expensive spirits. Birdie most likely could no longer taste the difference between the finest Scotch whiskey in the world or the rawest rotgut hooch, but he understood that Johnnie Walker Blue was a holy grail of liquor, and he'd wait until the gates of hell opened wide to get a chance to worship.

"Pour it again, boy," said Birdie when Justin finally returned to his perch at the bar. Birdie was trying to look hard-bitten as he said it, but the desperation glinted through the effort.

"I wouldn't want to waste any more of the good stuff," said Justin. "Why don't I pour you something house?"

"Don't be smart. That bottle up there. I've a hankering to taste it."

Justin shrugged and pulled down the Johnnie Walker Blue. He had already thrown away about a hundred bucks' worth retail, which is what Marson, keeping a wary eye on him from the corner of the bar, would make him pay. Still, it was having the desired effect. As he repoured, he watched Birdie's Adam's apple bounce. Justin pulled up when the glass was a third filled. The shock in Birdie's eyes was priceless.

"We were talking about Preacher," said Justin, still holding the bottle.

Birdie smacked his lips. "A bit more maybe, just for flavor."

"I'll fill it to the rim, Birdie, if you start talking."

"All right, boy. You keep pouring, because this is what I got. But it ain't just talk now. A deal's a deal. We start on something here, we're going to finish it, you understand."

Feeling himself close to getting an answer, Justin heedlessly pressed his advantage and put his hand atop the glass. "Go ahead."

"It ain't much, but it ain't nothing neither. Preacher, like I said, didn't never say nothing about who was doing the paying on our jobs. But this time he slipped up a bit, slipped up even though he didn't know he was slipping. Like I said, I was supposed to rifle the place, steal what I could. I was supposed to make it look like I slipped in for some easy cash. Preacher told me the client, she wanted it to look like a deranged druggie killed your mother dead."

"She?" said Justin.

"Picked it right up, didn't you?"

"You're saying the person who set you after my mother was a woman?"

"I'm just saying what Preacher was saying, is all. What you do with it is up to you. But it seems to include your father out, don't it? So figure what you need and then scrape up my money and we'll get to it. Now, give me my damn drink afore you get the urge this time to flush it down the toilet."

Justin stood there for a moment, let it sink in for a bit, and then pushed the glass forward.

Birdie looked down at it and then up at Justin, with a crocked smile on his crooked face. Justin filled the glass until the surface of the liquor domed between the edges of the rim. Birdie Grackle's eyes closed dreamily in anticipation. He reached for the glass with a shaking hand and was even able to get most of the Scotch in his mouth.

Justin was serving beers to two dudes in ripped T-shirts, their hair so wildly unkempt their dos could only have been carefully and obsessively kempt, when he noticed Birdie Grackle staggering out of the bar. As soon as Birdie left, Justin looked over at Cody, who nodded. A minute later Cody was gone, too.

Then Justin went back to serving the beers, thinking about his father, and trying to figure out who the hell was the woman who had so urgently wanted his mother dead. And though he didn't have a clue, he certainly had a clue who would.

18.

PINK SQUIRREL

Mia Dalton knew how to express incredulity on her hard features. Wide, shocked eyes, a wrinkled brow, an open gape leaning toward a smile, as if some dirty limerick had been recited in open court. *You have* got *to be kidding me,* the expression as good as shouted. *That is the most ridiculous thing I have ever heard.* It was quite the useful expression to flash in front of a jury during a damaging argument from the other side. One wide-eyed look at the jury and every sensible thing being said sounded like so much twaddle. She practiced the expression regularly in the mirror.

And now, in her office, she flashed her patented expression of incredulity at Detective Scott, but it wasn't aimed at him. Instead it was aimed at Sarah Preston, who had just said the very words Mia had been hoping she wouldn't hear.

"We're sort of still intending to go forward," said Sarah Preston, Mackenzie Chase's lawyer. "With that motion, you know, the motion for the new trial."

Cue the incredulity.

"Go forward?" said Mia, the expression still on her face. "We are all sorry that Mr. Flynn passed away, but passed away he has, along with the basis of your motion. We only kept this meeting because it was previously scheduled, but both Detective Scott and I fully expected you to withdraw your motion."

"I'm sorry, really, I didn't mean to disappoint you," said Sarah Preston with a nervous twitch in her lips. "If you want to reschedule or something, that would be okay, I guess."

Preston wasn't one of the usual members of the defense bar, or one of those public-interest lawyers always looking for a fight. She was, instead, a middle-aged, midlevel partner at a middling patent-law firm, without much litigation experience, who was representing Chase pro bono. How it pro'd the bono to help someone like Mackenzie Chase was another matter, but Preston seemed a bit of a squirrel, and in a matter like this, she was far out of her league.

"I understand you haven't spent much time in a courtroom, Sarah, but how the hell do you intend to go forward without a witness?"

"Well," said Preston, "you know, we do have Mr. Flynn's affidavit."

Mia laughed, raising her hands into the air for effect. "An affidavit. Sarah, you know as well as I do that without an opportunity for us to cross-examine Flynn, your affidavit is hearsay, which makes it useless."

"Yes, that is a problem," she said, pushing the glasses back up on her nose. Mia had met Sarah Preston before at bar association functions and political events, and Sarah had always come across as a bit dowdy, but her hair was glossier now and her lipstick brighter, and she was proving a bit harder to shove around than Mia had originally thought.

"A fatal problem," said Mia.

"You're probably right. But I've been looking at the Rules of Evidence, and I think there might be an exception for a statement like this." Sarah Preston reached into her bag, fumbled around, kept speaking as she fumbled. "Mr. Flynn in his affidavit claimed he lied on the stand. Which means he could have been prosecuted for perjury. Which means—wait a minute, here it is." She pulled from her bag a small blue book and leafed through it. "His statement would have been against his penal interest, and Rule 804(b)(3) of the Federal Rules of Evidence states—"

"I know the rules, Sarah," snapped Mia. "But the statute of limitations has already passed from the time of his testimony at the trial. So there was no penal danger."

"True, yes," said Sarah Preston, again pushing the glasses up her nose. "By just a few months, actually, which makes it harder."

"So you see—"

"But we do have some arguments."

"Arguments?"

"Well, you know, we could kind of argue that because Flynn's testimony was used by the state in the appeal, the statute could have been tolled until the appeal was ruled upon."

"Do you have any cases to support a position that ridiculous?"

"Not yet, but I have an associate looking it up for me in her spare time."

"She won't find anything, because it's not there."

"Then we'll have to make new law, I suppose," said Preston. "And Mr. Flynn was still on probation. Which meant the judge could have revoked his probation if the perjury was admitted."

"No judge will buy this, Sarah. Trust me, it's bullshit."

"Probably, yes," said Sarah, nodding. "And if so, I guess that's what the judge will tell me during the hearing."

Mia looked at her and then at Scott, who was smiling slightly, the son of a bitch. Mia had predicted to Scott before the meeting that she wouldn't have any trouble with the likes of Sarah Preston. Patent lawyers, she had told the detective, were the gym teachers of the bar, lawyers sure, but still.

Scott was now obviously enjoying seeing Mia being pushed around by a patent lawyer.

"Even if the statement is allowed in," said Mia, "it's not enough. Changed testimony by itself is insufficient basis for a new trial. The case law is crystal clear."

"But we won't only have the affidavit," said Sarah. "We'll have something else."

Mia looked again at Scott, who shrugged. "What something else?"

"We're going to present evidence about the real perpetrator of the crime."

"What are you talking about?"

"We're going to tell the judge who really did it."

"Who did what?"

"Who killed Mrs. Chase. And we'll tell the judge how we'll prove it to the jury. Newly discovered evidence. I think that might be enough for a new trial, don't you?"

Mia looked at Scott, who had suddenly leaned forward. "What kind of evidence?" said Scott.

"I guess we'll talk about that at the hearing."

"No, we'll talk about that right now," said Detective Scott. "If you have evidence about a homicide and a murderer on the loose, you need to turn that over."

"I'm sorry, Detective, really, but I can't do that."

Mia looked at Scott, then at Sarah Preston, then back at Scott, the incredulity not manufactured now, but real. "What the hell are you doing, Sarah?"

"I'm trying to represent an innocent man and save lives, Mia. How did Mr. Flynn die?"

"You know how," said Mia slowly. "An overdose."

"Then why is there a murder investigation going on?"

"It's routine with a death like that."

"Really? Because to me it seems if you were sure the death wasn't a murder, and wasn't related to the Chase case, you would not have hauled Mr. Chase's son into your office. Do you have any suspects in the Flynn murder investigation other than Justin Chase? Do you have any leads?"

Mia looked at Scott.

"If we do," said Scott, "we can't disclose them to you."

"And I can't disclose my evidence either. We gave you one name, Ms. Dalton, we gave you Mr. Flynn, our crucial witness. And next thing we know, he's dead."

Mia looked more closely at Sarah Preston. She was actually pretty sharp, for a patent lawyer. But there was something about her manner that was worrying. Maybe it was the shinier hair or glossier lipstick, but more likely it was the tone that underlay her words. She wasn't just taking a case or representing a client, she was more invested than that, no matter how hard she was trying to hide it.

"How did you get involved in Mr. Chase's case in the first place?" said Mia.

"I happened to meet Mr. Chase while he was in prison. He asked me to look into his case and I agreed. What I found raised questions, and then Mr. Flynn had some answers."

"You met Mackenzie Chase in prison?"

"That's right."

"What were you doing in prison?"

"I was doing volunteer work. Teaching a class."

"On patent law?"

"On Shakespeare. I was an English teacher before I became a lawyer. I was helping the prisoners put on a play."

"What play exactly?"

"Does it matter?" she said, dropping the little blue book back in her bag before standing. "I expect to be kept apprised of the Flynn investigation, if that's not too much trouble."

"We'll let you know what we can," said Mia.

"Good. I guess I'll see you in court."

After she left, Mia rubbed her jaw as if she had been clubbed. "What do you make of all that?"

"She's got nothing," said Scott. "She's playing for time."

"Which means she might expect to have something in the future. The Chase boy obviously told his father about our meeting during his visit in the prison. But I'm wondering what the father told the Chase boy during the visit. And this whole other suspect thing. Who do you think they have in mind?"

"No idea."

"Well then, Detective, I think you better get off your ass and grab one, before we're coldcocked in court."

19.

GIN GIN

The squat woman who answered the door squinted her squinty face at the figure standing in her doorway. The sun was shining directly in her eyes. The man before her was apparently more shadow than substance, and seemingly unfamiliar.

"What the hell do you want?"

"Hello, Aunt Vi," said Justin.

The woman put a hand up to shield her eyes and took a closer look. "Is that you, Justin?"

"It's me."

"Why, you been missing so long, sweetie, I thought you were dead."

"No such luck. Can I come in?"

"What for?"

"Just to visit."

"I don't got no money."

"I don't want money."

"If that's true, it'd be a first for your clan. Come on in if you want," she said, turning from Justin and shambling into the darkened interior. "And close the door behind you."

Violet was Justin's mother's sister. She needed a cane to support her weight as she made her way to a dark, plainly furnished parlor with the curtains drawn and the television on. Short gray hair, an untucked shirt over sweatpants, white sneakers. She had been a beauty once, with three kids and a doting husband, but alcohol had taken a toll on her looks. Now Violet had let herself go until she could barely make it out of the house to buy her Oreos and booze. But if you looked closely, beneath the folds of flesh ravaged by bitterness and drink, you could see the lovely creature she had been, and what she had been then was just as bitter and vindictive as what she was now. If anyone knew who might have wanted Justin's mother dead, it would be sweet Aunt Violet.

"Pour me a drink," she said after dropping into the lounger in front of the TV.

Justin found the small bar in the corner of the room and read the labels of the bottles all standing in a row. "Gin, gin, gin, and gin," he said. "What'll you have?"

"Gin."

"Anything in it?"

"Gin."

"I get the picture."

"And pour one for yourself," she said as she lit her cigarette.

"No, thanks."

"Too early?"

"By a couple decades."

"You always were the careful one." As she took the filled tumbler from Justin she gave him an appraising look. "But you don't look so careful any more. What did you do to your hair?"

"Nothing."

"There's the problem right there."

"You want to turn off the TV so we can talk?" said Justin.

"Why would we do something like that?"

He reached over, took the remote control off the small table next to the lounger, pressed the red button. Some soporific talk show died on the screen.

"They were going to give a recipe for jambalaya," she said.

"How are you doing, Aunt Violet?"

"How do you think?"

"That's what I figured."

It didn't take long to catch up on old times. There was no deep connection to revive, no store of fond memories to share. Aunt Violet was one of those estranged relatives who only showed up at the occasional Thanksgiving or Christmas celebration, or the occasional family funeral, to spew her bile. The other relatives shook in their boots when she approached with something to get off her chest. Even the dead ones.

Violet's ex-husband was now in Florida with some skank he had picked up in church. In church, could you believe it? And Violet's three children were scattered in states far from Philadelphia. She wasn't on speaking terms with the first, she was fighting with the wife of the second, and the third lived in Seattle. "I guess San Francisco wasn't far enough." The kids didn't visit much, which suited Violet fine, since a visit only meant the grandkids ran wild while her children talked incessantly about their lives, like everyone cared. "What is it with this new generation?" she said, the half-drunk gin in her hand. "All they care about is themselves."

Justin tried to catch up Aunt Vi on his life over the past five years, a heavily truncated version with just the least interesting details, but he stopped right in the middle when it became clear that Aunt Vi didn't give a damn, which was a relief. Neither of them gave a damn about the other; they were family after all.

"I visited my father in prison the other day," said Justin.

"How is the old bastard doing?"

"Not so well. He still says he didn't kill my mom."

"What else would he say?"

"Aunt Vi, you always know stuff, all the good stuff at least."

"I have a taste for the unvarnished truth," she said before taking another gulp of her gin.

"So what I want to know is whether you think my father is lying."

"What do you think yourself, Justin?"

"The moment I found her dead I knew it was him."

"And he'd have reason to have done it, too."

"Why?"

"Because your mother didn't love him."

"After all his infidelities, could you blame her?"

"I'm not talking about at the end, I'm talking about the very beginning. Your mother never loved your father, and that's the truth of it, the truth behind everything. She used him all along, like she used everyone her entire life, and that's why things turned out the way they did, you ask me. I'd say she deserved what she got."

Justin tensed his jaw for a moment. "That wasn't what I asked. I asked whether you thought he had killed her."

"It's all part of the same thing. You want the truth or you want the story that makes you feel all good and squishy inside?"

"The truth."

"Good," she said. "Because I have some to tell." She lifted her near-empty glass. "Fill me up and then buckle your seat belt."

20.

BITTERS

"What has your father told you about your mother?" said Aunt Vi.

"That my mother was the love of his life."

"Could be. And if so, there's the root of all his misfortune right there. Where's that drink?"

Justin took her glass and brought it to the bar. This was the second full glass of gin he had poured for her, and the first he had poured for her was most likely not her first of the day. As the clear liquor spilled into the glass, he imagined all the empty bottles piling up in the recycling bin outside.

"Eleanor married your father because he could support her the way she felt she deserved to be supported," said Aunt Vi, the filled glass now in her hand. "She wanted to be a poet, like she was another Sylvia Plath waiting to shock the world. As if the world isn't shocked enough already. But she knew she'd never earn enough to pay for her ink and her loft. Your father had a good job, and stood in line to inherit the factory. If she married him, she could keep her artistic pretensions."

"That's pretty cold," said Justin.

"You said you wanted the truth."

"Maybe not that much truth."

"Your mother was all ice, sweetie. But she was in love, actually, when she got married, just not with your father. She never fell out of love with her high-school sweetheart. You would think Eleanor would have gone for one of those angry boys in jeans, or a skinny misunderstood beatnik. But Austin was the high-school quarterback."

"Austin?"

"Austin Moss. Mr. Good Looks, Mr. Popularity. Everyone loved Austin, everyone wanted to be loved by Austin. He was in my class, older than Eleanor, and we'd had a thing for bit. You know, smeared lipstick in the back of the car, a loosened belt buckle, a tired jaw. And the way he purred, you could tell he liked it. We weren't going out or anything, but there was always the spark of possibility. I still remember how it felt when I heard the news in the hallway about my sister and Austin. Like a punch to the gut."

"You sound like you still haven't gotten over it."

"I never get over anything. That's my secret."

"That's a tough way to go through life."

She lifted her glass in a mock toast. "You might not believe it now, but I was the pretty one. I was the one that made the boys swoon. I had the tits of a pinup. Now they need to be pinned up before they reach my knees. But for her to be with Austin seemed a violation of the rules."

"Rules? What rules?"

"There are always rules in family, dear. That's why family life is so miserable. I was older by a couple years, but Eleanor was the special one. The favorite. My life turned dark the moment my parents brought her home. I remember staring at the little baby, thinking how beautiful she was, reaching in to touch her. And then she started crying, and my mother snatched her up, like she thought I was about to strangle her, and my father shushed me quiet, and they left me alone as they took her upstairs to fuss over her. And they never stopped fussing. And I was left to fend for myself, living under the shadow of the comparisons.

"'How come you don't get good grades like Eleanor? How come you don't have good manners like Eleanor? Eleanor won another literary award. Why don't you ever win anything? Why can't you dress more like Eleanor? Why do you have to dress like a slut?'

"Growing up with Eleanor was like growing up in a vacuum, because she sucked all the oxygen out of any room she was in. She was kind and sweet to me because she was in a position to be kind and sweet to me. And everyone always told me how lucky I was to have such a lovely little sister. And all I wanted was to pull out her hair like I had pulled out the hair of all her dolls. Because I knew the truth, that all she ever cared about was her own damn self. Your father learned that too late."

Justin felt strangely divided as his Aunt Vi spewed out the bitterness that had been eating at her like a cancer for almost the whole of her life. It was tragic in its way, how she had held onto it all these years, but it was not a surprise. He could always sense it in her during those family occasions: the cutting competitive remark, the dark expression on her face during unguarded moments. But as he saw his mother through Aunt Violet's eyes, he realized with a start that the vision wasn't shockingly off. His mother had been self-absorbed and a little selfish, and Justin himself had felt the sting of being on the wrong side of those aspects of her personality.

"Eleanor was the smart one," said Aunt Vi, "the artistic one. That was her role. I was the pretty one, the slutty one, the one that got the boys. The rules were simple. I wouldn't ever join the literary magazine and write poems about seagulls."

She downed the last of the gin. "And she wouldn't fuck the high-school quarterback."

"You know what, Aunt Vi? It's time for you to let that one go. All the bitterness, it just eats you up inside."

"Maybe I like the feeling."

"And that's why you drink?"

She looked down at her now-empty glass, lifted it up and shook it. "Give me a refill."

"How about some juice or something? Maybe toast?"

"You're useless," she said as she started to push herself out of the chair. She rose a bit, wobbled, and fell back down. "Crap. Do you notice the similarity in names? Your name is one purposeful letter away from Austin's. You were her memorial to the love she tossed away. No wonder you were always her favorite, why she ignored Frank and doted on you. The patterns repeat, don't they?"

"So why didn't she marry this Austin?"

"He couldn't give her the life she wanted. And your father was nothing if not a persistent suitor. From the moment he met her, he was lost, and eventually he wore her down. He promised her a nice house, time to write, a family, and a nanny to take care of the family. Though she didn't love him, she wanted all those things, so she allowed herself to be bought, it was that simple."

"Is anything that simple?"

"This was. Your mother confided in me, told me her situation with your father, asked my advice before she said yes."

"What did you tell her?"

"I had married for what I thought was love and it was already turning to crap. I told her to be smart and take the money."

"They seemed happy enough when I was a boy."

"Well, of course they did. Your father was still in love, your mother was still writing. But she grew a bit sour when her career never took off like she had hoped."

"I remember her at one point getting a little depressed. She would stay up in her room and we were told to stay away and fend for ourselves."

"She was paying the price for her choices. And the more she felt like her specialness was dying, the less she gave to anyone around her. Why the hell do you think your father started sleeping around? Why do you think he ended up with that girl you testified about at the trial, the one he introduced you to over dinner that night a few weeks before the murder? What a juicy morsel that was when it came out."

"Don't remind me."

"The papers had a field day. And everyone acted like your mother had been the one betrayed by his affair with that girl. But the truth was, my sister had been betraying your father the whole of the marriage by not giving him the two things he needed most. Other than oral sex, I mean."

"Aunt Vi, could you not."

She laughed, a throaty, vicious laugh. "What I meant was love and affection. The things my special little sister was never capable of giving to anyone."

"She loved me."

"Yes, dear, because you were so special, too."

"Do you think my father did it?"

"Did what?"

"Bludgeoned my mother to death?"

"My honest opinion? No. Truth was, he did still love her."

"So who did it if it wasn't him?"

"Who knows? Maybe it was a botched burglary. Maybe someone had been stalking her."

"Let me ask you a question. Was there a woman who might have wanted my mother dead? Someone serious enough to have her killed?"

"Other than me?"

"You?"

"She was my sister. Of course I wanted her dead."

"You cried at her funeral."

"Did I?"

"There were a lot of dry eyes, but not yours."

"Allergies."

Justin stared at the slumping figure of his aunt, and a wave of pity rushed through him. So many casualties. "Have you ever tried yoga?" said Justin.

"Are you kidding me?"

"No, I'm not. I could help you, start you out with a few basic moves. Yoga could smooth away some of your rough edges."

"I don't want them smoothed, don't you understand? My bitterness is about all I have left."

"That's too sad."

"Oh, stuff your tofu up your ass."

"You're right," he said. "I will."

He stood, leaned over her, kissed her sweaty forehead. She reached up a hand and touched his cheek, the same cheek that had been ravaged by the attack in his house. Her touch felt surprisingly good. He closed his eyes and saw his mother reaching out for him.

At the door, he stopped and turned around to take a final look. She was sitting in her chair. The TV was back on. She was smoking another cigarette. "Good-bye Aunt Vi," he said.

"What about the girl?" said Violet, face turned toward the television.

"What girl?" said Justin.

"Your father's little slut, the one he introduced you to. You're looking for someone who wanted your mother dead? What about her?"

21.

GRASSHOPPER

Derek does not want to understand all the twists and turns of Vern's master plan. If he tried to keep all Vern's sinister lines from snagging, he would only end up with an impenetrable tangle of fishing line and a hurting head. Making the plans and seeing them through is Vern's job. But what Derek does understand is that Vern is screwing up.

It was the untidiness of the last errand Vern sent Derek off to perform that first clued Derek in to the trouble. When you leave a dead body, there is no one left to give a description. That has always been Derek's primary advantage in the business. You look at Derek and you see someone who sweeps the floor at a McDonald's, or who attaches plastic leaves to fake plants. Cops cruising by always give him a wave, and Derek waves back, grinning all the while. And everyone feels good, and no one suspects anything, and Derek likes it just like that. He has always hidden in plain sight, with no one left breathing to paint a description.

But Vern's instructions were to leave the man with the long dark hair alive, to simply recite the script and then be on his way, and so he did it just as Vern told him to do it. But when the policeman came knocking, Derek had no choice other than to run. And as he ran, he glanced back to see if the policeman had yet come through the door. And when he glanced back, the man with the long dark hair caught a glimpse of Derek's face. Just a glimpse, but even a glimpse is enough when you have a face like Derek's.

Derek told Vern what had happened, and Vern told him not to worry about it. That Derek will have the chance, eventually, to shut the man's mouth but good. Still, there he is, the man with long dark hair and no TV, able to recognize Derek on sight, able to give a description. And when Derek complained again, Vern gave him one on the side of his head and told him to shut up. And so he did. But now when the cops cruise by, Derek's grin is not so secure.

So that was the first clue that things were falling apart. The second clue was that Vern was followed home last night.

As Vern staggered into their hotel, knocked woozy by his nightly dose of alcohol, he failed to notice the man slipping around the corner after him. Vern was too drunk to see it, but Derek does not drink. Derek was sitting on the stoop of the gated side door of the apartment house across the street from the hotel, scratching at one of his fleabites, when he saw the short man with the sharp, pointy face cautiously slide around the corner. The man moved carefully, his side almost rubbing up against the stone before he disappeared into the arched entrance of the hotel. The man left the hotel a few minutes later, walked beyond the hotel's entrance, turned around, and stared up at the wall of windows.

And that was the moment, seeing how badly Vern was screwing up, that Derek stopped believing Vern would ever get him a horse.

Derek did not tell Vern about the following-man when Vern lurched out of bed and plunged into the bathroom they shared with the room next door. Derek has learned not to tell

Vern bad news. All Vern does when confronted with a problem of his own making is to yell and spit right onto the floor, to ball his fists and blame Derek for everything. Sometimes he even cuffs Derek on the side of the head. Derek takes it because he needs someone to make the plans, and for now that is Vern, but the taking of it does not mean he likes it. And it does not mean he is not thinking of some way to cuff Vern back.

Derek is sitting on the stoop across from the hotel the day after, sitting there because Vern is lying on the bed watching TV in their little room. Vern always turns the volume so loud that it hurts Derek's ears. And there is the matter of the fleas that live like fat guests in their room. So Derek is outside, not thinking much of anything, just sad about the horse, when he sees the following-man again. The sharp-faced man walks into the hotel and a few moments later walks out of the hotel. He sees Derek watching him and he waves. Derek waves back and gives his grin. The man smiles at him before walking up and down the block, walking around the building, looking up to the top of the hotel. Then he comes over to Derek's side of the street, comes over, in fact, to a spot right next to Derek.

Derek is not so much afraid as he is curious. What is the following-man up to? Derek gets a closer look at him. His nose is long and narrow, his eyes are wide, his mouth is small, his hair sits up like fur. He almost looks like an animal, sharp and cuddly at the same time, like a dark-brown hamster, or a rat. Yeah, like a rat. Derek likes rats, feeds them when he sees them in the hotels that Vern picks. The man leans back against the wall with one leg propped behind him and his hands in his pockets.

"Hi," says the man without looking down at Derek.

"Hi," says Derek.

"What are you doing sitting out here?"

"The TV's too loud inside," says Derek.

"And it's quieter out here in the street?"

"Except when a truck goes by. But I like to be outside. I like to see things."

"Do you have a name?"

"Derek."

"I bet you don't miss much, Derek."

"I just sit and look."

"And see things."

"Sometimes."

"How about an old man, thin, his yellow hair combed back. You ever see him?"

"Tattoos?"

"On each forearm."

"Yes."

"I'm impressed. You must have really good eyes, Derek. He's staying in that hotel. Did you see him today?"

"Not today."

"He got in late last night, so he's probably still inside."

"Are you a friend?" says Derek.

"I'm like a friend, but not really."

"What's that?"

"More like a relative, maybe. The kind that you only see on Thanksgiving."

"I loved Thanksgiving."

"But not anymore?"

"Vern doesn't do Thanksgiving."

"Who's Vern?"

"The man I live with."

"Well, I'm sure he's very nice."

"He used to be," says Derek, "but not anymore."

"You staying in there, too?" says the man.

"Yes."

"The Parker Hotel. I've heard stories about the Parker. Do you like it in there?"

"There are fleas."

"I bet there are."

"You bet a lot," says Derek.

"You want to know something funny? You just figured out the biggest problem in my life. How'd you get so smart?"

"I do not try to be smart."

The man laughs. "That's your answer right there. Do you want to see a trick?"

Derek smiles eagerly. He loves tricks. "Yes, please."

The man reaches into his pocket for something and then sits down next to Derek. "My name's Cody, and I'm pleased to meet you, Derek."

Cody holds out his hand to shake, and Derek, wondering if that is the trick, holds back for a bit. Cody keeps smiling warmly, baring his teeth like a smiling rat, and Derek finally puts his hand in Cody's hand. Cody takes hold of it, but not roughly like Vern would, trying to control everything. He takes it gently, gives it a quick shake, and then turns it so it is faceup. When Cody removes his hand, Derek can see something in his own palm.

"A penny," says Derek. "That is a good trick."

"That's not the trick," says Cody, with a sly smile. Derek likes the way Cody talks to him, like Derek is an old friend instead of someone to shout at. A lot of people speak really slowly and raise their voices, as if Derek is deaf. Vern used to talk to him as nicely as Cody before he upped his drinking and turned mean.

"Now keep your hand outstretched," says Cody. "I'm going to try to take that penny from you, and you're going to try to stop me, but you can't close your hand or take it away until I make my move. Okay?"

"Okay," says Derek.

Derek holds his hand open with the penny in it, his tongue poked out of his mouth in concentration. Cody cups his hand with his fingers pointing straight down so their tips form a circle around the penny.

"Are you ready?" says Cody.

"Ready."

"Sure?"

"Sure."

"You sure you're sure?"

"I am sure I am—"

Just then Cody's hand darts down so that his fingers tap Derek's palm. As quick as a snake, Derek snatches his hand away and forms it into a tight fist. And when he feels the penny still in his hand, he starts laughing.

"What's so funny?" says Cody.

"I have the penny. You did not get it."

"You sure?"

"Sure," says Derek as he lifts his fist and opens it in front of Cody to show that he still has the—wait, wait—what is that in his palm?

"That looks like a quarter to me," says Cody.

"How?"

"It was just a trick."

"It is a good trick," says Derek, offering the quarter to Cody. "Here."

"Keep it," says Cody. "The old guy you spotted. Do you know anything about him? Does he hang out with anyone?"

"There sometimes is someone with him."

"Who?"

"Just a guy. Strong."

"Muscle, huh? That's good to know. Does the old man leave the hotel the same time every day?

"He goes out at night."

"Where does he go, do you know?"

"Out to drink."

"Anyplace in particular?"

"Down the street, that way. It has a name."

"A name."

"Like a person's name."

Cody turns his head to look down the street the way Derek pointed and then nods. "Dirty Frank's."

"Yes."

"Does he go with the muscle?"

"No. Alone."

"Do you know when he goes?"

"Only after it is dark. He does not like going out in the day. But when he comes back, it is late and he sometimes falls down."

"You think you could find me his room number?"

"Maybe. How did you do that trick? How did you change the penny into a quarter?"

"Want me to show you?"

"Are you allowed?"

"Sure I am, Derek, if you promise not to tell any other magicians. I wouldn't want to get in trouble."

"I promise."

"Okay. Let me teach you."

Cody then teaches Derek how to do the trick. He first shows Derek how to pick the penny out of someone's palm with one clean move. And then how to hide the quarter in the cupped palm. And then how to do the switch. He goes through it slowly, carefully, making sure that Derek understands each step, letting him practice the moves after each piece of the explanation. Cody makes what seems complicated into something very simple, and Derek likes that. And the whole time he speaks to Derek, he never raises his voice or slows his words.

"Now you have to practice," says Cody after he's shown him everything. "It takes a lot of practice."

"I will, I promise."

"Take the penny along with the quarter," says Cody. "I've got plenty of other tricks to teach you once you master this."

Derek looks at the following-man's rat face and feels something blossom in his chest, some certainty. This Cody does have tricks to teach him. Derek loves learning tricks. And Derek likes the way Cody talks to him. Much nicer than Vern. More like Tree, who Derek had liked the most of all the men who had taken care of the details, until that job in Harrisburg went bad. He missed Tree.

"Do you like animals?" says Derek.

"I love animals," says Cody.

"I like horses. I always wanted a horse. I would take such good care of a horse."

"I bet you would," says Cody. "Keep dreaming, Derek. Something will come up. It's amazing how many dreams come true."

"I know a trick," says Derek.

"Really, what kind of trick?"

"I can open doors."

"That's a good trick."

"Any door."

"I guess you can, so long as it's not locked."

"It does not matter."

"Even if it's locked?"

Derek just shrugs.

"Can you show me?" says Cody.

"If you want."

"Let's go," says Cody.

Around the block from the hotel is a maze of narrow streets, with some businesses, some houses. Cody walks slowly enough for Derek to walk beside him as Cody takes them through the neighborhood. He is looking for something, and on Manning Street he finds it. It is an old street, almost too narrow for cars, and the end of the block butts up against a building, so there are no pedestrians walking along the street. Cody walks up to the entrance of one of the houses and knocks on the door. No answer. He knocks again. No answer. He tries the doorknob. It will not turn.

"Okay, Derek," says Cody. "Let's see your trick."

As Cody backs away, Derek steps up to the door. It is an old door, with a deadbolt and a lock on the knob. Derek shields the lock with his body so Cody cannot see him work. It is a trick after all, and he does not want to give away all his secrets just yet. Working as quickly as he can, he picks the deadbolt pin by pin before turning it with the wrench and then brushing open the flimsy lock on the knob. When he is finished, with the door still closed, he backs away from the door.

"Done," says Derek.

"You're crapping me," says Cody.

"I do not need to go to the bathroom."

Cody looks at Derek, at the door, back at Derek. Then he steps up to the door and takes hold of the knob. It turns easily. And when Cody pushes, the door swings open. Cody ruffles his forehead as he looks again at Derek and then peeks his head inside the house.

"Nice," says Cody. "A flatscreen on the wall, a chandelier in the dining area, and some paintings of old dead people probably worth a load."

When Cody closes the door again, he looks at Derek but does not quite look at Derek. It is like he is looking beyond Derek, at something in the distance, even though all that is behind Derek is a brick wall.

"Hey, Derek," says Cody. "You ever just go in and just take stuff?"

"That would be stealing," says Derek.

"Yes, of course. You're right, that would be stealing. And you're too good a kid to do something like that, I can see that."

"But that is just me," says Derek. "You can do what you want."

Derek watches Cody's expression as it changes from puzzlement to surprise to calculation before he turns back to look at the unlocked door.

22.

GIMLET

Annie Overmeyer was drunk. Again.

She didn't mean to be drunk, again. That wasn't her intention, ever. Her intention, always, was to be the kind of girl she had thought she was destined to become as she stood awkwardly in the hallway of her high school, disappearing unnoticed into the pale green of the wall tiles, clutching her books tight to her chest. Like all young girls misfitting their way through high school, she had dreamed of the kind of woman she would grow into, sharp and funny and supremely competent, loyal to her friends, hip enough to be cool without being ridiculous, beautiful beyond belief and desired by all yet too preoccupied with her important and meaningful life to notice. But most of all she wanted to be good.

What did it mean to be good? Well, for starters, it didn't mean being drunk, again. Good women didn't get drunk. Oh, maybe they got a bit tipsy as they sipped Champagne at an art opening with their fashionable boyfriends or loving husbands. But not drunk, no, not liquored up by a pawing out-of-towner trying to get a little action while his wife knitted back in Ottumwa. And it's not like the red-faced conventioneer had to try so damn hard, like she was an ice princess up on her pedestal waiting to be thawed by a precise magical invocation. These days, give Annie anything with vodka and a little sophisticated patter and it was enough to raise her skirt. But this evening's stiff couldn't even follow that simple a script. It was all maudlin and sad, the rough economy, the frigid wife, the boy in the wheelchair. And have another drink, sweetie. And another. And why don't I get us a bottle?

She had put a kibosh on that one, not quickly enough to avoid the steady stream of Vodka Gimlets that sent her senses swirling, but quickly enough to avoid the rest of the pathetic playlet. Last thing she needed was to be in an overheated hotel room with a bottle of cheap liquor and some middle-aged man in his drawers blubbering about his son in the wheelchair. Maybe the photograph worked wonders in Ottumwa, but that was only one more reason to stay the hell out of Iowa.

So she was walking home alone, thank God, staggering a bit what with the heels and the alcohol, but on her way home. Which she never should have left that night. It hadn't seemed so wrong at first, she'd just had to get out of the apartment, couldn't stand another night of Lifetime, with the plucky heroine finding her inevitable redemption in the least likely of men. But she'd had no plans, no one special to meet, nothing definite on the horizon, and nights without plans these days almost always ended like this, with Annie drunk and the lingering scent of some slobbering out-of-towner on her neck.

Except this one had a coda that was worse than most.

When she bid her adieu to the gray hair and jowls, said good-bye abruptly and a bit too loudly, what with all the drink, said good-bye despite his protestations and the grip on her arm that she had to pry off finger by finger, she saw something painful in his eyes. Not the disappointment over thwarted lust she had expected, but something else, something worse: the sweet bath of relief. Like all along it hadn't been him trying to seduce her, but her, the big-city temptress, leading a God-fearing man of the heartland down the lascivious path toward hellfire.

Sometimes you only saw yourself clearly in the eyes of those you've left, and what you saw was a horror.

If she hadn't been drunk, she might have tried to figure out how the girl in the high-school hallway, who always intended to be good, had let her life slip so brutally away from her. But that was the question she had been drinking to avoid, and now, drunk and tired, avoidance was successfully achieved. No questions to be asked, no answers to be sought. As she approached her apartment building, a converted town house on Pine Street, she looked forward to nothing but the oblivion of a dreamless stupor-like sleep. She would lurch through the foyer and up the steps, scrape her key into the lock, kick off her heels the moment she stepped in the door, and collapse gratefully atop her king-sized bed, only to awake in the morning still in her skirt and shirt, with a line of drool marking the pancake on her cheek. Her life was too marvelous to—

"Annie. Finally. Where have you been?"

It took a moment to shift her focus from anticipation of the sweet relief of sleep to the man now barring her from her building's door, a small, fastidious man with pale skin and rimless glasses.

"Gordy," she said in a light, slurry voice. "I mean Gordon. What are you doing here?"

"Waiting for you. Wondering where you were."

"I was out."

"Tramping around, no doubt."

"Don't pout, Gordy." She closed her eyes and waved her hand at her mistake, remembering that Gordy didn't like the diminutive form of his name, being diminutive enough as it was. "Gordon. Pouting is unbecoming a man of your position. Yes, I was out tramping. Lawyers lawyer, doctors doctor, tramps tramp. None of us can help ourselves."

The man twisted his thin lips in disgust. "You're drunk."

"You think so? By golly, I was wondering why the world was spinning right around me, as if it were an amusement ride designed to make me throw up. Can you feel it? No? Then I guess you're right, it is only me. Funny, I only went out for a drink and here I am drunk. How does that happen, do you think?"

"I've been calling you over and over. Why don't you return my calls?"

"Because you've been calling me over and over." She looked a little more carefully at his neatly cut hair and his handsome face, lost her balance for a moment and regained it, saw the pain in his eyes and was strangely glad. Why should she be alone? "You're a sweet man, and we had fun, but we had this scene already, didn't we? And I'm of the opinion that the first is always the best. I'm moving on and you're going to go back to your wife, we both decided."

"You decided."

"Yes, isn't it marvelous?"

"My wife won't have me back. She's filing for divorce."

"It seems to happen more and more. A plague of divorces spreading about me like...like the plague."

"She says she can never forgive me and it's over. And she's right, it is over. I don't want her, I want you. I can't stop thinking about you. The way you feel and smell, the way you—"

"I get the idea."

"I gave up everything for you."

"And don't think I don't appreciate it."

"I love you, Annie."

"Maybe it's just something you ate. Did you have any shellfish? It's not the season, you know."

"I need you. I can't live without you."

"You'd be surprised what we can live without."

"Annie, I love you. Doesn't that mean anything?"

"Of course it does. To you. You're sweet," she said, swaying forward and placing a hand on his cheek. "But I need to get to sleep. Good-bye, Gordy...Gordon. Good luck."

He grabbed her wrist and jerked it down. "Why are you being such a bitch to me? Why are you acting like a drunken bitch whore?"

"Don't forget cunt," she said. "If we're going to pick out the juiciest of epithets, let's not forget the juiciest of all."

"You ruined me."

"You ruined yourself. Though I can't say I didn't enjoy watching. But don't tell me it wasn't worth it, darling. You blubbered like a baby in gratitude."

He twisted away from her, like her words were a slap, and then, while still holding on to her wrist with his right hand, he backhanded her face with his left. She could feel the force of the blow as it spun her to the right and drove her knee to the ground, but it wasn't painful. Yet. It would be, she knew, her face, and the bark on her knee from falling, once the alcohol wore off, would hurt like hell. Now she really had to get upstairs. She didn't want to be awake when the pain came.

"I'm sorry," he said, letting go of her and stepping away. "Oh, God, Annie, I'm so sorry. I don't know what came over me."

"I suppose now we're even." She put her hands on the cement and pushed herself to standing. Without looking at him, she staggered straight to her door. "Good-bye, Gordy."

"No Annie, please, you can't, I didn't mean—"

She felt his hand on her arm, and then the hand was gone. Along with his voice. Replaced with a constricted gasp like a death rattle. When she swung around to see what had happened, Gordon was being held back by an arm around his throat and his face was reddening alarmingly. Gordon was grabbing at the arm with his pale, manicured hands, but his flailing wasn't doing any good as the arm suddenly lifted him into the air. Annie's focus went from Gordon's face to the face of the man holding him aloft. A stranger, young, but without a touch of anger in his dark eyes.

"You're going to kill him," she said calmly.

"Death is relative," said the stranger.

"Before we turn all metaphysical and misty, why don't you let the poor man down before he croaks."

"If that's the way you want it," said the stranger before dropping Gordon splat onto the ground. Gordon, sitting on the sidewalk, grabbed his throat and gasped for air as the young man stepped over him as if the middle-aged man were a piece of trash. The stranger was tall and thin with broad shoulders, a bruised cheek, and dark shoulder-length hair. And he was way young, like a kid really, pretty much her own age.

"Who the hell are you?" she said. "And why are you playing superhero?"

"You don't remember me?"

"What, did I fuck you too?"

"In a manner of speaking, yes."

"Annie," said Gordon, still on the ground, hands still rubbing his throat. "Who the hell is this? Another of your toys?"

"Give me a minute," said the young man to Annie before he turned and stooped down so that he was face-to-face with the sitting Gordon.

"Let me tell you a story, Gordy. It is Gordy, right?"

"Gordon."

"Okay. So listen and think on this, Gordon. There was a Chinese Zen master who once asked a student if a heavy stone by the fire was inside or outside the student's mind. The student thought about it for a bit and then replied, 'From the Buddhist viewpoint, everything is an objectification of the mind, so I would say that the stone is inside my mind.' The master looked at the student for a moment and then said, 'Your head must be very heavy.'"

Gordon simply stared, as if there had to be more.

The young man lifted his hand and flicked Gordon in the forehead. "Lighten up, Gordon," he said.

Annie couldn't help but laugh.

Without rising, Gordon started crawling away like a crab. "Get away from me, you freak. Do you know who I am? I'm going to sue you into a Camden row house you touch me again."

The man with the long hair stood and turned around, and there was something in his hard stare that made Annie's throat catch.

"Wait," she said, the familiarity of the face coming into focus now. "I met you once. And I've seen...No, you're kidding, right? Are you who the hell I think you are?"

"Yes."

"Oh, Christ. And I thought this night couldn't get any worse."

23.

STRAWBERRY MULE

When she felt the cold kiss on the high arch of her cheekbone, Annie quickly opened her eyes. No, it wasn't all just a god-awful dream. The Chase boy was here, in her apartment, leaning over her like an accusation even as he gently held something up against her face while she sat, shoeless, on her couch.

"What's that?" she said.

"Ice."

"Wouldn't it be better in a glass with some alcohol?"

"No. Nice selection in your refrigerator, by the way. Diet ginger ale, an unopened carton of rotting strawberries, two desiccated limes, and a half bottle of cheap and bitter vodka swallowed by ice in the freezer. When was the last time you defrosted?"

"What did you say you were doing here?" she said as she put her hand over his, and took hold of the frigid plastic bag.

"I was saving you bodily from your disappointed suitor."

"Spare me the hero rap. I didn't need your help to handle Gordy. He's a pussycat, really, with such soft hands. It's just things haven't worked out well for him since he met me. Were you walking on by and happened to spy our little scene, or were you lurking?"

"Lurking."

She leaned back and closed her eyes. "You don't know how disappointed I am to hear that."

"Have you heard from my father lately?"

"Is that what you were lurking to ask me?"

"Partly."

"He writes me letters. I get one every month. They come as regularly as the cable bill. Sometimes I even read them. So yes, I have heard from your father."

"What does he say?"

"He coos like a pigeon. Sometimes I coo back out of pity. What are you doing here, Junior?"

"I have some questions."

"Maybe you should go to a priest; he's bound to have more answers than I do."

"I left any faith I had in priests on the floor with my dead mother."

She opened her eyes and stared at him. This was heading exactly where she didn't want it to head, yet there didn't seem to be too much choice. He had lurked, he had arrived with flash and violence, and he had questions. God save her from questions. Yet he wasn't hard on the eyes, Annie noticed, though in a generic sort of unshaven way, with a cute little bruise on his cheek that undoubtedly now matched hers. They were like coordinated T-shirts that read, "I'm with Stupid."

"Do you know how to make a drink, Junior?"

"I've had some experience."

"Fill me a glass with some ice and that vodka you found. Let me get out of this skirt and maybe you can ask your questions. I'll decide then whether to answer them."

"Fair enough," he said.

As she wiped off the blood and her makeup, and changed

into an overlong nightshirt, she heard all kinds of noise coming from the kitchenette, which alarmed her, but not enough for her to go see what the hell he was doing. She was back on the couch, legs curled beneath her, when he returned from the kitchen holding a glass filled with ice and crushed strawberries and a slice of lime. A spoon stuck out beyond the rim like a jaunty accent.

"What is that?" she said.

"It's sort of a Strawberry Mule, with a few necessary modifications based on the paucity of your pantry."

When she tasted it, her mouth fizzled with the clean, sweet flavor of strawberry. "It's pretty damn good."

He sat in a chair across from her. "There wasn't much juice left in the limes and ginger ale is not ginger beer."

"Still."

She took another sip and then a gulp. She needed something to help her deal with this serious boy out to find all the sad answers in his sad little life. In fact she would have preferred just the vodka straight, but this sure was tasty.

"You're not going to join me?" she said.

"I don't drink."

"And yet..." She lifted her drink in tribute. "So here you are, the grieving son, sober as a stone and trying to get to the bottom of the tragedy of his past, is that it?"

"I've gotten beyond the grieving part."

"Is there a beyond? And without drinking?"

"I could show it to you."

"This will do just fine."

"You know that my father is trying to get a new trial."

"After what happened to his friend, Flynn, I just assumed that was over. And to tell you the truth, it's a hell of a relief."

"Flynn's death was a relief?"

"What did you think, Junior, that your father was the love of my life and that I've been waiting dutifully all these years hoping they let him out so we can resume our torrid affair?"

"Something like that."

"I don't mean to disappoint you if you were waiting on me to be your stepmom, but he was just another mistake in a long line. And not the first, either. But seeing how it turned out, maybe the most spectacular."

He looked at her and struggled a bit to come up with the right words. "This thing you had with my father...what was it all about?"

"You go right at it, don't you?"

"I'm trying to understand what happened."

"I'll keep it simple for your simple little brain. It was a fling. They're messy and fun and stupid. And ours was drunken, which always adds to the hilarity. And of course, like most, it was a mistake."

"Were you in love?"

"God, you are grabbing all the clichés, aren't you?"

"That's all I have at the moment."

"I guess I felt something, but I don't know if it was love. It was dirty and grown-up and transgressive and thrilling in its perverse little way, all the things I couldn't help being attracted to, being as I'm nothing myself if not perverse. And it always feels safer with someone older, who has more to lose than you do. No future, you see, nothing that could really call for a commitment, which seems to be what I always fall for. There was an affair with an older professor in college that sort of began the pattern. And then your father."

"You didn't want to marry my father?"

"God, no. He was already married. And marrying him, what would I gain?"

"He was rich."

"Not that rich. And he was old. And he had a family. I didn't want to wreck your happy home, believe it or not. He said I was all part of this arrangement he had and I was ready to believe him. But he sure wanted to marry me. He kept on asking, and I kept on telling him the obvious, that he was already married."

"So it was all him."

"Not all. You know, when you're lying in bed with someone, naked, after, feeling some sort of glow..." She laughed at the boy's obvious discomfort. "However much you don't want to hear it, that part wasn't bad. But in bed you can feel a certain magical closeness that makes everything else seem distant. And I don't know, in those moments, with your father, maybe it seemed possible. And here's the kicker, Junior. Even now, somehow those moments, in bed with some old married guy, with both of us drunk and him pawing at my chest, those moments might just be the last innocent moments I have left in my life. When I can still feel like it was before."

"Before what?"

"Before the blood."

"Oh." He seemed to work at processing that, as if it didn't make sense that his own tragedy could have had any effect on anyone else. He was a little boy, wasn't he? "When did you hear about my mother?"

"Your father called me, but only after it was all over the news. He told me it was some sort of botched robbery, but still it was best if we didn't see each other for a while. He told me that he loved me and we would get through this, but all I wanted to be was through with him. From the first, I knew what had happened to your mother. I had killed her."

The boy leaned forward and said, "How did you kill her, Annie?"

Annie stared into his eyes, strangely focused now, a line of concentration pulling the skin taut on his forehead, and even in the swirl-whirl of her drunkenness, she sensed the danger.

"Wait," she said. "Wait one stinking minute." She looked at the drink in her hand like it had been poisoned, before putting it carefully down on the cocktail table in front of the couch. "When was the last time you saw your father, Junior?"

"A couple days ago."

"So you're bosom buddies now?"

"That was the first time I had spoken to him since his arrest."

"But you visit him after the Flynn thing blows up, and now here you are giving me the third decree."

"Degree."

"Whatever. What are you, your father's new lackey?"

"New?"

"I always thought your brother was the dutiful son, carrying your father's water like a water boy. But now here you are, bucking for a promotion to the top."

"I'm not working for anybody."

"But you are trying to pin something on me."

"I only want to understand."

"Then understand this, Junior. It didn't just happen to her. Or to you. Or the rest of the fucking Chases, who think the world revolves around them like they are the axis of existence. It happened to me, too. And it was crushing."

The boy tilted his head just a bit and looked at her as if he were seeing her for the first time. And at that moment she detected a certain sympathy in this Justin Chase that gave her an odd, tremulous thrill.

"Oh, yes," he said slowly, calmly, like a butcher trimming a steak. "Please. Tell me how crushing it was for you."

She felt just then, in his arrogant put-down, a shock of loneliness that was, in its depth and rawness, well-nigh unbearable. This boy didn't understand, didn't want to understand, was violently opposed to understanding. And he was no different, really, than anyone else on this stinking planet. No one wanted to understand, they either wanted to fuck her or look down on her, or go for the daily double like Gordy and do both at the same time. It was the sad state to which her life had fallen, and it actually would have been unbearable if she weren't already drunk. She picked up her drink, took a long fizzly gulp until there was only ice against her lips, felt the shock ebb, replaced by a warm velvety nothing, and she remembered why she drank in the first place.

"You want to make me another one of these, Junior?"

"I think you've had enough."

"That just shows how little you know. I'll make my own, I guess. Without all the accoutrement. Less luscious, more potent. But, despite how much fun we're having, we're through here. I have to get up for work tomorrow. And you need to be a shit to someone else. So no matter how much I've enjoyed your company, and you are certainly as welcome back as the plague, it's time for you to go."

"I didn't mean to—"

"Yes, you did. And I get it. I don't deserve to wallow. Only you get to wallow. That's fair. She was your mom. And he's your dad. And I'm just a whore."

He looked at her for a long moment, like he was looking through her. "You're not in a good place."

"And right now," she said flatly, "I want to be there alone."

He looked at her a bit more before standing and, without the pretense of an apology, which she appreciated, headed for the door. She watched as he reached for the knob and then pulled back.

"What did you mean by 'arrangement'?" he said after he turned around again. "You said you were part of an arrangement."

"Just something your father told me. Probably a lie, like much of what else he said."

"What did he say about my mother?"

"How well did you know her, Junior?"

"She was my mother."

"Exactly," she said.

"What is your mother like?"

"She's a happy little monster."

"Well, my mother wasn't like that at all."

"Then you shouldn't worry about it."

"Worry about what? What the hell are you talking about?"

"If you really want the truth, Junior, ask your brother."

24.

WILD TURKEY

Frank was still living in the house. Frank was still living in the house. Frank was still living in the fucking house, and even though Justin had known it to be true for all these years, he could still barely believe it.

When Frank, wearing a white shirt with the sleeves rolled halfway up his forearms, answered the door and stepped into the night, his face glowed palely from the dim outside lights, ghostlike. And the surprise expressed on his features made it seem like he was seeing a ghost himself.

"Justin? What the hell?" Frank looked around guiltily, as if he had gotten caught at something. "What are you doing here?" He glanced at his watch. "It's a bit late, don't you think?"

"I have some questions."

"Can they wait?"

"No."

Frank stared at him a bit, saw something in his face, pulled back a bit. "Is this about your visit with Dad?"

"Can I come in?"

"Okay, uh, sure." He opened the door wide and, like a barker at a fun house, gestured Justin inside.

Mom?

Justin tried not to look down when he walked in, but he couldn't help himself. His legs stopped moving and his gaze turned toward the floor of the foyer as if it were pulled there by the weight of the past six years. And what did he expect to see? The blood and the bone? The spreading red puddle? Maybe only the outline of her body still marked in the police chalk once the body was carted away by the coroner? Some stains are just too deep to clean. But all he saw were the sparkling marble tiles, the grout a spotless white.

"When was the last time you were here?" said Frank, noticing Justin's stop and his stare.

"That night."

"And not since?"

"No."

"Oh, that's right. You made the funeral but didn't have time to visit with the family right after. There must have been a game on TV or something."

"Something," said Justin.

At that moment he heard a creak from the stairwell. Cindy, Frank's wife, was standing on the steps, clutching at her robe. She was a small woman with a sharp, nervous face, prettier than Justin remembered, and she stared at Justin as if he had come bringing some very bad tidings.

"Hello, Cindy," said Justin. "Long time no see."

"Justin. I was so glad when Frank told me you were back."

"You look great."

"I look a mess," she said, pushing a strand of blonde hair away from her tense face. Her hair had been dark and mousy the last time he had seen her. "Is anything wrong?" she said. "It's so late."

"No, nothing's wrong. I'm sorry about the time, it's just I work weird hours and seem to have lost track."

"It's all right, Cin," said Frank. "Go back to bed." She stood motionless on the stairwell. "Justin, why don't you head on into the library. I'll be right with you."

"Sure," said Justin. "Sorry to wake you, Cindy."

"We're going to see more of you, I hope," she said. "The kids will want to meet their uncle. We've all missed you."

"Thank you," said Justin, though something in her voice let him know that the missing hadn't been all that painful.

From the wood-paneled library, he could hear bits and pieces of their hushed conversation, and something that sounded like a fearful "What does he want?" Well, what did he want? Hell if he knew for sure. And why had Cindy seemed so afraid to see him?

"Do you want a drink?" said Frank after he closed the door behind him.

"No."

"But you won't mind if I have one," said Frank as he went over to the small bar set in the corner and poured himself a half glass of Wild Turkey, their father's brand.

The library had been their father's office, and Frank hadn't changed it a whit. The bar was as it had been, the cut-glass decanters, the silver cocktail tools, the bottles lined up in a neat row. Justin's father was the first person to teach Justin how to make a drink, pressing him into service stirring up the Martinis for guests while Justin was still in grade school, more a trained monkey to his father than a son. The desk hadn't moved. The two leather chairs were set just so, as they had always been set just so. The painting of the horse was still hanging above the chair, symbolic of a failure of the lineage, since the Chase family had been ensconced at Radnor Hunt for generations but none of Mackenzie's brood ever rode. A quick scan of the shelves on the wall proved that the books hadn't changed much either. The same old leather-bound novels that only his mother had read, the same right-wing tomes placed in plain sight by his father. The whole room, the whole house, reeked, not of his mother's blood, the scent of which he had tried to catch and had failed, but of his own blighted past.

"How can you still live here?" said Justin.

"Have you priced real estate lately?" said Frank.

"Not for mansions, no."

"It's not quite a mansion, but it's bigger than we could otherwise afford. We moved in with Dad after Mom died, to take care of him. And we stayed on to take care of the house after his arrest. Sort of like triage in the face of tragedy. Then we didn't want to leave and sell the place before the appeal was resolved, as if that would send a message of some sort. And by then we had Ron, and the house worked for us, and it seemed just easier to stay."

"Doesn't it, like..."

"Creep me out every day of my life?"

"Something like that, yeah."

"It used to, I admit," said Frank, looking at his glass. "But you know, in a strange way, I find it comforting now. I think about her whenever I walk through the door. If we sold the place, the new people would just stride across the foyer without thinking of her at all."

"Maybe she'd haunt them."

"Mom wouldn't be much of a ghost," said Frank. He took a sip of his drink. "She'd probably just correct their verb tenses or something."

Justin laughed, because his brother was right. Of all the things haunting Justin, his mother wasn't one of them. "How was Uncle Timmy's funeral?"

"Sparsely attended," said Frank. "Although a cop showed up, which was interesting. The cop who handled Dad's case."

"Scott," said Justin.

"Right. You must have a good memory."

"Not that good."

"Dad said your visit ended badly."

"All the old crap kept coming between us."

"I know how that is."

"It comes between you and Dad too?"

"Between me and you."

"Oh. Yeah. Right."

"But he appreciated you making the effort. It meant a lot to him."

"He still says he didn't kill Mom," said Justin.

"Maybe because he didn't."

"Do you really believe that?"

"I want to. I try to. To be honest, I don't really think I have much of a choice."

"Why not?"

"Because he's my dad. Mom's gone. You ran away. Who the hell else do I have?"

"You have a wife and two kids. That should be more than enough."

"And yet..." He took a gulp from the glass, bit his lip.

"Tell me about the arrangement Dad had with Mom."

Frank looked up, slightly startled. "What are you talking about?"

"The arrangement, Frank. I was told to ask you, that you would know."

"Who told you that?"

"It's not important."

"The arrangement?"

"Yeah, the one that allowed Dad to sleep around like a pirate."

"Oh," said Frank. "That arrangement."

"Yeah."

"So that's what you came for. You might want to take a seat on this, Justin."

"I'll stand."

"Well, then I'll sit, if that's okay," said Frank before draining his glass and filling it halfway again. He walked around to the other side of the desk, dropped down into the chair. He leaned back, like Justin's father used to lean back, and rested the drink on his belt buckle.

"Mom and Dad's marriage," said Frank, looking at the whiskey in his glass so as to avoid Justin's gaze, "wasn't exactly what it appeared to be."

There was something about Justin's brother, sitting behind his father's desk, in his father's pose, talking about his father's marriage to his mother, that made Justin recoil.

"I know they were never quite the happy couple," said Justin, "and that he cheated on her."

"And Mom knew it and accepted it."

"No she didn't. She wouldn't."

"It's true."

"I don't believe you. Not for a second. You're trying to sell some crap that Dad must have sold you. Because my mother would not have stayed married to him all along if she knew."

Frank looked at Justin and smiled calmly. "She was my mother, too."

"So you know. She wouldn't have stood for it. She was too strong to have taken that from him, she would have left him on the spot. In fact, that's why I didn't tell Mom about Dad's affair with that Annie Overmeyer when he shoved it in my face. Because it would have ended her marriage, and I didn't want to be the one responsible for that. Because I was a coward. So I kept quiet. And she never knew. And then he killed her."

"And you've been beating yourself up about it ever since."

"I've gotten over it."

"It doesn't sound like it, Justin. You still sound so angry, so sad. But what if you were wrong, what if the whole scenario that has sent you spinning out of control is all wrong?"

"I'm not out of control."

"You were the brilliant one, the one with the great future. I got sucked into the family business because it was always assumed it was the best I could do, but you were going to make your own way. Northwestern. Penn Law. You were going to rise like a rocket ship, you were going to end up on the Supreme Court. And now you're tending bar in a dive."

"Zenzibar isn't a dive."

"But it's not the Supreme Court either, is it? And the guilt that pushed you off course is all bullshit. Because she knew, Justin. She knew from the first, and nothing you could have told her would have changed anything. Think about it. How could she have not known? She had a sixth sense. She knew what we were up to, always. Remember that time with the ink and the carpet."

"We moved the table an inch to cover the stain and she saw through it right away."

"She knew everything. She was just like that. And she knew what Dad was up to, too."

"He was more devious than we were."

"Not too devious for you to learn about his girlfriend."

"He wanted me to know."

"Because she knew. And she was happy about it."

"Don't be sick."

"Because they had an arrangement. That was what their marriage had become. He had his affairs, and she had hers."

"Fuck you, Frank."

"It's hard to fathom. Believe me, I know."

"It's a lie. From Dad. And I don't want to hear anymore."

"I didn't learn it from Dad. He didn't mention it at all until I found the letters."

"What letters?"

"Letters to Mom."

"From who?"

"We don't know, but they are worth reading."

Frank leaned forward and opened a desk drawer. He pulled out a few pages of copy paper and pushed them across the desk. Justin stared at them for a long moment, not wanting to see them, not wanting to know anything about them. And yet at the same time not able to look away. He slumped down into a chair, as if his legs had given out, and kept staring.

"Go ahead," said Frank as he pushed the pages a bit closer to Justin. "See for yourself."

25.

MUDSLIDE

Justin could barely read the pages. He shielded his eyes as if the letters burned white-hot and it hurt to even gaze upon them. He wanted to stop reading, but he couldn't stop. He wanted to throw the pages onto the ground, but he couldn't let them out of his hands. He felt he was doing something deeply perverse, violating his mother's privacy and invading her deepest-held emotions, even as he kept reading on and on.

No child ever wants to know the raw details of his parents' marriage. Whatever lies at that marriage's heart, whether it be derangement or joy, is best kept far away from the children, like household chemicals or prescribed narcotics. Children live in a world of myth, and fight to hold on to these myths at all costs, not because they are sweet and safe, but precisely because they are myths. Some things, even if beautiful, are better left unseen. Who wouldn't rather imagine their parents locked together in some silent and bitter misery then to actually see them blissfully fucking?

Especially blissfully fucking someone else.

Dearest E,
I've been thinking about you, about all you said, about your kindness and support.
—A

Dearest E,
You know the situation I am in, the vile power she has over me, you know how hard this is. But also, your love almost gives me enough courage. I think of your words, your kindnesses, your touch. If you can make the choices you have, suffer the pains, and come through it so beautiful and giving and perfect—yes, perfect—if you can do that, so can I. You know I love you, you know I need you, now more than ever. I think of you night and day, and each day I get closer.
—A

Dearest E,
Liberated. Empowered. Full of life. I was dead before you gave me your healing touch. Now I know love, and longing, and desire, and pain, and loneliness. Now I know life and I owe it all to you. We'll be together, I know it.
—A

"Where did you get these?" said Justin, after he stopped himself from reading the rest and slammed them facedown on the desk. The letters were forcing him to confront more facts about his mother that he didn't want to know. First there was the bile-ridden rant of Aunt Violet, and now the apparent love affair with A.

"They were in Mom's closet," said Frank. "Hidden in one of her shoeboxes, underneath the tissue beneath a set of red pumps."

"Why weren't they introduced at the trial?"

"Because I hadn't found them yet. Cindy and I didn't touch the closet for months, for years. We slept in the guest room. How could we sleep in the master bedroom? It was still their room. I sometimes dreamed that Mom was sweeping back into the house, saying hello and reclaiming everything. So for the longest time, I couldn't bring myself to do anything about her clothes. But when we decided that we might stay, Cindy said it was time, that Mom would rather the clothes be worn by someone than just sitting there to feed the moths. And she was right. So I packaged everything up for Goodwill myself, as a final gift to Mom. And as I did it, I found the box, and opened it to check that the shoes inside were matched, and there they were, underneath the tissue paper."

Justin grabbed the letters from the desk, glancing down again at them as he spoke, so his eyes were still hidden from Frank. "Do you have any idea who this 'A' is?"

"None."

"What does Dad say?"

"He doesn't know either. But he knew there was someone. He had a lover, and she had a lover, and everything was even, and everything was allowed. That was the life they created with each other, that was the arrangement."

"Yet he didn't bring it up at the trial?"

"He said he was trying to protect Mom's reputation."

"And you believe that?"

"I don't know. I think the fact that Mom might have been having an affair could have been seen as another motive, and to bring it up could be seen as just another attack on the victim, and so the lawyers decided not to go there. And because the letters hadn't yet been found, there was no proof."

"But there's proof now," said Justin. "These are copies. Where are the originals?"

"Dad asked me to give them to his lawyer in case they are needed in the hearing for a new trial."

"I guess there's been a change in strategy."

"What would you have him do, Justin? Just keep rotting in there for something he didn't do?"

"It sounded like a pretty good plan a few days ago."

"But not anymore?"

"So the theory is that the affair that got Mom murdered was not really Dad's but was instead Mom's."

"I guess so."

"Could our family be more fucked-up?"

Frank lifted up his glass in salute. "To the Chases. We put the fun in dysfunction."

Justin grabbed the pages off the table and stood up. "Can I take these?"

"Sure," said Frank, finishing his drink. "Take anything you want. Look around, it's all half-yours."

Justin took a step back and then eyed the oppressive library, with the old books and the painting of that horse. He hadn't thought about it, but it was true: this was all half-his, or would be once his father died. The books, the painting, the desk, the decanters, the whole damn house. Along with the business and all the assets that Frank had been living off for the last six years. And suddenly he knew why Cindy's face was so tense, and understood the hushed "What does he want?"

Not all this, that was for sure.

"Don't worry, Frank. I'm not throwing you out into the street. I wouldn't touch a stick of this fucking place."

Frank lifted up his empty glass, closed one eye, and squinted the other as he stared at Justin through the cut crystal.

"What do you see?" said Justin.

"You don't want to know."

26.

HURRICANE

"He's staying at the Parker," said Cody while Justin whipped up a Hurricane.

"The Parker?" said Justin as he dashed a dose of light and dark rums into his tin. "I never heard of it."

"It's the very definition of a fleabag flophouse," said Cody. "Shared bathrooms. Paper-thin walls. Meth busts. Fleas."

"I guess our Birdie Grackle isn't lying about needing the money."

"I haven't yet found out what name he's checked in under; there is no Grackle in the book. But apparently he's not alone."

"No?"

"He's got some muscle with him."

"That's disappointing," said Justin. He threw orange juice into the shaker, along with some simple syrup, a squeeze of lime, and a squirt of passion-fruit nectar. Most barkeeps just used store-bought grenadine in their Hurricanes, but when Justin showed up at Zenzibar he made sure there was always a plentiful supply of passion-fruit nectar behind the bar. Without it, a Hurricane was more like a damp mist in Flint.

"He stays in most of the day," said Cody, "but he spends his nights out."

"Where?"

"Dirty Frank's."

Justin laughed as he shoveled in the ice. He worked the shaker before pouring the drink and ice together into a Collins glass. "I guess he found a joint where his fleas could stage a family reunion."

"It's close enough, which is convenient, because he's pretty much a falling-down drunk."

Justin slipped a sliced orange over the glass, popped in a straw, and slid it in front of Cody. "How'd you discover all this?"

"In these matters," said Cody, lifting his drink and eyeing it appraisingly, "it helps to develop a source. And I found myself quite the interesting source at the Parker."

"How much do I owe you?"

"Four hours so far." He took a long draw of his drink through the straw. "That's nice."

"Four hours?"

"Well, three and a half."

"That means two."

"And a half."

"Fine. Want it now?"

"I can front you for it. I seemed to have stumbled onto an interesting opportunity."

"Another piece of bogus information?"

"Something surer. Give me a few days and I'll get my life and finances back to square."

"That would be novel," said Justin, grabbing his rag and wiping the bar to appear busy as Marson stared at him. "Now as much as I savor your company, I think it's time for you to find a less classy joint to drink in."

"I'm going to need hazard pay."

"You'll be fine. Just don't, under any circumstances, insult the bartender. She's great-looking, but she'll squeeze your head like a lemon if you give her any sass."

"I might like that."

Justin looked up, saw a gang of lawyers in suits making their way through the door. One of them waved, and Justin gave a brief nod as he kept wiping. "Befriend the old guy," said Justin out of the corner of his mouth. "Buy him some drinks, see what he has to say about himself, listen to his stories. He's full of stories."

"How's his breath?"

"Not good."

"Definitely hazard pay."

"Find out where he's been and where he's going." Justin took a wad of tips from his shirt pocket and peeled off a few layers. Just as he laid the bills on the bar, he eyed two men coming through the door behind the lawyers.

"What's that for?" said Cody.

"The drinks you're going to end up buying him. Now get on out of here, and you better be running when you do it."

"What's the rush?" said Cody as he pocketed the money.

"Those two guys that were looking for you?" said Justin. "They just walked in."

27.

BLOODY MESS

Cody didn't turn around and gawk. He didn't try to jump over the bar. Instead he stayed stock-still on his stool as his expression twisted from fear to terror before leaping the great void into sweet acceptance, as if he were relieved, finally, that the running and hiding was over. He lifted his drink with a shaking hand and took a long gulp as the two beefeaters—one tall and muscled with a golden tooth, the other short and wide—took spots at the bar on either side of him.

"Solly's been looking for you," said the tall one.

"And here I am," said Cody, waving his glass in the air.

"What can I get you gentlemen?" said Justin.

"What's he drinking?" said short-and-wide in a thick, nasally voice, a longshoreman in dry dock.

"A Hurricane."

"Looks tasty. I don't like tasty. Give me a rye. Neat."

As Justin poured out a shot of rye, he said to the tall one, "And you?"

"A Bloody Mess."

"I don't know that cocktail," said Justin.

"Well, this is what you do," said short-and-wide. "Lose a thousand dollars, go double or nothing on the Lakers giving twelve, lose that too, and then disappear. That's how you end up with a Bloody Mess."

"And I'll have one more of these," said Cody.

Short-and-wide slugged down his rye, slammed the glass into the bar with a belch, and said, "No time for that. Give me another quick bolt, and then we're taking a ride."

"No, thank you," said Cody.

"Oh, we're going, Cody boy," said the tall one. "Easy or hard is your only choice."

"Unless he wants to stay," said Justin.

"Shut up and pour," said short-and-wide.

"That is normally my motto," said Justin, reaching down and pulling up not the bottle of rye but a baseball bat, which he slapped on the mahogany with a home-run crack that shocked the bar quiet. "But not tonight."

"Who the hell are you," said the tall one, "Chase fucking Utley?"

"I'm the barkeep," said Justin, "and you're both outta here."

"It's all right," said Cody, "I'll just—"

"You two have till three to get your asses out of my bar," said Justin.

"You don't know who you're messing with," said the tall one.

"Three," said Justin as he lifted the bat off the—

And at that very moment, as if it were a magic trick, short-and-wide was jerked away from the bar and began to rise like a helium balloon into the air, his shot glass falling to the floor with a shatter. The pack of suits parted as short-and-wide floated toward the entrance. It took a moment to realize that someone big and burly and as tattooed as a sailor was hoisting him, seemingly without effort, out of the place.

Larry.

The tall goon started reaching for something in his

pocket, but his arm was grabbed and he was spun around until he was face-to-face with Marson.

"The bartender said you're flagged," said Marson, his jaw jutting like a fist. "Take it like a man."

"You're making a mistake, pally," said the tall one. "We work for Solly Heanus. He ain't going to like this."

"Yeah, well, Solly and I are old golfing buddies. Go back and tell your boss the next time he sends his boys into my bar I'm going to make him putt out every damn hole until he grips the club so tight he'll be bleeding from his ears. Now get the hell out of here."

Larry was coming back into the bar, still dusting the remnants of short-and-wide from his hands, as he passed the tall thug on his way out. Larry growled at him like a junkyard dog and the tall thug backed away.

As the atmosphere of Zenzibar slid back to its normal state of uproarious merriment, Marson looked at Justin, down at the bat, back at Justin. "Put that thing away," he said.

"Will do, boss," said Justin with a smile.

"And you," said Marson to Cody. "I'm charging you for the two ryes and the broken glass."

"Of course."

"And you might want to leave out the back entrance."

"Thanks."

"Now, I mean."

"Oh yeah," said Cody, snatching down the last of his drink before hopping off his stool and ducking beneath the wooden plank over the entrance to the bar. He patted Justin on his arm and gave a quick nod before he headed into the kitchen toward the back door that led up to the alley.

"Did that son of a bitch leave without paying?" said Marson after he cleaned up the broken glass.

"I'll cover it," said Justin.

"You bet you will," said Marson, heading back to his spot in the corner. "At customer rates."

Justin shook his head before he slid over to fill the lawyers' orders. He stuck limes in a couple of bottles of Mexican beer, poured a Martini, spent a good minute and a half pulling a Guinness, which was about as quick as you could do it and still do it right. As he circled the pint glass under the tap, drawing a shamrock in the foam, he saw Lee slide in with that slinky way of hers and sit next to Larry.

"Nice job there," said Justin after he made his way over to Larry.

"It appears I missed all the excitement," said Lee.

"Justin brandished a baseball bat," said Larry. "It was hot."

"And Larry put the muscle on some muscle," said Justin, "and did it so smoothly it was a work of art."

"I moonlight as a bouncer at Woody's."

"That must be rough," said Lee.

"Tougher than you would think, dearie. Everyone is in great shape and they like it rough."

"Just like Justin," said Lee.

"Oooh," said Larry. "So what were you and Cody hatching before the trouble started? It looked like you were whispering sweet nothings in each other's ears."

"I have a thing for failed gamblers," said Justin, looking all the while at Lee. She was perched high on her stool and leaning over the bar in one of her skimpier shirts, so that her breasts looked to be on the verge of spilling out. Eyeing her breasts was like waiting for the ball to drop in Times Square. The anticipation was all.

"You know," said Larry, staring now at Justin, "I'm a pretty hard-core gambler."

"Really?"

"I'm just saying, if that's your thing."

"I don't know if mah-jongg counts," said Lee.

"Want another on the house?" said Justin. "For bravery."

"Yes," said Larry as he checked his watch. "But I can't. I have a date."

"Is Quentin back?" said Lee.

"Who?"

"Good for you," said Lee. "You have to drop the ones that are bad for your soul."

"Preach it, sister," said Larry before hopping off the stool and hitching up his pants. "Just as long as you don't have to live it."

Lee watched him leave and then turned her attention back to Justin. "What happened to your cheek?"

"I fell while running."

"Sweetie." She reached and gently placed the back of her hand on the bruise. "You need to be more careful."

"Tell me about it," said Justin. "Will you be having your usual?"

"I usually do."

As Justin prepared the Martini glass, filling it with ice and a few splashes of water, chilling it in anticipation of the Cosmo, Lee said, "Sorry about the way our last night ended."

"Don't be." Justin reamed two lime halves into his shaker. "I've forgotten it already."

"Not all of it, I hope."

"No, not all of it."

"I wore the shoes."

She swiveled on her stool to show off her legs, flexing her ankles. Justin leaned over the bar and got a look. The lines of her legs, the bite of her calves, the sharp edges of her shoes, the flash of red from her soles, all of it caught him like a punch in the stomach. The attraction was so strong it could only be genetic. Justin figured that somewhere, billions of years ago, one of his male ancestors, crawling on finlike limbs along the ground of a tropical rain forest, had stumbled upon an alluring plant with a long slender trunk and spiky black-and-red roots. The creature took a taste and found a great source of nourishment, allowing it to survive a devastating drought. And ever since then, the men of his family—

"What about tonight?" she said.

"Tonight?" said Justin.

"Yes. And I promise no scenes."

"Let me think about it."

"Okay."

And he was, thinking about it, as he turned around and reached for the Cointreau. The excitement of the night had already raised the temperature of his blood, and thinking about the shoes, and the sex, and the smell of her, and the way her breasts were about to spill from her shirt as she leaned over the bar, he had pretty much decided yes, when he turned around again and saw, walking in the door, Annie Overmeyer, clutching a clutch and dressed to kill.

28.

ABSOLUT STRESS

Annie Overmeyer recognized the terrain. She had never been in Zenzibar before, actually. It was not her usual type of joint—it wasn't a hotel lounge replete with out-of-towners looking to buy you a Scotch, or one of the restaurant bars where ambitious bankers liked to shower you in Champagne Cocktails and clue you in on their upcoming top-secret deals as they slipped their soft, manicured hands up your skirt—but the landscape was familiar enough. She had wanted to become intimate with the geography of love, or the geography of success, or even the geography of marriage, however sticky and unfulfilling that might be, but all she had ended up mastering was the geography of saloons.

A pack of young suits stood at one end of the bar with hangdog leers and insouciantly loosened ties. Two craned their necks and gawked when she stepped inside. They'd be good for an hour or so of free drinks and pallid entertainment, for sure, but then she'd have to listen to stories about their legal cases or their golf games, and her lips would end up hurting from all the fake smiling.

And there were some bejeaned college kids in T-shirts and caps at one of the tables. They'd be all sputtery and beery and good rowdy fun, but the girls at the table would sullenly stare out at her like she was from a different planet and they'd all make her feel old.

A small group of women about her age, dressed in shiny halters and tight pants, or blousy shirts and sensible shoes, were together at the far end of the bar. Girls' night out. The fat one and the pretty one, the earnest one and the slutty one, all trying to look like on a girls' night out was exactly where they wanted to be. *It's so nice to get together like this, just us. We should do this more often.* It had never worked for Annie, the whole *Sex and the City* out-with-the-girls thing. It usually started with high expectations, but there was always a moment when she found herself huddled in the corner with a man while the girls looked on, lips pursed. And she knew what those looks meant. *Can't you spend one night without flirting shamelessly with some piece of beef? Aren't we worth a night with just us?* And the answer was always obvious, wasn't it? Because there she would be, in the corner of a booth, letting some random guy lick the wax from her ear. But that was the way it was when you were the slutty one.

A mature man eyed her from the corner. He had gray in his hair, his suit had the right heft, and there was a bright-white collar on his striped shirt, which always seemed to indicate enough self-regard to never wonder why a woman like her would be interested in a man like him. But there was something piggish in his eyes. He'd balk if a deal wasn't sealed by the third Mai Tai, and with his face it would take more than three Mai Tais to seal that deal.

Ah, the romance of the bar.

She read the map quick as a blink, weighed the opportunities, and dismissed them all just as a matter of sport. She wasn't here to throw another evening down the garbage disposal of her life. There was something very definite she wanted out of this night.

Swiveling on a stool at the bar was a tall brunette in shiny black fuck-me heels with red soles. Her long legs were crossed and she was leaning forward, on her elbows, shamelessly flirting with the barman. And then she spied the barman, Chase Junior himself, staring at Annie with that cold blank look of his. She smiled, warmly, as if surprised to see an old, old friend, and headed to an open stool next to the girl with the shoes.

"Hello, Junior," she said as she hopped onto the seat. "It wasn't easy finding you."

"I didn't know you were looking."

"I'm always looking." She turned to the woman next to her and was startled at how beautiful she was: a model's cheekbones, lovely lips, breasts a cough away from spilling out of her top and onto the bar. "Hi, I'm Annie."

"Lee," said the woman, languidly offering her hand. This Lee glanced up at Chase and then back at Annie with a curiosity now wrinkling her features. "Are you a friend of Justin's?"

"More like a friend of the family," said Annie, giving him a quick wink. "But we're old acquaintances. I met him when he was burning up that law school of his. And now look at him. We're all so proud."

"What will you have?" said Junior, his voice as flat as his stare.

"How about that donkey thing you made for me at my apartment the other night." She caught Lee turning her head toward Chase. "What was it called?"

"A Strawberry Mule."

"That's the ticket."

"Pick something else. We're out of ginger beer tonight."

"Too bad. I love ginger beer, whatever that is. Well, just give me something with vodka. Anything, it doesn't matter so long as it bites as it goes down." Annie leaned forward, nodding at the old guy with the white collar, who smiled back. "And bill it to him."

"Do you know him?"

"No, but he'll be picking up my tab by the end of the night, even if he doesn't know it yet."

"Why don't I just buy the thing for you myself, for old time's sake," said Chase as he started building the drink.

"Oh, Junior, that is so generous of you." She turned to Lee. "I just bet he buys you drinks all the time."

"No, actually," said Lee, her head tilted in puzzlement as she tried to figure out who the hell Annie was. "I always buy my own."

"In those shoes?" said Annie.

Lee smiled slowly but seemed genuinely pleased that Annie had noticed. "You like them?"

"Like them? I'm straight as a peacock in a pea patch, but even I want to lick them off your feet."

Lee laughed, and Annie caught Chase staring at Lee as she laughed.

"And it's not just me," said Annie. "Junior, given half a chance, you'd lick Lee's shoes right off her feet, wouldn't you?" She caught something just then in the look that passed between Lee and the Chase kid and said, "Or maybe you already have."

"What do you want, Annie?" said Junior.

"My drink. Desperately."

"Coming right up," said Chase, as he shook his shaker and then drained a light reddish fluid into a tall glass with ice. He put a slice of orange on the rim, dropped in three cherries speared on a toothpick, gave it all a stir with a straw, and slid it in front of Annie.

"What?" she said. "No umbrella?"

"It's not an umbrella drink. It's called an Absolut Stress."

"Feeling tense, are we?" she said just before she took a sip. It was way peachy, with brightness and just the bite she was looking for. "Nice," she said. "But it almost tastes like you're not drinking anything, which sort of misses the point, don't you think?"

"I'll be right back," said Junior before heading off to serve other customers.

Annie looked at Lee, who was trying for a moment to ignore her. "You come here often?" said Annie.

"Often enough."

"So what's he like in bed?"

"Excuse me?" said Lee.

"I'm talking about Junior. And don't even pretend any innocence about that. Let me guess. He's rough and distant, both, which are a brilliant combination when you're screwing the help, which, let's be honest, is what a bartender is, right?"

"I don't classify people like that."

"No? What are you, a lawyer?"

"I'm in investments."

"Stockbroker?"

"No," she said, as if she had been accused of something. "I'm an investment manager."

"Ahh, mutual funds. Vanguard maybe?"

"Maybe."

"A junior manager on a hot fund with a growing capitalization? One of a score of the company's up-and-comers who get their pictures in *InvestmentNews,* but the best-looking of the lot, no doubt. With the hottest shoes. And everywhere you go, all the middle managers at the companies you are investigating are lusting after you, hoping to trade a little inside information for a little more skin. And all the young men on the rise in your office are just desperate to throw at you all their upper-middle-class dreams. Kids and McMansions and top-of-the-line minivans. Vacations in Cabo. A house at the shore. Along with tedious nights of tepid role-playing sex. You be the cheerleader, and they'll be the football heroes, when in high school they were actually only mathletes."

Lee laughed at that.

"And you smile kindly as you brush them all off," continued Annie, "so you can spend your evenings drinking at a dump like this and nights screwing your bartender. And in the middle of it all, as he's pounding away, you detect a note of caring, and from him it's worth the world. Because you know somewhere in there is the key to every happiness you could ever hope for, if only he'll let you grab hold, and turn it, and open up his heart. But in truth, all he lets you grab hold of is his ass. And then the pounding is over, and though it was good, damn good, ridiculously intoxicatingly good, that's not all you were looking for. But by the time the glow has faded, he's retreated into his own little world and you are put in the position of a shrew, begging for more. No better than a wife. Worse than a wife, actually, because you're not the wife, and while you're there begging to be let into his precious little world, he's getting dressed."

Lee, no longer laughing, said, "Life's been tough, huh?"

"Tough would be a relief. Tough would be a vacation in Aruba."

"What happened to make you so bitter?"

"I finished my drink," said Annie before finishing her drink.

"So tell me, if you're so prescient. How does it all end?"

"Badly."

"Maybe not," said Lee. "Maybe I can pull it out. Maybe I have skills you haven't dreamed of. What makes you so sure it'll turn to shit?"

"He's a Chase."

Just then Junior returned from the far outposts of the bar and stood in front of Annie. "That guy over there wants to buy you a drink."

"Isn't life just so predictable," said Annie, leaning over and waving her fingers at the man with gray in his hair.

"What will it be?"

"Another of those stress things, but hold the fruit juice and the peach thing."

"That's just vodka and rum."

"Fine, but also hold the rum."

"Annie here says it's not going to work out between us," said Lee. "Annie says you're from a family of assholes."

"Annie would know," said Chase, looking not at Lee but only at Annie.

Lee looked at the two of them, back and forth. "I think I'm done," she said. She stood and dropped a twenty beside her empty drink. "It's time I start taking my own advice. I'll see you around, Justin."

"Sure," he said.

As Lee walked away, Annie turned and watched her go. "Aren't you going to run after her? Aren't you going to grab hold of her and tell her how much she means to you? Aren't you going to have your precious little scene?"

"I'm working."

Annie turned back and matched Chase's expressionless face with the smile of a victor. "But the shoes were something, weren't they? A little desperate, if you ask me, but something nonetheless."

"What did you tell her, Annie?"

"I sang her the sad song of my experience."

"What do you really want?"

"Another drink, Junior. I'm in the mood to celebrate."

"Buy it in another bar."

"You can't toss me, I'm not drunk yet."

"Doesn't matter, I'm not pouring for you anymore."

"Why, that's malpractice. I'll report you to the American Bartenders Association."

Annie stared at Chase a bit longer and felt something well inside her, the same thing she had been drinking to hold down. And suddenly her throat closed in on her and her breath came in quick gulps and she couldn't look at him anymore. She dropped her gaze to the scarred wood of the bar.

"Remember when you came to my apartment and you talked about your mother," she said in a voice as soft as that of a young girl on the verge of tears. "And you said you had gotten beyond the grieving."

"I remember."

Annie had always been so damn self-sufficient, she wasn't used to asking for anything. But now, here she was, asking for everything, and it hurt, it hurt like hell, and she didn't know why it scared her so much, but it did. She thought of cracking a quip, but she couldn't squeeze one out. So instead, she dropped her voice until it was so soft she could barely be heard, and then she dropped her heart's desire.

"Could you show me how?" she said.

"Show you how to what?" said Chase.

"Could you show me how to get beyond it? Please."

29.

CHAI

Annie Overmeyer let the water fall upon her like a cleansing rain. She was standing in a small shower on the tiny second floor of Justin Chase's tiny house. The showerhead was wide; the water flow was drenching. Like a cleansing rain. In November.

Even though Chase had told her there was no hot water in the house, that the water heater had busted and he had chosen to do nothing to fix it, it was still a shock, the cold sharp streams of water jabbing into her like thorns. At first she suffered through the burning cold pouring over her body to get the scent of the bar out of her hair and off her skin, as per Junior's instructions. But when she finally became acclimated to the cold, she found the shower bracing in a startling way. As if the water were reaching deeper than the surface, washing away more than the thick makeup she habitually applied before stepping out into the night. Washing away some mark that she couldn't identify but that had been staining her skin nonetheless.

Even so, she got out of there as quickly as she could. It was a cold shower after all.

Outside the shower, she dried her skin and hair with a rough towel before putting on a thick white terry-cloth robe that Junior had left for her on his futon. Even in the robe, she felt exposed, standing in some strange guy's house without her makeup or her bra. She heard a noise below, and thought of going down to see what Chase was up to, and to maybe take back some control of the situation, but he had asked her to head on upstairs after the shower, to sit down and wait for him. So she did, climbing the narrow steps with just the robe around her until she reached the third floor.

It was as small as the second floor but completely empty, the walls bare, the floor covered with pale-green mats, like some bachelor-pad fantasy of some demented Japanese salaryman. She couldn't help but look up to see if there was a mirror on the ceiling.

No mirror, but she knew the vibe all right, and what it foretold, and the disappointment she felt was like a slap. But, in all honestly, she had been braced for it. The shower, the robe, and now the kinky mat room. It was the story of her life: all her hopes, her mute yearnings that even she often couldn't decipher, everything always devolved into sex. She sat down, leaned her back against the wall that faced the stairs, crossed her arms and legs, and waited for Junior to come and show her how exactly he intended to solve all her problems.

And the truth was, how could she have expected anything else from a Chase?

Her anger grew at the sound of him climbing the stairs two floors below, the sound of him turning on the shower. She waited and grew angrier. She assumed he'd be finished with his cold shower as quickly as she, but he took his time. The shower turned off, he climbed out and stepped downstairs once more, and after a moment she heard the sound of him rising up the stairs again, the first floor, the second floor. In all the waiting, she wondered what he would look like, naked and erect, climbing up to her. Probably not too bad, actually. And maybe that was what she wanted all the time, maybe this whole help-me-get-past-it thing was just a ploy to bag herself another Chase. She was still angry, as she pulled her legs close and clutched them to her chest, but now she was angry at herself most of all.

And then he appeared, his long hair wet and loose, falling straight to his shoulders, his lean body wrapped in a robe of his own, dark and silken. And he was carrying a tray. With a teapot. And two gray Japanese mugs. Along with a book and some papers.

"What is this?" she said, her back still suspiciously against the wall. "Some ornate ceremony inducting me into your supersecret mystical society?"

"No," he said, sitting cross-legged in the middle of the floor and placing the tray beside him. "I just thought you'd like some tea."

"Lipton?"

"Chai."

"Sounds Jewish. What's that smell?"

"Cinnamon, cardamom."

"It almost smells good. Do you have some sake to go with it?"

"You don't want that."

"You're right. We'll just go with vodka."

"You don't want that either."

"You'd be surprised," she said.

He leaned over, picked up the pot, and filled one of the mugs. He lifted it with both hands and held it out to her, as if holding out an offering.

She sat there for a moment, back still against the wall, hands still clasped around her legs. Then she let go of her legs and scooted to a spot close enough so she could take the tea from him, but not so close that she couldn't kick him in the face if she had to.

"Is this drugged?"

"Do you want it to be drugged?" he said.

"Ahh, yeah. That's what I've been saying. Nothing like a little dose of phenobarbital to smooth out a tense evening."

"I'm sorry to disappoint you, but it's just tea."

She took a sip, mellow yet flavorful, with a comforting aroma that somehow felt like home, though not her home. "Pretty good."

He filled the other mug for himself and held it in both hands, closing his eyes for a moment as he inhaled the steam. He took a sip and opened them again, staring right at Annie.

"You asked me how I got beyond my mother's murder," he said. "It wasn't easy, it took me a long time. And it only happened after I had a revelation."

"Hallelujah. Born again, are we?"

"Not yet," he said with a wry smile. "When I think back on my life before my mother's death, it's like remembering a book I read long ago. I had these ambitions, I had this drive, this thirst for accomplishment. And none of it was rooted in what the accomplishments might actually be. I think it was all related to my relationship with my father, which was always more competitive than loving, but I can't blame him for everything, though I'd like to. These were my choices, this was my life. And then I found my mother's body, and it ended. It took me a while to realize it had ended. I continued on out of sheer momentum. There is something inside of us that drives us onward even when we no longer know where we're going or why. But eventually I discovered the truth of things: I was going nowhere for no reason."

"Aren't we all?" said Annie. "Isn't that the natural state of things?"

"Maybe, but when the illusions that undergird it all are stripped, it's a frightening moment. And for me, it happened with my mother's death, though it didn't become obvious until a little later when I sort of closed down."

"You cracked up?"

"I had entered a new realm, I just wasn't ready to accept it yet. I wasn't ready to accept the truth of all things, until I was given a book."

He took another sip of his tea, put the mug down, and reached to the tray, lifting up a small book, black and ragged and worn, bound in threadbare cloth.

"This book," he said.

She had seen such books before, in the hands of her family back in Minnesota, clutching them to their breasts as they sought salvation in some far-flung celestial future when they couldn't find it here.

"Oh snap," she said. "You're going to throw the Bible at me. I should have known. And now we're going to get down on our knees and pray together. If you were going to thump the Bible, you could have told me, and avoided all this tea-and-sympathy crap."

"It's not a Bible," he said. "It's a travel guide to a land I didn't know I was in."

"Oh yeah, and what's that? Iceland?"

"No," he said. "Someplace colder. The land of the dead."

30.

SINGAPORE SLING

Justin carefully observed Annie Overmeyer as she absorbed his words. He was telling her something he had never told anyone before, the absolute truth about his life now. He couldn't help but wonder how she would take it. Or why he was telling her in the first place.

The answer to the latter question might have been because she was flat-out beautiful and he was a sucker for beauty. Without her makeup or trashy clothes, she had the clean freshness of a wheat field after an afternoon shower. Her straw-colored hair, her high, freckled cheekbones, the pale flesh on her long legs. And there was something about the way she spoke, quickly and sharply, tossing out wisecracks that never fully succeeded in hiding the emotions underneath, that he found appealing. So yeah, he might not have wanted to fully admit it to himself, but no matter how perverse the whole thing, he was definitely attracted.

But the real reason he was telling her was because she had been part of it all. He regretted his snappish words to her in her apartment, not just because they were snappish but because they were wrongheaded, too. Annie Overmeyer had gone through the same maelstrom that had shipwrecked his life, and she had been damaged in her own way, and like him, she was still trying to recover. She deserved to at least hear what he had to say and to see if maybe what had helped him might help her.

"The land of the dead?" said Annie, looking at him with a furrow in her brow. "Are you crapping me?"

"There is a before and an after in my life, and the gap between the two is unbridgeable. The before seems like a story I've been told about a boy who strives for so much and then finds his mother murdered and then everything sort of goes blank. The after is this waking dream that I'm living through now, in which I couldn't for the life of me figure out where I was or what I was doing. Until someone I met, a stranger actually, gave me this book. And I started reading it, and somehow it resonated. I felt that it described more closely than anything else where I was and what I was feeling. And it told me exactly how to move forward."

"That must be a hell of a book. Can it predict the stock market too?"

"It's going down."

"Really?"

"Or up. So you asked me how I got beyond what happened. I did it with this book, and now, as that stranger passed it on to me when I was in so much trouble a few years ago, with solemnity and hope, I'm going to pass it to you."

He held the book in both hands, much like he had held the mug of tea, and offered it to her. She stared at him for a moment, looked like she was about to burst out in laughter, and then grew suddenly serious. She put down her tea, held out both hands, and received it.

And as soon as the book left Justin's hands, he was infused with an airy lightness, he felt joyful and giddy, free of the forces of gravity as well as the past, as if he might start to rise into the air in that very room.

"*The Tibetan Book of the Dead*?" said Annie. "Isn't that a druggie thing?"

"No," said Justin.

"Timothy Leary, LSD, all that hippie stuff?"

"No."

"Why are you smiling so much? Is this all a joke?"

"It's just I suddenly feel so much lighter."

"I bet." She hefted the book in her hand. "I mean this thing looks like quite the downer. I bet I'll be happy when I pass it on, too."

"You seem skeptical."

"Really? Now why would that be? Maybe because I'm not dead yet?"

"I understand your skepticism."

"Do you," she said. "Because you don't seem to. Junior, I hate to break it to you, but you're not dead yet, either."

"I guess it's all in your point of view."

"Should I get you a doctor's note?"

"I felt the same way before I started to read it. And it doesn't get any better once you start. It's like a treatise on gibberish by an addled professor, written in Greek. But I kept with it, and a pattern started to emerge, and the whole thing worked on me in a peculiar but liberating way. I hope it works the same way on you."

"You mean you hope I die too."

"I hope you find your way."

She looked at the book. "To tell you the truth, Junior, I don't think this is going to work. It seems like utter bullshit to me, no offense and all."

"No offense taken."

"Here," she said, handing it back to him. "It means a lot to you, I can tell, and I'd rather just keep self-medicating."

"No, you hold on to it," said Justin, "because if that's how you intend to continue solving your problems, you'll be needing it sooner rather than later."

She looked at him for a moment and then laughed. And he laughed with her.

"Okay," she said. "For future reference. Thank you. And I mean it. But if that's all you got, then it's getting a little late and I better be moseying on." She pushed herself to standing while clutching her robe closed. "Thanks for the...shower? The tea? The whole *Book of the Dead* thing? It was almost, I don't know, karmic."

"Don't leave yet," he said, reaching out and gently taking hold of her hand to stop her from walking away, and he noted a line of suspicion marking her features.

He let go, and she hunched her shoulders as she pulled her hand back. The small bone of her wrist was lost in the fold of her sleeve. And just that quick he understood. She thought he was on the make. A lothario trying to score. He considered it a bit. The shower, the robes—all to keep his third-floor sanctuary as pure as possible—would look like nothing more genuine than a cheap pickup line. *Hey, want to come up and wrestle on my tatami mats?* And yet, she had come, and showered, and put on the robe. And in a way, his heart opened to her a bit just then, because he knew, in her way, she was as much a seeker as was he.

"It's not what you think," he said. "I just have something else to give you. Something that might help in a...less metaphysical way."

She looked at him, the suspicion still there.

"It's not sexual, Annie. This is my sanctuary from the wretched universe of desire. This is my place of nonattachment. There isn't a safer place for you in the world."

She stared at him a bit more and then sat down again, a little farther away than before, perhaps, but she sat. And she opened her eyes wide, despite the furrow of suspicion still on her pretty brow.

"Remember when you said you thought my parents had an arrangement?" said Justin.

"That's what your father told me."

"But you never really believed it, did you?"

"I figured it might just be a line. 'She doesn't understand me. We have an arrangement. I'm leaving her, but the time's not right.' I've heard them all before. Sometimes all at once."

"Here," he said, lifting from the tray the copies of the letters Frank had given him and handing them to her. "My brother found these in my mother's closet."

He watched as Annie read them, her face reflecting first the puzzlement of trying to figure out what the letters were all about and then the rapt concentration that came from trying to follow the flow of words and ideas. He liked the way she read, immersing herself fully, as if losing awareness of where she was or who she was with. He seemed to remember that she was an accountant, and he could imagine her losing herself in the figures that danced like hard truths across her computer screen. It was a sort of meditation, with the numbers as a mantra, because, really, what could be more meaningless than an unending stream of numbers.

When she finished, she looked up at Justin with eyes that surprised him, because they were moist.

"She was in love with someone else at the end."

"So it seems."

"But was it an affair?"

"Apparently."

"Do you have anything other than these letters to prove it?"

"Just my father's word, but otherwise, no. But isn't it clear from the letters?"

"There's love, yes, but there's no sex."

"It's there between the lines."

"Sex is never between the lines. Between the sheets, yes, but not between the lines."

"Shakespeare's sonnets?"

"Drenched with sex."

"Really?"

"Read them again. If you're bumping knees, you can't hide it."

"You're overanalyzing this, Annie. Maybe the sex hadn't happened yet, but my mother was in love with this A. And my father was in love with you. So there was an arrangement, like he told you. Whatever guilt you might have been feeling is misplaced. You were a piece of their puzzle, not the cause of anything."

She thought about it for a while, then took a deep breath and smiled in a way that he felt, viscerally. "That was so sweet of you. Really sweet. Surprising, actually."

"Why?"

"Well, your father said you were an asshole."

"Dear old Dad."

"Who's A?"

"No one knows for sure, but I have an idea. My mother had a high-school boyfriend named Austin. My aunt thinks I'm named for him. I figure they might have hooked up again. I'm going to pay him a visit."

"Why would you want to do that?"

"I'm not as certain as I was about my dad's guilt. I'm trying to find out what I can about my mother's last days to see who else might have wanted to do her harm. And I have some information, however unreliable, that the person might have been a woman."

"That's why you found me?"

"Yes."

"So, do you think I did it?"

"No. But if I had thought your relationship with my father might have been the cause of her death, it's only fair that I try to find out if her relationship with this Austin might have been the cause instead. Maybe this Austin's wife got a whiff and decided to do something about it. It's just a shot in the dark, but it's worth taking."

"But that's not all, is it? You're not just out to clear your father."

"No. And this might sound a little weird, but in the book I gave you, there are prayers to whisper into the ear of the newly deceased to help them on their way in the land of the dead. I didn't know enough to recite them to my mother when I found her that night. But maybe, if I know what was going on in her life, I might gain a sense she didn't need those words, that she had enough of a sense of herself to know all the stuff in the book on her own."

Annie nodded at him as he spoke, as if she understood what he was saying, even though he knew she understood not a word. How could she? He had only given her the book a moment before. But she seemed to emotionally understand, and he liked that.

"So," she said, even as she kept nodding, "when are we going to meet this Austin guy?"

"We?"

"I have to go with you."

"That's not a good idea, Annie. I don't know what he'll be like or what will happen. And I think, considering the circumstances, we've about maxed out our appropriate amount of time together. I gave you what I felt I needed to give you, and now it's time for our ships to sail in different directions."

"I'm going with you, Junior."

"Oh you are, are you?"

"If everything you suspect is true, then he's me, don't you see? He's the other side of the equation. Whatever I went through, am still going through, he went through it too. And whatever he's going through, I might be able to help him, like you tried to help me. So don't even attempt to convince me otherwise. I'm going with you."

"You free Saturday afternoon?" he said, not quite knowing why he was saying it.

"I can get free."

"Good," said Justin. "Then why don't we catch up to Austin Moss while he's mowing the lawn at home."

31.

STINGER

Vern told Derek to be patient. They needed to wait for the right moment. Timing was everything. "Just keep yourself busy is all, until the clock strikes," Vern said before he went out drinking. And so Derek is following orders, like he always follows orders, and keeping himself busy.

They are now in their third house of the night. From the streetlight that bleeds through the front windows, he can see it is a really nice house. Comfortable. It reminds him of a hotel that Tree had conned their way into one night in Chicago, with fancy beds and paintings of the ocean on the walls. This was when Tree could still con anyone into anything, before he lost his breath from the cancer. Derek is hauling the flatscreen into the kitchen, while Cody cruises around upstairs looking for the smaller stuff.

Cody made all the plans for the night. He scouted out the houses, made sure they were empty, picked up the van, made arrangements for the stuff to be sold, and worked out the cut. He did all this even before he picked up Derek from the park off Lombard Street, near the basketball court, where Cody told Derek to wait for him. Derek can spend hours at the park unnoticed, which is much better than standing on the street while the crowd of addicts and drunks mill before the hotel. Cody came up with the idea of the park. Cody has a lot of good ideas.

Derek likes working with Cody. Cody never yells, he asks Derek's opinion even though Derek usually does not have one, and he does not like to linger. And Derek likes that Cody has taken the time to try to convince Derek that what they are doing is okay. Cody says that he is the one doing all the stealing. All Derek is doing is opening the doors and taking care of any alarms, like Tree had taught him. Tree had been a master of alarms, he had gotten his start installing them in Texas, before branching out. Working with Cody is like working with Tree before the cancer. None of the addict lies of Sammy D, none of Rodney's powdery nervousness, none of Vern's orneriness—just two guys working together. Like teammates on a baseball team. Derek has never played baseball, his Grammy would not let him play, afraid he would get laughed at or hurt, but Derek would have liked to play baseball with Cody.

The first two houses went smooth as a puppy dog's tail. Open the door, grab the easiest stuff to find, load it in the van, be on their way. Bam bam bam. It was so easy that Derek started helping out with the taking and the van was filling up as if by itself. This third house is proving to be no different. When Derek puts the flatscreen on the kitchen table, he goes back for the paintings, like Cody had told him to. By the time Cody is coming down the stairs into the living room, the walls are stripped, the little statues of naked women that Cody had pointed out are set beside the flatscreen, and everything is waiting to be moved to the van.

"What about the silver?" says Cody softly.

"Silver?"

"In the dining room."

"I did not know."

"No sweat. Just wait here and stay quiet."

Derek stands silently and still in the living room as Cody goes through the dining room, drawers sliding open and closed. Even when Derek hears something shuffling outside the front door, he does not move, does not say a word.

When Cody comes back to Derek in the living room, he has a small wooden case under his left arm, two long candlesticks, one in each hand, and a smile.

Derek points at the front door, and Cody's smile freezes into a grimace.

The scraping of a key, the turning of the knob.

Derek is standing to the side, by the stairs. The door will open away from him. He will have plenty of time to jump on whoever is coming inside and take care of him. Cody stands now a few feet in front of the door. Derek trains his gaze on Cody, wondering what Cody will do. Derek has plans for Cody. Big plans. But there is still so much he does not know about Cody. Like how Cody handles tight situations. Derek has found that his job is almost all tight situations. Derek does not let them bother him. He is just dim enough to be impervious to pressure, which relies on a grave understanding of the big picture to do its dirty work. But pressure sometimes makes the smart guys pee in their pants. And now Cody, who is definitely one of the smart guys, is getting his first taste.

The door starts to open.

Cody moves sideways toward Derek, away from the opening, and then scurries forward, still holding the stuff from the dining room.

The door opens fully, a shadow slips in, turns on the light, closes the door. It is a girl, young and thin, no threat.

Derek is just about to jump the girl when Cody steps in his way.

The girl turns and catches sight of Cody and opens her mouth to scream. She is pretty, with blonde hair and blue eyes, and with her mouth open like it is, it makes Derek think of his sister singing her hymns. A cry comes out, and Derek is readying to grab her and hug her and press her face against his chest so that the sound stops. But before he can move, Cody steps forward and thumps her on the head with a candlestick.

The girl stands swaying silently for a moment before collapsing in a heap. Cody turns to stare at Derek, and there is a look on Cody's face like he has done something terribly, terribly wrong and hopes Derek will not hate him for it.

"I didn't have a choice," says Cody.

"I know."

"I had to do something."

"I know."

Cody looks at him again, the pleading still in his eyes, as if he is begging Derek for some sort of forgiveness. Derek just nods.

Cody stoops down, drops the case and the candlesticks, gently places one hand on the girl's head and the other on her neck. There is some blood, but not much.

"She's fine, thank God," says Cody softly. "There's a pulse."

"What do we do?" says Derek.

"Let's just load up and get out of here," says Cody.

"Okay," says Derek. "What about her?"

"I think she'll be okay. She'll wake up with a headache, but she'll be okay."

"Okay."

"Let's get moving."

Cody picks up the stuff he dropped and carries it to the other stuff in the kitchen. Derek glances at the girl and then follows him. It does not take long to carry the stuff down the outdoor stairs and to load up the van. Derek handles the heavy stuff, sliding in the flatscreen and the paintings. Cody wraps the silver in a blanket so it won't rattle. When they are fully loaded, Cody twists the handle of the van door even as he shoulders it closed, so it makes almost no sound.

"I need to go back in," says Derek.

"Why?"

"The lights and the lock."

"Derek?"

"I need to lock the door and turn out the lights."

"Maybe you're right. I can do it."

"No, I will do it. It will not take long."

"Okay, go ahead. Thanks."

"I will be right back."

Derek climbs the outdoor stairs, his footfalls light on the wood. He steps quietly through the kitchen into the living room, still lit, the girl still lying on the floor.

As soon as Derek heard the sounds outside the front door, he assumed that it would be up to him to handle the situation, but Cody surprised him. Cody moved quickly and decisively, there was no panic in his movements. He looked as nervous as Rodney when he heard the sound, but he handled himself so much better. Derek cannot stop smiling when he thinks of it. This is going to work out, this is going to work out better than he thought. He just has to bring Cody in one step further.

Derek looks at the girl on the floor. She is nice, he can tell. She would have been one of the nice ones who said hello to him when they passed in the halls of the school, and said nice things about his projects or the T-shirts he wore. *Hi, Derek, how are you? It is always so good to see you. Did you have a good lunch?* And she is pretty. And the way her mouth opened, like his sister's mouth opened when she sang in the church choir, he is sure she would have a nice voice too. He has the fleeting thought of taking her with them, of putting her in the back with the paintings and the flatscreens, but he knows that would never work. That would be untidy, and his Grammy taught Derek to hate untidiness of any kind.

He steps forward to the door, locks it from the inside, and looks around to see if they have forgotten anything. It looks clean, it looks okay. He reaches for the switch and turns out the light.

Then he tidies up.

32.

DEPTH CHARGE

Mia Dalton was growing sick of this job. She had spent too long toiling in the sewers of the criminal law. Once her doubts about the Chase case were settled one way or the other, she would think about charting a new direction in her career. Maybe Mackenzie Chase's lawyer had it right, maybe patent law was the way to go. Intellectual property sounded so nicely intellectual. And no matter how deeply she burrowed through the dusty applications at the patent office, she wouldn't have to suffer through the noxious smell that was swirling around her right now, sweet, ripe, dark and coppery, nauseating in its meaning: the rotten scent of another rotting corpse. This is what her life had become, and no exfoliant was strong enough anymore to scour it from her flesh.

Scott had called her down, and though she had tried to beg off, he was adamant, and so here she was. The scent was faint enough in this room to let Mia know that death hadn't come so very long ago; this wasn't some body left to bloat and bleed its fluids all across the floor until it seeped into the level below. But that didn't make it any easier, because this body wasn't some lowlife drug-addicted liar like Timmy Flynn. This was a young girl with nothing but promise ahead of her. This wasn't just a violation of the penal code, this was a violation of everything that mattered in the world.

"Her name was Rebecca Staim," said Detective Scott, gesturing at the taped outline of a body sprawled on the floor. The victim was now in the morgue, and the scene was empty except for the two of them. "College student. Her parents say she was a good kid, never in any trouble. We've confirmed that she was exactly that."

"What's missing from the house?"

"What you would expect," said Scott. "Silver, some artwork, jewelry, a couple of high-end televisions."

"Is the robbery real or just a cover?"

"It seems real enough. It matches a wave of burglaries that have hit Center City in the last couple days. I got in touch with a guy I know in Robbery/Burglary. He says these break-ins all have an MO that matches this one: the family out, no sign of forced entry, the alarm disabled, only the most salable stuff gone. They figured a gang of roving burglars has come in to hit what they could before moving on. They've seen it before, but never ending with a murder like this."

"What's the theory?"

"The family was away, the burglars broke in, started ransacking. One of the neighbors noticed a van in the back alley, which matched what was observed at some of the other sites that were hit. The girl was in college and must have come home unexpectedly. She was killed before she could make a call or, if the neighbors can be believed, before she could even scream."

"Poor thing. So why am I here?"

"Some of the prints found at the murder scene match prints found in the other burglaries."

"No surprise, based on what you're telling me."

"But then the computer spit out another possibility, and

our analyst confirmed the finding. Prints from this murder scene match prints we found at Timmy Flynn's apartment. Prints on the phone that didn't belong to Flynn."

"Shut up."

"Why? What's going on?"

"No, I mean shut up, you can't be serious."

"As a heart attack," said Scott. "And at my age, at my weight, that's serious as hell."

"The same phone that called Justin Chase at about the same time Flynn died?"

"That's right."

"Shut the fuck up. Flynn's house is nowhere near the region where these other burglaries were perpetrated, right?"

"Right."

"Was anything of value taken from that shit hole?"

"No."

"So it's something else."

"The motive?"

"The connection. Was there any relation between this girl and Mackenzie Chase? Or Justin Chase? Or any relation at all between the families?"

"I don't know. We're just getting started here."

"Find out. Fast. Kingstree should be on this."

"He didn't pull this homicide."

"I don't care, there's a connection here, somewhere, and we're going to find it. Get him on the horn and get him down here. And make sure there's someone looking hard for anything that was taken in any of these thefts. All we need is one link to solve both cases at once."

"Will do."

"And you keep your eye on that Justin Chase. Maybe he got himself a new flatscreen TV."

"He didn't."

"How are you so sure?"

"He doesn't watch television."

"Everyone watches television."

"The kid doesn't. He doesn't drink or use drugs or seem to want anything material. It's just not his way."

"No one's too pure for money. Keep your eye on him."

"If that's what you want."

"That's what I want."

"One more thing," said Scott. "And this is peculiar and speculative, but something you should know. The fingerprint analyst I talked to mentioned something interesting in what she found. She said it offhandedly, like it was just an amusing piece of information, but it might be something to keep in mind."

"Go ahead."

"She said the prints that matched the phone were a little unusual. There was a larger-than-expected incidence of loops that pointed toward the pinky, something called ulnar loops, coupled with a lower ridge count than usual."

"So?"

"Well, she said it was interesting, is all. It's the kind of thing you sometimes find in Alzheimer's patients and might be a way to detect the disease before symptoms manifest themselves."

"Let's catch him first, and then cure him, okay, Detective?"

"But she said, and this might be more interesting, you also sometimes find these patterns in individuals with some sort of intellectual disability. The patterns weren't as obvious as you find with severely handicapped patients, so his mental functioning would be relatively high, but they were there nonetheless."

Mia felt a chill ripple down her spine. She tried to make sense of this and couldn't. Rikki had a niece named Julia who had Down syndrome, a lovely girl Mia often cared for. It was more than a pleasure to be with her; Julia was so full of love and joy it was almost as if Mia were touching something sacred when she ran her fingers through the girl's silken hair. But from the very first time she sat for the girl, she realized how strong Julia was, almost freakishly strong.

"How did this Rebecca Staim die?" said Mia.

"It's preliminary, but it looks like first she was banged in the head, because there's a pretty decent crease in her skull. But that didn't kill her."

"What did?"

"After she was down, someone lifted her head, took it in both hands, and twisted hard enough to snap her neck in two."

33.

AMERICAN SOUR

Justin spied the SUV standing outside his alleyway at the end of his run, the vehicle a monstrous black thing of the kind you don't spot much in the city because it is near-impossible to find a spot big enough to park it.

As he jogged toward the truck, he could see the back of the driver's head, a woman with silken blonde hair streaked with all kinds of expensive highlights and cut in a perfect line at the shoulders. It was like a glossy helmet, that hair, designed to be no different than thousands of others just like it, designed to look designer. And he imagined the face on the other side, hard and pretty and entitled, with big round sunglasses. All these suburban bottle-blondes had the same round sunglasses, as if purchased en masse from the Jackie O collection on QVC. When he passed her, he noticed that the sunglasses were exactly as he had imagined, forcing a smile at another vile prejudice confirmed.

Only a moment later did he recognize the face behind them.

He stopped, turned around, stared for a bit, wondering what she was doing there. When she saw him and smiled tightly, he knew she was there for him. He stood and wiped his face on the bottom of his shirt as he waited for his sister-in-law to open the door and climb down from the behemoth. She was wearing slacks—that's what they're called when you buy them at Neiman Marcus—and a string of pearls that peeked out from beneath the fashionably raised collar of her blouse. She had been earnest and pale and decidedly unstylish when she married Frank.

"I knocked at the house first," said Cindy. "When you weren't in, I decided to wait."

"I've been running," said Justin, and then he laughed at the obviousness of the comment. "What's up?"

"Do you have a minute?"

Involuntarily he looked around, as if for an escape route. He had never had a conversation with Cindy outside the confines of a family event and wasn't certain he wanted to start now. As he scanned the street, his gaze caught on a strange car parked at a meter on the edge of the square. There was someone sitting inside, which was a bit peculiar. He turned back to Cindy and thought about sending her off. He was already behind schedule for meeting up with Annie at Austin Moss's house; whatever Cindy wanted to get into, he didn't want to go into it now. But despite her obvious nervousness, there was a determined set to her jaw that told him he didn't have much of a choice.

"Sure," he said.

"Can I park the car here?"

"Car?"

"Well, technically it's a truck."

"I guess you and Frank are doing okay."

"Can I park here?"

"No."

"Will cops ticket me?"

He glanced back at the parked car with the figure inside. The car was brown and boxy, the figure had a big head and sloped shoulders and looked a bit...*Damn.* He waved at the figure sitting in the car.

"There's a cop sitting right there," he said.

"Staking out the parking spot?"

"Something like that. Give me a moment, okay?"

He headed over to the car, watching the man inside watch him as he walked on over. When he reached the driver's door, he scooted low so that his head was equal height to the window. He waited for it to roll down.

"Neighborhood watch?" said Justin.

"Of a sort," said Detective Scott. He sat slumped in the front seat, looking at Justin over reading glasses perched low on his nose. A folded newspaper was in one hand and a pencil in the other.

"I feel safer already," said Justin.

"Not too safe, I hope. People are dropping like stones in the big city. I'm keeping my eye on things, hoping I might be able to avert another tragedy."

"I can take care of myself."

"The morgue is full of folks who could take care of themselves."

"What are you really doing here, Detective?"

"The Jumble."

"You any good?"

"Not really. Here's one, see if you can help. R-Y-S-W-E-C."

"Harassment?"

"No, that's not it, there's only one S. Did that guy who gave you the warning come back yet?"

"No."

"He will. You have any idea who sent him?"

"No."

"You'd tell me if you did, wouldn't you?"

"I don't know."

"Leastways you're honest. Can you describe him for me?"

"I only got a glimpse."

"A glimpse might have been enough. And if he's the guy I think he might be, you're lucky you're still alive."

"I guess I've got good karma."

"Your father thinks he's going to find a fall guy for your mother's murder. You have any idea who he has in mind?"

"No."

"I'm supposed to find out. And to hound you if necessary until I do."

"Then it's a good thing you're a hound dog. Can you do me a favor?"

"Sure."

"See that big black SUV parked illegally on the corner there?"

"The Escalade."

"Right. Could you make sure it's not ticketed?"

"Who's the girl?"

"My sister-in-law."

"I must say, Chase, you get around."

As Justin approached Cindy after his visit with Scott, he thumbed the car. "It should be okay there. So, you want to talk?"

"If we can."

"Sure," he said. "Come on in. Why don't you make some tea while I take a shower, and then we can get down to it."

34.

DARJEELING

He tried to figure out what she wanted while the cold water beat upon his neck. It had something to do with his visit to Frank. It had something to do with the fearful way she had stared at him from the steps that night. It had something to do with everything, but exactly what, he had no idea. Cindy and Justin had never gotten along in the years between his brother's marriage and his mother's death. He hadn't wanted it to be cool between them, he had hoped she'd be the sister he had never had, but there was some barrier of resentment coming from Cindy, always, which made Justin always wonder what Frank was saying behind his back. Or it could have been simply that Justin in those days was an asshole.

"I found some Darjeeling in the cabinet," said Cindy when Justin, in jeans and a T-shirt, joined her at the table, two mugs steaming on the tabletop. "But I couldn't find your sugar."

"I don't have sugar."

"No sugar?"

"White poison."

"I thought that was cocaine."

"I don't have that either, but I have some honey if you want."

"I'll drink it straight, thanks." She lifted her mug and took a sip, smiling slyly. "You seem to be doing okay. I caught a whiff of some very nice perfume. Jasmin Noir, I believe. Bulgari. It's nice to see you're keeping busy."

"She was just a friend," said Justin.

"Past tense?"

"Yeah."

Cindy glanced down, gathering her words. "You look good. A lot better than you did before you left."

"That's not saying much, considering my condition then. I look okay, but you..." He stopped talking and gestured at her up and down. "You look transformed, like a different person."

"Thank you," she said, beaming into the compliment, although Justin hadn't meant it as such. "When did you come back?"

"A few months ago."

"I didn't know you had returned until you showed up at the house. Frank never told me."

"Things are still tense between us."

"But even so, I knew something was up. He's been drinking more than usual lately, which means he's been drinking a lot."

"I seem to have that effect on people."

"We've missed you here."

"No, you haven't."

She looked at him, her eyes blinking the truth, before she broke contact and took another sip.

"So where were you? What adventures did you have?"

"I went out west. It seemed just so American to head out there and find myself. So Jack Kerouac."

"Did it work?"

"No."

"What did you find instead?"

"That Kerouac is dead."

"You didn't have to leave Philadelphia for that."

"Tell me about it."

"I know it's been difficult for you," she said, "and I'm sure no matter how you might minimize the difficulties with flippancy, the last couple years haven't been easy ones. But think about this for a moment, Justin: at least you had the chance to run away. Frank didn't have that option. He was married, and had a baby, and the business needed looking after, and there was the house. And your father's legal case kept going and going and going, through all the appeals. Whatever other plans he might have had for his life—that we might have had for our life together—they got lost in the shuffle."

"Frank made his choices," said Justin.

"No, Justin. You made your choice to leave the whole mess in his lap, and Frank was left to try to put the pieces together."

"What do you want from me, Cindy?"

"I want you to know that we're doing better. That things have calmed down. However hard you think you had it, it was just as hard for Frank. Or harder. You can see the consequences on his face. You look young still, but he's aged twenty years in six. And he's so wound up he has to drink himself to sleep at night."

"Then he should get some help."

"But there have been moments, lately, when your brother smiles at the little things. Like when Ronnie makes a catch in Little League and he looks so surprised. Or when Ellie rolls on the floor like a little wound-up dog and laughs. Things are getting better. It might be hard to believe, but things are approaching normal. After years, it's like we can finally exhale. We thought we could almost put what happened behind us and look to the future with some sort of hope. We thought we'd reached some sort of equilibrium. And then you showed up."

"I'm not trying to cause problems, Cindy." Justin glanced at his watch.

"Do you have someplace to go?"

"I planned to meet someone. I have some questions I need to ask."

"About what happened to your mother?"

"Maybe."

"What the hell are you up to, Justin?"

"Since I've been back, questions have been raised about my mother's death. You know about my father's motion for a new trial, and Tim Flynn's changed testimony, and his strange death. Maybe you don't know that the cops think it might have been a murder and that I might have had something to do with it, which is why that cop is sitting there on the square. Or that this bruise on my cheek came with a warning that I should stop asking questions about what happened to my mother."

"From whom?"

"I don't know, but it might not have ended with just a bruise if that policeman outside hadn't shown up at my house when he did. All of this has got me thinking. I'm not out to upset anyone's equilibrium. I'm just trying to find out what really happened to my mother."

"To what end, Justin? What the hell are you trying to do?"

"It's my mother. Doesn't the truth matter?"

"I don't know anymore. But I do know that Frank is starting to lose it again. And my family is starting to suffer. And you need to think about what might ultimately happen as a result of your muddying the waters, of all you might be putting at risk."

There was something in her tone that struck a nerve, and Justin suddenly remembered why they had never gotten along. It was as if she had internalized the twisted family dynamic between Frank and Justin and thereby treated her brother-in-law as the enemy on some sort of family battleground, projecting toward him a condescending bitterness. And he could feel it now, just as he had always felt it, and it twisted something inside him.

"You mean your wonderful house, Cindy, that's not really your house? Or the stylish new hair, or the black gas-guzzler parked on the square? You came here to tell me that I'm risking your wonderful new lifestyle, is that it?"

She stared at him with a hard, defensive anger, but there was something else in her eyes, some pleading that he took as a sort of shame. Like he had hit on it exactly, but not exactly. Yes, he was threatening her sweet upper-middle-class lifestyle, but there was something else, too, something else that he wasn't getting.

She was about to spit out a reply reflexively bitter and hard, it was in her expression as her mouth opened to deal her crushing riposte, and then she stopped herself. She took a moment to smooth the lap of her slacks, pushed her chair back from the table, stood.

"Good-bye, Justin. Thank you for the tea," she said before heading toward the door.

"If I'm full of shit, tell me," said Justin to her retreating back. "Don't just take it and walk away. Tell me off, but first tell me why everyone is suddenly so worried about what I might discover. What the hell are you so afraid of, Cindy, if it's not losing your damn lifestyle? What are you protecting other than your stuff?"

She stopped and just stood for a long moment, the line of her back hunched and angry. But when she turned around, what he saw was not anger but fear.

"Do you really want him back in our lives, Justin? Do you really think that's the best for anyone but him?"

35.

COSMOPOLITAN

For Annie they were always there, on the other side of things, mute specters haunting the dramas of seduction and submission she playacted with married men. The wraiths glowered sullenly from the darkened corners of plush bars, where Champagne sloshed over the rims of thin, languid flutes. They stared from behind the kitchen doors that swung open to dark, intimate restaurants, where family budgets were wrecked upon the shoals of overpriced wine lists and racks of lamb. And they writhed in anguish over the hotel beds where the stage productions reached their terribly unsatisfying Act III climaxes, each apparition with the same ghostly face, pale mouth open in voiceless outrage, there but not there, always felt, never heard.

Except for that one time at the Bellevue.

This was years after the Eleanor Chase murder. Annie had been sitting on a dark leather seat at the poorly lit bar on the nineteenth floor, sitting under a marble archway, drinking a Cosmopolitan because the red of the drink matched her heels, waiting for Brad. Brad was from legal at the insurance company she was accounting for at the time. She should have known better than to hook up with a guy named Brad, really now, but he was old enough to prick her fancy and his suits were well made and, more than anything, he was persistent. Annie didn't admire persistence—she thought it showed a bullheaded obliviousness to the facts of the world—but that didn't mean it didn't work with her. Sometimes it was easier just to say yes. *Oh, all right, if you insist.* And so here she was, on the nineteenth floor of the Bellevue drinking a blur of vodka mixed with all manner of extraneous stuff, waiting for the oh-so-persistent Brad. There were to be more and ever more drinks, there was to be a picked-over dinner, there was a waiting hotel room.

That's what she liked about the Bellevue, one-stop shopping for adultery.

She was halfway through the drink, it didn't take long actually, when an older woman lifted herself onto the seat next to hers. She was pretty and coiffed, her shoes were sling-backs, her fragrance was expensive, and she was wearing a sharply tailored suit that showed off her waist, like she was dressed for a wedding or some other sort of an affair. Annie figured that made two of them. The woman ordered a glass of wine from the bartender. Annie rolled her finger over her own half-empty Martini glass to signal her readiness for another. They sat side by side in quiet for a number of minutes, drinking.

"Waiting for someone?" said the woman, finally breaking the silence.

"He's late," said Annie, nodding sadly at the sad character flaw the lack of punctuality signaled.

"He's going to be later than you think," said the woman.

"How prescient of you," said Annie. "Maybe I should shake your head and ask about my investments?"

"Oh, he'll come to the bar." The woman scanned Annie up and down. "He'll show up for sure. He's a tabby who likes his catnip, and you are all of that. But he's a coward at heart, trust me. He abhors scenes, and when he sees me sitting here with you, he'll back out on tiptoes like a frightened little boy."

"You know who I am," said Annie, the tingling in her neck making her suddenly aware of exactly who this formidable woman might actually be.

"Oh, dear, I know you better than you know yourself. Here, let me show you something. You have time for a picture show while you're waiting, don't you?"

"I think I'm going to need another drink."

The woman gestured to the barkeep for another round before pulling a wallet out of her bag and snapping it open.

"This is our son James," she said. "He's in high school now. He's in the school play, *West Side Story*. He didn't think he'd get a part, but he's so excited, even if he's a Shark, not a Jet. And this is Janice. She's in middle school. She's a foot taller than all the boys and takes it personally. And this is Ryan. Ryan has issues. I had to quit my job to take care of Ryan. He's very sweet, he's an angel, truly, but, well, he has issues."

"It's all very touching," said Annie, draining her second Cosmo. "I'm about to burst into tears."

"I just thought it would be nice if for once you saw all the people you were actually fucking."

"You're swearing at the wrong person here. I'm just an innocent girl in the big bad city."

"You are anything but, dear heart."

"Shouldn't you be showing the pictures to him?"

"He knows already who they are. And who I am. And I guess he's going to learn who you are too, deep down, because you can have him."

"Excuse me?"

"He's yours, dear. Not his money, of course, whatever there is, his children and I will get that. Along with the house. And half his future earnings, which are not as much as you would think, considering my parents are still paying half the mortgage. But you can have him. All of him. With my blessings."

"What if I don't want him?"

"Well, we don't always get what we want, do we? And fair warning, that thing he does in the middle, when his face gets all red and his eyes bulge and his pudgy little body goes into that grotesque spasm, like he's Joe Cocker? It's not a heart attack, you'll just wish it was."

When the woman slipped off the chair, she took a few bills out of her wallet and dropped them on the bar. "For the drinks," she said. "If you see him, please tell him not to come home."

"Where should I tell him to go?"

"Don't tempt me."

"Who's Joe Cocker?"

The woman stopped fussing with her bag and looked straight at Annie for a moment before snapping it shut. "He always did like them young," she said.

That, of course, was the end of Brad. It wasn't the sob story about poor little Ryan with his issues, or even the moxie of the wife that killed the evening for him. It was the heart-attack image. There were many things in this world that Annie could stomach—way too much alcohol, a plate full of snails, even dentures in a glass—but Brad's paroxysmal orgasm was not to be one of them.

Still, even as Annie went about the familiar process of forgetting Brad, the wife stuck. It was the way she had dressed for their confrontation—that suit, those shoes—and the sense of occasion that she gave it. Their tête-à-tête in the bar was a big moment in her life, a declaration of independence from being merely the cuckolded spouse, and in that bar she had given voice to all the silent specters haunting the edges of what had become of Annie's sad, spoiled existence, the ghosts of those cheated-on wives, each manifesting a singular face. But the face on each was not the face of Brad's soon-to-be ex-wife, no, instead it was the face of Eleanor Chase.

Which was why Annie was standing in the parking lot of an Applebee's on some trite suburban boulevard, the restaurant flanking the one road leading into a subdivision with bright, tasteless houses all lined up in a row. The kind of dreary subdivision she had always expected she'd end up in, married to some charmless stiff like Brad, with kids pulling at her hem and calling for her attention as she drank herself into a regular afternoon stupor. Sometimes the sad fact that her dreams were no less mind-numbing than her reality was all that kept her going. She was standing there, waiting for Justin Chase to arrive, so they could both meet this Austin Moss, who had taken her tiresome suburban dream and made it his own.

For Austin Moss, Eleanor Chase's apparent lover, was not just Annie's mirror image, but possibly the instrument of her exorcism. In her own bitter way, that woman at the bar at the Bellevue had made it clear to Annie exactly who she had been betraying with every adulterous kiss. And the woman on the receiving end of each of these betrayals, in Annie's mind, had always been Mackenzie Chase's wife. That was why the murder of Eleanor Chase had haunted her so: it was the physical manifestation of each of her betrayals. But if Mackenzie and Eleanor truly did have an arrangement—a line he had given Annie but which she had never quite believed—and if Eleanor was finding love and solace outside her marriage, then there was no betrayal there. And maybe, God, maybe, all those silent specters would just fade away, leaving her with the possibility of a future free of ghosts.

"Where have you been?" she said to Justin when he climbed down off his motorbike. "I've been standing here like a streetwalker for half an hour."

"You make any money?"

She was about to take his head off for that crack, but his smile was so good-natured that she just shrugged into it. "Enough for an Applebee's lunch," she said, "so long as I don't order a drink."

"How could you bear an Applebee's lunch without one?"

"Good question."

"I had an unexpected visitor," said Justin.

"Anything interesting?"

He looked at her for a moment and she could see him thinking about something. The way he was thinking and looking at her at the same time made her feel strange. What was she doing, blushing? Christ, she was. Where the hell did that come from?

"How would you feel if I could prove that my father didn't kill my mom?"

"Relieved. Thrilled, actually."

"It would wipe out all remnants of the guilt, I suppose."

"Uh, yeah."

"But how would you feel about him getting out of prison? Coming back into your life?"

"I hadn't even thought of that. I don't know. I think we've both moved on."

"But he's still sending you letters."

"What's going on, Justin?"

"I don't know. It was a strange morning. Are you ready?"

"Are you?"

"Sure, I think," he said. "The last address I had was 1350 Mantis Drive."

"It will be that way," said Annie, pointing up the street. "When you told me to meet here, I figured it had to be that development. I scouted it out. Just a loop and a cul-de-sac, with no connecting streets. There's only one way in. And as far as I can tell, one way out, too."

"Inside a coffin?"

"It is the suburbs."

"The address is a couple years old, but nothing else came up on the Internet. He's probably not there."

"Probably not. But you never know."

"No, you never do," said Justin, looking at her more closely than she was comfortable with. "Come on then. Let's see what my mother's lover has to say."

36.

RUSTY NAIL

The houses on Mantis Drive were all alike, two-level tract homes built to sell when tract homes were still selling. The driveways were wide, the lawns green, the trees remarkably uniform, as if they were all planted at exactly the same moment in time, which they were, about a decade and a half before. The house at 1350 was like the others, only better tended. The trim was freshly painted, the lawn freshly mowed. A battered white van was parked in the driveway, and a thin man in ragged jeans was high on a ladder set by the front door, laying a fresh coat of beige on a window frame.

"Can I help you two?" he said from the ladder after Justin and Annie had made their way down the driveway and then along the path that led to the front door. The man kept on working as he spoke, and from the angle, Justin could only make out an unshaven jaw.

"We're looking for Austin Moss," said Justin.

"Good luck with that," said the man as he smoothed on a swath of paint. "Seeing as he's been dead for about three years."

"That's too bad," said Justin. "How'd he die, do you know?"

"He got hisself run over. Right on the street. Which happens sometimes when you're walking around drunk as a skunk. I always thought if you got to be drunk, it's better to be it behind the wheel than out in the open without no protection."

"An accident, was it?"

"Some say."

"What do the others say?"

"Oh, folks are always saying."

"Does Mrs. Moss still live here?"

"That she does," he said as he leaned forward and worked on a corner of the sill. "What kind of business you got with the missus?"

"Are you her painter or her social secretary?" said Annie.

"I do more than just painting around here," said the man, without stopping his work. "I cut the lawn, do the plumbing, clean them gutters, keep the weeds in check. I guess you could say I'm Mrs. Moss's handyman."

"I can't imagine a place like this," said Justin, "with a house this new, provides much work for you."

"You'd be surprised at that, you would," said the man as he carefully dipped his brush in the paint can hanging from a hook on the ladder. "They put these things up in a hurry, and that's the way they seem to want to come down. The name's Eddie, Eddie Nicosia of Nicosia Home Repairs. Like on the side of the van. You got any drains need unplugging or a tilting deck, I'm your man."

"We'll let you know if anything comes up, Eddie. Is Mrs. Moss in?"

"She expecting you?"

"Not exactly."

"Fair warning then," said Eddie from up high. "Janet don't like no unexpected visitors."

"I guess we'll just have to take our chances," said Justin.

He looked at Annie, who curled the edge of her lip in amusement at the nosy handyman and then knocked on the door.

Rap rap. Rap.

As they waited, Justin glanced up at the man in time to see him carefully place his paintbrush on the edge of the can and start climbing unhurriedly down the ladder. There was something disconcerting about him, the way he slowly yet menacingly descended the ladder, the note in his voice that was sure of way too much. When he reached the ground, he pulled a rag out of his pocket and started wiping his hands, all the while watching as the door opened.

"Well, well, what have we here?" said the woman who answered the door.

"Mrs. Moss?"

"Oh Christ, and I thought the election was over," she said, her voice slightly slurry. "No, I'm not going to vote, I never vote. On principle."

"And what principle is that?"

"I don't give a fuck. How's that?"

"Pretty good, actually," said Justin.

The woman in front of him was tall and thin and seriously unsteady, standing in the doorway with one hand braced against the doorframe, the other holding a cigarette. She had a weathered face that had once been quite pretty and a voice as leathery as her skin. She swayed slightly as she stood before them in a loose sweater over a pair of jeans.

"Don't tell me you're selling magazines for college. You two are a little old to be undergraduates."

"Do you have a moment?"

"Not really," she said before pausing to suck the half-life out of her cigarette. "It's Saturday, which means I'm scrapbooking."

"You're into scrapbooking?" said Annie, with a false

enthusiasm.

"No," said Mrs. Moss. She slowly turned her attention to Annie and stared for a bit, as if it took a moment for her lidded eyes to focus. "Do I know you?"

"I don't think so, Mrs. Moss."

"Yes, I do, and call me Janet. Mrs. Moss was my mother-in-law. If I ever grew into her, I'd slit my throat. No, I know you, I just don't remember yet from where. But it will come to me, it always does, only usually too late to do any good. So what do you two trespassers want?"

"We were actually looking for your husband."

"You're a little late. Did he owe you money?"

"No."

"Good, because I don't have any. Who are you again?"

"My name is Justin Chase."

"Chase, huh?" she said, tilting her head and staring at him for a long moment while her mouth slowly turned down, as if she were slipping back through the turbid currents of her life into bitter memory. "Oh."

"Yeah."

"You're the son. The one that found her. And now I recognize you," Mrs. Moss said as she slowly wagged her cigarette at Annie. "From the newspapers. Don't you two make just the cutest couple? I mean, considering. Is she, like, your mom now?"

"Can we come in, Janet?"

"I suppose you two got something on your minds."

"That we do."

She slowly lifted her chin and narrowed her eyes until they were almost closed. "What exactly?"

"I'd like to talk to you about my mother."

"It was a long time ago, and a lot of water has rushed

through the basement since then."

"And your husband."

"Also dead."

"But still. And I have something you might want to see."

"What could you possibly have that would interest me?"

"Can we come in?"

She stared at the two of them for a moment more, passing her gaze from Justin to Annie and back again.

"Why's she here?" she said, pointing her cigarette at Annie.

"Solace," said Justin.

The woman stared at him for a moment longer without an ounce of amusement on her weathered face. "That's a good one," she said, almost collapsing backward as she stepped away from the doorway, inviting them into the house.

37.

CAN OF BUD

If Annie Overmeyer knew anything in this world it was that men lied. They lied about their wives, their money, their emotions, the size and dependability of their cocks. The outright inevitability of their lies was one of the things she liked most about being with men, besides the sex and the drinking. Who doesn't like having her vision of the world confirmed night after night, in one bar after the other, one bed after another?

But still, she couldn't help feeling a little disappointed when she caught Justin Chase in his first lie. She was sitting with Justin and that drugged-out Janet Moss in the horrid living room of her horrid little tract house. You could tell the room once had looked okay, in a Seaman's-discount-furniture sort of way, but over the years a cancerous clutter had taken hold. When you live in a place, things dropped here or there cease to register and, after a while, take on an air of permanence. Little knickknacks, piles of magazines, a broom in the corner, a jacket tossed on a table. The clutter in the Moss house had metastasized. And it smelled like bird poop.

"I like your home, Janet," said Justin, which, considering the size and simplicity of his own house, could not possibly be the truth.

"We bought it when it was still spiffy and new," said Janet, sitting deep in a greasy old easy chair. "As was our marriage at the time. Would you like something to drink, the two of you?"

Justin glanced Annie's way and then said, "No, thank you."

"That's good," said Janet Moss as she lit another cigarette, "because I didn't really want to get up again."

In a black cage hanging from a stand in the corner of the room, a small yellow bird spread its wings, jumped from one perch to another, pecked the air, let out a series of satisfied chirps, dropped a small white load.

"How did you meet your husband?" said Annie.

"Pure chance," she said. "I had just happened into a bar to meet a friend—I've never been much of a drinker—and there Austin was. I liked his looks right off, and he must have seen something in me."

A desperate lush, thought Annie, nodding with sympathy.

"Neither of us were exactly young when we met," said Janet. "We had been around the block a bit, so we both knew how lucky we were to find each other. And then we found this house, bigger than we ever expected, and out of our price range. But I loved it, and they almost threw the mortgage at us. We were giddy, we felt like we had been pulled out of something and saved."

"Pulled out of what?" said Annie, suddenly curious.

"Out of the muck our lives had become, I guess. Walking into our house the first time after the settlement, it was the richest I had ever felt. It didn't last."

"What happened?"

She took a deep, noisy drag from her cigarette. Rising smoke curled in front of her eye as she tried to sort out her past. "What always happens," she said finally.

Just then, Annie heard the sound of a refrigerator being opened in the kitchen, a rattle of cans, the exhale of carbonation when a pull-top was popped. The canary rustled excitedly in its cage.

"Is somebody here?" said Justin.

"That's just Eddie," said Mrs. Moss. "He helps me out. He's been doing that for five or six years now. It's good to have someone."

Annie leaned forward and looked hard at this woman sinking into the chair as if it were swallowing her whole. "It must have been a shock when your husband died," said Annie. "We heard it was an accident."

"It was something," said Mrs. Moss. "We'd been having our problems, that was no secret. We'd been having our problems for a while. That was just the end of them, I guess. It let me keep the house, though."

"How?" said Justin.

"I had lost my job, and the mortgage had adjusted up. But after the accident, with the insurance and all, there wasn't really a problem anymore."

"I guess it all worked out that way," said a voice from the kitchen. Annie looked up and there was the handyman, that Eddie Nicosia, leaning against the doorframe with a can of Budweiser in his hand, and his hips thrust weirdly forward. He was thin and sharp-faced, with twisted teeth, and his very posture was of a belligerent alpha, which seemed a bit strange seeing as it wasn't his house to alpha in.

"You want something, Eddie?" said Justin.

"Just a beer," said Eddie, standing there, rolling his hips and showing absolutely no intention of taking the hint and shuffling off.

"These people have come to talk about Austin," said Janet. "They want to ask about Austin and the Chase woman. This is her son."

"Is that a fact?" said Eddie.

"The one that found her dead and bloody on the floor."

"Oooh," said Eddie. "That must have been tough for a kid like you."

"This is a little private if you don't mind," said Justin.

"No, go ahead," said Eddie. "I don't mind at all."

"You said you had something to show me," said Janet.

Justin looked at Eddie a moment more, as if he were measuring something, and then turned back to the woman in the chair. "Apparently, my mother knew your husband," he said.

"She knew him for a long time, well before I did," said Janet. "Never let him go, as a matter of fact."

"What do you mean?"

"There's always someone in the past, isn't there? And the comparisons never stop. If only...Why didn't I...With her I could have...Mine is Edgar, Edgar Monelli. Sweet boy. Now he owns a bank. But the whispering disappointments quiet down if the ghosts stay out of the marriage, don't you think? Edgar had the sense to keep out of our lives."

"And my mother didn't?"

"I assumed that's why you were here."

"In the back of my mother's closet," said Justin, "my brother found some letters addressed to my mother that were kept in a shoebox. There's no name at the end, just an initial. An A."

"What kind of letters?"

"It's hard to say."

"Try," said Eddie.

"This doesn't involve you."

Eddie gave a little snort and then took a long drink of his beer, his Adam's apple bobbing as the can was drained.

"They look like love letters to me," said Justin to Janet. "And I wanted to know if the A in the letters was your husband."

"Not if they're love letters," said Janet Moss.

"Excuse me?"

"Let me see," she said, snapping her fingers.

Justin took a piece of paper out of his pocket, unfolded it, and leaned over to hand it to the woman in the easy chair. She glanced at it just for a second, purposefully not reading it, before handing it back.

"It's his handwriting, all right. That careful little scrawl. You know how many love letters that son of a bitch sent me?"

"Anything else?" said Eddie.

"Don't let us keep you," said Justin.

"I'm not letting you do nothing. Either of you want a cold one?"

"No," said Justin.

"I'll just get me another then." He pushed off the doorframe and headed back to the refrigerator.

"When did you find out about the relationship between your husband and my mother?" said Justin, after Eddie had moseyed off.

"I knew about it. The way you know about things in your bones."

"Did you catch them at something? Did your husband confess?"

"I just knew."

"They always know," said Eddie, back at his spot in the doorway. "The wives. Shit, my first wife could smell it on me afore I walked in the door. I'd be getting out of the van and she'd be hurling them pans at me."

"How did your husband react to the news of Mrs. Chase's death?" said Annie.

"He was devastated, disconsolate. He drank to excess. Well, he always drank a bit to excess. This was more than excess."

"And you?"

"She was in the way. And then she died. And there was hope. And guilt, too, a little, I admit." She looked at Justin and Annie and then rushed her words as if she had been caught at something. "About being so satisfied at someone else's death, I mean. I guess you know about that, dearie."

"I only felt horrible," said Annie.

"Mostly I was just glad."

"That's pretty harsh," said Annie.

"She put herself right in the middle of what we had. It wasn't perfect, our marriage, it wasn't a model, I admit that. But it was ours. And it was all I had. And yet there she came, like she was going to save him. Save him from what? From me? And it went to crap after that. It was never the same, even after she was dead. I thought it might all just go away, but it didn't. And then, a while later, Austin moved out."

"He wasn't living here when he died?" said Justin.

"He was living in town. A new life. He helped with the house, but he wanted to sell it. Wanted me to move into an apartment to save money. The same type of crap apartment I was living in when I met him."

"And then he died," said Eddie. "You got anything more? 'Cause I got to get back to work."

"No one's stopping you," said Justin.

"Oh, I'm not leaving Janet with the likes of you two. She's tired, and there's no telling what you could push her into. You want me to walk these people out, Janet?"

"I think so. I am tired."

"It's time," said Eddie. He took a step into the living room, leaning forward aggressively from the waist, jutting out his jaw. "Let's go, folks."

"We're almost done," said Justin.

"No almost about it."

Justin stood up and calmly turned to Eddie.

"If you give us a moment of privacy, we'll be out of your hair in a jiff."

"You ain't ever getting in my hair, flash. You know that sign that says BEWARE OF DOG? Well, I'm the big dog around here."

Eddie took a step toward Justin in that aggressive lean of his. The two were face-to-face now, staring each other down.

Annie felt an electric thrill ripple through her as the canary chirped excitedly in its cage and Eddie took another step.

38.

ELEPHANT'S EAR

Justin took a hard look at Eddie Nicosia, standing there like a pit bull in front of him, and immediately did the calculation.

It was a weakness, he knew, judging a man by whether or not he could kick the man's ass, but Justin was still a creature of testosterone and so couldn't help himself. Whenever things got dicey in the bar, like when those two yahoos came in for Cody, he did the same calculation, gauging weight, fitness, the crazy glint in the other man's eye. He covered this Eddie Nicosia in weight and fitness, and Justin had some skills to be sure, but the spark in Nicosia's eye let him know it wouldn't be an easy or pleasant thing to take him on. Once in Reno he had seen a too-rowdy drunk with the same aggressive posture, the same nasty spark. The bouncer, a guy named Pete, outweighed the drunk by a hundred pounds, but still, before Justin could register the blade hidden in the drunk's pinwheeling right hand, Pete's ear was on the floor. From that point on, they called Pete "Vince."

Justin's quest for nonattachment in this world only went so far. He weighed his attachment to his body parts against what he could gain by holding his ground, and it wasn't close. Time to go. He put his hands together and switched on his mask of serenity.

"I understand completely," said Justin to Eddie Nicosia before turning to face Janet Moss. "Thank you for your time, Janet. We won't bother you further."

Janet Moss waved him away, the cigarette smoldering in her grip. "It wasn't a bother. My marriage was a bother."

"You two need any help finding your way out?" said Eddie.

"No," said Annie, standing and looking at Justin with a crease of disappointment in her forehead. "We're good, really, since that's the door right over there and we can actually see it from here."

There was silence between Annie and Justin as they walked past Eddie's ladder in front of the house, down the driveway to the street, and then up along Mantis Drive toward the subdivision's entrance.

"You really showed him," she said finally.

"What did you want me to show him?" said Justin.

"Some gumption, maybe?"

"Gumption?"

"Ever hear of it?"

"Where are you from, anyway?"

"Minnesota."

"Lot of gumption out there, I suppose."

"Loads. Wisconsin has cheese, we've got gumption. Your father would have put that jackass on his butt."

"My father's in jail," said Justin. "There's an old Zen saying: Ride your horse along the edge of the sword; hide yourself in the middle of the flames."

"What the hell does that mean?"

"I don't know. What did you think about our Mrs. Moss?"

"She's a disaster," said Annie. "Bitter, angry, totally drugged out. I liked her."

"You liked her?"

"Sure. Life hasn't turned out for her, but still she's got her house, her boy toy, and her sense of humor."

"Boy toy? Are they...you know?"

"Absolutely. Couldn't you see? He stood in that doorway like a rooster guarding his coop."

"What do you think she was on?"

"Valium, OxyContin, something. And I caught the sweet whiff of pot somewhere, so she's mixing and matching."

"I bet old Eddie Nicosia has all kinds of fun stuff in that van."

"Along with a mattress and shag carpeting maybe. He's a real handyman. Janet's a little lost is all. Once she gets her bearings back, she'll kick that son of a bitch out of her life and get started again."

"Is it that easy?"

"I've always hoped so."

"Convenient how her husband died so suddenly, leaving her the house and his insurance."

"It was, wasn't it?"

"And she didn't seem to like my mom much."

"My God, did she hate her. That was the only true thing that came out of her mouth: the vitriol she felt for your mother."

"And she said she felt guilty about my mother's death. You don't think..."

"I don't know. When you're mixed up in some triangle and things go terribly wrong, the emotions are always confusing. I know that firsthand. But there was something about the way she described your mother's effect on her marriage. It wasn't like your mom was stealing her husband from her. I've been on the other side and know how that would play out. Mostly she would have described your mother anatomically, because for her that would have been the threat. But here it was more like your mother was just getting in the middle of something, of some sort of agreement, and Janet Moss didn't want her meddling."

"She said that after my mom's death, she thought her marriage had another chance. It seems that a lot of people in her orbit end up conveniently dying. How long did she say Eddie had been helping her out around the house?"

"Five or six years, I think it was."

"Maybe he's been more helpful than just painting shutters, plying her with pills, and dipping his wick. Maybe I should check him out a bit."

"How are you going to do that?"

"I'm a barkeep," said Justin when they reached the parking lot of the Applebee's. "We have our ways."

"Thanks for letting me come," said Annie hesitantly, like she had something else to say but didn't know how to phrase it. She looked down and kicked at the ground. "It helped a bit to see that the situation was bigger than just me."

"It always is," said Justin. "You know Whitman?"

"The candy? The chocolate sampler? What does that have to do with anything?"

"'For every atom belonging to me as good as belongs to you.'"

"Where did you read that, Junior, on the inside of the box?"

"Exactly."

"Uncle Walt's always been my favorite. Sexy, like chocolate. You'll let me know what you find out about that creep Nicosia?"

"Sure," said Justin, not meaning it.

He watched her retreat a bit, turn, spin around once to smile and wave good-bye, and then head for her car. He watched the way her back arched, her arms swung, her long legs loped on the asphalt. And he tilted his head in disappointment as he watched her go. This, he knew, was the end of the line for Annie Overmeyer in his life.

It wasn't that he didn't want to screw her. Of course he wanted to screw her. Justin wanted to screw everything in heels; send a horse by in Manolos and he'd neigh. In fact Justin really, really wanted to screw her. Really. And he sensed he wouldn't have the urge to be up and out as soon as he caught his breath with Annie Overmeyer, that he wouldn't mind lingering a bit, talking things through, losing himself in the rough edges of her voice, wincing happily at her defensive jokes. But in the middle of it all, with their arms and legs twisted in a delirious tangle, with those beautiful lips of hers locked onto his, with that straw-colored hair swirling around them both like a pale saffron robe, would she be thinking about him? Or his father? Or maybe both, comparing one with the other? Technique. Size. Yikes. No, Justin was all up for perversion, but some things were just too damn perverse, and that was one of them. It might have been different if he were a different kind of kid and his father were a different type of man, but his father wasn't, and Justin wasn't, and this thing wasn't going anywhere, ever.

And so good-bye, Annie, and good luck.

He was still feeling disappointment at the end of this tender yet ghostly embrace when Eddie Nicosia's white van rattled out of Mantis Drive and headed south. Justin kicked the bike to life and followed.

Normally Justin would stay as far back as possible from the van, being that a motorcycle was easier to keep track of in the rearview mirror, but Eddie's van, with its solid back doors, didn't have a rearview mirror. And the passenger-side mirror was conveniently cracked. So he wasn't as worried about being spotted as he followed up and down, here and there, along the broad corridors of Montgomery County, all the while doing his best to stay out of the view of the driver-side mirror. Still, it wasn't as easy as you would suppose. Justin had no idea how many white vans there were in the world until he tried to follow one. There were fleets of white vans on the street, zooming here and there, diving in and out of the lanes of traffic, toting plumbing supplies or flowers, trolling for kids, all of them keeping Justin in a cloud of doubt as to which of these white vans belonged to the louse.

But when he spied what he hoped was Eddie's white van turn into a parking lot, he caught the plain block letters on the side reading NICOSIA HOME REPAIRS. He slowed down and pulled to the curb.

Eddie was now parked exactly where Justin had figured he'd be parked, in front of a bar. The Kork & Keg was a ragged little roadhouse wedged between a desultory strip mall and a 7-Eleven. Pabst on tap, charred pieces of gristle served with French fried potatoes, Sinatra on the jukebox. The Kork & Keg.

Justin had seen the way Eddie had sucked beer from the can in Mrs. Moss's living room, absorbing the alcohol as neatly as a protozoan absorbed oxygen. After a hard day's work at the Moss estate, doing whatever strange things he did there, Eddie Nicosia would certainly head off to his regular joint for a quick pop. And he might stay for a couple of quick pops more. The only thing Justin didn't know for sure was whether Eddie would leave on his own power or be swept out with the dust and the vomit.

Justin rode into the parking lot and parked next to the van. He slid off his bike, looked around as he walked to the back of the van, and tried the doors. Locked, of course.

He walked over to the bar's entrance and checked out the

closing time. Two. Same as Zenzibar. Too bad. On the way back to the bike, he kicked at one of the van's rear lights, cracking the plastic. It felt surprisingly good, which was a pretty good indication that Justin was losing perspective. So be it. Back on the bike, he slipped it into gear and drove off, all the while thinking about how Marson was going to react tonight when Justin told him he would have to leave a little early.

39.

FUNKY COLD MEDINA

"Is that a new shirt?" said Justin to Cody as he built Cody's drink behind the wood at Zenzibar.

"Silk," said Cody, tapping on the bar, looking around more insistently than usual.

"Take it easy. I don't think Slammer and Jammer are coming back."

"Not as long as you still have that bat and Larry's sitting next to me," said Cody, glancing quickly to the side. "I'm just a little amped tonight."

"And what's that around your neck?"

Cody fingered the thick gold chain. "Something I picked up. Remember I told you I had stumbled onto a moneymaking opportunity? Well, it's starting to pay off. And I owe you for it."

"Me?"

"It never would have happened if you hadn't sent me"—he glanced at Larry on the adjacent barstool, talking to the guy next to him, then leaned forward and lowered his voice—"if you hadn't sent me on that mission, you know. It was in the middle of that where I fell into what I fell into. I could hook you up with a piece of fine merchandise if you wanted it. A fat plasma or something shiny. At prices you would not believe."

"Thanks, but no thanks," said Justin as he measured the Peach Schnapps and Southern Comfort before loading them into his silver shaker. "I'm trying to get rid of my junk, not add to it."

"Who doesn't want more junk? This is America, baby."

"You ever listen to Dylan?"

"That creep that comes in here every so often and starts talking politics? Nah, why would I do that?"

"Why would you?" said Justin. A jigger of vodka, a jigger of Blue Curaçao. A shovel of ice. "Did you ever make it to Dirty Frank's?"

"Like I promised. And I found your buddy too."

"Charming, isn't he?" said Justin as he capped his tin and gave it a quick shake before straining the bluish mixture over a stack of square cubes in a tall tumbler.

"I sort of admired him."

"You must have been really drunk."

"No, really. The old guy is sick as a dog and yet he's still in there fighting the fight. I could see a bit of myself in him."

"God, I hope not." Justin filled the rest of the glass with cranberry juice, put a lime on the edge and gave it a stir, turning the whole thing a bright purple.

"What's that?" said Cody.

"It's called a Funky Cold Medina."

"You're kidding me."

"I kid you not. I don't name them, I just make them. Try it."

Cody brought the drink to his lips, taking a small sip and then a longer one. "Wow. What's that taste that sort of pulls it all together?"

"Peach."

"Yes, it is," said Cody before taking a gulp. As he did, the door to the bar opened and Lee walked in.

She was dressed conservatively, like she had just come

from the investment firm, high neckline, sensible black pumps. And there was something crisp in her step as she made her way to the bar; she was coming in to deliver a downgrade rather than to relax into a drink. Justin winced a bit as she came right up to the bar and stood next to Cody.

"Hello, darling," said Larry, leaning forward to talk across Cody. "We missed you."

"I took the day off yesterday. How are you?"

"Miserable as usual."

"Attaboy," she said, staring at Justin for a bit before turning to Cody.

"Is that a new shirt?" she said.

"As a matter of fact," said Cody.

"Nice. You seem prosperous tonight, I must say."

"Things are looking up."

"For both of us then," she said. "What's that you're drinking?"

"It's called a whatchama-something-or-other, I think, but it's pretty damn good."

"You want one?" said Justin.

"How about just some tonic water and lime?"

"Gin or vodka?"

"Ice," she said.

"Coming right up." He grabbed a glass and filled it with ice, poured in the tonic water. "I called," he said softly.

"I know."

"I wanted to see how you were doing."

"Is that what it was?" she said, her voice not so soft. "Because I just thought it was a booty call."

Cody coughed midsip, spraying purple on his new shirt and over the bar. "I'll be right back," he said before retreating from the scene.

"That was a little harsh," said Justin as he wiped the bar.

"But true," said Lee, taking Cody's seat.

"Maybe."

She watched as he squeezed a half lime into the tonic, threw out the hull, slid a slice of lime atop the rim.

"Where's your friend?" she said when the tonic water was in front of her.

"She's my father's friend," said Justin, "not mine. And she's gone."

"Out of town?"

"Out of my life."

"That's too bad," said Lee. "I liked her. She has a cruel honesty about her."

"Yes, she does."

"I found it surprisingly refreshing." She lifted her drink and took a sip. "She forced me to see things a lot more clearly."

"I suppose that explains the tonic water and lime, with just ice. Are you sleeping better suddenly?"

"Much. You want to know something, Justin? Your whole 'rare beauty of nonattachment' thing is utter bullshit."

"Maybe."

"Definitely. It's a coward's way of not getting hurt. But it only goes one way with you. You count on the attachment from the other side, you even cultivate it. Sweet smiles, kind gestures, that puppy-dog look in your eye. Just so you can call up late at night, have your fun, and then talk about your nonattachment as if you were some Buddha in training instead of just another horndog."

"You're right."

"I'm right? That's all you have to say? That I'm right?"

"I'm a bartender," said Justin flatly, "and to a bartender, the customer is always right."

Lee stared for a moment before taking hold of her drink and lifting it as if to dash it smack into Justin's face. He didn't move, didn't so much as flinch, knowing he deserved a drenching, totally. But then she gained control of herself, snatched down a gulp, and slammed the glass back to the bar. She lifted her purse and rummaged for a bit before grabbing a bill and tossing it beside the near-empty glass. "For the drink," she said.

"It's on the house."

"It should be on your head," she said, "but I want to pay for it. Good-bye, Justin," she said as she stood from the stool. "I hope you find what you're looking for."

"And what exactly is that?"

"That's the problem right there," she said before turning and striding away from the bar.

Justin stared at her back, her legs, her lustrous black hair. She stopped at the door to say something to someone, glancing back as she talked. Even from that distance, the beauty of her eyes shone.

Justin knew that when she left the bar, she was leaving his life, and he felt an unaccountable sadness. But he couldn't tell if the sadness was from losing Lee or the convenience of a Lee. Were all his efforts to keep from getting too close to her a sad acknowledgment of his inability to deal with how important she might already have become in his life? Or was she right, was she just a handy body and was he just a horndog? And which would make him feel better about himself? He was at a loss, which was why he had reverted to the cold and level affect of a professional barkeep.

Damn, he had been in the job too long; he needed to find another profession. Personal trainer? Dog walker? Sanitation engineer? He watched as Lee gave him a final toss of hair before heading out the door.

Annie Overmeyer, he said to himself, nodding in appreciation. Who knew that honesty was so damn contagious?

"Nice show," said Larry. "You should have charged tickets."

"Yuengling?"

"Let's try something a step above."

"How about a Stella Artois?"

"Yes, please, I'm feeling a little Brando-ish. Stella! I guess we're both in the same boat. Me with Quentin, you with Lee."

"We're not in the same boat at all. You still care."

"Dude?"

"You want my advice on your Quentin problem?" said Justin as he tilted the chalice and poured from the tap. "There's a place you can get to. It's hard to find and it's easy to fall out of, but there it is, that place. It is the sweetest place you've never been and it's called I Don't Give a Crap. Book yourself a ticket."

"Nice mood you're in."

"Yeah, well, I'm tired of saying good-bye."

He slid the beer in front of Larry and headed over to Marson. "I need to leave a little early," said Justin.

Marson looked impatiently at his watch. "When?"

"About an hour before closing."

"You know, Justin, this is a job, not a resort."

"I know what it is," said Justin. "And I have to punch out early. And instead of giving me crap, you should say, 'Sure thing, Justin, I'll cover for you.'"

"Sure thing, Justin," said Marson, with an edge in his voice. "I'll cover for you. This time."

"Thanks, boss."

When he made his way to the end of the bar, taking orders all the way, Cody was back on his stool, his shirt matted wet where he had tried to clean it.

"That was a little sticky," said Cody. "Didn't mean to get in the middle of something."

"There's nothing to get in the middle of anymore," said Larry.

"So it's over between them?"

"I'm not sure what it was," said Larry, "but whatever it was, it sure isn't anymore."

Without comment, Justin grabbed Lee's glass, threw out the lime and the straw, dumped the rest in the sink, and ran the glass over the scrubber. When Larry turned away, Justin leaned toward Cody.

"What did you mean when you said that the old guy was still fighting the fight?"

"Hustling, I meant. Looking for the big score. I figure most guys that age have given up already, are left sucking down all the second-rate liquor they can buy with their Social Security checks. But your old geezer, he's still in the game."

"What game?"

"Well, he was telling me how he was right on the edge of a big-time score that was going to land him flat on easy street. Something to do with some insurance scam. He was going to buy himself a house smack on the beach in Honduras, drink beer all day, and hire native women to sit on his face through the night. And he said if they happened to smother him with their tender thighs, then he'd go out happy."

"A classy guy."

"It didn't sound so bad, actually."

"This sound like a ten-thousand-dollar dream?"

"No way. He was talking big money, fuck-you money, he was talking about being richer than sin, and that's pretty damn rich in my book."

"Interesting."

"I asked him if I could get a piece of that action."

"What did he say?"

"He told me to stick my dick up my ass."

"I bet it sounded better in his Texas drawl."

"That it did," said Cody. "The way he put it, it almost sounded like fun."

40.

BOOKER'S

The parking lot of The Kork & Keg in Blue Bell was mostly empty, a couple of beaters, a black pickup. No white van. Justin parked his bike near the entrance and sauntered inside.

"Don't be wasting your time stepping in," called out the barman with a sharp, high-pitched voice. "We're just about to be closing." He was a burly older man in a white shirt and a dirty red vest, distinctly unfriendly. He leaned against the far end of the bar as if his hip were planted there, his thick arms crossed, his head tilted toward the television.

The joint had a long bar to the right, tables in the middle, and booths on the left, with a door leading to the kitchen straight back. It was the kind of place that served food only because the state required that kind of bar to serve food. Justin had worked a couple of bars like this in his day, sad hard-drinking roadhouses where the only ones left at the end of the night were the hard core who were bumming drinks instead of leaving tips, because they had already poured all their monies down their throats. Two guys sat morosely at the wood, their hands gripped around their beers as if afraid someone would snatch them away. Another man sat alone and pondered the imponderables, like how to crib a final drink. A couple of old-marrieds hissed at each other in one of the booths.

Justin hopped onto a stool. The bartender ignored him as he watched some noxious cable news channel. Justin sat there, drumming his fingers. It wouldn't be long, he figured, and it wasn't. The barman turned from the television and gave Justin a look of disgust before taking a noisy breath, pushing himself off his perch, lurching over.

"I said we're closing. You're not deaf as well as dumb, I'm supposing. I already gave last call. Which makes you, my friend, shit out of luck."

"Just a quick drink," said Justin calmly. "I won't be long."

"You're right you won't be long. I told you twice already, last call's been rung."

"And here I am to answer the bell."

The barkeep stared at Justin for a moment, and then said, "The doors get locked at two. If you're still inside, then you'll be cleaning up with me till I unlock them again. So drink fast, friend. What will it be?"

"How about a Tequila Sunrise."

"Right away."

"But hold the tequila."

"Hold the tequila? What will you be wanting in it, then, vodka instead?"

"Just the juice and the grenadine. But charge me for the real thing, that's fine."

"A late-night vitamin C fix for you, is that it?"

"Something like that," said Justin. "What kind of grenadine do you use?"

"Are you busting me balls now?"

"I just want to know."

"He just wants to know, like it is any of his business what goes into his damn drink. Well, if you must, we use Rose's here."

Justin winced. "That's mostly just high-fructose corn syrup. Have you ever made your own?"

"Can't say that I have."

"It's not too hard if you ignore all the hard ways to do it. Just squeeze a pomegranate in a juicer, heat the juice enough to mix in an equal amount of sugar, and then for each cup of juice, add an ounce of pomegranate molasses and half a teaspoon of orange-blossom water. Simple as that."

"Pomegranate molasses?"

"You can get it at Whole Foods."

"I don't eat quiche, and I never took to chemistry."

"All righty then. If all you've got is Rose's, hold the grenadine as well as the tequila. I'll just have the orange juice. Over ice. And maybe a dash of cranberry for color."

"You seem to know your way around a drink."

"I work at Zenzibar in Center City."

The bartender tilted his head. "On Sixteenth, is it?"

"That's the one."

"Nice place, that. And what are you there, a waiter?"

"I'm behind the wood."

"A fellow pour man, is it? It's grand to know you, then. The name's Rosenberg," said the bartender, reaching out a hand.

"Rosenberg?"

"You got a problem, friend?"

"None," said Justin as he took hold of the outstretched hand and gave it a shake. "Justin."

"An old comrade of mine, he works down the street from your place now," said Rosenberg as he poured the juices from his plastic pourers into a glass with ice and pushed it toward Justin. "By any chance do you know Crowder?"

"That knucklehead? Sure."

"We poured drinks together at the Irish on Locust until they booted us both into the street."

"What happened?"

"He was too generous with the merchandise and they said the clientele was getting too young for me to relate to."

"That's raw."

"But they weren't wrong on either of us, to be truthful. The place, it got discovered by a gaggle of goslings. The management wanted me to put myself out on Facebook to play to the crowd. I asked if they were pulling my pud. They weren't. I told them I wished they would, because I could use the action. You sure you don't want anything in that juice?"

"I'm sure."

"A twelve-stepper, are you?"

"Something like that."

Rosenberg slapped a shot glass on the bar and filled it to the brim with tequila. "You wouldn't mind if I happen to take your shot for you, then?"

"I was hoping you would."

"I was a twelve-stepper too, until I stepped off," said Rosenberg. He lifted the glass. "Sláinte."

Justin peeled a Benjamin out of his wallet, dropped it on the bar. "I'll have another when you get the chance."

Rosenberg eyed the bill for a bit and lifted his chin to stare at Justin. Just then one of the laggards at the bar spoke up.

"Hey, George. Let me have another. One final pint for the long dusty road."

"The last call's been rung, Tom," said Rosenberg still staring at Justin. "The pub's a-closing, boys."

"You made that guy a drink."

"I said it's closing time, I did," announced Rosenberg,

pushing away from the bar and heading over to Tom. "Snatch down what you've got and then be getting the hell out of here. I'm locking up."

"What about him?" said Tom, jerking his thumb at Justin.

Rosenberg turned to glance back at Justin for a moment. "He's a cousin, he is."

"From the old country?"

"Sure," said Rosenberg, "as long as by the old country you be meaning Philadelphia."

"Family?" said the gray guy next to Tom. "That's almost sweet. I love my family, so long as they stay the hell away from me. Let's have one last drink and celebrate all our families."

"Let's not," said Rosenberg. "Especially since you was tapped out an hour and a half ago, Johnny boy. Come on, lads, let's be going on home now. I'm tired as a fifty-cent whore on payday, and me dogs are barking."

It took Rosenberg a while to clear the place out; it was like herding cats that were drunk and had to piss one last time. As Rosenberg worked, Justin took a rag from the bar and started wiping down the tables, one after the other, lifting the chairs and setting them upside down on each tabletop after it had been wiped. By the time the last dawdler was being pushed out, all the chairs and stools were up except for Justin's. Rosenberg twisted the lock and stepped back behind the bar.

"You need to sweep?" said Justin.

"They got a woman who opens up in the morning to do that. I just need to get everything in order back here and set the alarm. Another, you say?"

"Sure," said Justin.

Rosenberg filled up Justin's glass with juice, and then filled up his shot glass with Justin's tequila. He downed it with a wince. "If you'll be taking my professional advice, you'd do better with something a bit smoother next time."

"What do you like?"

He leaned forward. "Promise not to tell anyone, but when I first came to this country, I discovered bourbon. And that was it for me."

"Why don't you make me a Bee Gee OJ, then," said Justin.

"What the hell's that?"

"Bourbon, orange juice, grenadine. But hold the grenadine and hold the bourbon."

"What kind of bourbon am I holding, if I may ask? House?"

"Don't insult me. I'm a man of fine and distinctive tastes."

"The best we've got is Booker's."

"One twenty-eight?"

"That's the stuff."

"It's a little stiff, isn't it?"

"You're man enough for it, I can tell."

"Then let's make it a double."

"I don't know why, Justin," said Rosenberg as he poured the juice into Justin's glass and then filled his own from the narrow bottle he pulled off the top shelf behind him, "but I do indeed like drinking with you, even though I'm the only one doing the drinking."

"It's because I'm the one doing the paying."

"Maybe so," said Rosenberg, lifting up the shot glass and admiring the color of the light shining through. "Here's to being single, drinking doubles, and seeing triple." He winked at Justin before taking a sip. "Ahh, that's mighty good, that is."

"Careful," said Justin. "That's strong as an ox."

"Don't be worrying about me. An Irishman is never drunk as long as he can hold on to one blade of grass and not fall off the face of the earth. Okay, son, so what can I do for you, pour man to pour man?"

"I'm interested in a guy."

"Funny now, you don't seem the type."

"I want to know his story, and I think you just might have it. His name is Eddie Nicosia."

"Ah, the Snake. I should have known it was he you were after."

"Why's he called the Snake?"

"It's a long story," said Rosenberg. "Literally, I suppose. But for this, you're going to need to order yourself another drink."

41.

ANACONDA

Justin knew he was courting mortal peril. And he wasn't thinking about Eddie "The Snake" Nicosia, who surely wouldn't take kindly to Justin's snooping, or the strangely shaped thug who had slammed Justin's face into his floor, or the DA, as obsessed with Justin as Ahab with his whale, or Birdie Grackle himself, who, if there was even a little truth to his story, could suddenly turn his talent for killing upon Justin if he discovered that Justin was jerking his chain about the money, which Justin most assuredly was. No, beyond all these physical threats was a bigger threat by far.

Hope.

His late night of drinking with Rosenberg had sowed his soul with all kinds of possibilities, and hope was the deadly snake slithering among the resulting stalks. For what was hope but a liar, preoccupied with the droughts of the past and the harvests of the future while it killed off the present with its bland blandishments? Justin should have been sitting on his tatami mats, seeking harmony and acceptance, looking to quiet his mind and lose himself in the riotous beauty of the now. That's what he should have been doing, but instead he was flirting with hope as it climbed up his leg, wrapped itself around his chest, and hissed sweet nothings into his ear.

Perhaps Birdie Grackle has been telling the truth all along, and it was he, not your father, who killed your mother. Perhaps he had been hired by Austin Moss's vengeful wife and the sinister Eddie Nicosia. And perhaps you are not in any way to blame. And perhaps your father will be released from his Hades of jail and be the parent you always hoped he would be. He'll toss the pigskin with you in the yard, and take you to ball games, and give you sage advice, and finally accept what you've become. Oh, how perfect the world would be if you actually found the truth, and the truth set your father free.

This was now the sad state of his life. No matter how unattached to the false illusions of the world he thought he had become, he was still a sucker for hope. It was like a leprosy of the soul, and all he could do was try to hide its corrosive effects on his emotions.

"I didn't think you'd be back," said Justin's father. They were again in the visiting room of the prison, sitting across from each other at a table, surrounded by other grim visitations and the shabby vending machines. And once again they had chosen to forgo the allowed embrace at the beginning of the session.

"I'm surprised I'm here myself," said Justin. "But I need to know something."

"You're looking for some sort of definitive answer from me, yes? Your generation and its psychobabble about closure. I've always believed it's better to close your mouth and just get on with it."

"Tell me about my mother. About your relationship with her."

"What is there to tell? I loved her."

"But not only her."

"I am not a narrow man."

"Did she know all along about the others?"

"Do you want the truth or just some salve for your psychic wounds?"

"I'm not sure."

"Of course not. You're like everyone else in this soft, polluted world. You'd rather sit comfortably by the fire with your delusions than face the hard reality of things."

"Frank said there was an arrangement."

"Every marriage is an arrangement."

"Not every marriage is open."

"Let's say ours was expanded."

"Which means that you cheated like a jackal and she let you. Is that the story?"

"It's amazing how children always think they understand the emotional lives of their parents, when there is little they understand less. The truth is, Justin, when it came to stepping outside the marriage, your mother stepped first."

"Now I know you're lying."

"Doesn't it ring true, though? Was she ever one to wilt into the background? She stepped out first, but I knew enough not to blame her. Something had changed in our relationship. It happened slowly and then all at once. You could blame time, blame me, I don't care. But after a decade or two, we were simply going through the motions. Inertia keeps more marriages whole than love ever did. And it kept ours together, too. There were things I could have done, I suppose. Bring flowers, escape with her to Aruba, pretend to care more than I did. But I had pressures in the business, and there was a social calendar, and things just went on as they went on. And all along I thought she was content, even as I became more dissatisfied. And then I got a call from a woman. She wouldn't identify herself, but she told me that my wife was sleeping with her husband and that I should put a stop to it or she would. I didn't know whether to believe her or not—it seemed far-fetched—but I decided to ask your mother. Whatever she was, your mother wasn't a liar. She told me she had been dissatisfied for a long time and that, yes, she had done something about it."

"With whom?"

"That she wouldn't say. Your mother always had more discretion than did I. And I reacted as you would expect, with anger and jealousy. And not just jealousy because she was screwing someone behind my back. Jealousy that she had someone else and I didn't. I had always assumed if one of us was pirate enough to be cheating it would be me. To tell you the truth, I admired what she had done."

"So what did you do about it?"

"I had an affair myself, something tawdry and harsh. I thought it would even things, but it didn't. It actually made me feel worse. The next was not as tawdry. And slowly we settled into the new rhythm and our marriage, such as it had become, expanded. We wouldn't share our experiences, but it was understood that if the opportunity arose, we were free to take advantage of it."

"That sounds skeevy enough to make me want to puke. Why didn't you just split?"

"We almost did. A number of times. But there were you and Frank. The money would have to be divided, with all the headaches. And we sort of liked it the way it was, the freedom and security all at once. Paradoxically, through all of it, I felt closer to your mother than I had in years."

"I don't understand."

"Maybe we suddenly saw the whole as more fragile. When we were together now, it was because we wanted to be together. And when we had sex now, it was—"

"I get the picture."

"Do you?"

"As much as I ever want to. Frank showed me the letters he found."

"Yes, he told me."

"Do you know who 'A' was?"

"No. As I said, she didn't give much information, your mother. But I could tell it was serious. I felt her pulling away. And by then I had found something a little more serious myself."

"Annie Overmeyer."

"Yes. Annie."

"Did you love her?"

"She was intoxicating. Maybe it was her youth, maybe her midwestern matter-of-factness."

"Did you want to marry her?"

"I thought about it."

"But if you were so happy with Mom then, why?"

"Because I wasn't happy with myself. What do men feel when they spy a woman that attracts them? Not just someone to screw, although yes, that of course. But also someone who offers a different kind of life. Bohemian maybe, or literary, or earnest and political, or sybaritic. You see her, maybe across the table, or the room, or the street, and you wonder. What would you be with her? How would she perfect you? And it is that, more than the swell of a young breast, that clenches the gut. I knew what I was with your mother, and I wasn't sure I liked that person very much. Maybe I hoped I'd be someone different with Annie."

"What exactly did you want to become?"

"Younger, optimistic, full of energy and plans. A man with a future. What I was before."

"So it was pure narcissism."

"I won't deny it. Isn't everything?"

"Did you ever tell Mom about her?"

"No. Not specifically. I didn't know how to. When I introduced you to her, I thought you would tell her. But you never did."

"No."

"Why didn't you?"

"I didn't want to hurt her. I thought she was the dutiful, pining wife and mother."

"Yes, well, self-deception is humanity's most universal trait. I had just about resolved to tell your mother myself, not just about the affair but that it was getting more serious than I intended, when she was murdered."

"And you were conveniently free, without the headache of splitting the fortune and paying out alimony."

"Do you think I would kill your mother so as not to pay alimony?"

"I don't know, Dad. Why didn't you tell any of this at the trial?"

"It wouldn't have helped. And I didn't want to drag her reputation into the mire with mine."

"Noble."

"Is that why you came, to berate me more than you already did through your testimony at the trial and then by your absence? Consider me berated. Are we through?"

"Austin Moss," said Justin.

His father stared at him and blinked.

"He's the A of the letters," said Justin. "He was the one having an affair with Mom."

"Austin Moss? I know that name. Your mother was going out with him when I started dating her. Austin Moss? I never thought much of him, he seemed weak to me. Never a threat. I don't think he could be it."

"I checked it out with his widow. I showed her the letters and she identified the handwriting. He's A."

"You checked it out?"

"She must have been the woman who called you."

"That's a hell of a thing. Austin Moss."

"But there's more."

"Justin, what have you been doing?"

"On my last visit, you dared me to test my truths. So I did."

"You actually listened to something I said?"

"Hard to believe, isn't it? And this is what I found, Dad. This Mrs. Moss, the one who probably called you, is mixed up with some smarmy handyman named Eddie Nicosia, who has insinuated himself deep into her life. She pays him a monthly stipend that he cashes, along with her Social Security widow's check, at a bar each month. In exchange he runs her errands, warns off anyone who is crowding her, fills her prescriptions and stashes the pills in his own little medicine cabinet, doling them bit by bit to keep her on his string. But the drugs aren't his only mother's little helper. His nickname is the Snake, which he gave to himself in honor of his favorite tool. And I have it on good authority that we're not talking about a little garter snake here, more like an anaconda."

Justin's father sat back and looked at Justin with a puzzlement creasing his features, like he was trying to stare down an optical illusion.

"It's time, Mac," said one of the guards, who suddenly appeared over Mackenzie Chase's shoulder.

"Give me a minute, please," said Justin's father. "Just a minute more."

Justin waited until the guard nodded and backed away. Then he leaned forward and continued in a soft voice.

"Mrs. Moss isn't this Eddie Nicosia's only meal ticket. He has a veritable stable. He uses his pet to insinuate himself with lonely women. They keep hiring him to take care of their houses.

And to run their errands. And to make their lives a little less lonely, not to mention the sage financial advice he can give due to his years of experience in bankruptcy court. And after a long day of servicing his clients, he goes to a bar to blow off steam and brag about his conquests. Sometimes when he blows off steam, he does so by picking a fight with some hapless bystander. But this one time, when the hapless bystander turned out not to be so hapless and the thing got out of hand, our friend Eddie started with the threats. 'Watch your step, punk. I could have you killed quick as a snap. I done it, too. More than once. You want to be next?'"

Justin's father listened to all this with rapt attention. Justin could see him work it out, the implications. And suddenly he could see something else press itself onto the surface of his father's hard face, something bright and painful all at once, like a snake within a field of desiccated stalks.

"You said Mrs. Moss is a widow," said Justin's father. "How did this Austin die?"

"He was run over by a car," said Justin. "Or run down, one or the other."

"When?"

"A couple years after Mom died."

"How long has this handyman been wrapping himself into this Mrs. Moss's life? Was he there before your mother was killed?"

"I believe so, yes."

"You don't think..."

"I don't know what to think," said Justin. "But she told me how she thought she had a chance to save her marriage after Mom died. I just thought this was something you should know."

"My God," said Justin's father. "It is what we've been looking for. It is better than Timmy. What to do about it, that is the question."

"Time, Mac," said the guard by the door. "Your son has to go."

Justin's father stood, and Justin stood with him. They stared at each for a moment, unsure of what to do with their arms, their hands.

"I think I should tell the police," said Justin finally.

"The police? Don't be a fool. They'll just bury it."

"There's a detective I've grown to trust a little bit. I'm going to tell him."

"And be done with it yourself."

"That's right."

"Okay, then. You deserve the peace. But to keep them honest, I'll tell my lawyer too. If she has it, they'll know they have to keep digging. Do you have anything concrete to give her? Evidence?"

"Nothing, except for the letters."

"She already has those. Witnesses?"

"Not really."

"Well then, we have no choice but to trust the police just a bit. My God, Justin. I would never have thought. You of all people. Never. I don't know how to thank you."

"Maybe that's because you never thanked me for anything before in my life."

"I'm going to have to learn."

"It might not be anything," said Justin. "It might be all wrong."

"It's something," said Justin's father. "It's a possibility. And in here, that's everything."

They stood there a bit longer, even as the guard came over for a third and final time.

"Okay, then," said Justin's father before hesitantly and stiffly reaching out a hand.

Justin stared at the hand for a moment, and then took hold of it and gave it a little shake. It was an awkward moment, over in a flash, the tiniest of gestures. But it was also the first time he had touched his father since he had found his mother dead on the floor. And somehow, for some reason, it made his heart sing.

A song of hope.

42.

CHAMOMILE

The car parked on the edge of Fitler Square was boxy and brown, with the familiar squat figure sitting inside, drinking coffee and writing on a folded newspaper. Justin hadn't seen the car when he went out for his run, but it was there when he came back. His habits had become so regular that a guy like Detective Scott could set his watch by Justin's running times. He couldn't tell if that was a good thing or a bad thing, but for some reason it made him think of Annie Overmeyer.

He shook her out of his head as he ran over to the car. It was a cool morning, the sky congealing with clouds for a rain that was coming. While jogging in place, he knocked on the roof to get Scott's attention.

"Nice morning, Detective," he said, in a series of breath-catching syllables.

"'Tis all of that," said Scott.

"I was actually looking for you when I went out."

"Something came up."

"A Starbucks?"

"Their lemon squares are quite tasty. A little expensive for a cop, but I have so few other joys in this life."

"Sitting in a car all day, drinking coffee," said Justin, shaking his head. "I bet you have to pee something awful."

"At my age, the only time I don't have to pee is when I'm peeing."

"I have a bathroom in my house. You're welcome to use it."

"Thanks for the offer, truly, but I'll just keep my eye on you from out here."

"And if you want I'll brew us up a fresh cup of chamomile to calm down the nerves frazzled by all that caffeine."

"Drinking tea is like kissing your dog. It's warm and wet, sure, but where's the kick? If I need to, I'll just pick up another Venti at the Starbucks and use the bathroom there."

Justin stopped the jogging and leaned forward, putting his hands on the windowsill. "Come on in and have the tea. I don't have any lemon bars to go with it, but I do have a story you might want to hear."

43.

VICODIN

Mia Dalton stood behind the glass and examined the man seated alone at the table in the green interrogation room. He was wiry and hard-looking. His boots were dirty, his jaw was unshaven, his unkempt hair thick and ruffled. He sucked his crooked teeth to pass the time. Staring at the rumpled figure of Eddie Nicosia made Mia feel like an alien, not from another country but from another planet.

"I don't get it," she said.

"I wouldn't think you would," said Scott, standing by her side, holding a file and a paper bag.

"We're each part everything if we're honest enough to admit it. I look at plenty of guys and feel something stir. But if what you're telling me is true, the standards for gigolos have plummeted beyond my capacity to understand."

"You don't think he has a certain sexual animalism?"

Eddie Nicosia stuck a finger in his ear, swirled, extracted, examined the tip.

"Like a mangy three-legged dog," said Mia.

"They say his cock is huge."

"Well, that explains that. When you're done interrogating him, give him my number."

"Any particular way you want me to play it?"

"Set him up one way and then scare the hell out of him. He won't admit to anything, but it should be interesting to see how he reacts."

"Will do."

"And don't be gentle."

"My guess," said Scott, "is that our boy Eddie Nicosia hears that a lot."

Mia kept her gaze on the suspect as Scott left her side and a moment later entered the room behind the glass. Nicosia, sprawled in his chair, didn't change his posture when the detective walked in. He simply lifted his head and followed the detective as Scott made his way to the opposite side of the table, dropped the file and bag onto the tabletop, and took a seat, all without so much as looking at the suspect.

"When can I get the hell out of here?" said Nicosia.

Scott didn't respond, he simply opened the file, took out a stack of papers, tapped the stack on the table to neaten its edge, and began asking for Nicosia's name, address, occupation, all things they knew already. Nicosia's impatience showed as he spit out the answers.

"Now, just as a matter of protocol, Mr. Nicosia," said Scott, "I'm going to read you a list of your constitutional rights and then ask you to sign a statement to indicate that these rights were read to you and that you understood them."

"Isn't this a bit over the damn top for a broken taillight?"

Mia watched the ritual unfold at Scott's slow pace as he began reading the document to Nicosia. She had watched many of the detective's interrogations and was always impressed by the simplicity of his technique. He didn't threaten or browbeat, he didn't lie to catch another lie. He was calm, and polite, and there was always a sense that he was a little on the suspect's side. All of it made Timmy Flynn's claim that he had been forced into lying about Chase a bit far-fetched. But there were occasions when Scott seemed to take the case a bit more personally, when a child was dead or a woman in the hospital, and on these occasions he would often lose it, pounding the table with a brutal anger as he squeezed out what answers he could. Mia would always wonder which Scott would show up. It appeared to be the calm one today.

After Nicosia signed the statement, Scott carefully placed it into the file and then reached into the bag and, one by one, pulled out a series of sealed plastic bags with labels on the outside, each containing a number of orange pill bottles.

"We found these in your van, Eddie," said Scott. "Hidden beneath a mess of screws and bolts in one of your tool cases."

"Shit," said Nicosia, "is that what this is all about? They don't mean nothing."

"Valium, OxyContin, Tylenol No. 3, Vicodin, all controlled substances under state and federal law. And your name is not the name on the labels. Were these prescribed for you?"

"Not for me, but they was prescribed. You can check it out. I just filled some prescriptions for friends of mine."

"Gloria Nader," said Scott, reading now from the labels. "Miranda Holmes."

"Call them up, they'll tell you. These are old ladies that need help running errands. I do stuff for them, you know what I'm talking about. I also take care of their houses, their yards. You know."

"Yeah, we know."

"I provide services. And sometimes I fill prescriptions when they need them filled."

"Ida Switt," read Scott from the labels.

"I'm just helping out, being a good Sumerian. Since when is that a crime?"

"Do you keep some for your personal use, Eddie? Or to sell? Is that what this stash in your truck is all about?"

"You got me wrong here, I'm telling you."

"So tell me."

"It's these ladies," said Nicosia, leaning forward, like he was passing a secret just between the two of them. "They're old as dust, they forget. It's dangerous for them to have too much all at once. They'd take a couple, forget they took them, and take some more. Next thing you'd know, the bottle is empty, they're dead on the floor, and I'm shit out of luck. So I keep the bottles in the truck and dole out just enough to fill their little weekly pillboxes, you know, seven daily doses at a time. It keeps them healthy and alive."

"Mildred Payne," said Scott.

"Go ahead, call them all," said Nicosia, "and they'll tell you they like what I provide. That they've come to depend on me. You want the numbers? Call whoever the hell you want."

"Janet Moss."

"You hear what I'm saying? Call her."

"We already did," said Scott.

"Good, then you know. She told you, didn't she?"

Scott didn't answer, he simply looked down at his file as if the secrets of the universe were written there.

"What did she tell you?" said Nicosia.

"She told us that you did what you did without her knowledge."

"That's a lie. She gave me the prescription, gave me the money, even paid me for the time. You can find the damn checks if you want. And I told her I wasn't going to give it all to her at once. That woman is so whacked, I give it to her all at once you'd be spending the next week fumigating the house. She's crazy enough to want to die."

"She wasn't talking about the drugs, Eddie."

"Then what the hell was she..."

Eddie Nicosia stopped midsentence and stared at Scott for a moment before his face creased with an emotion close to fear and Mia felt a shiver of anticipation. Even after all these years, whether in the interrogation room or in the courtroom, these moments where the truth of things were slowly revealed never got old. And she sensed that here, now, the doubts that had been plaguing her since the Chase case concluded would somehow be confirmed or dismissed, and either result would ease her burden.

"What did she say about me?" said Nicosia to Scott.

"You know what she said."

"Oh crap."

"That's right."

"But she got it wrong. I swear she got it wrong."

"Then let's go over it. How long have you known her?"

"Five, six years."

"How'd you meet?"

"I was doing gutters down the street. I had some time, so I was knocking on doors, looking for another job. She answered, gave me the eye, you know."

"And you knew she was having trouble with her husband after he moved out."

"More than trouble. She told me everything, yeah. That's the way it always is. I'm like their confessor. I hear about their marriages, their bunions. It's harder work than you could imagine. You ever seen a bunion?"

"And you knew she was struggling to keep the house," said Scott, "and that her financial problems would become more severe if he divorced her. But you also knew there would be an insurance windfall if he died."

"She told me that, yeah. We talked about the options, yeah. I didn't know the amount of the insurance, just that there was some. So all of that's right. I won't deny any of that. I'm trying to be honest here."

"Try harder. You were servicing her at the time—that's the way you put it, right? And she was paying, right?"

"Getting her money's worth, too."

"And you were afraid the money train would stop."

"It looked likely."

"And so you ran him over with your van."

"No, I didn't. I swear."

"But that's what she said you said."

"It's not true."

"You didn't say that to her? Is she lying? Should we haul her in?"

"I think I need a lawyer. I thought this was just about my broken taillight. You said I could have a lawyer, right? That thing I signed. Well, hell, before I say anything else, I want a lawyer."

"Do you have a lawyer already?"

"Not one I don't owe money to. But you said you'd get me one, right?"

"Yes, I did."

"Okay then. That's what I want."

The detective calmly put down his pen, leaned back, put his hands behind his head like he was enjoying a day at the shore.

"If that's what you want, Eddie," said Scott, "if that's what you really want, then we'll stop the conversation right here right now. We'll have to lock you up for a bit, until your lawyer shows, but that will only be a couple of days. When we end up back here, you'll just have to answer the same questions. And if you don't talk based on your lawyer's advice, we'll just have to assume that everything Mrs. Moss told us represents the truth. Which means we'll have no choice but to charge you with murder. With the drugs we found, and all those Social Security checks you cashed, the bail on a murder charge will be pretty high. A million maybe. And unless you can come up with a cool hundred thou, you'll stay in jail until the trial. We're a bit backlogged now, so figure a year, maybe more."

"Fuck you. I can't be here for no year."

"And after the year's up and we have the trial, we'll see what a jury thinks of the whole mess, with all these women paying you all kinds of money to run their errands and service them in all your clever ways. But if that's the way you want to play it, if you really want a lawyer, Eddie, that is your constitutional right, and we would never, ever want to impinge on your constitutional rights."

"It sounds like you're doing a pretty damn good job of pinge-ing anyway."

"So, should I get you that lawyer?"

Nicosia sucked his teeth and rubbed his jaw and did a decent imitation of a man trying to decide whether to bluff with his pair of twos or to chuck the damn thing in.

"I told her what she said I told her, yeah," said Eddie finally, rubbing a finger along the hard edge of the metal table.

"Was it the truth?"

"No."

"Then why did you say it?"

"Look, I'll be honest."

"In these moments, that's always a good idea."

"I got these women, the ones with their names on the pill bottles, taking care of me. It's a sweet play, really. And we both get from it, you know? These women, sometimes I'm the only loving they got in their lives."

"That's pretty sad."

"Innit? But there it is. They need me. And, with the state of my business and my debts, I need them too. It's a mutual thing, you see. Symbolic, you understand. So I been hearing all this crap from Janet about her husband the creep and all, and then, bam, he gets run over. Hit-and-run. No suspects. And I see a way to make the thing we have, with the financial benefits, a bit more solid. A way to become like a hero in her life, and no one's the wiser. So I tell her I done it."

"What you're telling me is, it wasn't murder, it was fraud."

"Pshaw. A little white lie ain't fraud."

"Lying about a murder isn't a little white lie."

"Now you're getting all technical on me. Maybe it had a pinkish hue."

"What about the time before?"

"What time before?"

"When that Chase lady was killed."

"What, the one that got aced in her home?"

"That's the one. Did you just tell Mrs. Moss you did that, too?"

"I didn't tell her nothing about that. Why? What did she say?"

"Mrs. Moss knew there was something going on between her husband and the Chase woman before the murder, right?"

"She might have mentioned to me there was something between her husband and some woman at some point."

"And she was upset about what was going on between them, right?"

"I assume she was. Who wouldn't be?"

"And then the Chase woman was killed."

"Look, the husband was still living there then. Maybe I might have wet the wick once or twice there while he was out, she sure wasn't getting it from him, but I don't ever get too involved if the husband's still there. Too many guns in the world, you know what I'm saying."

"You didn't know that the husband and the Chase woman were together."

"I would have been more shocked than anyone."

"Why's that?"

"Look, I never said nothing about that one. Nothing. In fact, Janet never told me who the woman was until after she was killed. We wasn't that close yet, not until her husband moved out. And anyway, it was that Chase guy that did that, wasn't it? You convicted him, right? How the hell would I take credit for that? And I sure didn't do it...But wait. Wait."

"What, Eddie."

"The son of the Chase woman was just at the house and he was asking questions and...Oh, now I see."

"What do you see?"

"That little fucker is trying to pin his father's crime on me. That little fucker wants to make me the fall guy. And you're the sap that's letting him."

"We're just trying to find the truth here."

"Now it all makes sense. I was wondering how that taillight got broked. That little fucker."

"You got anyone working for you, Eddie?"

"What, in the business? Nah, the way I work it, I need to work alone."

"No assistant? No mentally challenged helper to keep you on schedule?"

"I'd have to pay him, right?"

"I suppose."

"Well, there you go."

"What about a guy named Flynn? Timmy Flynn? You ever run into him?"

"Who is he? A cop?"

"No."

"A name like that, he should be a cop."

"Take a minute, Eddie," said Scott, standing up. "I'll be right back. Don't go anywhere."

"You mean that door, it ain't locked?"

"No," said Scott. "It's locked."

Mia watched as Scott left the room. A moment later he was by her side. "What do you think?" he said.

She stood there a moment and looked at Nicosia. He was about as vile a specimen as she had seen in a long while. They had a raft of stuff they could get him on: fraud, embezzlement, drug counts, maybe even prostitution. Not to mention that broken taillight. And she was inclined to nail him on all of them. But that would be about it.

"It's not there," she said. "Book him on what we have and keep him overnight, but it's just not there."

44.

LATTE

Annie Overmeyer had a suspicion that needed to be scratched. And she might not have been willing to admit it to herself, but she had something else that needed scratching too. Deep in the still-tender recesses of her largely galvanized heart lay the hope that this visit just might relieve both itches.

The suspicion part was rooted in the letters that Austin Moss had written to Justin's mother and the way Janet Moss had described her relationship with her husband. Annie had been the other woman enough to know there was something in both that didn't feel right.

Annie became involved with married men for all the right reasons. They were safe. They were attentive. They bought her Mai Tais, one after the other. They were fun in a what-the-hell-let's-debase-myself-a-little-more sort of way. And they somehow filled the emotional needs she chose not to deal with in other, less productive ways, like sitting in some badly decorated office and blathering on about her father's cold demeanor and all the affection he didn't shower on his little girl. Sure, the sex wasn't always that terrific, but these married men sure did appreciate the hell out of her body. And that right there was the key.

The notes she received from her married lovers, breathless letters from the romantics or shorthand text messages thumbed into a BlackBerry from the terminally busy, might have started out with paeans to emotion—*oh my heart, oh my soul, oh my love*—but always ended with not-so-oblique references to the carnal—*your lips, your breasts, your...* Yeah, yeah, yeah. They wanted to screw her, she got that. It was always there, behind every drink, every dinner, every line. Whatever they were trading, sex was the currency. And it was precisely that, the sex, that was missing from Austin Moss's letters. And it didn't matter that Eleanor Chase might not have had the body of a twentysomething anymore; sex was sex, and if it was burning somewhere, it would have come out on the page.

Buttressing Annie's suspicions about the letters had been Janet Moss's description of her marriage. *We felt like we had been pulled out of something and saved,* she had said of her relationship with her husband. *It wasn't perfect, our marriage, it wasn't a model, I admit that. But it was ours. And it was all I had.* There was much in all of this that tolled familiar to Annie. She had thought she would feel a kinship to Janet Moss in Moss's role of the long-suffering wife. The cheated-with and the cheated-on are both inextricably linked; one can't exist without the other, and both, in their way, are willing participants in the epic drama of infidelity. But there was a whiff here of something else that Annie could relate to even more strongly: marriage as a saving grace, a blissful fading into a secure and contented future.

Annie had felt the urge herself, to give up the life she was living and give herself over to something, anything. She had been proposed to a number of times by these married men, and she had considered it, more seriously than she would like to acknowledge, not because of love, because she hadn't been in love, or because the sex was so brilliant, because it was usually as pedestrian as an old lady shambling down the street with tennis balls stuck onto the feet of her walker. No, she had considered it because she was tired, exhausted actually, lonelier than she would ever admit, and wanted it to end. All of this, to end.

Someone once said that marriage was the death of hope, and he was half-right. The true seductiveness of marriage, to Annie, was not a matter of settling but of suicide. The dream was to see all the impossible hopes, all those futile expectations, bleed through sliced blue arteries into a bathtub, before something new and shiny arose from the red-stained water: a lovely little corpse pushing baby carriages, attending PTA meetings, steaming vegetables, flirting with handymen. To even imagine the peace of it now was to swoon in anticipation.

Janet Moss, she sensed, had made that exact deathly leap with Austin Moss. And though her marriage wasn't perfect, containing, as Annie imagined, neither love nor, more significantly, sex, it was all she had. Until it was under threat by Eleanor Chase. But what was Eleanor Chase offering if not sex? That was the question Annie was coming back to the Moss house on Mantis Drive to discover.

And what would be the result if she was right? Then she'd have a nugget of information. That she would have to share. With Eleanor Chase's youngest son.

And there it was, the second itch.

Because there was something about Justin Chase that snagged at her consciousness like a grappling hook. Maybe it was that he wasn't grappling at her whenever he was around, or maybe it was his preternatural calm, so different from her scattershot energetic approach to ruining her own life. Or maybe it was the sheer perversity of doing both father and son. Whatever it was, she couldn't deny that she felt a ripple of thrill run through her as she turned at the Applebee's and made her way down Mantis Drive. Because after she found out what she expected to find out, she was going to have to give Justin a call. And they'd have to meet. And they'd have lattes at some Starbucks and they'd sit across from each other at a small round table and lean their heads one toward the other and talk softly as they tried to figure it out together. And somehow, more than anything, that was the goal of this whole expedition.

It was dark out, the sky thick with clouds, a light rain falling. But the Moss house was well lit, both the first and second floors. Quiet and dry and well lit, a refuge, a home. Everything Janet Moss had bargained for. Somehow put at risk by Eleanor Chase. Of course she would be pissed. Who wouldn't be? Annie would have scratched the meddling woman's eyes out, but that was just Annie's way. Janet Moss maybe had handled it differently.

Annie parked her car on the street right in front of the house. She pulled her jacket tight and jogged through the rain, down the empty driveway to the little path that led to the front door. She stood beneath the arched overhang and rang the bell once, twice.

Through the side window by the door she could hear the bell ring, and another sound beneath the bell, faint and high-pitched. She turned around and checked behind her while she waited. Empty. A dead suburban street deadened further by the rain. She turned around, pressed the bell again, and banged on the door. Nothing.

Though she had gotten the phone number from the Internet, she hadn't called first, afraid that Mrs. Moss would somehow get that creep Eddie Nicosia to oversee their conversation if she had been given a warning. Now she took out her phone and made a call.

She heard the phone ring inside. And ring. And ring some more until it was picked up, finally. She started talking after the hello until she realized it was a machine. She shut her phone, felt a chill, pulled her jacket closed, and remembered how drugged out Janet Moss had seemed, how barely in control.

She knocked again, calling out "Mrs. Moss?" before taking hold of the door latch and pressing down with her thumb. The latch depressed. She pushed the door open slightly, heard the high-pitched sound more clearly, a whistling. And in addition, she could pick up, slipping through the sliver of doorway, the sound of a distant television.

"Mrs. Moss? Are you there?"

Nothing.

She pushed the door open and stepped inside, into the lighted foyer. "Mrs. Moss?"

Nothing.

The television was on upstairs, she now could tell, some fatuous show going on and on about celebrities, a show that Annie often watched herself before lurching into the alcohol-drenched night. Gently closing the door behind her, Annie looked around. The place seemed quiet, not so much empty as deserted. And there was a smell, something beneath the smell of the bird, something furry, like a wild animal had been let loose inside. She moved into the well-lit living room with its sense of lapsed order. In the corner was the canary cage, the newspaper on the bottom still piled with droppings, but now the door was open and the bird gone. She spun around, suddenly frightened, looking for the bird.

The high-pitched whistle had grown louder. A kettle on the boil? Expecting the loosed bird to dive at her head at any moment, she ducked down and stepped through the living room into the kitchen. A mess on the table, dishes in the sink, the kettle shaking on the stove. She went over and turned off the burner. The whistle faded slowly before dying.

She headed out of the kitchen and toward the stairs that led to the second floor. When she reached the foot, she called out again. No response, no sound other than the television. With a steadying hand on the baluster, she began to climb.

As she rose, the furry smell strengthened and twined with something sharper, darker. The two smells together frightened her even more than the emptiness. She let the sound of the television guide her, upstairs and then to the right, to a darkened hallway that ended at an open door leading to a room lit only by the dim flashing of a television. She walked past a couple of closed doors, the furry smell growing stronger. A chirp from the bird came from someplace distant. She stopped, looked around, saw nothing winging its way through the air. Slowly she stepped forward through the open doorway.

A bedroom, with a sharp, smoky scent, like an oily cigarette. The bed at the far wall empty, the television on against the near wall. And in the corner, facing the television, a figure sprawled on an easy chair. Mrs. Moss, drugged enough by her pills to have fallen asleep watching TV, after having forgotten that she had put on the kettle. Most likely smoking, which explained the scent. The whole thing was too sad for words. Annie, ready to help her into bed, reached to her right and switched on the light.

Blood.

Everywhere.

Drenching the woman in the chair, staining the wall.

Blood.

Before she knew what she was doing, Annie bolted toward the bloodied Janet Moss. The blood was no longer flowing, but still wet and glistening. When she reached the chair, she caught sight of the woman's right arm flopped over the side of the chair, ending with her hand dragging on the carpeted floor, loosely gripping a gun.

"Oh God," she gasped.

She bent down, put her hand on Mrs. Moss's bloody chest, pressed hard, felt nothing. The pressing shifted the body slightly and the head bobbed forward. There was a burned patch of flesh on the side of the woman's head closest to the gun. On the other side a great gap had been gouged by the gunshot. Annie gagged, backed away, fell to her knees, retched and threw up on the floor.

Then she heard something rise above the nattering of the television. A thump.

And she suddenly remembered that the upstairs lights had been on when she arrived.

45.

SUNSET BOULEVARD

Cody was a mess.

Not that he looked a mess, sitting at the bar with a shiny gold jacket, a sharp black shirt setting off his gold chain, a silver-and-gold Rolex on his wrist. He looked killer. But his fingers were tap-tapping frenetically on the bar, and there was something both nervous and haunted in his eyes, like he had just looked into a mirror and seen a specter behind him reaching for his neck.

"What can I get you today?" said Justin after he had worked his way down the crowded bar to Cody. "I learned this drink called a Sunset Boulevard that would be right up your alley. Want to give it a try?"

"Does it have vodka?" said Cody, looking over his shoulder.

"Yes, it does."

"Then is the other stuff really necessary?"

"You okay?"

"Yeah, fine. But why don't you just give me the vodka."

Justin squinted at Cody. "Okay if I add some tonic and lime to make it go down easier?"

"Sure, anything, but don't skimp on the main course."

"Coming right up," said Justin as he turned and reached for a bottle of Skyy. He poured a couple of ounces into a highball with ice, put in a spritz of tonic, squeezed in some lime, and slipped a fresh slice on the rim.

Cody grabbed at it hungrily and closed his eyes as he swallowed half at once. When he opened them again, he looked like a guy who had been slapped in the face and was glad for it.

"Has anyone come in looking for me?" said Cody.

"Stewie and Louie from the night before?"

"Them or anyone else. Especially anyone else."

"No."

"If anyone does, you don't know me, never saw me."

"Who are you again?"

"That's right."

"What happened?"

"I just read something in the paper that made me a little sick."

"Box score?"

"Obituary."

"Someone you knew?"

"Not really. I only ran into her once. But it stayed with me, you know?"

"Sure I do," said Justin, giving the bartender's flat, noncommittal response and regretting it immediately. Cody was in some sort of trouble and Justin was offering only the barkeep's reflexive detachment. The rote interaction made him feel cheap. Just doing what he had done on his father's behalf—following a lead, asking questions, turning what he had found over to the cops—had given him a peculiar satisfaction. His investigation was the exact opposite of drifting; he had taken some control and he felt ready to take more.

"I think maybe I need to get out of here," said Cody.

"That's a good idea," said Justin. "Go home, get some sleep, start fresh in the morning."

"I'm talking about out of here. Here. What do you know about Tallahassee? I've heard good things about Tallahassee."

"That must have been a hell of an obituary."

"You got any money you can lend me quick? I need a stash to get me to Tallahassee."

"Is that a Waylon Jennings song?"

"Hey, Justin," said Marson from the far end of the bar, a look of disapproval on his face and a telephone in his hand. "You got a call."

Justin tapped the bar and pointed at Cody in encouragement before heading over to take the phone.

"It's getting busy," said Marson.

"I'm on top of things," said Justin.

"There's a party over there that's been waiting."

"Then the sooner I take this, the sooner I can get to them."

Marson waited a second longer with his normal sour attitude before handing him the phone. Justin took the phone, turned his back to his boss, and said into the handset, "Chase."

"Justin?" said Annie Overmeyer, in a voice rent with terror. "Justin? Oh my God."

46.

BLOOD AND VOMIT

As a thick nausea spread in her gut, Mia Dalton stood within the twining scents of blood and vomit and stared at the lump slumped in the bedroom chair, tastefully covered by a shiny yellow tarp. The local police were already describing Janet Moss's death as an apparent suicide, and while the bloody tableau beneath the tarp certainly backed up that assumption, Mia couldn't help but think that something here was wrong as hell.

And even though she was way out of her jurisdiction and had no authority here, she was going to do something about it.

She retreated from the stench into the hallway and down the stairs, where she took a spot next to Scott, who was standing beside the empty birdcage.

"When is he getting here?" she said to Scott.

"He just reported in," he said. "A few more minutes. He wasn't so happy about the whole thing. He was at the ball game."

"Poor little fellow," said Mia. "One way or the other, this is part of the whole, and Kingstree needs to be aware of it. Quite the tender little scene outside, wouldn't you say?"

"It brought tears to my eyes," said Scott.

Mia was referring to Justin Chase and Annie Overmeyer, who were sitting side by side on the curb, in the rain, leaning their heads together as they talked. Even though soaked to the bone, the girl's clothes were still bloodstained and her skin blood-smeared from her encounter with the corpse of Janet Moss. And it appeared that the son of Overmeyer's former adulterous paramour was actually trying to comfort her.

"What the hell are the two of them doing together?" she said. "Do we have any idea?"

"Somehow they found each other."

"The son and the lover. It sounds like a *Reader's Digest* version of D. H. Lawrence. Am I the only one who thinks it's creepy?"

"No."

"Do we believe her story about why she was here?"

"It sounds just far-fetched enough to be true."

"And the mysterious figure who ran out of the house after she got inside the bedroom?"

"Probably her imagination run wild. It's tough seeing your first corpse."

"That was a tough sight for anyone, no matter the number. When you brought Chase over, did you get any sense about what he thought of this?"

"He was worried about her."

"Such a tender heart."

"And he was wondering how this affected his father's case."

"It damn well better not," said Mia. "And what the hell happened to the bird?"

A local detective by the name of Dechert descended the stairs, his head ducking down to avoid the low ceiling. He was a soft-spoken man in a sharp blue suit, his hands still covered in latex. Plenty of suburban cops would have thrown Mia out on her ear for horning in on his crime scene, but Dechert seemed grateful for the help. She admired that, as well as his manners.

"Any idea when your witness is coming, Ms. Dalton?" he said.

"Momentarily."

"We found something else we'd like him to look at."

"What exactly?"

"Something a bit alarming. Come on up and take a peek if you want."

Mia winced, not sure she wanted to go back into that room with its bloody stink, but then nodded. Dechert led her and Scott up the stairs and into the bedroom again. Mia had to put a hand over her mouth and nose to stand the stench, but neither Dechert nor Scott seemed to be bothered. Cops. She was surprised they weren't eating hoagies while standing over the body. She'd seen that before, even seen stray bits of shredded lettuce drift down onto the blood.

"Over there," said Dechert, gesturing with one of his gloved hands toward a low table set beside the bed. The table lamp was on and the drawer open. Mia and Scott both leaned over to look. A bunch of junk, tissues and keys, cheap costume jewelry, glasses, loose pills. And, in a little clearing in the middle of all the detritus of Janet Moss's now-ended life, a glassine envelope filled with some damp reddish clumps of powder next to two silver earrings with diamonds set into the dangles.

Mia looked up at Scott and without turning to Dechert said, "What's in the packet?"

"We haven't tested it yet," said Dechert.

She turned toward the suburban detective. "Have you found anything else that points toward intravenous drug use? Needles, burnt spoons, a kit of any sort? Anything?"

"No. It might not be what it looks like. We'll have it sent to the lab right away."

"When you do," said Scott, "have them check it for fentanyl."

Without turning from the suburban detective, Mia nodded her agreement. She and Scott both had the exact same idea, but something was wrong. It was too damn obvious, the whole damn thing. "Detective Dechert, did you move stuff around in the drawer to uncover the apparent drugs?"

"I didn't touch a thing," said Dechert, "and neither did anyone on our team. We just slid it open."

"So that little clearing was made by someone else."

"Maybe so. Interesting. Don't move anything before I get a photograph."

When Dechert left the room for a moment, Mia said to Scott, "Do those earrings look familiar?"

"No."

"That's because we've never seen them before except maybe in a photograph, hanging from a pair of earlobes. Go out and get Chase and bring him up here. See if he can identify them."

"You think they're his mother's, don't you?"

"Just get him, all right?"

"This is screwy as a lightbulb."

"You bet it is. And make sure that Annie Overmeyer sticks around. I've got some hard questions for her."

"Dechert might want her first."

"This may be his jurisdiction, but he's going to have to wait in line."

When Detective Scott returned about five minutes later, he didn't have Justin Chase in tow. Instead he brought in Eddie Nicosia, handcuffed and accompanied by Detective Kingstree.

Nicosia had a pale, pained expression on his face, like he had been dragged up the stairs by his ankles.

"What the hell's going on?" said Eddie Nicosia to Detective Scott. "Your cop wouldn't tell me a thing the whole ride down. What the hell is going on, and what the hell is that smell?"

"Be quiet, please, Mr. Nicosia," said Mia.

"I'm not talking to you," he snapped at Mia before turning his attention back to Scott. "I'm just asking, what the hell are you blaming on me now? I didn't do nothing."

"Shut up," said Mia, sharply enough to quiet the creep. "Where's Chase?"

"Gone," said Scott. "Along with the Overmeyer girl."

"Didn't you tell them to stay put?"

"Sure I did, and Dechert asked them to stay, too. I guess it didn't take."

"He asked them, did he?" said Mia. "That's putting the hammer down. He didn't have anyone keeping an eye on them?"

Scott didn't say anything, he just shrugged resignedly at the working of the suburban police force running the crime scene.

"What the hell am I doing here?" said Kingstree. "It was the seventh inning of a tie game."

"There may be a connection between what happened here and what happened to our pal Timmy Flynn."

"What kind of connection?"

"That's what you're here to find out."

"Are we ready?" said Dechert, sweeping into the room with a photographer trailing.

"Ready," said Mia.

Dechert motioned the photographer toward the open drawer and then faced Eddie Nicosia.

“Detective Dechert,” said Mia, “this is our Detective Kingstree. He’s here to observe, if that’s all right. And this is Eddie Nicosia. He was—how would I say it—*involved* in Mrs. Moss’s life.”

“I didn’t do nothing,” said Nicosia. “I been locked up this whole time.”

Dechert eyed Nicosia for a moment and then said, “That’s fine, Mr. Nicosia. We’re not accusing you of anything. We just have some questions. This way, please,” he said as he took hold of Eddie’s elbow. Slowly he led him over to the tarp atop the body in the chair. Mia motioned for Kingstree and Scott to follow and keep tabs on what was happening before she backed away into the hall.

She didn’t want to hear the words that were being passed back and forth, she just wanted to catch Nicosia’s expression. How much of this was a surprise to Eddie? How much of this was inevitable? Nothing he said would be of interest—he was a lying scumbag of the worst stripe—but his raw expressions might tell her something.

And this is what she saw on Eddie Nicosia’s face when Dechert lifted the yellow tarp: shock, yes, definitely shock.

This tragedy, this apparent suicide as judged by the suburban cops, was nothing that Nicosia had anticipated in the least. Not that he seemed the most emotionally prescient of guys, but still, you would have thought he was close enough to see it coming if it had been coming. That was the first thing she saw on Nicosia’s face.

The second thing was bereavement. A crushing bereavement that shut his eyes and forced out tears and bent his knees so that Kingstree had to keep him from tumbling onto the floor in grief. How did you like that? Eddie Nicosia had a heart as soft as his exterior was slimy. Some things just couldn’t be gauged, and the human heart was one of them. Twenty years on the job and it was something she still had to learn every damn day.

She had seen enough. The sight of the bloodied and blasted skull, the stained housedress, the sweep of the arm ending with the gun, Nicosia's tears, the smells of death, all of it drove the low-level nausea that had been percolating in her gut up and into her throat. She gritted her teeth and bolted down the stairs, out into the thick, rainy night.

She raised her chin and closed her eyes and let the soft rain spread its cool fingers over her hot face. She wanted to think it through, what this all meant, but her thoughts were chased out by the nausea. She'd been to enough crime scenes, she should be used to it by now. But there was something that was eating at her. Worry? Guilt? Had she blown it six years ago when she went after Mackenzie Chase with all her claws bared? That's what the dead woman seemed to represent in there, that was the message of her apparent suicide. And maybe that was the cause of the distress she was feeling. That or the chewy piece of veal she'd had for dinner.

When her stomach calmed, she opened her eyes. Scott was waiting for her in the covered area by the front door. She thought she detected a smirk on his face, but when she got closer, she realized it wasn't that at all.

"You okay?" he said, his evident concern evidently all too real, which for some reason pissed her off.

"Worry about yourself," she said, a little too quickly. "What did he say?"

"It was her gun, all right. It had been in the drawer by the bed where they found the earrings."

"Did she know how to use it?"

"He didn't think so. He had gotten it for her a couple of years ago after some burglaries in the neighborhood, though he claimed she had been too afraid to load it. The clip was supposedly in the drawer too and he doubted she knew even how to slip it into the gun, not to mention chambering a round. He figured it was safer for everyone that way. She would just wave it around if anyone showed up."

"Well, someone showed her how to do it," said Mia. "What about the drugs?"

"He was adamant that other than her prescribed pills and a little pot, she wasn't a user."

"Forensics will tell us the truth on that. And the earrings?"

"He had never seen them before."

"I bet not. Find out what you can about the dead woman's husband."

"Other than that he's dead?"

"Dig a little, Detective. Find out why he's dead and how. And you said Chase was at the bar when he called before you picked him up to bring him here?"

"That's right."

"Find out when he started his shift and see how it coincides with the time of death here."

"You don't think that—"

"I don't know what the hell I think, except that something is wrong here. Did Kingstree find any link between that Rebecca Staim who died in that apparent robbery and Mackenzie Chase?"

"Nothing. Absolutely nothing, other than the print that matches the one we found on Flynn's phone."

"Tell him to keep looking, and to check on all the prints they find here, especially on the gun and the clip. This is the third crime scene I've been to in a very short time that is somehow related to the Chase case. An apparent overdose. An apparent robbery. An apparent suicide. And we're supposed to think that nothing is going on?"

"Apparently."

"I hope to God it ends here, but I doubt it will. We might have to consider whether we have a serial killer on our hands. But for now, I'm out of here."

"Where are you going?"

"Home," she said as she started down the walk. "When I throw up, I prefer to do it in my own damn toilet. Get what you need from Dechert and then find out what the hell is going on between Justin Chase and the Overmeyer girl."

47.

OOLONG

Later, they would tell themselves it just happened. But of course, that would be a lie.

It never just happens. It is always preceded by an intimation, a curiosity, a flash of fantasy that immediately embarrasses, and most of all a yearning, sometimes as raw as a hard-core blue reel flickering on a stained white sheet pinned to the fringes of your mind, and sometimes as soft and as lovely as a prayer. But there is always something first, and then, if the fates conspire, it happens.

"You have to think about it," said Justin, after the blood and the death and their escape from the scene, but before anything more.

"I don't want to think about it," said Annie.

"It's like an elephant. If you try not to think about it, it just gets bigger and bigger."

"Then I'll think about the elephant."

"Don't try to run away from it, Annie, because you can't."

"If I agree to think about it, do I get to hit a pillow with a baseball bat?"

"Why would you want to do that?"

"I took this anger management class and they had me

hitting a pillow with a baseball bat. It didn't help much until in my backswing I took out a vase. That felt pretty good."

"I'll be sure to hide my pottery."

They were sitting cross-legged on the third-floor tatami mats, Justin Chase and Annie Overmeyer, freshly scrubbed and in the robes, facing each other but still well apart with the teapot and their cups between them. They had been sitting in the rain outside the Moss house and they decided, on the spur, to get out of there, not to tell anyone, not to let the cops know, just to leave. So they did, in Annie's car. When she stopped the car on Fitler Square to drop him off, she broke down into tears. So he invited her into his house for some tea to calm herself. When she took off her coat and spied the blood on her still-wet dress, she started shaking from more than the cold. So he told her to go upstairs and take off her stained clothes and wash the blood and the scent from her skin. When she was out of the freezing shower and enveloped in terry cloth, he brought her to the third floor to cleanse her emotions. This last part wasn't going so well.

"If the goal is to forget what happened tonight," she said, "why don't we just drink something stronger than the tea?"

"But it's an oolong," said Justin.

"I meant alcohol."

"I know."

"Generally I've found if I want to forget something, drunkenly collapsing into a pool of my own vomit really does the trick."

"That itself is an image I'd like to forget. Look, just give this a try, okay? And I'll do it with you so you won't ever be alone. Sit up, straighten your spine. Good. Now even out your breathing. In. Out. In. Out."

"How about in, in, in, pop."

"Annie."

"Okay, fine. In, out, in, out."

"Slower."

"In. Out. In. Out."

"Feel it in your diaphragm."

"In. Out. In. Out."

"Good, now close your eyes and feel yourself floating, like you're in a great, warm pool of water. I'm closing my eyes too, and I'm floating with you."

"Okay."

"We're just floating, calmly, together. Do you see me?"

"No."

"Look. Keep your eyes closed and look. I'm right there beside you."

"What are you wearing?"

"Don't you see me?"

"Yes. I see you. Nice robe."

"I got it at Goodwill. Now we're falling, slowly, together, falling, until we find ourselves right back at that house on Mantis Drive, right at the front door."

"Yuck."

"It's open. We float inside, together. We rise up the stairs, together. We smell that awful smell. Keep breathing. In. Out. We turn toward the room and, still floating, we glide forward, slowly, toward the open door. We slip inside the room, and there she is, Janet Moss, in that chair."

"Can we stop now?"

"No."

"I want to turn around."

"This is no longer a choice, this is inevitability. We're facing her, or what is left of her. And we move forward, together, closer to the corpse, and closer still. Do you see her? Everything about her?"

"Oh God."

"Can you smell the death?"

"Please, Justin."

"Can you?"

"Yes."

"You're hovering there, staring at her. Now open yourself to what you are feeling. You've spent a lifetime choking back your emotions. But this time, don't hold them back, let them rise within you. Like water pouring into an earthen jug, rising higher and higher within you. What do you feel?"

"I'm afraid."

"Okay."

"And sad, unbearably sad."

"Okay."

"And desperate."

"For what?"

"For everything. For my life. It's my life."

"It's her life."

"No, you're wrong. It's me. With the gun in my limp hand, with half my head missing."

"It's not you, Annie, it's her. But this is good, you're experiencing the emotions viscerally. Everything you're feeling is right. Let it rise within you, all of it. Taste it, smell it, let it overwhelm you."

"I don't want to."

"Yes you do. Let it flow, let it keep flowing."

"I can't."

"Let it pour in. Feel every drop of it as it rises. The more you feel, the less you'll find. The deeper you reach, the closer you'll come to finding the true peace within your own soul. Trust it. Feel it."

And, shockingly, at least to Annie Overmeyer, she did. Trust it, because he told her to trust it, and somehow, for some strange reason, she trusted him. And feel it, because finding herself back in that place, that hellhole of blood and death, she couldn't help but feel the pain and fear, the sadness, the despair.

And it was new, in a strange way, all this trust and feeling, because she had spent so much of her past self-medicating with drink and tawdry sex to desperately avoid those very two things. The emotions felt thick, and red, like a scratchy Hudson's Bay blanket, and they wrapped around her tightly, suffocatingly. She could sense her tears squeezing out beneath her lids and something rippling through her chest, which she realized were sobs. And it should have been unbearable, all of this emotion spilling out as she hovered before the dead body of Janet Moss, mourning the dead woman, mourning her own spoiled life and dead future, it should have been the darkest of pain.

And yet it wasn't. It wasn't. And she couldn't figure why. The more she felt, the less it hurt. The more she cried, the warmer became the swathing blanket around her. And in her mystified state, she turned and saw him, next to her like he promised, his hard, gentle face, his long hair, his solid body wrapped in silk. She saw him floating next to her, and suddenly she knew why she wasn't choking on it all. It was him, his kindness, his gentleness, the way he took her more seriously than she took herself.

Still floating there, before the dead body of Janet Moss, she reached out a hand to him.

Justin had thought this whole exercise was only about helping her exorcise her own emotions. But when he found himself once again face-to-face with the bloody suicide, a spectacle Detective Scott had showed him only briefly upon their arrival at the Moss house, he found a flood pouring into his own sterile pool. The only corpse he had ever before seen was that of his mother, and so the blood of one brought back the pain of the other. And the guilt. The anguished loss. The hatred and impotence. The love, spilled carelessly onto the floor along with the blood. And the certainty he had held then that his father had done this brutal thing. And the uncertainty he held now, facing this horror, about the very same fact. Because maybe this was all a result of what he had told Detective Scott. Maybe Scott had called this woman about the suspicions. And maybe this woman had killed herself out of guilt at what she had done, hiring someone named Preacher to hire someone named Birdie Grackle to kill Justin's mother.

And as all these emotions rose from some hidden chamber in his mummified heart, rising up to fill his throat and nostrils, he felt something else, something he had felt quite recently, an emotion that scared him more than all the others. Yes, hope. He felt the dark song of hope stirring his blood once more, and he assumed, logically, it was once again about his father maybe leaving that prison and entering again his life. But then, with his eyes still closed as he floated in that room of death, he turned his head and there she was, Annie Overmeyer, tears streaming down her pretty face, her hand held out to him like a gift, and he knew he was wrong. The song of hope he was feeling was not being sung about his father just then, it was being sung about her, about Annie Overmeyer.

And he took hold of her hand.

And she squeezed his palm.

And he squeezed back.

And then it just happened, as simple as that.

Holding hands they pulled themselves one toward the other, twisted their necks so that even with their lids still closed, their eyes stared one pair into the other, and they kissed. They kissed. And for both of them it was sweet and soft, slippery and electric, and frightening in the best of ways. Frightening like a shattering work of art, like a glimpse into the future, like a choice. And, strangely, in a way that neither understood, for both Annie Overmeyer and Justin Chase, that kiss was like coming home.

48.

BRAMBLE

Derek is in the small park off Lombard Street, sitting cross-legged within the boughs of a prickly bush. He is not far from the wooden bench that faces the now-empty basketball court where Cody knows to look for him, but he is far enough away that he can stay concealed in the shadows if he must. Derek senses the danger in his position, this tense moment between arrangements, and so he knows to stay hidden. And yet he needs to be able to be found too. So now it is only about waiting. Derek is good at waiting, even if he is waiting for nothing other than one hour to pass into the next. Waiting is one of his great talents, along with picking locks and death. But tonight he is not waiting on the hours, he is waiting on his future.

Derek hasn't seen Cody since that last break-in, where they took hold of the big flatscreen and the paintings and all that silver stuff. The very next night, Derek was waiting right there on the bench, expecting Cody to show up like he had the night before and the night before that. But Cody did not show. Each night after that, Derek sat in that park until it was so late he was sure that Vern was back from the bar and already passed out on the bed. Then Derek slipped into the hotel room and lay stiffly on the floor at the bed's foot, trying to figure out what happened to Cody.

At first he thought that Cody simply forgot, but Cody was too organized to forget about Derek. And then he thought that Cody sold the stuff for so much money he did not need Derek anymore. But even though Derek himself does not understand much about money, he has never seen anyone who ever had enough, not his father or Sammy D or Rodney or Vern or even Tree, after he was riddled with the cancer and had no use for it anymore. Then he worried that maybe Cody was arrested with the stuff. But then, if Cody talked, it would have been the police instead of Cody coming to the park for Derek. Yet still no one came. So for the longest time, he could not figure out why Cody disappeared. And then, on the third night, he had a frightening thought.

Could it possibly be the nice girl who came unexpectedly into the last house they robbed together? Cody moved so swiftly and decisively that Derek figured what happened was no big thing to Cody, but now he wonders. Is Cody upset about knocking the girl to the ground with the candlestick? That would be a strange thing, to be so upset about something that came so naturally and that had already happened. For Derek, the things he does in these houses just sort of disappear. Nothing that Derek does ever lasts much beyond the doing.

But once, he and Rodney stayed a few days in Cincinnati after doing a job and Rodney grew more and more nervous reading the newspapers until they were forced to slip out of the city in the dark of night, stealing a car to take them into Kentucky before grabbing a bus that was going west. That memory is enough to strike a note of worry in Derek's heart. Because if what happened to the girl appeared in the newspapers, and that is why Cody did not show, then Derek is in serious trouble.

It is never a sure thing for Derek to find someone new to take care of him, someone who can appreciate and put to use his talents. The only thing that is sure about Derek's life is that after one of his special friends disappears for whatever reason, it is up to Derek to find another. At first it just happened. Sammy D found him when he was still a kid, running from his father after they let him out of jail again. And after Sammy D died from the drugs, Rodney swooped in like he had been waiting for the opportunity all along. But after Rodney, a number of possibilities fell through until Tree stepped up. And then it was only in prison that he met Vern. It is always hard for Derek to get someone to understand exactly what Derek needs, and what Derek can do in return.

It would have been smarter for Derek just to stay away from the park, from the street, to hide in the room until the final job is done and he and Vern can get out of the city and start someplace fresh. But he does not want to get out of the city with Vern. He does not want to go anywhere anymore with Vern, not after what happened tonight. He and Vern are through for good, the only thing is that Vern does not know it yet.

Derek has been hit before, sure. Rodney, when pressed by fear, sometimes would slap Derek hard on the back of his head if Rodney thought Derek was making too much noise or even breathing too loudly, which Derek, with his asthma, could not ever help. And Sammy D, by the end, would smash away at anything that stood between him and his fix, including Derek. Yet nothing either of them could do to him would ever approach the beatings given to Derek by his father after his father's blind bouts of drinking. He would treat Derek worse than the dog, and it was a crime, really, the way Derek's father treated that dog.

So Derek has been hit before, plenty of times, and he can take it better than almost anyone, but that does not mean he likes it. Soon enough Vern is going to learn exactly that.

Vern hit Derek when Derek, breathless from his race away from the house with the old lady inside, tried telling Vern what happened. Derek ran from the house, across a couple of backyards, and jumped a fence to get to a street that was not connected to the street with the house. It was a hard sprint, and Derek's heart and lungs were still sprinting even after Derek reached the car and climbed inside. Vern grew angry, not just at what Derek was trying to tell him but because the words became lost in Derek's loud asthmatic gasps for breath. And when Derek tried to tell about the part where the girl walked right past the bathroom where he had been hiding on the second floor, and Vern wasn't sure what he was saying because of the loud breathing, he cuffed Derek hard right above the ear.

"Shut up that racket and tell me what it was you did, you little idyet," said Vern after the hitting.

And Derek, surprised at the blow, because Vern only ever hit him before when he was drunk and did not know what he was doing, leaned back in that car and just stared for a moment, trying to catch his breath and work things out at the same time, which is really one thing too many for Derek to try to do at once.

And then Derek said, as slowly and clearly as he could, "You did not say there would be someone else."

"What the hell you mean, boy?" said Vern.

"There was someone else."

"If there was, I didn't know."

"It is your job to know."

"Did you do it?"

"I did it."

"Did you get the thing for me?"

"I did it."

"Did the other person see you?"

"I was running too hard to find out."

"He must have heard you. You might have ruined everything, you worthless cur. I should a known not to trust no fool cretin idyet with something this big," said Vern, starting the car. "Should have done this one myself."

And Derek said nothing more in return, but it was all pretty much decided right then, not just from the being hit but from the untidiness of it all. If Vern cannot be trusted on the most basic parts of a plan, how can Derek trust him at all? Which is why he is taking the risk, sitting in the shadows of that prickly bush, waiting for Cody. Though more and more, as time passes by, he is expecting Cody never to show. Which will be a problem, because Derek is done with Vern, and he needs someone new to take care of him, and he wants Cody to be the someone new. But it will not be the first time his plans for someone new have fallen through. It is always a dangerous moment, making the approach, and more dangerous still if the approach is rejected, and dangerous not just to Derek. Because if you learn about Derek, then one way or the other you have to be taken care of, one way or the other you have to be tidied up.

So he is sitting in the shadows, not on the bench, wondering who will come. Will it be Cody, ready to take Derek as his charge and shelter him on their path through the world? That would be so nice. Cody promised him a horse, and Derek wants that horse so badly. Or will it be the police, led by Cody to this very spot? That would be bad, that would be rough for someone, there would be shooting, violence, someone would get hurt, maybe even Cody. Or, worst of all, will Derek wait there for night after night, and in the end no one would ever come? No Cody. No cops. No one. Nothing. Derek has not been alone in a long time, he does not know if he can make his way by himself. How do you find the jobs? How do you make the arrangements? How do you deal with the money? Derek is less frightened of the coming of the police than of the coming of no one.

But whatever shows up, something will change. He still is going to deal with Vern, though he would rather deal with Vern alongside Cody than after Cody.

"Derek?"

Derek hears the whisper from afar and slinks a bit farther into the shadows. He looks around and sees only a single familiar figure walking hesitantly to the bench. He scans behind the figure, scans the sides of the park, the street, looking for anything suspicious. Nothing.

"Derek?"

Derek rises to his haunches, readying an attack.

"Derek?"

"Where have you been?" whispers Derek, just loud enough to carry to Cody.

Cody spins around, trying to find him in the darkness. "Derek?"

"Are you alone?"

"Yes, yes. Of course."

"Where have you been?"

"I've been...I've been...Derek?"

Derek crawls from under the bush, stands, takes a step forward. A stray bit of streetlight hits his face. He shies away from it even as he waits for the gunshots from the police, the gunshots that would end everything, the final kiss of death in a life formed from that very thing. But there are no gunshots, there is nothing, only Cody, trying to say something, trying and failing.

But Cody does not really need to say anything more, does he? He knows about the girl, it is in his voice, it must have been in the newspapers after all. And still he has come, and he has come without the police, which means, well, which means everything.

49.

MAXWELL HOUSE

The knock on the door was loud and heedless. Just the kind of thing Justin Chase, out of principle, refused to heed.

Still floating within the lovely layers of slumber, he turned onto his side, buried his head into his pillow, and let himself drift down, down, deeper down. When the knocking came again, he simply wrapped the pillow more tightly around his head.

"Are you going to get that or what?"

The voice was close enough to startle him out of his sleep. He turned over, and there she was, leaning on an elbow, staring right at him, her face still thick with sleep, her eyes slit in annoyance, her breasts bared and ripe enough to be angry.

Annie Overmeyer.

And when he saw her, he had a moment of desperate panic. Justin had spent an inordinate amount of effort to ensure that he never actually went to sleep with anyone so he could always awaken alone. It was bedrock in his life, no wake-up surprises, no awkward mornings full of playacting and lies. And yet here she was, in the flesh, a physical manifestation of everything he had been working so hard to avoid. He blinked at her, at first uncomprehending and then, a few seconds later, with puzzlement as the memories of the night before slowly returned.

It took him a moment to remember it all, and to process its meaning. But when he finally did, he flung himself at her, wrestling her onto her back, grabbing her thin wrists in his hands, rising over her until he stared down at those suspicious brown eyes.

Another series of heedless knocks on the front door.

"There's someone downstairs," she said.

"Screw him," said Justin before leaning down and kissing her, hard.

She twisted her shoulders and jerked her head away. "I have morning breath."

"Screw that, too," he said, kissing her again.

She tasted funky and sour with a faint edge of morning rot, yes, and still it was the most electric thing he could ever remember.

To Justin, the single most attractive part of the barkeep's credo was to never try to save a soul from behind the bar. He viewed with great suspicion the evangelical urge rampant in this country. Believe what you want, but leave everyone else the hell out of it. And yet Justin now had the unfamiliar impulse to grab the world by the lapels and shout out the truth. Like he had just discovered, that very night, for the benefit of all mankind, fire.

Justin had thought he had mastered the whole sex thing—and we're not talking technique here—though if reviews given before the mirrors in the ladies' room at Zenzibar were any indication, his technique was spot-on. No, what he thought he had mastered, through much rigorous practice, was a method of moving past the mutating messiness of emotional connections and experiencing with heightened awareness the brilliant physical clarity of the sexual act. Like the distilled flavor of a single malt, or the perfect breathless note sung by a beautiful soprano. He believed he had successfully found in sex that which he was valiantly seeking to find in the entirety of his life, the ecstasy of the moment, unfettered by the past or the future, unfettered by the illusions that corrupted the universe. Whole, contained, rhythmic, tantric, peaceful and timeless, pure. It was like meditation gone blissfully feral. What could ever be better?

Well, sex with Annie Overmeyer, that's what.

Sex with Annie was sloppy and acrobatic, rushed and slow all at once, hilarious, exhausting, and rich on so many levels it was impossible to keep track of what the hell was going on except that so much was going on. It was a Mahler symphony compared to the single note he had been experiencing before, and it was flat-out fabulous. Who the hell knew that emotional sex was the better sex after all?

That was what he wanted to shout to the world. Emotional sex, give it a try.

And that the swirling, twisted nature of the emotions he was feeling matched the swirling twisting of their limbs and tongues as they spun around in his bed and performed all kinds of tricks didn't much matter. And "twisted" was the operative word, absolutely. Because he wasn't just feeling something strangely powerful for this woman beneath him, or above him, or beside him, depending on the snapshot moment, no. He was also feeling a bizarre pull from his past, something about his father and his mother and the way he was before everything crashed around him, stuff that was way better left unfurled. Especially the stuff about how his father had been lying in this very same position with this very same woman. Yet combining explosively with all of this, he was also feeling an almost painful yearning for his future, a future maybe not controlled by loss but instead by possibility, if such a thing could even be imagined.

And here it was, all of those emotions, so damn bright they were limned in pain, embodied in this act, this woman, this kiss. It was enough to leave him breathless, even if she wasn't just then sucking the breath out of him.

And then the knock again, louder than before, and a familiar voice calling out and reaching up to them through door and window. "Chase. I know you're in there. Open the hell up."

"Maybe you better get that," she said.

"I don't want to."

"Okay."

"But maybe I should, considering."

"Considering what?"

"Considering who is at the door and what happened last night."

"Last night." She twisted him off her, turned away from him, contracted her body into a lovely curl. "I had almost forgotten."

"It has nothing to do with us. With this."

"No?"

"No."

"It's pretty to think so, isn't it?"

"I won't let it."

"Go get the door," she said.

He rose from the bed, a move for him as natural as breathing, but it felt wrong suddenly, like he was abandoning a newfound truth.

"You'll stay, right?" he said to her as he put on a T-shirt and reached for a pair of jeans.

"I have to get to work."

"Please."

"We'll see," she said. "That's the best I can do."

"I'll make some tea."

"Coffee."

"How about I brew us a pot of something strong, like Earl Grey?"

"Earl's a weenie. I need coffee."

"A woman who knows what she wants. I think I have some somewhere," he said before heading down the stairs.

As he reached the ground floor, he could see the unsmiling face staring in through the front window. "Come on in, Detective," said Justin after he opened the door, "and I'll make you something to drink."

"I didn't come to socialize," said Detective Scott. He stepped through the door and stopped, suddenly, like he had walked into a wall. "You alone?"

"At this hour I'm always alone. I'm making some coffee. Want some?"

"Coffee, huh?"

"Late night last night."

"Maybe I will have myself a cup."

"Good," said Justin. As he walked to the kitchenette and started opening cabinet doors in search of the coffee, Detective Scott ambled over to the small dining table and pulled out a chair.

"We were looking for you last night," said the detective.

"It was getting a bit heavy. I needed to get out of there."

Behind a cloth sack of basmati rice, Justin found a yellow-and-brown can. He opened the plastic lid and took a sniff. Fresh enough, he supposed.

"How'd you get home?" said Scott.

"The girl drove me."

"The girl, huh? Nice-looking girl."

"I hadn't really noticed," Justin said as he filled a kettle with water and put it on the burner.

"Why are you lying to an old dog like me?"

"Habit?"

"That was one screwy crime scene."

Justin kneeled down and took out a French press from deep within a rarely used corner cabinet next to the stove. He began ladling coffee into the press. One tablespoon. Two tablespoons. Three tablespoons. "It all looked pretty straightforward to me," he said without looking at the detective. "I mean, the gun was in her hand, right?"

"That it was."

"Any note?"

"No note, but we found some interesting stuff that we wanted you to look at. Of course, you had disappeared."

"But you knew where to find me."

Scott took a photograph out of his jacket pocket and tossed it on the table. "You ever see these before?"

Justin leaned over and gave it a look. A pair of dangling diamond earrings in a drawer, next to some other stuff. There was something about the earrings that tolled familiar, but Justin couldn't figure out what.

"I don't know. Why?"

The detective pulled the picture back. "They seem to match a set of earrings that were found missing after your mother's murder."

"Let me see them again," said Justin quickly. When the detective gave him the photograph, he looked more closely. And he remembered his mother, dressed to the nines, leaning over him and giving him a kiss as he sat in his pajamas in front of the television with Frank. Hanging from her ears, glistening like a constellation of stars...

"Oh my God," said Justin just as the kettle started whistling.

"And we found some powder right next to the earrings," said the detective as Justin went over to take the kettle off the stove. "Powder that might link up to the drugs that killed Timmy Flynn."

"That's almost hard to believe," said Justin as he poured the heated water into the French press and fitted in the filter.

"You're telling me."

"But it all makes some sense, doesn't it? If Mrs. Moss was responsible for my mother's murder, then she might have kept the earrings that were stolen from the scene. And later she might have sent that sleazebucket Nicosia to kill Timmy Flynn to keep my father in jail, which would explain the powder. And somehow she must have gotten scared that it all would be figured out, and that was why she killed herself. It seems a clear enough connection." He paused a moment, tried to make his next comment feel as offhand as possible. "The only mystery is how she would have found out that you were looking at her."

"I called her and asked her some questions about your mother that night, that's how."

"So that's it. Don't you see?"

"Yeah, I see it all right," said the detective as Justin slowly pressed the plunger on the French press. When it was down as far as it would go, he poured a mugful for Scott. "I don't have milk or sugar, but I could put in soy milk and honey if you want."

"Soy milk and honey?"

"Sorry."

"I'll have it black."

"Good choice," said Justin as he set the mug before the detective.

The detective took a sip and winced. "You having any?"

"I don't drink coffee."

"Well, aren't you something." He took another sip. "This whole scenario of yours is pretty damn neat, wouldn't you say? I been doing this for longer than you've been alive, and they don't come tied any tidier than this. If I didn't know better, I'd suspect someone had tied the bow himself."

"That's because you don't want to admit that maybe you made a mistake six years ago."

"Yeah, well, here's the thing, Justin. When I was your age, sure, last thing I ever wanted to admit was that I blew it. It was a pride thing, I was swollen with pride. I made detective four years in, and for weeks on end I strutted around like a mummer on Broad Street. But at my age now, the only thing that's swollen on me is my prostate. I am more than ready to let go of my mistakes, if they are mistakes."

"Maybe my dad is one of them."

"You think?"

"I don't want to blame anyone, Detective. But if my dad didn't kill my mom, then I am partly responsible for putting him in there. I want to be responsible for getting him out. And maybe I'll have my dad again. Maybe things will end up being the way they were before."

"What would the Buddha say about that?"

"Frankly, I don't give a damn."

"You ever hear of a girl named Rebecca Staim?"

"No."

The detective looked at his coffee. "She was a Penn student, one of those foolish kids who think they can change the world. Took a semester off to do volunteer work in Guatemala, that sort of thing. A kid bound for disappointment, but who knew what she'd accomplish before that happened. She was killed a few days ago in a burglary gone bad."

"I'm sorry."

"Yeah."

"And?"

"She was the one fatality in a wave of successful burglaries that hit Center City last week. And here's the thing. There's a connection—tenuous as hell, but a connection nonetheless—between what happened to her and what happened to Flynn. And maybe to what happened last night, too."

"I don't understand."

"Neither do I, yet. But I will, trust me on that. You know anyone who has suddenly seemed to fall into some money?"

Justin thought about that for a moment and then felt a chill. "Not me," he said, trying to cover his reaction.

"I know not you. What would you do with all that cash? Buy a bigger TV?"

Justin laughed a little too loudly. Scott stood.

"Thanks for the coffee, though it was more than a little stale and could have used some fixings. We're not through here, you know."

"I know."

"And I'm going to need to talk to that Annie Overmeyer, too."

"I'll let her know if I see her."

"You do that." The detective stepped over to a coat flung on the couch. He picked it up by the collar, gave it a quick look, found the bloodstains right off, and then held it out for Justin. "And you might want to give her this too."

Justin took hold of it sheepishly.

"You don't think it's weird?" said the detective.

"You ever been crazy for someone, Detective?"

"In my time."

"Tell me, how weird was that?"

50.

SOMETHING WET

The spate of violent deaths seemingly stalking his family's past was not what scared Justin to the bone. And while the peculiar vulnerability he felt now when he thought of Annie Overmeyer was as alarming as it was delicious, that wasn't it either. Nor was it the questions that still had to be answered about Birdie Grackle, that murdering son of a bitch, or Cody's strange new affluence, which was the first thing Justin thought of when Detective Scott asked about anyone falling into money. No, what terrified Justin the most was that, in the course of a single night, he had reverted back to that which he had been before blood and death twisted his life onto a new course; he was once again a young man with a future. Not as young, true, and with a future not quite as bright, absolutely, but still.

He felt the frightening power of all his possibilities as he sat stiffly and waited in the visiting room at Graterford. This was no longer just a visit with a lifer in prison, this was a visit with his father, who might soon be released and become again an integral part of his life. And in a way, that made it so much harder.

When his father was finally escorted through the locked door, Justin stood and wiped his hands on his jeans.

"Justin."

"Dad."

There was an awkward moment as they stood face-to-face, Justin noting a bruise beneath his father's eye. Justin's father reached out his hand. And Justin gave it a shake. And then quick as a breath, as if embarrassed by the press of flesh itself, they took their places across from each other at the table.

"How's it going?" said Justin, looking away from the bruise.

"The same. Every day in here is the same."

"You getting by okay?"

"What choice do I have?"

Justin turned his gaze directly on the bruise. "What happened to your eye?"

"Do you want the details?"

Justin thought for a moment. "No, not really."

"I didn't think so."

They talked about nothing for a bit—the weather, politics, Frank and Cindy and the kids. They talked about nothing because Justin was somehow afraid of what was behind the door of the huge something he was there to talk about, afraid of the disappointment that would inevitably be found there. And was it inevitable? Of course it was; he was dealing with his father. But when the nothings petered out, he gathered his courage and said finally, "I have some news."

"Good news?"

"Not if you're Janet Moss. She killed herself last night."

"My God."

"She shot herself. In the head. This was after a detective asked her some questions about Mom. And in her house they found a set of earrings."

Justin's father leaned forward. "What kind of earrings?"

"Earrings that matched the description of a set that was missing from our house."

Justin watched as his father absorbed the news and made the calculation. After a moment his father softly banged the table with a fist. "Who knows about this?"

"Just the police for now. And they might have a link between her and what happened to Uncle Timmy."

"My lawyer's name is Sarah Preston. She needs to know everything. Everything, Justin. Will you do that for me?"

"You know what this means?"

"It only means I'll still be here tomorrow."

"You don't seem as excited as I thought you would be."

His father pressed his lips together and lowered his voice like he was telling a secret. "You know what kills more people in here than a shiv in the shower? Disappointment. If you start getting ahead of yourself, each day is like a kick in the teeth. Just tell everything to Sarah."

"Okay. I will."

"Good boy."

"This is going to do it, Dad. You're going to get your new trial."

"We'll see." His father looked away, as if struggling to take it all in while keeping his emotions in check, and then he turned back to Justin and stared at him for a moment, as if he were studying a stranger's face. "And if I do get the new trial, then what?"

"The prosecutors won't move forward. They can't. Any first-year law student could punch a hole the size of the Holland Tunnel through his case. The whole thing will be dismissed."

"And then what. I mean, what will it be like between us?"

"You'll be out."

"Thanks to you."

"I didn't do much of anything. I just—"

"Stop. Justin. For six years I've been telling everyone who would listen that I didn't kill your mother. Others, like Frank, might have believed me, but you were the one who actually did something about it."

"Maybe that's because I had something to do with you being in here in the first place."

"You just told the truth, son. I don't hold that against you, I never really did. If I vented, it was just because in here everyone needs a target. I know I wasn't much of a father."

"Dad, stop."

"No, listen. I was the worst I could possibly be, arrogant and self-absorbed and intolerant of any of my own flaws that I saw in my boys. I was a bastard, and when I cheated on your mother, even though it was part of our arrangement, I was also cheating on you. I choke on my own bile when I think of the way I was." He wiped his eyes with the back of his hand. "Of all the things I regret in this world, I regret that the most."

"You were what you were, but that's the past. We've all moved on."

"Some failures you never move on from."

The guard from the door stepped over. "It's time, Mac."

"Thanks, Rondell. This is my son Justin."

"Nice to meet you, Justin."

"He graduated Penn Law."

"That's pretty fancy," said the guard. "Very nice. Where do you work now?"

"Zenzibar," said Justin.

"International, huh? Good for you. You must be proud as punch, Mac."

"I sure am. I'll be there in a minute, Rondell." He waited until the guard was back at the door. "He's a prick except when there's family around. But Justin, what I wanted to say, if I ever get out of here, I swear I'm going to make amends for the way I was before. I'm going to be the kind of father you deserved. I know it's too late, I know I can't make up for what I was."

"Dad."

"What I want to say, and it's hard for me, but it's this. I love you, son. I never told you enough."

"You never told me at all."

"Maybe it was too scary for me to express, but I did. And I do. And everything will be new if I get out. I promise."

"Okay, Dad."

"I just wanted to say that."

"Okay."

"I guess it's time."

His father stood and Justin stood with him. They stared at each other awkwardly for a moment. Justin saw more tears in his father's eyes and had to look away for a moment. His father reached out a hand and Justin took it. And they shook. And then, suddenly, before Justin even knew what was happening, they were hugging, hard, like they hadn't done in years, like they hadn't done ever. And Justin felt something wet on his neck. His father's tears? On his neck? It was impossible and it was happening.

Sometimes, against all odds, the deepest, most unlikely dreams come true.

Justin watched through his own tears as his father pulled away, nodding with an exaggerated show of self-possession even as he wiped his eyes and nose with his palm. And while Justin watched his father turn and make his hunched walk to the exit, Justin felt the peculiar lift of a young man with a future when the future begins to come into focus and it is lovely beyond imagining.

But before Justin's father reached the door, he stopped and turned around again and came back to Justin, gripped his shoulder, pulled him close so he could whisper.

"Could you do one thing more for me, son?"

"Sure, Dad. Anything."

"That girl I was seeing, Annie? Annie Overmeyer? She's still living in the city. Find her and tell her I'm going to get out, finally. Tell her to hold on a little bit longer and then we'll be together, forever, just like I promised."

51.

CHAMPAGNE COCKTAIL

His name was Mark from King of Prussia. He traded stock options for some firm with three names on Market Street that Annie Overmeyer had never heard of and he smelled of a cologne notable for its not-so-subtle hints of oak and arrogance. He was talking now about a killing he had made in the market that very day, amused at his own brutal cleverness. A Rolex sprouted on the hairy wrist of the hand that was wrapped firmly around a glass of high-priced Scotch; his other hand rested heavily on her thigh. When in the midst of a whispered comment his tongue burrowed into her ear, it was as blunt and wet as a salamander's snout. And every time he squeezed her leg, it was like he was crushing her soul.

It had started with Mark from King of Prussia like it always started with the Marks from King of Prussia, with a drink. The trader had been sitting at the other side of the bar, and he had given her the eye, his trading eye, she assumed. She had smiled back, out of mere politeness or, maybe more truthfully, out of long-ingrained reflex. And next thing she knew a Champagne Cocktail was coming her way.

"This is from the gentleman over there," had said the barkeep as he presented her the drink, seven words like seven slaps on the face, coming as they did from Justin Chase.

That cold son of a bitch.

It was her own fault for letting him seduce her in the first place. Not seduce her into bed—there was no trick in that, a line as stale as week-old bread and a bottle of Jack or Jim was all it took—but seduce her into thinking that his being with her was maybe more than just another notch on his futon, albeit a notch supercharged with a little oedipal hot sauce. There is no fool like a slutty fool, as Annie insisted on proving again and again.

Their morning had been as brilliant as their previous night, sweet and rough and wildly romantic, and neither had been touched with the lubricating mendacity of alcohol. For a moment she let herself believe what before she had always known to be lies. But when he came back up the stairs after dealing with that cop, he was already someplace else.

"I need to run an errand," he said.

"Good, because I have a report I need to finish at work."

"I'll call you there."

"I might answer."

"You'll answer," he said, and he was right. She would, he had made a believer out of her. A believer in what? In the stupidest of things, that something bright and full of promise might reach down and save her life. Justin ex machina? Why not, why the hell not? And the kiss that followed was just as passionate as all that had come before it, just as true, and when it came to kisses, she knew true. It carried her home on a cloud. She went to work late, hid at her desk, and spent the day waiting for his call.

And waiting. And waiting. Not that she didn't deserve it. Not that the city wasn't full of men who had spent untold hours waiting for her calls just as she was waiting for his. But there she was, waiting. And waiting.

She knew she was in trouble when the delivery boy brought the flowers, a large bouquet of daffodils and daisies and white roses. Her heart soared and swooped in flights of rapture. White roses. Who could resist? She was like an actress reciting to herself her acceptance speech while waiting for her category to be called at the Oscars. But the boy gave her not a glance as he passed her desk and placed the flowers on a desk at the other end of the hallway. For Phyllis, a truly sweet woman whose face, at that very moment, Annie wanted to rip off her skull.

She swore she wouldn't call him, swore she wouldn't knock on his door, but it only took a few moments of pacing in her apartment after work, exasperated and hopeful and heartsick all at once, before she started dressing for an evening out. And where she was headed wasn't in doubt from the moment she picked out her brightest red lipstick and spikiest heels.

Zenzibar.

When Justin saw Annie Overmeyer walk into his bar, he felt a disappointing lurch of emotion.

The lurch was disappointing because he had spent hours on the tatami after visiting his father, working to rid himself of the emotional attachment he had felt for Annie just the night before. That emotion was all based on illusion, he knew, lies about a future that existed only in his fevered imagination and would never survive the mutable onslaughts of reality. *Fear it not. Be not terrified. Be not awed. Know it to be the embodiment of thine own intellect.* It was all a trick of the mind that would immediately be exposed upon his father's release from prison. Better to drain its power now rather than wait for it to drain his sanity. And so he had worked hard on letting the emotions flow through him and out of him, and hoped that would be the end of it.

And then, of all the gin joints in all the world...

He had been trying to have a serious conversation with Cody between serving other customers, hoping to glean what was really going on with him, when she made her entrance. And he wasn't having much luck with Cody, either. Something had happened to him, something strange. Cody was nervous, hyper, scared absolutely, and yet full of a weird optimism about his future.

He was making Cody's third Sidecar of the evening, drinks that Justin was still paying for in exchange for the detective work, when Cody had said, "When I get back, I'm going to buy this place."

"Let's keep our ambitions modest," said Larry, who was sitting beside him, "and say that when you get back, maybe you'll actually buy your own drinks."

"No, I'm serious. I always wanted to own a bar."

"How are you going to afford a bar?" said Larry.

Cody winked. "I can't talk about it."

"Afraid someone else will jump at the opportunity?"

"There you go."

But there was something in the wink that wasn't all hope and cherries, something cheerless and frightened. Cody was into something way over his pay grade, and Justin couldn't help but think about what Detective Scott had asked regarding whether anyone Justin knew had fallen into money. Or how shaken Cody had seemed by an obituary he had read. Or, and this concerned him the most, how Cody had thanked Justin for setting him on the path of his newfound success.

"You haven't run into that old guy since your visit to Dirty Frank's, have you?" said Justin.

"No. Why?"

"Just thinking," said Justin. "He's not a guy you want to hitch your wagon to."

"Don't worry. A guy like that is all pipe dreams and desperation. I know what that's like. I'm getting as far away from pipe dreams as possible. The thing I have going is as real as they come, and don't I know it."

"Good," said Justin.

"It's as real as a kick in the balls," said Cody.

"We should have a going-away bash," said Larry. "Buy a cake, blow up some balloons."

"You really know how to party," said Cody.

"I might be depressed. Do you think I'm depressed?"

"You're not depressed, Larry. The problem is you're sober. Buy him a drink on me."

"Which means on me," said Justin.

"Exactly."

"So when are you leaving?" said Larry.

"I don't know exactly," said Cody. "First I need to build up my bankroll and pay off my debt to Solly."

"How are you going to do that?"

Cody leaned forward and tapped the bar with a finger. "I think my luck has turned. I've made enough in the past few days for one more bet, with everything riding, and then I'm off into the sunset."

"And if you lose?"

"I won't," said Cody. "My luck has turned. And I happened to get word of a sure thing."

"There is no such animal," said Larry.

"Maybe not, but truth is, it doesn't really matter. I could go clean or I could go dirty, but either way I'm going. Things are getting a little tight here, don't you think? A little closed in."

"I know exactly what you mean," said Justin, sliding Cody's drink in front of him.

"I'm going to miss you, pal," said Larry.

"I'll send you punks a postcard."

"Hey, Cody," said Justin softly, leaning forward as he said it so Larry couldn't overhear. "You're not into something you shouldn't be, are you? I mean, nothing you're into so deep you couldn't get out of it even if you wanted to."

Cody just looked up at him, and his eyes were about the saddest things Justin had ever seen.

And that was when Annie Overmeyer walked into the bar and Justin's emotions lurched, a combination of yearning and regret that sent his jaw shaking.

She came right over, looking as fresh and bright as a ripe pomegranate, sat down on an empty stool, and waited for him to make his way over to her part of the bar.

"Hi," she said to him, and he had to fight the sudden twining urges to kiss her and to cry. But he knew for a fact that the only way to maintain his equilibrium was to pull the emotion stirred by this woman out by its root. He wasn't going to let false and evanescent attachments get in the way of the possibility of something new and rich between him and his father. And when the right moment appeared, whenever that was, he was ready to tell her the truth of things. So instead of kissing her or bewailing his fate, he simply leveled his gaze and reverted to perfect barkeep form.

"What can I get you?" said Justin.

"What can I get you?" said Justin.

And there was something in the calm, dead expression of his eyes that told Annie everything she needed to know. She knew why he hadn't called, she knew why the flowers weren't for her. He was one of those men who lose themselves in the moment and then, on reflection, pull away, jerk away, run away like fearful little boys and hide in their callousness. And as sudden as that, the doors started closing in her mind, one after the other, slam, bam, one after the other until she was as locked up as an accountant at a meeting of the board.

"Something tall and wet," she said, knowing how to play it now, the way she played it every stinking day of her life.

"Fruity?"

"Definitely not fruity. Why not something sparkly and gay to remind me of a fundamental truth of the world."

"And what's that?"

"Men are shits."

"All men?"

"Maybe I'm being too harsh. There might be a nice guy in Toledo. I'm just talking about the ones I sleep with."

He stared for a moment and she hoped to see some hurt, or maybe embarrassment, or at least a little regret. But that's not what she saw at all; what she saw was nothing. A barkeep's nothing. And all she could do was laugh.

"Is something funny?" he said.

"Me," she said. "I'm hilarious. I never fail to crack myself up." She turned her head from him, she had to look away, it was too painful. Some guy at the other end of the bar was staring at her. He nodded. She smiled reflexively and turned back to Justin. "The silly thing is, I was actually waiting for your call. Like I was sixteen again."

"Something came up."

"It always does. Trust me, this I know better than anyone."

"Look, Annie, I need to talk to you. The thing that's come up—"

"You don't need to explain. Last thing I want is an explanation. Too bad you're not married. Then your excuse would be easier, you could just use the kids."

"I'm not looking for an excuse."

"Little League. Girls' soccer. That's why men invented these things. Don't tie yourself into knots, Justin. Whatever happened just happened and that's that. You're not my type anyway. Your hair is pretentious, your place is too small, and you need some furniture."

"Furniture?"

"That whole futon on the floor is so undergraduate. And you want to know something about tea? I hate tea."

"Who hates tea?"

"I do."

"No, really. No one hates tea. It's like fresh air."

"That too. And your coffee sucked."

"Can we talk, please?"

"We just have."

"Don't do this, Annie."

"You're right, it's not you, it's me. Blame it on me, baby, that's fine. I can take it."

He stared as if he were seeing something new in her, something he didn't like. Good, now they were even, because she had seen something just like that in him. He glanced at her one more time before he turned away and walked to the other end of the bar. She breathed deep and tried not to think.

When he came back, he was holding a Champagne Cocktail. "This is from the gentleman over there."

"Fuck you," she said, the streak of authentic anger in her voice sharp and surprising. But she sure as hell had taken the drink.

And now here she was, snuggled next to Mark from King of Prussia, whose cologne was making her sneeze and who thought the Champagne Cocktails he had been plying her with were actually going to seal this deal.

Even as Mark was telling a story about a cockroach on the trading floor and one of the runners who was offered four figures to eat it, Annie kept her eye on Justin. He moved with a lovely grace behind the bar, mixing and pouring, pirouetting as he reached to get a bottle. Just as graceful as he had been in bed. Screw him.

See, that was the problem, she still wanted to. She turned and gave Mark from King of Prussia a taste of her tongue. That would keep him interested, that would be good for another two drinks at least.

When she looked up again, Justin was talking to that girl from the time before—what was her name?—Lee, that was it. God, she was beautiful, so beautiful Annie had winced when she walked into the bar, winced like every other woman had, as if she had somehow stolen a few watts from each of them. And now Justin was leaning forward and whispering in her ear, and Lee threw her head back and laughed. Laughing, Annie was certain, so that her perfect white teeth just caught a bit of the light. She was good, and, as always, her shoes were fabulous.

This was more than she could take, this she had to get away from. She lifted her drink, gazed at the bubbles collecting on the edges before rising to the top, and then downed the thing. It tasted like Paris in the springtime. She had never been to Paris in the springtime. If she ever went to Paris in the springtime, it would not be with a stiff like Mark from King of Prussia.

She leaned toward him and nipped his ear in her teeth. “I’ll be right back.”

“I’ll be here, doll,” he said.

"Good."

She gathered her purse, slipped out of the booth, made sure Justin was watching as she headed, not to the restroom, but to the front door of the bar. She hesitated a moment before walking out, not just on Mark from King of Prussia, but on Justin Fucking Chase too.

On the whole damn city, to be honest about it. It was time to go someplace else. Austin. Vegas. LA. It didn't much matter, just so long as it wasn't here.

Heartsick.

Justin watched Annie Overmeyer leave the bar and he felt heartsick. He never knew what that word had meant before; now he swore he'd never feel it again.

Lee watched him as he swiveled his head to follow Annie's progress out of the bar. "I guess it didn't work out," she said.

"What didn't work out?"

"Her," said Lee, looking at the now-empty doorway.

"Who, Annie?" said Justin, getting back to the business of mixing drinks. "There was nothing to work out. She was part of the past, but not my past, someone else's past."

"Your lips might say it, but your eyes give you away."

"You want another drink?"

"No, I have dinner reservations. Buddakan."

"Sweet. Someone nice?"

"From work," she said. "He's been pestering me for years. And yes, he's nice. A regular nice guy. I'm going to try sincere, see how it tastes."

"I bet it tastes fine."

"Maybe, but I came in for a quick pop just to hedge my

bets." She glanced at her watch. "Oops, got to go. It's good to be late, but not too late."

"You're going to devour him," said Justin.

"And he'll love every minute of it," she said before reaching out and patting Justin on the cheek. "Take care, sweetie."

"Sure," said Justin.

He watched her leave, the gorgeous and sweet woman whose bed he couldn't wait to leave, watched her walk out the same door that Annie Overmeyer had walked out a moment before. They were the lucky ones, the two of them. If he could leave himself behind, he'd toss down his towel and walk out that selfsame door without a backward glance.

When he made his way back up the bar, Cody was telling him good-bye, telling him that he had a place that night to be, but Justin ignored him and stood right in front of Larry.

"You know what you should do?"

"What?" said Larry.

"You should stop feeling so sorry for yourself and get your ass to Pittsburgh."

52.

MOTHER'S MILK

A few minutes later, as if cued by Justin's foul mood, Birdie Grackle stumbled through the front door of Zenzibar. The old man regained his balance, looked behind him for the offending limb that caused him to stagger, and upon seeing nothing there but the smooth tile floor, turned around again, sucked his teeth, and, with an exaggerated hitch in his step, angled his way toward an open stool at the bar. He climbed up, leaned forward, tapped at the mahogany with an oversized knuckle, and let out a woodchuck's shrill whistle.

Justin finished serving a customer at the far end of the bar and slowly made his way to the old man.

"Why, Birdie Grackle," said Justin without mirth. "As I live and breathe."

"At your service, doctor, as always," said Grackle, his big dentures loose in his mouth, causing his words to be a mite mumbled. "It's a rare pleasure seeing you again."

"I thought you had crawled under a rock and disappeared."

"No such luck for the ladies or the bottles," said Birdie with a tap of the bar and a rheumy wink. "Or for you neither, I suppose. I'm like them bats in that cave outside San Antone, I am.

Fifteen minutes after dusk, there I come, swooping out like an avenger from hell, ready to feed."

"For once, your imagery is apt. What can I get for you?"

Birdie smacked his lips as he examined the bottles lined in rows behind the bar. Finally, his gaze hooked on something high up on the wall. "How about a little more of that fancy blend you shoveled at me last time I was here. I must admit, it left a haunting impression on my tongue."

"Johnnie Walker Blue?" Justin reached up, pulled down the bottle, examined the label for a moment. "I don't know. It's a bit expensive."

"Don't mind the expense, doctor. I'm good for it. You can just take it out of what you owe me."

"What I owe you?"

Birdie smiled his fearsome full-dentured smile. "Now don't go squelching on me, doctor. A deal's a deal, and we had a deal."

"We had no such thing."

"You been smoking that wacky weed, boy? Didn't your momma tell you that stuff kills the memory? I said clear as day, if we started on something, we was going to finish it, remember?"

"We never started, Birdie."

"You must be smoking something, you don't remember you giving me the go-ahead. That's the only reason I gave out my clue. And I must say, I was mighty impressed the way you ran that doggie to the ground."

"What the hell do you know about it?"

"A man like me, he keeps his eye on his investment. Oh, I been watching you, and watching that cop watch you, too. I got myself a good idea of everything what's going on."

Justin felt a chill just then. Cody had said that Birdie

wasn't alone, that he had a companion. Justin would have spotted Birdie if he was spying, but maybe not the muscle.

"How's your daddy doing?" said Grackle.

"He's doing."

"Always better than not doing, that's for sure. Things are working out?"

"They look like they might."

"Then all is as you could have hoped. I figure I earned my fee. So what's the problem, boy?"

"You didn't finish anything, Birdie."

"No?"

"I found someone who might have fit your description, but even if she was the right one, you had nothing to do with what happened to her. She killed herself."

"Is that right?"

"I saw the scene with my own eyes. She put a bullet into her head. I'm sure it's a disappointment for you, Birdie, but you weren't needed. Let's say I pour you one more drink, we call it even, and then we part our ways forever."

Birdie's slick dark tongue slithered out of his mouth and licked his upper lip. "I could go for the drink part, that's for sure."

Justin eyed the old man for a moment and saw the need in his eye. It was almost out of pity that he opened the bottle and started pouring into a lowball. When he poured in two shots' worth he stopped and looked up at Birdie. Birdie was staring at the glass, not moving to grab it as of yet, just staring, waiting. Justin tilted the bottle until the thick brown liquor rose to the rim.

"Thank you, doctor," said Birdie, reaching for the glass.

He lifted it for a moment, but his hands started shaking so badly he had to put it down again and slide it to himself. His head lowered and he slurped at the glass until the level of liquor was secure enough that he could lift it without risking a drop. He drank deep as if it were water from a tap, and his eyes fluttered as if he were in the throes of something obscene. It was almost enough to get Justin drinking again.

"That's the stuff," said Birdie when he had downed half, "to put an atheist on his knees."

"I'm glad you like it, because it's the last of anything you'll ever get from me. Our game is through."

"You think it's that easy, boy? We had usselves a cash deal. And like I told the nurse at the sperm bank what helped me out that time—cough it up."

"I'm not paying a cent, Birdie."

"You'll pay," he picked up his glass, let the light cut through the amber color, and then took a gulp. "One way or t'other."

"Are you threatening me?"

"Not you, because you the one going to pay me. Only a fool would do something that stupid. But there's that brother of yours, that—"

"Leave him out of this."

"Or his wife, what comes visiting you in that big old truck to get whatever you're slipping her."

"That's enough."

"But I'll end up with my ten thousand, one way or t'other."

"For what, you old fraud? What the hell did you ever do for me? You're a con man, and not even a good one. And now the con is over. Get out of my bar."

As Justin said those last few words, he took hold of the half-full lowball. A bartender never leaves alcohol in front of a customer he is finished with. It is not up to a troubled patron on the other side of the wood to decide how long to stay, how long to ruminate, when to erupt. When a bartender decides that a customer is done, the barkeep pulls their drink as quick as that, and that's what Justin was doing.

But before he was able to slide it away, Birdie grabbed at it with two gnarled hands and started pulling it back, pulling it back with all the desperation of a man dying of thirst fighting over the last dreg of muddy water. There was a tug-of-war as the old man strained to lift the glass to his trembling lips and liquor sloshed within the walls of glass. With a final fraught yank, Birdie Grackle pulled the glass free, splashing half of what remained across his face. Staring at Justin, he lifted his chin and drained what was left, his Adam's apple bouncing with ferocity. The sound of the glass slapping down on the bar and a growly sigh came at the same time.

"Mother's milk there," said Birdie Grackle as he wiped his face with his hand. He stared at Justin while he licked the wet from his fingers one by one.

"You must have had a hell of a mother."

"She was that and more. So I guess that's it, that's all we got. This little romance of ours, it's over. Fitting then that I've got for you a good-bye gift. Something to remember old Birdie by."

Onto the bar the old man placed a little box, wrapped in blue paper and bound by a red ribbon tied into a bow, and slid it to Justin.

"There's nothing you have I want," said Justin.

"Open it."

Justin gave the old man a look before he slid off the ribbon and ripped away the blue paper. Slowly he lifted the top off the small cardboard box. He stared at the contents for a moment before putting the top back on.

"What did we agree on?" said Birdie, his head dropping low so he was staring at Justin now through his wild, weedy eyebrows. "Ten thousand dollars? Minus the drink."

"What did you do?" said Justin. "What the hell did you do?"

"I did what I do," said Birdie Grackle. "What did you think was going to happen? You got three days, boy. If you don't have the money, get it from that brother of your'n."

"What makes you think I won't start yelling bloody murder?"

"You won't tell them cops because what would they think, except that maybe your daddy, he ain't as not-guilty now as he might look. And you won't tell your daddy because you got your own secrets to hide from him, don't you, you randy piece of jerky. Three days."

Justin took a deep breath and took the top off the little box again. A bird, small and yellow. A canary. Justin poked at it with his finger. It was real all right, he could feel the tiny bones right through the feathers. It was real and it was dead.

"What's the matter?" said the foul old man. "Birdie got your tongue?"

53.

A STEAMING PILE

Justin had to admit this about Birdie Grackle—he was a raw and bracing piece of reality.

Justin knew better than to check out from the present, with its hard and beautiful truths, and turn his face to the future, which was nothing more, really, than a shade of an image of an idea of a hope. But that is exactly what he had been doing, losing himself in a blizzard of conjectures about his father and Annie and his own little life. Would his father get out of jail? Would they have the kind of relationship he had always hoped for? Would Annie be his lover or his stepmother or disappear entirely from his life? He had been busily constructing castles in the sky when Birdie Grackle sauntered into Zenzibar, sucked his big fake teeth, and presented his truths flat on the bar like a steaming pile of crap.

It might not have been a pleasant thing to smell, but it sure as hell did wake him up.

Because what did Birdie represent, really, but reality itself, namely the truth about what happened to Justin's mother, the truth about the guilt of Justin's father, the truth about Justin's own responsibility for a host of crimes? And being face-to-face with Birdie Grackle left Justin face-to-face with the most awful truth of all: that he still knew nothing. And it seemed that everything he had done since Birdie first walked into the bar had left him further from knowing anything at all.

But even in his state of perfect ignorance, he still had to deal with that human piece of excrement. He had been avoiding doing anything about Birdie because all the alternatives were rank. But there was no choice now. This man, who claimed to have killed his mother and now who was claiming to have killed Janet Moss, needed to be dealt with, and fast, before someone else ended up dead. And as far as Justin could see there were only three options: turn him in, pay him, or kill him.

What he wanted to do was kill him, brutally and quickly, with a maximum amount of blood spilled about his rotting carcass. It shocked and horrified Justin how much he yearned in his gut to stick Birdie Grackle's chest with a knife or to inside-out his brains with a Louisville Slugger.

But no matter how satisfying it might seem in the imagining, Justin was no killer. Even if he was certain that Birdie had actually killed his mother, even if he had more proof than the old con man's say-so, he still couldn't do it, it wasn't in him, thankfully. A murder like that could only arise from a deeply held belief, of which Justin proudly claimed none. And in his state of pure ignorance, even the idea of murder was anathema. No, Justin would have to bask in the satisfaction of some sort of karmic justice, knowing that a cockroach like Birdie Grackle would inevitably come back to life as, well, a cockroach.

But if he wasn't able to kill the son of a bitch, neither was he willing to pay him. From the moment Birdie stepped into the bar, he was looking for a payday. He had something else going on other than this ten-thousand-dollar scam—Cody had made that clear—and so Birdie might just end up with his score, but he wasn't going to get it from Justin, because Justin would sooner pull out a toenail than pay it.

No, Justin wasn't going to kill Birdie, and he wasn't going to pay him either. Which left one crappy option.

54.

SCREWDRIVER

Mia Dalton had a headache, and it was Justin Chase who was giving it to her. Each word was like a cymbal clash right next to her ear. Nothing he said made sense, or maybe everything he said made sense, but because she couldn't be sure which was which, the whole thing was giving her a headache. *Clash clash.* Listening to Justin Chase was like playing chess with a Russian: you began seeing plots everywhere.

Generally, in the middle of an interrogation, Mia always asked questions on the slant; the answer she was seeking was never directly related to the question. She searched instead for hesitations, improbabilities. You never ask for the thing you really want to know from those on the other side of the desk because they might tell you what you don't want to hear and then where the hell would you be? But now, after hearing the strange story of Birdie Grackle, from the moment he first strode into Justin's bar until the last unsettling meeting just the night before, she broke her rule.

"Justin," she said, "do you want your father to get out of jail? I mean really?"

"He's my father," said Justin.

Mia looked at him for a moment and then smiled in

admiration. She had asked a straightforward question and Justin Chase had answered on the slant. Too bad he never took the bar, he would have been a hell of a lawyer.

The phone rang. She picked it up and heard her secretary tell her there was a call for Detective Scott. "It's for you," she said to the old man.

Scott grunted as he pushed himself out of the chair. He grabbed the phone and barked his name into the handset.

"Okay, good. Did you check the book?...How about the description? Anything?...Remember, he wouldn't be alone. There'd be some muscle with him...Yeah, it would be hard to miss the tattoos. What about a walk-through?...Just do it so we can say we did it, or Dalton will be chewing my ass...You don't got to tell me. Okay, good. Oh, and Kingstree, it's the Parker, so don't go in alone."

He hung up the phone, gave Mia a look she couldn't decipher, and eased back to his chair right next to Justin's. "Kingstree gives his regards and told me to watch out for frostbite."

"What did that lunkhead learn?"

"No Birdie Grackle registered at the Parker," said Detective Scott, "as well as no one named Birdie and no one with the last name Grackle. Though it is the Parker, which means that a photo ID is not strictly required before they put a name in the book. And the description Chase gave, old alcoholic with yellow hair and bad dentures, fits about half the current residents. Kingstree is going to go floor by floor to see if he can pick up anything other than a rash."

"Who did you say followed him there?" said Mia to Justin.

"Just some guy," he said.

"Who?"

"I don't want to get him involved."

"You already did. A name would help."

"No."

"Okay, so here we are," said Mia, rubbing her temples in an attempt to relieve the pain. This whole thing was like a screwdriver in her brain. "You've told us this story, which we can't corroborate, about a guy who claims he killed both your mother and Janet Moss, six years apart. And because of the fentanyl we found in the drugs in her drawer, we can assume, if he killed Janet Moss, he killed Timmy Flynn, too. So we have three possibilities. Either you're lying, or he's lying, or we have some sort of serial killer on our hands. But since we can't confirm anything you said, it makes it more likely that someone is lying."

"I'm not," said Justin.

"Good, since that is settled, then he is probably lying, which makes the most sense. Scott here is going to do everything he can to find this"—she looked down at her notes—"this Birdie Grackle, and if he succeeds he'll bring the old man in for questioning. And, of course, the old man will deny everything. So in all likelihood, nothing will come from it, but we'll try."

"What about the bird?" said Justin, indicating the small box he had put on her desk.

"It's a bird, Justin. We'll have Eddie Nicosia look at it, and we'll have our scientists see if we can compare it to anything left in the cage, maybe compare DNA with some of the feathers or dung, but you and I both know it could have come from anywhere. Go into a pet shop, buy a yellow canary, twist its sweet little neck and put it in a box."

"But how would he even know there was a bird there?"

"You knew," she said flatly, and saw Justin wince at the accusation that it all might be a fraud that he himself set up.

"But what I'm trying to figure out, Justin, is what you're doing here. Mrs. Moss's apparent suicide seems favorable to your father's cause. His attorney has already called, asking if we're ready to dismiss the case and release him."

"What did you tell her?"

"I laughed, but it was more out of reflex than conviction. The way things stand, your father's motion for a new trial looks pretty solid. But now you've just given us the possibility that Mrs. Moss didn't kill herself out of guilt and regret, but that she was helped along. Which throws everything into doubt."

"Maybe she hired him originally," said Justin, "because my mother was having an affair with her husband, and then, six years later, he killed her for the exact reason he said, to extort money from me."

"Well, you see, Justin, the second part might be true no matter who did what six years ago. This Birdie Grackle might have seen an opening, conned you into thinking he had killed your mother, and then killed Mrs. Moss for the ten thousand he wants from you. Meaning he might actually be a murderous son of a bitch, which, if true, would ruin the whole suicide-out-of-guilt theory and leave your father smack in jail. Which leaves me again wondering why you're here."

"I just want to tell the truth."

She looked at Justin and then at Detective Scott, who seemed strangely content with that answer, and then back at Justin. It was such a simple response—the boy just wanted to tell the truth—but it left Mia again feeling that he was manipulating her for some reason of his own.

"Thank you, Justin. We both appreciate you coming. We'll have the...the thing in the box tested and then we'll get back to you."

"Which means you're not going to do anything," said Justin.

"We're going to do what we can," said Mia.

"He said if I didn't pay him the money, he was going to kill someone else. Maybe my brother."

"Then maybe your brother should take precautions," said Mia.

Justin stood up and nodded, as if he were trying to control some emotion roiling beneath his placid surface. "Thanks for all your concern," he said before walking out of the office, closing the door behind him a little too loudly.

"You were pretty cold," said Scott.

"Just living up to my rep. Wouldn't want to disappoint Kingstree. Keep your eye on him. There's something about him I don't trust."

"I think the kid was telling the truth, Mia. I could sense he was holding back something before and I guess this Birdie was it. He maybe mentioned something about it outside the prison, but it didn't really register."

"Why was he holding it back?"

"Because he didn't believe the old man."

"Then why this meeting?"

"Maybe because now he does."

"And he gets to screw over his father at the same time, which is a nice daily double. With this kid there always seems to be a hidden agenda."

"It's not so hidden."

"No?"

"Whoever it was who killed his mother, he wants that son of a bitch to burn."

55.

MORE WILD TURKEY

When his brother Frank saw Justin standing in the doorway of the house, he lunged at him, grabbed him tight, hugged him like he was a long-lost brother suddenly found.

"I talked to Dad," said Frank, still hugging away.

"I bet you did."

"You're amazing. You did it."

"I didn't do anything," said Justin, "and we'll see what happens."

"It's a chance," said Frank, letting go and stepping back to get a look at his little brother. "You gave him a chance."

"It wasn't me, really."

"Do you think the lady who killed herself really was responsible for what happened to Mom?"

"I don't know."

"We'll never find out for sure now, will we?"

"No," said Justin. "No, we won't."

"Let's celebrate," said Frank, backing into the foyer. He called up the stairs. "Cindy. Justin's here. We're having a drink." He turned to Justin. "Let's go into the library."

Justin stepped into the foyer and once again couldn't help but look down at the floor. Still impossibly spotless. He didn't want to be here, in his father's house, which still stank of death to him, even though he knew it truly smelled more of potpourri and Lysol, but he didn't see he had much choice. His attempt to turn in Birdie Grackle had not only failed, but it had hurt his father's chances of getting out of jail. Nice move, Justin. Now he was trying to avoid the third and final option for dealing with Birdie Grackle.

In the library, Frank went right to the bar and picked up a bottle. "A nip?"

"You know I don't drink," said Justin.

"But this is a special occasion," said Frank, putting some ice from the bucket into a glass. "We're getting our father back. If that doesn't put a drink in your hand, I don't know what will."

"It's not a sure thing that he's getting out."

"He thinks it is. Oh, and he wanted you to talk to his attorney."

"I'll do it tomorrow."

"He'll be pleased. I wonder what it will be like, the moment he gets free," said Frank, lost in reverie. He twisted the top off the bottle and started pouring. "We'll be waiting in the rain, the cleansing rain, like in a movie, and out he'll step. And everything will start again. Do you think it will be just like it was?"

"It can't be," said Justin. "Not without Mom. I need money."

Frank stopped pouring, looked up at Justin for a moment, his expression turning from lost to found in an instant, and then put another shot and a half into the glass. He took a long sip before walking slowly to the desk. He sat down, leaned back like a banker, looked at his glass as he rubbed his thumb along the rim. "How much?"

"Ten thousand dollars."

"I don't have that kind of money in the house."

"But you can get it quickly."

"The company has been struggling lately. We lost our best salesman when we lost Dad. I don't know."

"I need it right away."

"Can I ask why?"

"No."

"How much trouble are you in?"

"It's not me that's in trouble."

"Then who?"

Justin was looking at Frank, unsure of what to say, when there was a knock on the library door. The brothers turned their heads quickly, as if they had been caught at something. And there was Cindy, standing in the doorway in a pleated fifties dress, as if expecting company all along.

"Congratulations, Justin," she said without an ounce of cheer.

"There's nothing to celebrate yet."

"No? Because Frank's been celebrating since he came back from the prison. He's going to celebrate himself to death."

"I just had a few," said Frank.

"He's very excited about his father getting out of jail, as he should be," said Cindy. "As are we all. Do you happen to know of any houses for rent in your area? We're suddenly looking."

"I'm sure you won't have to leave."

"You don't think your father will want his house back? He already mentioned that Overmeyer woman to Frank. He expects her to move in here with him. And it won't be long until he reclaims the corner office that Frank has been using to keep the company alive. I think he wants everything just the way it was."

"Five years in jail will change anyone," said Justin. "I'm sure he's different."

"You're suddenly sure about a lot of things, Justin. How did that happen?"

"Maybe you'll join the company after Dad gets out," said Frank. "That was always his dream, his two boys working for him. You could take the bar, be our corporate counsel."

"No, thank you," said Justin. "I might have been a law student before, but now I pour drinks. Unless Dad wants me to work the occasional cocktail party for him, I'll go my own way."

"That's so noble of you," said Cindy. "So now, only Frank has to deal with him."

"Cindy, if you'll excuse us," said Frank, raising his glass in dismissal, "we're conducting some family business here."

"Oh dear, I wouldn't want to interrupt that. I just wanted to say thank you to Justin. Thank you, Justin."

"You're welcome."

"He's the hero of the day, all right," said Frank.

"And we're all so happy," said Cindy.

Justin looked around, saw not an ounce of happiness on either face, and knew there was none on his own. Cindy gave Justin a final bitter look before leaving the room and shutting the door behind her.

"She's not so enthused about the new way of things," said Frank.

"And you?"

"He's my father. I have no choice but to be enthused. What was it you needed, ten thousand?"

"Yes."

"In cash?"

"Yes."

"This isn't—"

"No."

"And you really, really—"

"Yes."

"Okay, then. I'll juggle some firm accounts and take it out tomorrow. I'll call it a fee for investigative services."

"Thank you."

"Anything else?"

"Don't tell Dad."

"That was assumed."

"And stop drinking so damn much."

"Why should I? It's a celebration, isn't it? We're going to have to put up banners." Frank lifted his glass. "Daddy's coming home."

56.

BOMBARD OF SACK

The insight came to him in, of all places, a lawyer's office. It arrived like a satori, swift and devastating, a fork in the eye. And like a fork in the eye, it pierced something fragile, and afterward nothing ever looked the same again.

It wasn't enlightenment, for in that moment of vicious perception Justin saw the raw truth that he was never about the search for enlightenment; he wouldn't have recognized enlightenment if it approached him with a name tag and one hand clapping. "Hello, I am Enlightenment," would say Enlightenment, and Justin's true self would reply, "Get lost, dude. Can't you see I'm busy?" And what he was busy doing was hiding. The meditation, the tatami mats and ceremonial teas, the calm words coming from an apparently calm center were all fronts. What he was really searching for was an emotional desert to call his own. Before his mother's murder, he was a member of the human race, with all its untidy ambitions and messy emotions. After his mother's murder, he was as good as dead, and eager to stay just that way.

But all of that was about to change.

"Tell me about yourself, Justin," said Sarah Preston.

"There's not much to tell," said Justin. "I pour drinks at Zenzibar on Sixteenth Street."

"How nice. That sounds exciting."

"Not really."

"Oh, I'm sure it is. You must be like Bogart in *Casablanca*."

"Hardly," said Justin.

They were sitting almost knee to knee in front of her office desk at her law firm on a high floor in one of the city's office towers. The floor was a warren of little offices, each with a secretary out front, the kind of beehive that had been waiting for Justin out of law school. It gave him the creeps to be up there, as if he were in an alternative history of his life. In the office next door was probably another Justin Chase, toiling on a brief that meant either a small bump or a small dent in some huge corporation's quarterly profits. Was the other Justin Chase happy with his high salary, his blonde wife, his shiny BMW? Most likely ecstatic, the son of a bitch.

"Well, I'm glad you came," she said. "I've heard so much about you that it's really exciting to finally meet you in the flesh."

"You've heard so much about me?"

"From your father, dear. He is so proud."

"No, he's not."

"You'd be surprised."

"Don't you want to talk, like, about the case?"

"In time. I've heard the outlines of what happened from your father, and read the reports in the newspaper. Of course, I'm going to need the details from you before we go to court. Still, I thought it was important that we meet face-to-face and get to know each other."

"Why?"

"Because we're going to be spending a lot of time together." She looked at him and pulled back a strand of hair. "On the case, I mean."

"So you do meet-and-greets with all of your witnesses?" said Justin.

"Just the special ones."

Sarah Preston was tall and thin, dressed quite stylishly, with just a bit too much makeup. Even the rouge, though, couldn't hide a certain grayness, not just in her overly coiffed hair, but in her pallor. She was trying quite hard, Justin could tell, to be charming and ingratiating. Trying way too hard. As if she were coming on to him, except she wasn't. Of course she wasn't.

"Your father said you found this Mrs. Moss on your own," said Sarah Preston.

"It wasn't as hard as it might seem. My aunt was a big help, as were some others."

"Who else?"

"Just...I don't know." There was something in her manner that made him hesitate to bring up Annie's name. Eventually the lawyer was going to have to hear about her, but since everything he told her was bound to get back to his father, he wasn't ready to go into all of that, at least not just yet.

"How well do you know my father?" he said.

She smiled brightly, and the effect was like a beam of light hitting her face. "As well as you can know someone in prison, I suppose. He's a very intelligent man."

"Yes, he is."

"And very gentle."

Justin tilted his head at that. His father was a lot of things, but gentle was not one of them.

"And you're representing him pro bono?" said Justin.

"Our firm asks that we all do some pro bono work as part of our firm culture. It's in that spirit that I've taken on your father's case."

"I'm a little surprised that he qualifies. We don't really talk finances, but I thought he had plenty of money."

"Your father's assets are all tied up in litigation. The house, his stake in the company, all of it was transferred to Frank to keep it from creditors. Whatever cash he had went to his defense lawyers, and he never received the life insurance payout, for obvious reasons."

"But he could get you paid if he wanted to."

"Maybe, but I'm glad to do it for him without payment," she said, which was about the most unlawyerlike thing Justin had ever heard a lawyer say. "It's an honor representing your father."

"An honor?"

"He's quite a man," she said. "Unique. And on top of that, he's an innocent man sentenced to jail for the rest of his life. How many lawyers get a chance to right such a wrong?"

"And you're sure he's innocent?"

"Aren't you? After the suicide and the evidence they found in the Moss house, what else could you think?"

"That's right," said Justin. "What else?"

"That's why I am so excited to meet you, Justin." She leaned forward and patted his knee. "You're a big part of his life, and I have the feeling we're going to be seeing a lot of each other."

There it was again, the sense that she was coming on to him. He pulled back, stood up from the chair, wandered around the office, knowing all the while that she was staring at him. It was a fairly large office, bigger than most of the others he had spied while being led down the hallway, a partner's office. But even so, the furniture was stock and the photographs on the walls were routine shots of Philadelphia: the fountain in Logan Square, the art museum, Independence Hall. Nothing too personal, no family photos. And her left hand, the one that had patted his knee, was bare of rings. He started having a weird feeling about this room and this woman and being here, like he was touching something soft and moldy.

"How did you meet my father?" he said.

"He was one of my students," she said, swiveling around in her chair to follow Justin's wanderings.

"Students?"

"I was an English teacher before I went to law school. My passion was Shakespeare. When I was still trying to make partner, I was advised that I needed some public-interest work to burnish my credentials. So, though I am embarrassed to admit it, I only started teaching in the prison to get ahead at the firm. Shakespeare for the incarcerated. A stupid idea, I suppose, but it worked. There was much more interest than you would imagine, and the discussions were quite lively. Truth is, I learned more about Shakespeare from the inmates than I ever did from my professors or at the Old Vic. Last year we were putting on *Henry IV, Part 1*, when your father joined the group. In all my classes at the prison, I had never met anyone like him."

"I bet not."

"He was so quick, and had such keen insights. And Justin, you'll like this. He told me he had a son that reminded him of Prince Hal in the story. He was referring to you."

"I don't know the play."

"Oh, you should read it. Fabulous. Prince Hal is the play's true hero, who fights the battle at the end that saves his father's crown. Stirring, actually. The performance was quite well received by the other prisoners. Here, let me show you."

She stood, went over to her desk, pulled open a drawer, and pulled out a photograph in a simple wooden frame.

"Here," she said. "I cast your father as the king."

"He liked that, I'm sure," said Justin as he took the photograph.

A group of men, scraggly in their prison togs, with just a few accessories to define the character each was playing. The men stood around Sarah Preston, who looked much less spiffy in the picture, her hair not done, her face not made-up, her clothes not Nordstrom. Something had changed in Sarah Preston from when this photograph was taken, and Justin, sadly, had an idea of what that was.

He picked his father out of the photograph right off, standing next to the lawyer with a Burger King crown on his head. There was a bearded inmate with a pillow under his shirt. There was a young prisoner with another crown and a sword. And off to the right, an old man, also with a sword, who looked a lot like...No, it couldn't be.

"Who's that?" said Justin, pointing at the old man with the sword.

"Hotspur," said Sarah. "He's the villain of the play, the great warrior trying to unseat the king. It's Hotspur who fights Prince Hal at the end."

"No," said Justin, "I mean who is he, for real?"

"Vern."

"Vern?"

"Yes. Vernon Bickham. He was in for forgery or something. But I think he's out already."

"Vern," said Justin.

And then he stopped speaking. Because this Vern wasn't just another old man with bad teeth who looked a lot like Birdie Grackle. He was an old man with bad teeth who looked enough like Birdie Grackle that he could have been Birdie Grackle's twin. Except the sleeve of the shirt on the arm holding the sword was rolled up to the elbow and there, on the forearm, was Birdie Grackle himself, with a crown of thorns. No twin at all.

What a peculiar coincidence, thought Justin in the first blush of recognition, when his mind was still befogged by the shock of it all. What an amazing coincidence. And then the fog lifted and the amazingness of the coincidence fell apart as the reality of what it all meant slammed into him.

Like a fork in the eye.

57.

MOUTHFULS OF VODKA

The knock on the door came when Annie Overmeyer was packing to pack it all in.

It was late, and she was a little drunk, and that would have been the obvious explanation for why she was throwing shift and shirt into her bag. But her packing to leave, to flee actually, was no drunken folly. It was, instead, a failure of the alcohol to soothe what normally it soothed.

She had tried drinking it away, the emotions that had overwhelmed her the night Justin Chase had spurned her completely, the anger and self-pity, the hurt, the sadness, the pathetic yearning to be something other than she was. She had tried to drown it all and yet, unhappily, alcohol had failed her. It had been such a friend, along with bad sex and the occasional vampire novel, just what she needed to keep her mind from the truths of her life. But the bottle wasn't working just now, the vodka she had downed didn't numb. Instead it perversely made her more aware of what had happened to her life.

There should have been a warning label on the bottle. *Caution: life as viewed after drinking contents may appear more pathetic than you can bear.*

You get into a habit of low expectations, which gives you a sort of contentment. You go through life as if through a mist, seeing little farther than your nose and scorning all that only appears wispy and faint. Then a bolt of lightning splits the mist and gives you a glimpse of all you might be missing. And doesn't that just ruin the hell out of your day? That's what Justin Chase had been in their night together, a bolt of lightning that allowed her a glimpse of all she had let drift out of her life.

It wasn't the sex, which was fine, really, but still just sex. She could find cocksmen in any dive in the city that could give Junior a run for his money. And it wasn't that he was so super-special a guy. Really, all that Zen crap was fake nineties bullshit that made her teeth ache. And, to top it all, he was just a bartender; Mark from King of Prussia pulled in more in a month than Chase could dream of making in a year behind the bar. And no one knew better than Annie how much she liked her creature comforts: facials at the spa, a bright new pair of shoes that lifted her calf just so. So what was it?

It was their way together. Lying in bed beside him—and yes beneath him and above him, too, belly to belly, hand to hand, tongue to breast—there was no subterfuge, no abject neediness, no sense of obligation or payment owed, no unbalanced emotions or subjugation. They weren't there making up for childish slights, playing out their adolescent neuroses, searching for the emotionally distant daddy or seeking revenge on the cheerleader who cut them in high school. It was just easy and fun and intimate in such a naked way that it seemed almost obscenely pure. She'd had, for a single evening, the type of relationship that she had always thought was merely the mewling fantasy of romance novelists and lonely country-club wives. She had glimpsed what was, for her, the holy grail: a relationship of equals without the usual dose of self-loathing.

It had been a lie, of course. Justin Chase had proven to be no different than every other self-satisfied scoundrel who had talked his way between her legs, just a more convincing actor with a unique line of patter. But the promise of the thing she had glimpsed, that intimacy, was what she had tried unsuccessfully to numb with the vodka and why she was packing now. Because it had exposed with the brightest of lights what was truly absent in her own life, and how much less she was settling for night after unsatisfying night. And if she couldn't drown that promise in mouthfuls of vodka, then she would do the only other thing that was sure to numb her spirit.

And so she was packing, filling a suitcase for a quick and unplanned getaway to Minnesota, to her girlhood home, so her parents could give their unbidden advice and tell her exactly what she should do with her life. A week in that gray Lutheran landscape and she'd be pawing at the door like a dog, desperate to head off to some new place, any new place. Mom and Dad were always good for that. Every day at home was like Thanksgiving, filling her soul with the true spirit of thankfulness that she was not, thank God, living at home anymore. Minnesota was such a great place to be from.

And then the knock at the door.

Her first response was annoyance. When she was half-drunk and in the middle of a self-pity party she didn't want anyone trying to sell her on vacuum cleaners or Jehovah. But then she wondered how the solicitor had gotten past that front security door without ringing her up first. And then she thought about Mrs. Moss, dead in her chair, and the glimpse she caught along that darkened hallway of the strange figure tearing out of the house. And then she grew scared, damn scared.

Another knock, the muffled sound of a voice.

She grabbed hold of a lamp from her bedroom and headed into the living room. Something jerked back her arm like she was being grabbed. A jolt of terror hit before she realized the thing jerking her back was just the power cord. She kneeled down and pulled the plug before advancing again, the twelve-dollar piece of pottery and pressed steel a pitiful little cudgel.

More knocking.

"Who the hell is it?" she said, gripping the lamp more tightly.

"It's Justin," came the voice. "Justin Chase."

She lowered the lamp and leaned her back against the door. "I know your last name, Junior. What do you want?"

"There's something I need to say."

"Then say it."

"Through the door?"

"Sure."

"Let me in, Annie."

"No."

"No?"

"No. We both had our fun, and you made yourself perfectly clear that all you wanted after was to get the hell away and stay away. I understand, it's a characteristic of the species *malepenus stupidius*. And you're right, we can both do so much better. It turns out I have a date tonight with that guy who you let buy me a drink. We're going ballroom dancing."

"I didn't know you liked ballroom dancing."

"I don't, but he's an investment banker. Do you know how much he makes?"

"No."

"Enough for me to spin like a top if that's what he wants."

"Come on, Annie. Open up. I don't want to make a scene for the neighbors."

"They're used to it by now. I could set up bleachers, sell tickets."

"Okay, you're right. I'm an asshole."

"A pretentious, self-righteous, narcissistic asshole."

"Exactly."

"Say it."

"I'm a pretentious, self-righteous, narcissistic asshole," he said. "Not to mention the king of the bullshitters. I pretended to see the world more clearly than everyone around me when all the time I was the world's biggest dupe, a Zen faker who was twisting ancient *kōan*s to convince himself of the virtue of taking the easy road out. Which makes me a fraud and a coward too. And I sing like a hoarse crow. Do you want to hear?"

She could feel herself weaken with every word, every confession. Even if it was only a new line of patter, it was having an effect, but then the best lines of patter always do.

"I wouldn't say you were the king of the bullshitters," she said through the wood as she pushed herself off the door, turned around, twisted open the bolt. "More like the idiot prince."

She heard the knob turn, and slowly the door opened, and then there he was, so close it was almost shocking. He was big, bigger than she remembered, and strangely disheveled. It wasn't like him to look so unkempt, as if he had been run over by a huge animal. She watched him stare at her for a moment, and then his gaze drifted slowly downward.

"It works better if you plug it in," he said.

She followed his gaze and noticed the lamp in her hand. She had forgotten she still was holding it. The reality of it, the hard feel of the pottery, brought her out of some sort of trance and back into her situation.

"I was taking it with me to the bath," she said. "It puts a

sizzle into the enterprise. What do you want, Junior?"

He stepped through the door, closed it behind him and stared at her, stared so closely it was like he was peering through her flesh.

"Is there something on my face?" she said.

He stepped toward her and put his thumb on her lip, and she felt a spark jump between them. He rubbed her lip gently with his thumb and then, with the same hand, he caressed her cheek. She wanted to be immobile, as still as a statue, not even dignifying his unsubtle attempt at seduction with a jerking away, but her neck betrayed her and bent into the touch. His hand slid from her cheek into her hair and he gently held her in place as he leaned toward her and kissed her.

He kissed her and something went weak inside. Her eyelids fluttered, her bones wobbled. She sagged into his hard body and let go of everything.

Crash.

The shock of the sound pulled her away. She looked down. The lamp lay in shards about her. She stared at the ruined lamp for a long moment, trying to piece everything together, and then she looked up at him, tilting her head.

"So that's what this visit is all about. A little breakup sex, huh, Junior? You're all pathetic, the whole lot of you."

"No, you're wrong. Not about us being pathetic—we are, me especially—but about why I'm here."

He stepped forward and kissed her again, hard, and she responded, again. She closed her eyes and felt his lips and his tongue, his teeth, his hand on her back. And she felt the sun on her face, the wind in her hair, the foamy surf roll over her feet, and then, above the roar of the ocean she heard his voice: *This is from the gentleman over there.*

She jerked her head back and pushed him away. He stared

at her, looking drowned-rat miserable, some strange pleading in his eyes. She had seen that before, the pleading stare, and it only left her cold. Next thing he'd be on his knees begging for one more night in paradise. Men were such predictable shits.

"Go to hell," she said, "and on your way close the door behind you."

"My father's probably getting out of jail," he said, in a flat, soft voice.

"I know, Junior. I found that woman's body, remember."

"How do you feel about that?"

"What do I care, really? If he didn't do it like you were saying, then he should be out. I know you were pretty happy about it."

"I went to see him after that cop came to the house, and he told me he wants you back."

She thought about it, the timing, the meaning, everything. She thought about it and ran it through her processor a couple of times. "Ahh, yes. Of course."

"I wasn't going to—"

"Step on your father's toes? What are you, his wingman? Or are you his pimp? Either way, you make me sick, the both of you. I suppose you two put your heads together and decided the way it was going to be. Like two guys at a bar sizing up the opportunities. You take the brunette, and he gets me?"

"It's not like that. It's just—"

"What the hell are you doing here?"

He kissed her, but she didn't respond; she wasn't going to respond until she figured out what was going on. She stood there and let him kiss her while keeping her lips as immobile as marble. And beyond strange, it felt good, it felt great, way hotter than tonguing. She could stay there for hours and let him kiss her marble lips, her marble neck, her hard marble breast. It should have been her who pushed him away, but he was the one who stopped, who took hold of her biceps and held her at arm's length, shaking her back into the moment. She was such a sucker.

"If he gets out, what would you do?" he said. "Do you want to be with him?"

"That ship sailed long ago."

He kissed her again and the marble cracked.

"Are you sure?"

"You want me to show you?"

"How?"

"Stay."

"I can't."

"Fuck you."

"Not yet. Look, I learned something that has made me question everything."

"Everything?"

He kissed her quickly, familiarly. She leaned into it and they kissed again, longer. What was she doing? She didn't care. She just wanted him to kiss her and kiss her. And it wasn't the vodka making her lose control like this, his kisses had burned the alcohol right out of her. She kissed him until he pushed her away.

"Maybe not everything," he said. "But him. My father. I'm questioning what everything that happened really means. And what I'm going to have to do about it. I need to find out more and I think I have a way to do just that. I don't want you to be part of it. But I want you to wait and let me learn what I need to learn and do what I need to do. And then, whatever happens, I'll come back for you."

She felt woozy, drugged, and because of it she didn't have any biting comment to throw in his face. All she could do was repeat his request.

“You want me to wait,” she said.

“Yes.”

“For how long.”

“I don’t know.”

“Okay.”

“Okay?”

“That’s what I said, Junior.”

“Okay.”

“So get the hell out of here and do what you need to do.”

“Okay,” he said. He looked her up and down. “Were you really going dancing with that investment-banking asshole who was trying to pick you up with a goddamn Champagne Cocktail?”

“He was just being polite.”

“Like a piranha.”

“You brought it over. My gosh, Junior, I’ve never heard you so acidly judgmental before. It exposes a flaw in your character. I like it.”

“Are you still going out with him?”

“Do you want me to?”

“No.”

“Then I won’t.”

“Good.” He tossed her a lopsided smile that was entirely too damn charming, and then backed toward the door. “I can ballroom dance if that’s what you want.”

“I bet you can, Junior.”

“Is that what you want?”

“Please, no.”

“Thank God.”

After he left she cleaned up the mess of the broken lamp before going back into her bedroom. The suitcase was still there, half-full. Piece by piece, she took her clothes out of the suitcase, folded them neatly, and put them back into her bureau. At one moment she heard a peculiar sound and stopped to try to identify it.

It was a song, a stupid Beatles love song. And strangely enough, she was humming it.

58.

TEZÓN AÑEJO

Justin was setting up the bar at the beginning of his shift when Frank walked in.

The hour was more contemplative than exuberant; the couple drinking at the wood seemed to be there out of quiet celebration rather than frenetic need. It was Justin's favorite time at work, the expectant stillness before the coming rush. You could feel it in the very air, the Pavlovian salivation as the minute hand rose, the thirst from a thousand office cubicles about to descend upon a hundred different bars, the concoctions about to be mixed, the eyes about to be gleefully glazed, the soul-crushing compromises of the day about to be frantically drowned. It was all coming, the whole wholly misnamed happy-hour thing, only not just yet. Just yet was the calm.

"What can I get you, Frank?" said Justin to his brother. "Wine again?"

"I think we're beyond wine right now. Maker's over ice."

Justin checked his watch.

"Shut up, little brother. I have your money, now pour me a drink."

Justin nodded his head some, like he was thinking about it, and then did what he was told. When he pushed the drink forward, Frank returned the gesture, pushing forward a thick white envelope. Justin slipped it behind the bar without looking at it.

Frank raised his glass. "To Dad," he said before taking a slurp. "Yabba dabba doo."

"Thanks for this," said Justin.

"It wasn't so easy grabbing hold of it all." Frank swirled his glass a bit so that the liquor wobbled. "This is about as liquid as we get these days. But there were some escrow accounts that were just hanging around."

"Escrow? You can't touch escrow accounts, they don't belong to you, they still belong to the customers."

"Between you and me, Justin? No one's looking."

"Frank."

"No one will know."

Justin took the envelope from the shelf where he had slipped it and slapped it on the bar. "Put it back."

"You said you needed it, right?"

"That's what I said, but things have changed a bit."

"You're not buying drugs with it, are you?"

"No."

"Too bad," said Frank before draining his drink. "You can make a killing selling drugs. I should have been a pharmacist. You get to wear those nice blue shirts, and you can always give fifty-nine instead of sixty pills and bank the extra."

Justin looked at the envelope for a moment, thought about what he had still to do. An instant later the envelope disappeared again beneath the bar.

"I'll get it back to you," said Justin.

"Sure you will," said Frank.

"Sooner than you think. I thought I'd have to spend it, but I think now it's just going to be a temporary decoy."

"Either way," said Frank, circling his finger around his now-empty glass.

Justin pulled the bottle and filled the glass. "Go easy on that."

"Why would I want to do that?"

Just then Cody stepped in the door, hitched up his pants, looked around nervously before heading to the bar and hopping onto one of the stools. Justin slid over to him.

"You're in early."

"I got a game to watch and could use a little courage."

"You won't get it here."

"You never know, it's a pretty important game. If it turns out right, I'm off the hook. If it turns out wrong, I'm going to have to work out what I owe. Something over time, maybe paid with services of a discreet nature to be rendered on request in the future. Fortunately, I now have a card to play."

"I didn't know MasterCard made deals like that."

"Which is why I'm cuing the courage."

"What can I get you?"

"That thing you were making me the other day."

"Sidecar."

"Yeah, that's the ticket."

"Right away," said Justin. He grabbed his tin, poured in the brandy and Cointreau, started in on the lemons. "You see Larry around? He wasn't in yesterday."

"He took a trip," said Cody. "To Pittsburgh."

"Good for him."

"It won't work out, it never works out. Life doesn't let you have happy endings."

"You never know," said Justin, sliding a scoop of ice into the shaker. "Maybe your bet will come in."

"Truth is, Justin, I expect to lose. I always do. And life seems eager to exceed my expectations."

When Justin finished mixing the drink, he rimmed a glass with sugar, cracked open the shaker, and poured. He slipped an orange twist on the edge and slid it to Cody. "One Sidecar."

"Thanks."

"Don't leave until I talk to you," said Justin.

"Sure thing."

"I'll be back in a sec."

He gave the couple another round—Vodka Martini for him, Cosmo for her—and then went back to his brother, who had finished his second already.

"What say one more?" said Frank.

"Did you drive here?"

"Just pour."

Justin refilled the glass. "I'm visiting Dad tomorrow."

"You and he are suddenly getting quite chummy."

"I've only visited a few times."

"Chummy, chummy, chummy." He emptied half the glass. "Such chums you've become."

"You actually sound jealous."

"No, just curious. All the time growing up it was like we had picked teams, you and Mom versus me and Dad. And at the trial, it was exactly the same as you worked to railroad him into jail."

"Railroad?"

"But now, suddenly, you're like Dad's new best friend."

"Mom always loved you."

"Fuck you. You don't have to tell me that."

"Not because you were her son and she had to," said Justin. "It was more than that. But she was concerned that you were too close to Dad, that he was unduly influencing you. She always hoped you would end up teaching, like you once said you wanted to."

"I was a kid when I said that."

"And she was sad when you ended up working for him."

"What's your point?"

"That maybe you don't need him like you think you do."

"He's our father."

"Yeah, but just the idea of him getting out is causing you to throw more and more of that crap down your throat."

"I'll have you know Maker's Mark is not crap, it's actually quite tasty."

"And it's not making Cindy so happy."

"Neither do I, so Mark and I, we console each other."

"Have you ever thought, Frank, it might not be the worst thing if it doesn't work out like we think it might."

"He's getting out, Justin. He's coming home. And you're the one that did it. You're the hero."

"I'm no hero."

Frank started laughing. He finished off his drink and slammed it on the bar. "I'm your brother," he said. "You don't have to tell me that."

Justin watched Frank lumber out of the bar with that sad, too-careful step Justin had seen so often after first slipping behind the wood in Reno, and he suddenly envisioned how poorly the endgame would affect his brother. Justin had become so self-absorbed he had bumbled on this dangerous path without worrying how his bumbling impacted others. Typical. And whatever he had done so far would taste mild as club soda when compared with what was to come.

Marson marched in from the back with his clipboard to count Justin's bank and make sure the bar was stocked for the rush. "You're low on quarters," said Marson. "I'll get you more change from the safe."

"Someone told me the stock market popped today," said Justin. "We might need some more of the top-shelf stuff for when the traders come marching in."

"I'll take care of it."

"I'm not going to be able to make it tomorrow night."

Marson stopped marking up his clipboard and lifted his chin. "That's your shift, Justin. I let Chip go to open that shift for you."

"It can't be avoided."

"The word on you was that you were flaky but reliable, that you never missed a shift. That's why I brought you on board. But here you are traipsing in when you want, getting phone calls and leaving early, and now missing shifts. What the hell's going on?"

"Something's come up."

"Your shift tomorrow night has come up," said Marson, looking down at his clipboard. "And you'll be here, or don't bother coming back."

"Then you better give Chip a call."

Marson's head jerked up. "Are you quitting on me?"

"I don't have to. Your ultimatum did it for me. And I actually want to thank you for it."

"If you're quitting tomorrow, then you're finished now," said Marson. "Hang up your towel, punch out, and go."

"There's a call for you, Mr. Marson," said a waitress.

"I'll be right back," said Marson. "Don't touch the till."

"You can trust that I won't," said Justin.

"That's the shame of it, Justin, because I know that I can."

Cody was finishing his Sidecar at the bar when Justin ambled over to him. "Another?" he asked.

Cody checked his watch. "Something quick."

Justin snatched a shot glass and slapped it on the bar, grabbed a squat brown bottle from the premium rack, filled the glass to the rim.

"Tequila?" said Cody.

"Not just any tequila," said Justin. "This is Tezón Añejo. Pure blue agave, slow-roasted, ground by a millstone of volcanic rock, aged in oak for two years."

"So how do I rate such an honor?"

"It's a celebration," said Justin. "I just got fired. Drink up."

"What's going on? You never got fired before, you were always the one who left."

"It's a new era."

Cody lifted up the glass carefully. "To new things," he said before lapping up just enough of the tequila to stop it from spilling. "Wow."

"Yeah. I need something from you."

"Whatever you need, you must need it bad."

"That I do."

Cody looked at Justin for a moment and then snapped down the rest of the shot. "Yowza, that's good."

"Ready?"

"Sure."

Justin leaned forward and lowered his voice to a whisper. "I need to buy a gun."

59.

DUPLEX

Justin's father was speaking, words were coming out in a seemingly sensible order, but they held no meaning. Justin sat across the table from his father in the Graterford Prison visitors' room and heard the audible ebb and flow of sentences as they streamed across his father's lips, yet still it was as if he were watching a dumb show. That is what happens when you finally realize that every word out of your father's mouth is a stinking lie.

Justin now fully understood the truth in that old weathered book pressed urgently upon him so many years before. *Fear it not. Be not terrified. Be not awed.* In the past Mackenzie Chase's words had the capacity to terrify and destroy Justin; all manner of damage could be done with an indelicate suggestion or a barbed comment. But no longer. Now that Justin understood everything his father said to be a lie, and that any meaning his father's words might carry existed only in the convoluted workings of his father's own befouled consciousness, his father's words were suddenly devoid of threat.

"It's just amazing to me that she could have done it," said his father. "That this woman, whom I had never met, could wreak such devastation on our family is unfathomable. It makes what happened to Eleanor seem even more horrible."

"It's unfathomable, all right," said Justin.

"And yet you tracked her down."

"I got lucky."

"Luck had nothing to do with it," said Justin's father.

Now see, there was an interesting comment that took some close interpretation, because while it wasn't quite a lie, it certainly wasn't the truth either. That Justin had found his way to Janet Moss certainly had little to do with luck, Justin was now well aware of that. He had been led there, step-by-step, by this very man sitting across from him. But Justin's father was implying that it was Justin's pluck and perseverance, along with a pressing curiosity and keen intellect, that had led Justin on that path, and this certainly was a lie. It was more Justin's gullibility, and his fervent wish to disavow the truth, that sent him to Janet Moss, and his father well knew it. It was becoming almost a game to try to find every level of lie in his father's words, in his every breath.

"Have you told everything to Sarah?" his father said.

"Most," said Justin.

"You need to tell her everything, son. We can't have any surprises in court."

"I have another appointment scheduled. She seemed more interested in getting to know me as a person than in pumping me for information. As if we're going to be seeing a lot of each other in the future. Why would she think that?"

"I'm sure she's just thinking of the case," lied Justin's father. "She's a patent lawyer, and I don't suppose she has much trial experience. She must just want to get to know her witness."

"I'm sure that's it," lied Justin right back.

His relationship with his father had entered a new and quite interesting phase. Before, Justin's father would lie and

Justin would sort of believe him, would want to believe him. What son doesn't want to believe his father? And so there was a troubling inequity in their roles, a carryover from the awe and fear Justin had felt for his father since toddlerhood. But now, after experiencing his fork in the eye, a wonderful balance had been achieved. Justin's father would lie and both of them would be aware that he was lying. Justin wasn't sure if his father was aware that Justin was aware that his father was lying, but that was only a matter of time. As it would only be a matter of time for Justin's father to figure out that everything Justin was saying now was a lie. And when that happened, when both of them became aware of the full extent of each other's lies, then they would have finally reached across the generational divide as equals. Sweet harmony.

Hey, nothing's perfect.

So Justin watched with a surprising amount of satisfaction as his father lied to him about the past, the present, and the future they would have together.

"I want to take a trip when I get out of here," said his father. "I want to reconnect with you."

"That would be nice."

"A cruise maybe."

"We're all a little short of cash."

"So then we'll just go camping. You, me, and Frank."

"And Cindy?"

"Sure, and Cindy too. And the kids. The whole damn family."

"And that Annie Overmeyer?"

"No, not Annie. She's not important, Justin. She never was. Just us. Just family. That's all that really matters."

One, two, three, four. He had to restrain himself from pointing at the lies as they slipped out of his father's mouth. It could be like a game show. Welcome to this episode of *Find the Fib*, with your host, Mackenzie Chase. It astonished Justin that he hadn't seen it all before. And just by being there, and nodding along, Justin was lying just as much as his father was. That was all part of this new relationship.

"I'd like that, Dad," lied Justin. "I really would."

God, it was beautiful, the symmetry of it all. And now it was time for Justin to raise the level of his game to match his father's. It was time to play the caring son faced with a dilemma.

"I have to tell you something, Dad. I have to tell you the real way I found Janet Moss."

"You told me already."

"Not totally. I've been holding back."

"Justin?"

"Just listen, Dad," said Justin, and then he leaned over so he could say the next part in a whisper that only his father could hear. "A guy came into the bar one night, an old guy named Birdie Grackle. You ever hear of him?"

"No," said Justin's father. "Never."

"This Birdie told me a strange story, that he was a Vietnam War vet who had become a killer for hire."

"Jesus."

"And that one of the people he had been hired to kill was Mom."

"What?"

"And that he was actually the one who had killed her."

A look of shock crossed Justin's father's face, a look of generic shock, mouth open, eyes wide, brow furrowed. The expression was as much a lie as everything his father had said that day. Justin fought to stop a smile.

"Who did he say hired him?" said Justin's father.

"He didn't know for sure, but he said he did know it was a woman. That's what led me to Janet Moss."

"Do you think this Birdman—"

Oh, thought Justin, that was good, the misremembered name, that was fabulous. His father was taking it up a notch. "Not Birdman, Birdie."

"Birdie. How perfectly awful. Do you think he's telling the truth?"

"I don't know, Dad. I don't really know. But he gave me a little turtle pin that looked just like the little turtle pin I had given Mom and that came up missing after the murder. I tried to bring it in to show you, but they snagged it in the metal detector."

"I don't believe this. This is crazy."

"Yeah, it is," said Justin. "But then something really strange happened."

Justin's father pulled back a bit. There was no feigning his concern this time.

"This Birdie Grackle told me he'd kill the person who had hired him if I wanted. He said he'd do it for ten thousand dollars. I didn't tell him to pound sand because I was still trying to find out who might have hired him. And then Mrs. Moss killed herself."

"So it's over. He should just disappear. Which is just as well, probably."

"No, it's not, Dad. If he killed Mom, he's going to have to pay, don't you think?"

"I don't know, Justin. If he's as dangerous as he said, then isn't it better just to leave him be? You said he was old, he's probably sick as a dog. Just let him die."

"Maybe, if I could. But he came back to the bar two nights ago demanding his ten thousand dollars."

"What? Why?"

"He said he killed Mrs. Moss for me. He said he made it look like a suicide just to help me out."

"He must be lying."

"I'd think so, but there was a bird at the Moss house when I first talked to her. It was missing when they found her body. This Birdie Grackle handed me a box, and inside the box was the very same bird. And he said something would happen to Frank if I didn't pay him the money."

"That son of a bitch." Was there something truly aggrieved in his father's exclamation, or was Justin imagining it?

"Exactly," said Justin, powering on. "And I had to do something, right? But I didn't want to go to the police right off, because I didn't want anything to affect your case. So I got the money from Frank."

"What?"

"And tomorrow I'm going to set up a meeting."

"You're going to pay him off?"

"Sort of."

"Sort of?"

"Dad, if he's telling the truth, he's the one who killed Mom. We can't do nothing. We have to do something."

"What can you do?"

"There were some fingerprints at Mom's murder scene that they never identified, right? Well, I carefully pulled his whiskey glass right off the bar and put it in a bag. It's got his prints all over it. It's filthy with his prints. Tomorrow I'm going to set up a meeting with the old bastard. But before the meeting I'm going to give the glass to the police with the whole story. They'll check his prints with the ones they found at the house. If they match, they'll be waiting when this Birdie Grackle shows up to get his money."

There was suddenly something truthful coming from Justin's father, something so pure and honest that it hurt a bit to see it. Justin had been enjoying the whole mendacity of their encounter a little too much, and now, to see something so raw was a little unsettling. And what Justin saw now in his father's eyes was panic.

"Justin, that sounds too dangerous. Justin—"

"It's all set up, Dad. And when they match his prints, you'll be out, totally free. They won't even wait for the hearing. This Birdie Grackle will be behind bars, you'll be free, and we'll be together, Dad. Finally. Just like you want."

"Justin, no."

The guard stepped over to their table. "It's time, Mac."

"No, not yet," snapped Justin's father. The prison guard didn't step away this time.

"It's fine, Dad," said Justin, standing from the table. "I'll be fine. But now I have to go. I have to make preparations."

Justin's father came to his feet, scurried around the table, and reached over, grabbing Justin's arm. "Justin, stop. Listen to me."

Justin wrapped his arms around his father, pulled him close, hugged him tightly. "If things go right, Dad," said Justin into his father's ear, "you'll be out of here day after tomorrow."

"You have to listen. You can't—"

Justin let go of his father, pushing him away as he pulled back. "You have to go. Sleep well."

"Justin, stop."

As Justin backed away, his father pressed forward before he was stopped by the guard. Justin took a long look at his father's face. Panic and fear and maybe hatred too. It was impossible to read it fully, there was so much going on, but the expression on his face at that moment at least was sincere. Justin took a final look and then turned to leave.

"Justin, Justin," said his father.

Justin stopped, and stood there without turning for a moment. This was it, the last chance for anything truly honest to pass between them. There was something his father wanted to say, needed to say, was desperate to say. A last chance at something. Would it be another lie or the truth, finally?

Justin turned around. "What, Dad? What is it?"

His father's face was no longer a seething pool of emotion. It was friendly and calm, with a smile Justin recognized all too well, a bartender's smile. It was all so tragic it seized his heart.

"Where will you be tonight, Justin?" he asked.

"Home, Dad," said Justin, choking on the sadness as well as the words. "I'm going to be home. All night."

"I'll try to phone."

"That would be great."

"Wait for my call."

"I'll be waiting."

"Bye, son. I love you."

Justin nodded, thinking those might have been the very same words Justin's father said to Justin's mother the morning he left her to go to work. The morning he left her to go to work before giving the okay later that afternoon to whomever the hell he hired to beat his wife to death.

60.

MOLOTOV

In a dank alley, on the dark edge of dusk, illuminated by the sallow of a yellow lightbulb and enveloped by the stink of a Dumpster behind which he stood, Justin Chase felt, at last, after six years of hiding, strangely at home.

If you had asked him before Birdie Grackle had shown up in his life, he would have told you he felt most at home within the emptiness of his third-level room, with its floor of tatami and its bare walls. But now, giving in to the force of events that had overtaken him like a rogue wave, he had let his emotions rise and take control, roiling and messy as they inevitably were. Those emotions had led him from hope to lust to despair to outright fury. And now here he was, smelling the rotting vegetables and stinking fried gunk tossed into the garbage bin. Putridity inside, putridity out. Perfect equilibrium at last.

Ahh, humanity.

So why was he here, in the alley behind Zenzibar, the bar from which he had been fired the night before, waiting to purchase an illegal firearm? Because he had tried to turn Birdie Grackle in, and that had not worked. And then he had intended to pay him off to get him out of Justin's life, but that was before he learned the truth about who the hell Birdie

Grackle really was and why he had shown up at Zenzibar that first night. There was no way that son of a bitch was going to get a dime from Justin Chase. Which left one option.

A streetlight's dim glow bathed the far end of the alley. Suddenly, within the glow, was a shadow, as much a boy's as a man's, thin legs, thin shoulders, a head of long bushy hair. The silhouette was as distinguishable as a fingerprint.

Cody.

Justin had set the handoff here because he never knew anymore who was staking out his house. He had headed west from Fitler Square, cut through a couple of alleys, walked north and east and south again, all the while checking behind to see if he was being followed. The fact that he sensed nothing only deepened his suspicion. Where was Detective Scott? Why was he not following him like a hound dog? Had the detective found someone else to tail? Had he stopped caring? After a long circular walk he allowed himself to slip into the alley behind the bar and wait.

Cody approached slowly, and with a slight limp that hadn't been there the day before. His face stayed in shadow as he grew closer. In his hand he held a paper bag. Justin stepped out from the shield of the Dumpster. Cody reflexively flinched.

"It's just me," said Justin.

"Are you sure you want this?" said Cody.

"I'm sure."

"No good can come from this."

"You'd be surprised."

"I'm afraid I won't be. I got you a Glock forty. The clip is full, like you asked. Smith and Wesson cartridges. I can get you more ammunition if you need it."

"I won't need it. Let me see."

When Cody stepped forward to hand over the bag, his face was sliced by a shard of yellow light. His eye was black and swollen shut, a side of his jaw had swelled to the size of a grapefruit.

"What the hell happened to you?" said Justin.

Cody backed away into the shadows. "The sure thing wasn't so sure."

"I thought if it didn't come through, you were going to work it out."

"Solly didn't like my plan. Solly apparently didn't like my teeth either, since his boys knocked two of them out."

"Maybe you need the gun."

"I can either fight or run. What do you think I should do?"

"I see your point."

"I have some options, though. Well, one actually. A partnership of sorts. I have until tonight to decide if I should pursue it. It's not something I'm looking forward to, but it could be lucrative as hell."

"That sounds good."

"It would be nice to get rich, but the price is pretty damn steep. Don't know yet if I can muster up what it takes to pay it."

Justin opened the bag, pulled out the black automatic, hefted it in his hand. It was solidly heavy and it shone dully in the yellow light.

"Do you know how to use that thing?" said Cody.

Justin gripped the handle, pointed the gun at the Dumpster, and ejected the magazine. The magazine was full. In one smooth motion, he pulled the slide open, checked the chamber, let the slide snap back into place. He aimed the gun at a box in the alley and squeezed the trigger. He could feel the ping as the firing pin sprung forward. He nodded with satisfaction as he slammed the magazine back home.

"I guess you've handled one before," said Cody.

"This one place I worked had a Beretta nine millimeter

behind the bar. You had to be trained to use it before you poured. The pull's pretty light on the Glock."

"They eased it up. Guy who gave it to me told me to keep my finger out of the guard until I was ready to kill something."

"This is just what I need."

"And I thought I was in the deep."

"It will all be over tonight. It's just a matter of who shows up."

"Who do you think it will be?"

"You don't really want to know, do you, Cody?"

"Not really. All I know is that from what I see in your eye, I sure as hell don't want to be on the wrong end of it."

"How much?" said Justin as he put the gun back in the bag and rolled the top up tight.

"Four hundred."

Justin took out of his back pocket the thick envelope his brother had given him, opened it, and slipped out four bills. Cody stared, transfixed by the wad, before stepping forward and taking the money.

"I guess it's a big night for both of us," said Cody.

"I guess so. Good luck, dude."

"You too, Justin. It's probably the last time we'll see each other."

"Probably."

"You made a good drink."

"You drank a good drink."

"I think you made them better than I drank them. I'm going to miss you, man."

"Me too."

There was an awkward moment where they stood there, the two of them, unsure of what to do next. And then a strange emotion swelled in Justin's throat. Cody wasn't really a friend, he was more a business associate, the kind that continually drift in and out of your life. Losing touch with Cody wouldn't normally have caused even a burp's worth of distress, but suddenly Justin was feeling like he was losing his oldest and dearest buddy. And actually, thinking about how much Justin had cut himself off from the world in the last six years, maybe he was.

Then the strangest thing of all happened. The two men hugged. How it happened Justin wasn't sure; one moment he was standing there, wondering why he felt so rotten, and the next he was hugging Cody. A man hug, with the gun, all hard jabbing angles, between them.

"Now get out of here," said Cody when they stepped away from each other, "before I start crying into my beer."

"When the hell did you ever order a beer?" said Justin.

"Buy me one next time I see you."

"Done," said Justin, backing away. He took one last look at the small silhouette before turning, certain he would never see it again.

61.

A PINSKY

The first person Derek ever killed was a kid in the neighborhood named Pinsky. Pinsky was a huge pink-faced kid who pushed around the little kids and often made fun of Derek. Derek was used to being made fun of. Pinsky was not the only one who harassed Derek when he was a boy and Pinsky was not even the worst. But Derek always knew who was mean to him and who was nice, and Pinsky was mean to him.

But that was not why Derek had to kill Pinsky.

One afternoon, Derek was walking along the creek in the woods, looking for salamanders and kicking at the leaves, when he heard a wild screeching in the distance. He moved carefully through the trees until he saw Pinsky playing with a cat. But the cat was not playing, the cat was screeching. Pinsky had tied the cat to a tree trunk and was trying to set the cat's tail on fire with a small plastic lighter. As the cat clawed frantically and Pinsky snorted with delight, the dark scent of the cat's singed fur hit Derek like a scream.

Derek does not remember how he crossed the ground and grabbed hold of Pinsky. It happened so fast, all of it. But he does remember the feel of Pinsky's head jerking this way and that and Pinsky's legs kicking out as Derek squeezed harder and harder and harder. Until Pinsky's head stopped its jerking. And the kicking ceased. And the weight in Derek's arms went slack. And all that Derek heard was the squealing of the cat and some strange pounding in his ears.

It took Derek a while to calm the cat enough so he could loosen the knots and untie her. Pinsky did not do anything to stop him. Once free, the cat bolted away, stopped and looked back, and then disappeared. With the cat gone, Derek himself retreated from the scene and hid behind a tree. He waited for Pinsky to wake up.

And waited.

And the longer he waited, the more agitated he became, pacing back and forth, jumping up and down, slamming his head into a tree trunk. He was agitated not because of what he had done—he had only done what he had to do—but because he was certain now that everyone would be really, really mad at him. Not his Grammy, who took care of him whenever they took his father away and who never got mad, but everyone else. So mad, maybe, that nothing would ever be the same. They would not let him in the school anymore, they would not give him free ice cream at the drugstore. Finally, he became too restless to stay and he tore off home, ran up to his room, bit his lip over and over as he waited for them to come.

But they did not come. Not that day, not the next. Even after they found Pinsky's body, they did not come, at least not for him. Two other boys were picked up by the police and questioned, but never Derek. It was like they could not see him, like he was wearing an invisibility cape. But that was not all. With Pinsky gone, things were better at school. Kids were nicer to him, there were more smiles, everyone was a little bit happier.

Except, of course, the Pinskys, who eventually moved away and were never heard from again.

He never thought he would ever do it again, ever. But the second time it happened, the second time he squeezed someone until they stopped being, there was no choice about it again, the way that guy had jumped on Sammy D in the dark like that. And after that first time with Sammy D, Sammy kept making sure it happened again and again. And Derek did as he was told, as if Derek had no choice in the matter, until the killing became less a big deal and more of a habit. And then less of a habit and more something that gave Derek a sense of pride.

But still, even now, after all those times, and after learning that he is good at it, he never forgets the agitation he felt as he waited for Pinsky to get up and tell everyone what he had done. Terror, self-hatred, self-pity, anger, sadness. Like the worst pain he had ever felt, knowing that what happened could never be undone and how much trouble he was going to get in for doing it. The memory stands beside him, always, like a ghost. It is the image of that frightened kid in the woods, banging his head against a tree trunk, that makes him so careful in his jobs. And it is why he is happy that Vern finally gave him the job this evening. It is a bit of untidiness that has been weighing on Derek and that Derek needs to clean up.

But tonight, even though he is happy about the one job, the ghost beside him is spinning with agitation. Because tonight, Derek is not only going to kill once, he is going to have to kill twice. He knows who the first one will be, but who the second will be is still undecided.

"Derek." A loud whisper in the park. "Where are you?"

Derek stands and slips from beneath the prickly bush where he has been hiding. Cody is standing in the shadows by the bench, looking around.

"Here," says Derek.

Cody's head spins toward him. "Oh, wow, yes. I didn't see you. Where were you?"

"Hiding."

"Hiding? Why?"

"I hide sometimes. Especially before a job."

"You don't like doing the jobs, Derek?"

"They are just jobs. But sometimes I hide."

"From what?"

"Nothing."

"Maybe you shouldn't be doing something that makes you want to hide."

"What else would I do?" says Derek. There is something lumpy on Cody's face. Derek reaches a hand to Cody's face. "What happened to Cody?"

"I had a disagreement with some guys."

"About what?"

"Money."

"Do you need more money? Because I can get you money. If you help me, I can get you lots of money."

"I know, Derek," says Cody. "But I don't know."

"It is just a trick, like the trick with the penny and the quarter. Come on, I will show you."

"I don't know."

"There's money at the place I am going tonight. Lots of money. I am just supposed to pick it up. You can have it if you need it."

"How much?"

"A lot. A pile, Vern said. Come on."

Cody steps away and doesn't do anything. He just stands there, his body still, and Derek waits patiently, waits for a decision. Something will have to happen here, he cannot just let

Cody wander around knowing all he knows. He trusts Cody, but Rodney taught him that trust is for fools. So he waits, waits for Cody to decide.

And then Cody nods, like he does not want to nod, like a hand is behind his head pushing it up and down and up and down. Nodding.

"Good," says Derek. "Glad. Let's go."

Derek heads out of the park. He looks back once and Cody is not moving, but suddenly Derek is not worried. He knows Cody will follow. The money will drag him along. And the next time he looks back, Cody is there, walking behind him, hands in pockets and shoulders hunched, but walking with him to the job. Their job now.

Derek has mapped it out in his head and made a pass in the afternoon with Vern to remind himself exactly where he is going. This way, and then that, and then this. Winding his way through the streets, avoiding the park, and coming up through the alley to the back part of the little house just the way Vern showed him.

"Stand there," says Derek, pointing to a spot between the door and a wedge of the street just off the alley.

Cody steps where he is told. "Who lives here?" says Cody.

"Just a guy," said Derek.

"I think I know someone who lives near here somewhere," says Cody.

"A friend?"

"Sort of."

"That is nice."

"This guy inside. What did he do?"

"He has money," says Derek, taking the slim pack of tools out of his pocket. He runs his finger along the slot of the lock and then picks out a wrench that fits the hole.

"But what did he do to deserve what you're going to do?"

"Vern makes that decision. I just do the job."

"Vern, huh?"

"He tells me what to do. He plans the jobs and takes care of the money and takes care of me. I need Vern, or someone like Vern."

"You said the money was inside."

"For Vern." Derek takes his eye off the door and looks at Cody, jiggling in the street like he has to pee. "But you can have it if you want."

"Then what about Vern?"

"You would be Vern," says Derek. He turns back to the door, looks at the lock for a moment, and then puts his hand on the knob. It turns sweetly.

"Uh oh," says Derek.

"What?"

"It was not locked."

"What does that mean?"

"It means he is waiting for me."

"Maybe we should go."

"No, it is okay. Vern said I needed to talk to him to get the money."

"And then you'll go."

Derek puts a finger up to his lips before he opens the door just wide enough to slip inside. He waits for Cody to follow. Cody eventually does.

"What do you do now?" whispers Cody.

"Find the job."

62.

MAD MONK

Justin, sitting cross-legged near the back wall of his tiny third-floor room, about ten feet from the stairway, felt something stir downstairs, something so slight it was less a stir than the thought of a stir. He wondered if he imagined it, but even so, he lifted his hands from his knees and put them in the pockets of his loose silk robe. With his right hand, he fingered the grip of the gun.

This wasn't the first time his nerves had sparked at a scrap of sound. He was trying to maintain his cool, the cool he'd need in the coming confrontation, but he was failing. Three days ago he would have been better at it, would have let the fear and fret flow out of the pool of his being, leaving nothing but his barkeep's level affect, but three days ago he still believed in the tooth fairy. He had lost the equipoise he had been pursuing since he had been handed the book in the asylum, had lost the very notion that his being was a pool, had lost it all and was glad. For he knew now there was evil in the world, just as there was evil in his blood, and no placid little pond was enough to fend against its awful hand.

It was the photograph in the lawyer's office that showed it to him plain, once he allowed himself to accept the truth of it.

It wasn't a strange and remarkable coincidence that his father and his mother's murderer were in the same prison at the same time. It was as natural as breathing, because they both were one and the same. And what of Birdie Grackle? He was merely a rancid figment of his father's deranged imagination. He was bait leading Justin to find an alternative suspect to present at the precious motion for a new trial. And Justin, always the sucker, took the bait like a hungry marlin and towed that boat right into the harbor.

But Justin's father was still stuck in jail, which left Justin with Vernon Bickham to deal with. Vernon Bickham had been up for release and thereby held something of great value that Justin's father might never know, freedom. And so Justin's father had sent Vernon Bickham out into the world to wreak all kinds of havoc in order to win Justin's father's freedom. And it didn't matter who Vernon mauled in the process. Uncle Timmy? His changed story was enough to get the motion for the new trial heard but not granted; his newfound lie would have fallen apart on the stand, so he had to go. And Janet Moss? She was doomed as soon as Justin found her, because as a suspect, she was first-rate until the cops looked closer, so Vern had to stop the cops from looking closer. And Justin? He was first tempted by the ghostly Birdie Grackle and then beaten and warned to stop looking into his mother's murder, all so he could be duped into searching the ruins of his past for his father's answer.

Cody had mentioned that the man he knew as Birdie Grackle was going to hit it rich on some insurance scam, and Justin could very well imagine exactly what he had in mind. One million dollars, the insurance payout on the death of Eleanor Chase, denied by the insurance company because of Mackenzie Chase's conviction. But it would have to be paid if he was found not guilty. And the benefits would be signed over, immediately, either legally or extralegally, to one Vernon Bickham if all went as planned.

Son of a bitch.

But the extra ten thousand, that wasn't Justin's father's idea, that was Bickham's own little play, to tide him over until the million came through. Justin could see it on his father's face in the prison visiting room, the disbelief and then the anger when he realized this whole brutal attempt to get himself out of his life sentence could founder on the shoals of the greed of his own fictional character, Birdie Grackle. Because if the cops got wind that Janet Moss hadn't really killed herself in grief over what she had done, but had instead been murdered for maximum evidentiary impact, the ruthless cavalcade of lies and death would all be for naught.

So now Vernon Bickham was coming. Or Vernon's muscle that Cody had warned him about, no doubt the homunculus that had delivered the brutal warning in this very house, was coming. Or maybe both of them were coming. But all that was important was that someone was coming. Justin had made sure of it, by telling his father about the fingerprints and the plan to go to the police, leaving this one night as his father's one chance to nip the destruction of his carefully laid plan in the bud. Justin's father would unleash his hound, and someone would be coming, because there was too much at stake for him not to come, and Justin would be ready.

He had left the doors to his house open and had left the lights dim, except for the bright light burning on the third floor, all to lead his killer up to him step-by-step. Resting on the tatami mat in front of Justin was the envelope, the money fanning out of its opening in an eye-catching display of the most delicious mint green. And in the pocket of his robe, opposite the gun, was a voice recorder, ready to be flicked on as soon as Justin heard the inevitable footfalls rising up the stairs. No matter who showed, he would refuse to give the money to anyone other than Birdie, because with Birdie there would be a moment of conversation before the violence flared, Justin was sure of it. The Birdie Grackle who had stepped into Zenzibar, no matter how unreal, couldn't resist a little crowing, a tall tale or two, the deranged aphorism. And Justin would let him talk. Justin wanted the world to hear what Birdie Grackle had to say, he wanted the world to be certain beyond certainties about his father's guilt.

And then Justin would kill him, and in so doing, kill his own father's hopes dead.

Another sound from below, just as faint as the first, as much a ghost of a stir as anything else. But it was enough to let him know. The fingers that were tapping on the edge of the gun's grip now wrapped around it. The first bullet was already chambered. He turned on the voice recorder with his left hand and placed his right forefinger on the outside of the trigger guard.

Derek is not happy. Vern said the back door would be locked, but the door was not locked. Vern said that the job would not be expecting him, but something in the small house gives Derek the sense that he is very much expected. The lights on the first floor are dimmed, but not off, so that Derek can conveniently make his way through the kitchen without banging into the stove or table. And there is a brighter light bouncing down the stairs, as if a sign. *I'm up here, expecting you.* Vern told him the job would not be armed, but if Vern is wrong about everything else, he might be wrong about that, too.

Derek backs away from jobs if they feel wrong to him. If something does not match the information he has been given, or if something starts making Derek afraid, he will walk. There have been enough close calls in his time for him to want to avoid any more, even if the people who take care of him get mad. Sometimes very mad. But he simply says, "You do it if you want," and they shut up. Usually they work out a new plan and Derek then does what he has to do. But one time Rodney beat him over the money they lost by Derek's backing away. That was just before their last job together in Baltimore. But by then, Derek had already met Tree.

Derek wants to back away from this job, things do not seem right. But Cody is with him now and he does not know if Cody will give him another chance. And the money that is waiting for him is what he needs to get Cody to go with him when he leaves the city. He is done with Vern, wants to be with Cody, and does not want to do what he will have to do to Cody if things go wrong. So he does not turn around like his head is telling him to. Instead he turns to Cody and whispers.

"The money is upstairs."

"Do we have to do this? This place smells familiar."

"Were you here before?"

"No, never. But..."

"But what?"

"I think we should go."

"After we get the money."

"But you're not just going to grab the money, are you?"

"He saw me."

"That was his crime?"

"It is like the girl in that house," says Derek. "My Grammy always told me to clean up after myself."

"We're going to hell."

"I thought Kentucky."

"Kentucky?"

"Someone told me there are horses in Kentucky."

"Yeah, there are horses in Kentucky."

"And no one in Kentucky will hit you in the face."

"I suppose not," says Cody.

"Derek is going upstairs for the money. Will Cody wait?"

"I guess."

"Good," says Derek before heading for the light. He reaches the stairwell, stops, looks up and listens. Nothing to see and not a peep. But someone is up there, he can tell. He remembers the house, the first level, the second level, the empty third level with the soft green floor. The job will be there, on the third level, waiting for him. Derek hopes the job does not have a gun. It will be so much easier if the job does not have a gun. He thinks of just turning around again, but Cody is behind him. And Kentucky is in front of him. And the job is the only thing in the way.

Slowly he starts climbing the stairs.

Justin heard a shuffling static downstairs, as if someone had turned his TV on to a distant UHF station. Except he didn't have a TV downstairs. He gripped the gun a little tighter. Vernon Bickham hadn't come alone.

This wasn't a surprise, but it wasn't welcome either. First it meant that he might be outgunned, which was a sickening thought. But even more sickening was the possibility that he might have to kill a second man. Justin was shaky on this whole kill thing. He had a gun, yes, and he meant to use it, yes, but on Birdie Grackle only, a cackling figment of his father's imagination. Vernon Bickham was the actor intoning Grackle's lines, true, but it was Birdie he was out to kill. Shooting Birdie would be like shooting a piece of his father's rotten soul; killing Birdie Grackle would be the same as killing dead his father's dreams of freedom.

But what about this other guy? A lug, no doubt, hired muscle, just a tool being used by his father's tool, and by the sound of the voice none too bright. Justin used to watch James Bond movies and wonder how Bond could so casually dispatch all the hired hands manning the missile launch sites. Dr. No was evil, sure, but what about the saps who signed on for the cash? Maybe just to support their families. Shooting them, one after the other in an orgy of stoolie death, to Justin seemed a bit harsh justicewise. But at least Bond had the fate of the world to consider; what was Justin's excuse for dispatching some hired hand?

A creak of the stairs answered his questions: self-fucking-defense.

He took the gun out of his pocket, no need for subterfuge now. He aimed the muzzle at the opening to the steep and narrow stairs, and put his finger inside the trigger guard. If there were two, he couldn't wait. The narrow stairway was his best chance. He'd have to go all Thermopylae on their asses.

The creaking turned to footsteps. He gently stroked the trigger with his finger. The footsteps rose higher up the stairs, the climber not anymore trying to hide his presence. How arrogant was that? Like death presenting a calling card. And then he heard a voice.

"I'm coming up."

The voice was slow, thick, with a lazy tongue, the voice of a big child trying to enunciate each word very carefully. Justin recognized it right off, the voice of the strangely shaped man who had beaten him in the first floor of his house and given his rote warning.

"Who the hell are you?" said Justin.

"Derek."

"What are you doing in my house?"

"Birdie told me to come."

"Did he send you the last time when you shoved my face into the floor?"

"Yes. Can I come up?"

"Why?"

"To get the money. Birdie told me to get the money."

"He did, did he? Are you alone?"

"Only I am coming up the stairs."

The last couple of answers comforted Justin a bit. This Derek hadn't lied about beating the hell out of him or being alone, maybe he wasn't lying about just being an errand boy sent for the money.

"Stay where you are," said Justin. "I have the money, but I'm only giving it to Birdie himself."

"He cannot come."

"Where is he?"

"Somewhere else."

"It has to be him. Go down and find Birdie and tell him to come himself. I'll be here, waiting."

"I cannot tell Birdie that."

"Why not?"

"Birdie would be mad. He hits me when he's mad."

"Then you should find a better companion."

"I am trying."

"Don't come up."

"I am coming up."

"Don't."

Justin waited nervously as the footsteps started up the stairway again. The gun suddenly felt heavy in his hand. It was one thing letting your baser instincts take you on a ride—anger and lust both could be so damn exhilarating—but it was a whole different thing when the other party was there in the flesh. How could he shoot someone like Derek?

He was still wondering that same thing when the strangest sight imaginable became visible in the doorway.

Derek likes the sound of the job's voice. He does not sound mean or arrogant, mostly just scared. That is good. But the way he is talking makes it clear to Derek that Vern was wrong again and the job has a gun. But even though he has a gun, he does not sound like someone who wants to use it. Occasionally, a job will have a gun but not know what to do with it. Or even if the job knows what to do with it, he does not want to do what he has to do with it. It is not easy jumping over that barrier. Derek had leaped it with Pinsky, but there was a cat involved. There is no cat here, just Derek. Derek is able to do what he has to; the job, maybe not. That is an advantage.

But Derek does not want the job to see his face. He likes working in darkness; the shadow is his natural habitat. Some people can look at Derek's face and see everything he is thinking. "You got no guile," Rodney used to say, whatever "guile" means. Derek just assumes it means that Derek is not a good liar. One look at his face, and the job will know exactly what Derek intends.

With the old druggie guy, the place was too dark to get a good look, but the room on the third floor is brightly lit. There is no way to get into the room and to the job without the job seeing his face. Then if something goes wrong, the agitation will start again. Somehow Derek has to turn off the light in the upstairs room before the job sees his face. He should have done it before, gone into the basement and cut all the power like Tree taught him, but Vern said the job would not have a gun and he was afraid Cody might leave if he did not move quickly. So now here he is, up the stairs, and Vern was wrong again.

From the sound of the voice, Derek can place the job toward the back of the room, just in front of the wall opposite the stairs. There is only one way to go into the room so that the job does not see his face.

Derek turns around and walks backward up the stairs, turning his head away from the entrance as he reaches the top landing. Then he raises his hands high and stands at the entrance with his back to the room.

"What are you doing?" says the job.

"I need to get the money," says Derek. He takes a step backward into the room, his hands still up in the air. His back feels like there is a cockroach scratching at the skin between his shoulder blades. Derek is feeling the gun aimed right at his back. That is interesting. He takes a step further back and the scratching grows deeper. It feels good.

"Don't be an idiot," says the job. "Get out of here."

"I am an idiot," says Derek, examining the area around the door and finding exactly what he is looking for. "But I need to get the money."

"I have a gun."

"I know."

"I'll shoot you."

"I am only doing my job."

"Where the hell is Birdie?"

"He said he had to give someone a message."

"Who?"

"He does not tell me things."

"Turn around."

"You will shoot me if I turn around."

"No, I won't."

"Promise."

"I promise."

"Okay," says Derek.

Derek lowers his hands and begins to slowly whirl to his left. As he does, he reaches his now-hidden right hand toward the light switch he had spotted beside the door. In one quick and savage sequence, he clicks off the light, leaps to the side, and rolls with all his weight toward the man with the gun.

As soon as Derek feels his weight slam into the man, a huge sound explodes next to his ear.

63.

BLACK-EYED CODY

There was an instant after the lights went out that Justin was functionally blind. It was only a blink and a half, if that, before his eyes adjusted enough to see clearly what had happened. But by then it was too late.

Before the lights went out, the strangely shaped Derek was standing just inside the entrance of the tatami room, his arms up in the air. The way he was standing, he was like an optical illusion; by the mere shape of him, it was impossible to tell if Derek was facing Justin or not. But if he was facing Justin, then the hunched figure was made even more grotesque by a face that was full of short cropped hair, like a freak show attraction or a Magritte painting. Justin had his gun pointed right at the man's back, but there was no question of firing. He had been indoctrinated by too many movie westerns, he wasn't going to shoot a varmint in the back, especially a varmint that seemed as limited as Derek. So Justin told Derek to turn around, and as Derek began to turn, the lights suddenly went dead.

In the instant it took for Justin's eyes to adjust to the darkness, Derek was gone. And then something huge and hard slammed into Justin's left side. His finger slipped on the trigger and the gun went off with a shocking crack as a blue flash spurted from the barrel.

Before Justin could recover from the trauma of the shot, something grabbed hold of his right arm, and his arm was slammed elbow first into the mat. Another futile explosion. Justin tried to bring his hand around so that he could shoot off this huge mass of muscle that had latched onto his back, but as he tried, his arm was slammed again into the tatami floor, and suddenly he wasn't anymore gripping the gun, just gripping air. And something close to steel was wrapping itself around his neck.

He could feel him now behind him, this Derek, one arm around his neck, another gripping his head, putting unbearable pressure on Justin's nose.

Justin tried to kick himself violently into his attacker, but the kicks swished empty in the air. He grappled at the arms entombing his face and neck, grappled and failed, his own feeble hands no match for his attacker's iron limbs.

He reached backward, felt the short bristly hair on the man's scalp, tried to slip his gouging fingers down to the eyes, but this Derek was burrowing his face so hard into Justin's spine that it was impossible.

The darkness grew darker, Justin kicked for air. He grabbed one of Derek's tiny ears and twisted, and twisted harder, and tried to pull the damn thing off, eliciting a roar from behind him.

But things were growing blacker, and the struggle to breathe overtook him. He let go of the ear to grab futilely at the unmoving arm around his neck. He kicked again, involuntarily this time, listlessly and again to no effect. He felt things slipping away, his breath, the light, his anger and fear, his hatred.

And in a moment of stillness, he heard the words from the book he had been given in the asylum, the very words he had wished he had known to whisper into his mother's ear as she lay in her blood on that marble floor, words being spoken now directly to him.

The time has arisen for you to seek the path. They came to him, those words, in a soft, lovely voice, a voice as familiar to him as his own breath. *Your breathing is about to cease, and you are about to experience that reality wherein all things are like the void and the cloudless sky.*

It was the voice of his mother, guiding him through the next stages of his existence. *At this moment, know thyself and abide willingly and peacefully in that state. For I, too, am with you.*

And he felt just then the strangest bit of grace, as if his greatest fear had been soothed, as if his mother had found her salvation, as if she were coming back to help him find his own, as if the sufferings of the world were already peeling off him like the bitter skin of a rare and precious fruit. And he could simply close his eyes and drift away into the void. Toward the voice. Toward the sweet and loving voice of his mother.

A light burst through his closed eyes, a painfully bright light that jerked him from the realm of utter peace and dragged him back into a harsh and painful reality. A reality where some deranged goon was choking him to death. His eyes opened and, even as the brute strangled him from behind, there was someone standing in front of him with a gun in his hand.

"Let him go, Derek," said the man standing in front of Justin, in a voice familiar but wildly out of place. A few blinks later, as the disappointment of being jerked back from the lovely void alighted off him like a flock of birds, Justin knew exactly who it was standing there with the gun.

"I need to finish," said Derek.

"No, you don't," said Cody. "Not this one. Let him go."

"But Vern will be mad."

"Don't worry about Vern."

"I need Vern."

"No, you don't, not anymore. Let this one go and I'll take care of you."

"Promise."

"Yes, I promise," said Cody.

"Okay."

A blast of fresh air gushed down Justin's throat as the brutal pressure eased on his face and neck. Justin greedily gulped down more air, even as he grabbed at the loosened arms, trying to pull them off.

"What the hell?" gasped Justin. "Cody?"

"Shut up, Justin," said Cody. "There's nothing you can say that will help. Let him go, Derek."

Justin, completely released now from Derek's grip, collapsed onto the tatami mats, still wheezing, grabbing at his own neck, as if the arm were still wrapped around it.

"He saw my face," said Derek, standing behind Justin.

"He won't say anything."

"How do you know?"

"I'll take care of it. That's what you want me to do, take care of things, right?"

"Yes. I have to go. Will you go with me, Cody?"

"Sure I will."

"Away from the city."

"That's the deal."

"As soon as I tidy up Vern."

"I figured that would have to happen. Just leave Justin be."

"If that is what Cody wants."

"That's what I want. Now go downstairs and wait for me."

Cody stepped aside and watched as Derek walked by him and started climbing down the stairs. Cody, still with the gun, weighed it in his hand as he looked at Justin.

"Nice shooting," said Cody. "You riddled him."

Justin struggled up to lean on an elbow. "I wasn't trying to kill the kid. The gun just went off."

"Twice by accident?"

"Sort of."

"I told you they loosened the pull."

"It was looser than I thought."

"I'm going to have to take this back to protect you and the innocent people of Philadelphia, if there are any left." He gestured at the envelope and the mess of bills scattered now over the floor. "Is that the money you were going to pay that Vern guy?"

"All of it but the four hundred I paid you."

"I'm going to have to take the money, too."

"You're not serious."

"Why don't you pick it up for me. And don't forget I have your gun."

"There's that, true."

"And I saved your life."

"Yes, you did. Who the hell is that guy anyway?"

"That's Derek. I met him outside the hotel when I followed your guy Birdie."

"He's a menace."

"You don't know the half of it." Cody waved the gun. "Let's go, I need to get the fuck out of here, and fast."

"You're serious."

"As a fifth of bourbon, baby." Cody leaned over, picked up the empty envelope, tossed it at Justin. Justin stared at Cody for a moment, and then rose to his knees, crawled over to the money and started stuffing the envelope with it.

"When you were talking about the partnership opportunity you had been offered, was it with that Derek?"

"He's something, he is. An actual phenom, except he doesn't throw speedballs."

"Then what does he do?"

"This and that."

"He was sent to murder me."

"It's his special talent."

"And he's going to tidy up Vern."

"He's very neat."

"For a killer, you mean."

"He's a force of nature is what he is."

"Like a monster."

"More like a gun." Cody raised the Glock and hefted it in his hand. "All he needs is someone to aim him. And I'm going to be the one to do it. That's what he means by taking care of him."

"And you can't find him something honest to do?"

"Like make little Kewpie dolls? He's a fricking genius at what he does. You should see the way he opens locks, the way he goes about his business. He's a better killer than you are a bartender. Between the two of us, Derek and me, we have one talent. But so far he's been aimed at all the wrong people. Maybe I'll aim him at the right ones for a change."

"Have Derek, will travel, all wrongs righted, for a price?"

"There's a lot of crooks who want to kill other crooks. And you want to know something, Justin? I don't have a problem with that, especially as I'm going to have to buy some new teeth."

"Even if it's for the right reasons, it's wrong, you know that."

"Do I? Derek's a killer, sure. But so is this, and you went out and bought it from me. What did you intend to do with it, Justin? You meant to kill, for what you thought were the right reasons. So how will what I'll be doing be any different?"

"He's going to eat you alive."

"Maybe, and maybe he's already started. You don't want to know my dreams lately, rough stuff. But there are some benefits to the whole arrangement, too. Like the money. And the power's not bad, either. And along with the money and the power will come the women."

"When did you decide all this?"

"For certain?"

"Yeah, for certain."

"When he had his arm wrapped around your neck."

"So you agreed to it all to save my life."

"That's one interpretation."

"What's the other?"

"I'm sick of being poor, I'm sick of being the guy who's afraid his bets won't come in. I'm sick of getting beat on by two-bit leg breakers. Let those assholes be afraid of me for once. Are we done here?"

Justin gathered up the last of the bills, put them in the envelope, tossed it to Cody. "Yeah, we're done. And you're taking my money because?"

"Because I have the gun."

"It's my gun."

Cody opened the envelope, riffled the bills, took out four hundreds and tossed them onto the tatami. "Something tells me I'll be needing it more than you."

"Be careful, they loosened up the pull."

"I'll send you a postcard. Remember that favor you owed me?"

"Yeah, I remember."

"Well, here it is. All I'm asking is that you keep your mouth shut about me and Derek. I'll take it from there. Can you do that for me?"

Justin looked at Cody for a long moment, not sure what the hell to do. Then he decided. Cody had just saved his life, he owed him something. And Justin sure as hell wasn't a masked avenger out to right all wrongs, he was just a guy with one goal in his life now, and stopping Cody wasn't it.

"Good luck," said Justin finally.

"Name a drink after me, maybe."

"Something fruity?"

"Not anymore. My tastes are changing."

"How about a Black-Eyed Cody. Tequila, salt, pickle juice, shot of Tabasco. It'll taste like a punch in the face."

"Sounds wicked. Perfect."

With a final nod, Cody headed down the stairs.

And Justin lay down on the tatami, surprised to find how calm he was. It is funny how focused the mind can become in the face of mortal danger. All he needed was a deranged hit man to attack him every morning and his life would be perfect. He thought through what had just happened, how Cody's life was going to be twisted in all bad directions from here on in, and how he himself had dodged death's dance. And then something that Derek had said hit him with the full force of its meaning. He had asked where Birdie Grackle was and Derek had replied, *He said he had to give someone a message.*

What kind of message, and to whom?

Justin lurched to standing and staggered toward the stairs. He caught his balance and then made his way as quickly as he could down to the second level, where his futon lay open on the floor. Beside it was a small crate, turned over to create a table, and on it was a lamp and his cell phone. He picked up the phone and made a call.

"Yes?"

"Frank?" said Justin. "Is everything okay?"

"Who is this? Justin? Yeah everything's fine, sure. You ready to give back that money already?"

"Well, not really. Something came up. But is anybody there? Is everything okay?"

"Sure, kid. What could be wrong?"

"Just do me a favor, all right? Don't let anybody in the house. Hunker down for the night. Or better yet, take Cindy and the kids on a jaunt and hunker down in a hotel somewhere."

"What are you talking about? What's going on?"

"Just trust me on this, okay? I'll tell you everything later, but it could be a tough night for someone. I'm getting out of here myself. Just do it."

"You sure?"

"Yeah."

"Okay, little brother. I'll do it. And you'll tell me about everything tomorrow, including what happened to my money?"

"I'll tell you what I can," said Justin.

When he hung up, Justin paced a bit. He was going to follow his own advice and get the hell out of Dodge himself. Or at least out of this death trap of a house where there was no place to hide. He wondered a moment at where he would go, and then made a call. The phone rang. And rang.

No answer.

64.

ARISTOCRAT ROYAL

"All I have is some vodka and ice," said Annie from the kitchen. "Will that do?"

"In a pinch," said the old man in a growly Texas drawl. He was standing in her living room, leaning forward at the waist, his lips cruelly pursed. "And just between you and me, what say we forget about the ice."

"How many fingers?"

"A handful," said the old man. "It's been a day."

"Yes, it has," said Annie, pouring a little for herself over ice and a good long pour for the stranger. He had buzzed up from outside, claiming to be an old friend of Mac Chase and asking if he could come on up and talk to her a bit. She had hesitated, but when he mentioned that he also knew Justin, her curiosity had defeated her caution and now here he was, a decrepit old man with yellow hair and false teeth, wearing a ratty checked jacket, standing loose-limbed and ragged in her apartment.

"This is about it," she said, bringing over the glass. His sallow eyes lit up at the sight of it, as if it were half-full of some magic elixir rather than the cheapest vodka in the State Store. "The bottle's dead."

"You with that glass is about the two prettiest things I ever done seen," he said when he took the drink from her hand before raising it high. "As we say in Texas: To wine, women, song, and vice. To syphilis, the clap, crabs, and lice. I've had them all, the best ones twice."

She laughed at that as the old man slurped down a slug of the vodka. The bawdy toast was so inappropriate coming from this strange and desiccated man that she couldn't help herself. She was feeling unaccountably confident and strong, able to laugh off things that would have bothered her before, as if Justin had performed a sort of alchemy, transmuting her from a substance dreary and leaden into something far shinier.

"So how do you know Mackenzie?" she said.

"Oh, we're old friends. You mind I set a spell?"

"No, please sit. Of course."

"Thank ye, ma'am," he said, dropping onto the couch. "Not everyone is so hospitable to an old man already most ways out the door."

"You look better than that, Mr.—"

"Bickham, Vernon Bickham. My friends call me Vern."

"You look healthy enough to be with us a long time, Mr. Bickham."

"You lie nice, almost as nice as you look," said Vern. He took another slurp. "Old Mac sure could pick them."

"So how did you meet Mackenzie? In school?"

He laughed at that, and she felt immediately stupid, like Flounder in *Animal House*.

"No, missy, we was in the shack together."

"Oh," she said, taking an involuntary step back. But of course, she should have known from the ravaged look of his face and the tattoos peeking out from his shirtsleeves. "Then how do you know Justin, too?"

"Oh, the boy and me, we had our run-ins, though I don't expect that we'll have any no more, seeing as how things turned out."

"And how have things turned out?"

"Why don't you sit down, miss."

"Is something wrong with Justin?"

"By now I'm sure everything's righted up perfectly. Sit on down. I got a story to tell that you'll want to hear."

"I'm not sure I do."

"Maybe I don't blame you."

Annie looked at the old man carefully, trying to figure out what he was after. Probably money, and she was ready to pay him just to get him out of there. It had seemed a clever idea letting him into the apartment at first, trying to wile out what information she could for Justin, but it seemed not so clever now. The man scared her for some reason, even though he was old enough that it seemed she could turn him into dust with one well-placed kick. Just being close to him, she didn't feel so new and shiny anymore. She took a seat as far away from him as possible.

"After I got out of the army," said Vern, waving his mostly empty glass in the air for emphasis, "I fell in with a guy named Booker. He was one of them smart guys, you know, ugly as sin and always reading books, which is how he got his name. We did us some jobs, Booker and me, small stuff, you know, E-Z Marts and such. We was doing all right, nothing spectacular, but old Booker he kept on telling me that the big one was right around the corner. So one day, we're holed up in some motel outside Laredo and he tells me he got me a job that pays hourly. Now I'm not interested in no such job, I got myself some standards after all, but he tells me it ain't the job that matters, it's where the job is. Right across the street from the Laredo National Bank."

He lifted his glass and emptied it.

"How about some more of this bug juice?" he said.

"I told you, I killed the bottle."

"What else you got? Whiskey? Wine? Hell, I'd even take a beer, just to lubricate the bladder, you know what I mean?"

"I don't have anything."

"Why that's...that's...that's un-American. How are we going to peaceably pass the time without anything to drink?"

"Maybe you should head off to a bar," she said with a slight smile, "and find some better company."

"No need for that, missy, we'll figure something out I suppose. There's always the Lysol." He put his glass down on the coffee table and rubbed its rim with his thumb as if he were figuring it out. "So there I was, in Laredo, waking up early in the morning to bus tables in a twenty-four-hour diner. I was a table-bussing fool, I was, and my share of the tips wasn't so bad at that, but all the while I was keeping an eye on the bank. And I got me a bead on who's going in that bank, who's going out, who opens up and when. I tell everything to Booker, and Booker, being the brains, he sets it all up."

Her cell phone started singing a jaunty little tune in the kitchen. Annie jumped up to answer it, but the old man shook his head.

"I think we should let that be," he said.

"It's just the phone," said Annie.

"I know what it is," said the old man as he reached into his jacket and pulled out a gun. "Let it ring and sit back down."

The tune continued.

She sat back down, just like he said, right back down. She wasn't one to obey orders, but suddenly, in the presence of the old man's aggression, she felt strangely hollow. The sight of the gun, along with the still-raw memory of Janet Moss without half her head, had scooped out something inside her. Her spunk was punked by fear. The phone kept singing until the song died with a final burp.

"It's a kidnapping deal, right?" continued the old man, the gun now resting on his thigh, as innocuous as a cobra. "We bust into the manager's house before dawn. I stash the family into a bedroom and keep them there with a gun. Booker, he takes the manager to the bank to open the safe. If it all runs smooth, we make out like bandits. Which is the way it should be, don't you think, since that's what we were?"

"Do you want money?" said Annie, her teeth clenched to stop them from clattering. "Is that why you're here?"

"You got money?"

"Not much."

"But you got something, don't you? Jewels or something. You got to have something. Everybody's got something."

"I have some jewelry. You want me to get it? Please let me."

"In time. But right now we got other fish to fry. Relax yourself, because I'm going to be here awhile. You got a cigarette?"

"Somewhere."

"Light me up, sweetie."

She hopped up with an alacrity that bothered her. There was a pack of cigarettes in a drawer in the kitchen. While there she checked her phone quickly. The call was from Justin. Oh yes, Justin. Just the image of him calling gave her a shot of strength. She thought of grabbing the phone and making a desperate call, but when she craned her neck to check out the living room, the sallow eyes of the old man were tight on her. She took the cigarettes and a pack of matches and brought them back to the living room, lit two, handed one to the old man. He put the stick in his mouth and sucked it greedily before coughing out the smoke.

"Smooth," he said.

The phone started up again, and they watched each other as the ringtone sang and then died.

"Who called before?"

"Just a friend."

"If it really was a friend, she won't be calling no more, or I might get a bit jittery. And you don't want me getting a bit jittery, what with no more alcohol to soothe my nerves. So I was telling you about Laredo and that plan of ours. Son of a bitch, damn if it doesn't go as smooth as the skin on your soft, pretty cheek. The family, they don't make a peep, the vault is stuffed to the gills with payroll, Booker empties it out like he was a vacuum cleaner. A hundred and fifty grand, said the paper. The sweetest score of my life until I gets to the place where we was supposed to meet up at the car, and the car is gone. Booker booked with all the cash, that sly son of a bitch. I should have known never to trust no one what read all the time."

He took another inhale and coughed himself sick. He glanced around halfheartedly for an ashtray before flicking the cigarette toward Annie. She flinched, even though the butt never got near her, landing instead on the carpet, where it smoldered until she put it out with the sole of her shoe.

"It took me three years to track the some-bitch down," said Vern. "Booker had moved out of Texas, changed his name, broke with his friends, was living like a ghost. But even a ghost has a mother. Once I found her, stashed out in California with a new name, it wasn't so hard to find him. She didn't want to say nothing, but cracking her was easy as cracking walnuts. Utah, she told me. A small town out of Provo called Spanish Fork."

"What do you want?" said Annie.

"A girlie like you, what I really want is to screw you till you're blind. How would you like that?"

"I'd rather you shoot me."

He laughed, a wet arrogant laugh. "It ain't necessarily an either-or proposition. In my heyday you might have ended up happy and dead at the same time. Sadly, I'm not up to the screwing part no more. Used to be all my limbs was loose and limber, all but one. Now they's stiff as boards, all but one. No, all I can do now is pass the time until the coast is clear. The hotel I was staying at got a sudden infusion of cop, so I needa hide out a bit before I hightail out of this stinking town. And you and me, we're going to pass the time together."

"A movie would be more entertaining."

"I don't go to the movies. It's no fun having to pee every five minutes, you miss the good stuff. You got any music?"

"I'm not in the mood."

"You care too much about mood, you never get yourself laid. Put on something nice. No reason we can't have usselves a little party while we're waiting."

"What are we waiting for?"

"You're waiting for me to leave and I'm waiting for someone to die. Put on something nice and soft to ease the blood, none of that modern crap that only gives a headache."

Annie stood up from the chair and, with shaking knees, went over to the credenza with the stereo. She went through her CDs and found Miles Davis. Just the kind of noir fusion cool to handle a deadly kind of night. She put the disc on and let the first tense notes of Bill Evans's piano shift through her. When she turned around again, the old man was standing right in front her.

"Want to dance?" said the old man.

"Not on your life," said Annie.

"Aww, go on now." He reached up with his left hand and thumbed her cheek. "No reason Mac should have all the fun."

She backed away until she was up against the credenza. He leaned into her and she felt something sharp on her hip. She looked down. A shiny narrow blade bridged the gap between his hand and her dress. As she stared at it, he twisted his hand slightly so the blade glinted as the point of it dug into her flesh.

"Just put your arms around my neck, sweet Louise, and let an old man grab a sweet whiff of your hair."

He was so close his smell assaulted her with a foul familiarity, the usual old-man-on-the-town getup, Brylcreem and Aqua Velva, along with rotting breath and the not-so-faint whiff of bacteria chewing through the sweat on his parchment skin. There had been nights when she willingly endured just this smell as she allowed some other reeking old man to run his hands all over her body so she could cadge another drink or two. She had thought she was through with all this, somehow Justin had convinced her of that, but it was as if her hidden life were pursuing her. She wasn't through, she would never be through, because she would never deserve to be through. And the prick on her hip was just a reminder of exactly what she deserved instead.

"Usually I only dance with men who buy me enough drinks to get me drunk," she said bitterly.

"I would if I could, sweetheart."

"I know you would," she said, her voice dead. "What do you want?"

"I just want to dance."

She closed her eyes as she rested her elbows on his bony shoulders. He reached around her with his left hand and jerked her body close. She let him take hold of her and felt the bulge of the gun in his jacket press into her side. He placed one bony hand on her butt even as he leaned his unshaven face into her neck. The rasp of his tongue, the scrape of his teeth, the credenza digging into her back, the pinch of the knife in her hip. It would have been too excruciating to bear if she hadn't earned every inch of it.

"You mentioned something about the way things turned out for Justin," she said. "What happened?"

He kissed her neck before pulling away. "You ain't dancing," he said. "You're just standing there."

"That's the way I dance."

"Ohh, now that's shockingly sexy. Look at you, so concerned about that boy's fate." He pulled her close again. "I wonder if Mac knows about you and that son of his."

"I don't care what Mac knows."

"Good for you. Truth is, I don't care much neither." He gave her neck a dry lizard lick before pulling his upper body away. "You taste like high-class tequila," he said. "Sweet vanilla with a tang of salt. I could just eat you alive."

"After you carve me up?"

He laughed as he lifted the knife from her hip and rested the flat of it on her cheek.

"Spanish Fork City," he said, his lips centimeters from her own, his knee grinding her crotch, his left hand rising to grab hold of her hair. "You want to hear?"

"No," she said. She dropped her hands to his chest and tried to push him away, but his grip on her was surprisingly strong. Pushing him away was like trying to push away a corpse. She thought of the bulge in his jacket and slipped her hand beneath the lapel as if she were caressing his chest, but he laughed as he knocked her arm away, even as he pressed the knife harder into her cheek.

"Don't get no ideas," he said in a low growl. "It didn't take nothing to find a screw as ugly as Booker in a town that small.

He had married a widow with three kids and a house, had bought a bookstore, had joined that freaky church out there and become almost respectable. It's bad enough becoming respectable, but doing it with my money, well, some things is beyond forgiving. The son of a bitch spied me coming up the walkway to his shop and pulled a runner out the back. I burned it down and then headed to his little picket fence. Just the kids and the wife in residence, and none of my money. The wife wasn't much to look at, the house was tiny, the noses on them kids was running, but still all of it pissed the hell out of me. So I patted the kids on they's heads and told the wife where I'd be the very next day and then signed off on her face. And after seeing my work, he showed, with a sack of cash. There wasn't but fifteen thousand in the bag. Booker said he could get me more in time, but I didn't want to put him out. So I put him down."

He flipped the knife and ran it down her cheek. It felt hot and slippery sliding down, like it was creating an itch and scratching it all at once.

"See," he said, backing away from her now, the knife held in front of him, "sometimes all it takes is a little signature."

She reached up with the back of her hand and wiped it across her slick cheek. As she did, she could feel her flesh separate, her cheek slip sickeningly apart. When she pulled the back of her hand away, it was smeared thickly with blood.

"When he gets out," said the old man, as he reached into a pocket, pulled out a yellowed handkerchief, and handed it to her, "you tell old Mac not to forget his friend Vern."

"Okay," she said, taking the wretched thing and pressing it to the wound.

"You tell him I'll be waiting."

"Okay."

"That I'll be expecting—"

There was a knock on the door, a loud double rap. Birdie smoothly reached into his jacket and pulled out the gun.

She knew who it was, had no doubt, and her heart leaped, not with hope but with fear. Fear that this old man would do to Justin what he had just done to her. No, it would be worse, the old man would shoot him dead, would shoot him cold, as a further message to Justin's father.

"Keep your mouth shut," he whispered.

"Okay," she said.

"I locked it when I came in. Just let him go away."

Another knock.

"Liquor delivery," called a voice she didn't recognize, an old voice. "I got a liquor delivery for Miss Overmeyer."

"Liquor?" said Vern. "You ordered liquor?"

No, she didn't order liquor, what a ridiculous thing to have ordered. She had her liquor bought for her by old men like this murderous piece of crap. But if she denied it, this Vern might start shooting.

"Oh yes, I did, yes. For a party I'm having next week. I had forgotten."

"Well, answer the door then, why don't you?"

"I'll send him away."

"Don't do something that stupid. Let's have usselves that party now." He waved her toward the door with the gun. "Go on."

She followed his orders, keeping the handkerchief plastered to her face as she went over. Go away, she thought to herself. Go away. Go away. And when she opened the door, that's exactly what she intended to say. Go away. Run away. And then the old man would kill her, but he'd be safe. With each shaking step, she repeated it. Go away. Go away.

When she reached the door, she leaned against it for a moment, unsure of what to do. Go away.

Another knock shook her. "Miss Overmeyer, I have your delivery."

She unlocked the latch and looked behind her. The old man put the gun behind his back and nodded. She opened the door just a crack, saw an old black man in an ugly sport coat at the door, and felt relief overwhelm her. She recognized the old man somehow, wasn't sure how, but it didn't matter, it wasn't Justin. Justin was still safe. She opened the door a little wider and whispered to the old man, "Go away."

And then someone else grabbed her wrist, hard, and yanked her into the hallway as the door closed with a *slam-bang* behind her.

65.

ANOTHER BLOODY MESS

Justin didn't notice the blood right off after he snatched Annie out of the apartment. When the door opened, from his vantage beside Detective Scott, he could see only her wrist, with some strange splatters on it, like she had been cooking tomato sauce. He grabbed at the wrist and pulled her out of the doorway and shoved her unceremoniously to the side as the door slammed shut.

He was standing quite deliberately between her and the door when it opened again and Birdie Grackle stared out at him, something shocked and hard on his face.

"I'm still here, you son of a bitch," said Justin.

Birdie threw out a fist and Justin lifted up his hand to block it before he noticed the stained silvery blade. Something sharp bit into Justin's palm even as he pushed hard against the blow. The old man staggered backward and the door slammed shut again.

Justin jammed his bleeding hand beneath his armpit and stood in front of the door, waiting for it to open again so he could do some damage of his own, when something smashed into his side. As he fell to the floor, he slammed onto something irregular and hard even as he turned and saw that it was Detective Scott's big black shoe that had sent him sprawling.

And then the shots came: one, two, threefour, right through the damn door, pocking holes and splattering splinters.

Detective Scott, from the other side of the doorway, kneeling low with his gun out and his back pressed safely to the wall, stared at Justin like he was too much the fool to even bear, which he absolutely was. That's when Justin turned around to see what he had fallen onto and realized it was Annie. And her face was a bloody mess. And his first thought was that he had done that to her.

"Oh my God, Annie, I'm sorry, I'm sorry."

"About what?"

"Look at you," he said, on his knees now, holding her up and caressing her hair with his bleeding hand because he was too afraid to caress her bloody cheek. "I'm so, so sorry."

"You didn't do it," she said. "He did it. All you did was save me."

"Oh."

"Where did he come from?" she said, gesturing to Scott.

"He had given up trailing me and was trailing you. I spied him outside and dragged him up here."

"My hero."

And then another shot from inside the apartment sent shards of door wood flying.

"Stay down," shouted Detective Scott, and Justin obliged, taking hold of Annie and cradling her in his arms. A door down the hall opened, and Scott turned, showed his badge, and yelled, "Get back inside."

The door closed right up.

"What are we going to do?" said Justin.

"We're doing nothing, son. You're staying right there with the girl. I'm going in."

Scott, still kneeling low, leaned toward the door and banged on it twice.

"Mr. Bickham, this is the police."

No answer.

"Put your gun down, sir, and no one need get hurt."

No answer.

Detective Scott reached a hand over and tried the knob. It turned, and the door opened slightly. He shoved it open and backed away from the entrance.

Nothing.

"This is the police, throw your gun out the door."

No answer.

With his gun in front of him, and remaining low, he swung into the doorway as nimbly as his years and weight would allow. There was no gunfire, no shouting, just an old detective attempting to stand while firecrackers went off in his knees.

Justin started to get up himself, and Scott, without taking his eyes off the interior of the apartment, said, "Where the hell you going?"

"I was just—"

"You were just staying right where you are."

"Yes, I was," said Justin.

"Good," said Scott. Then, without a sideways glance, he headed in to find the son of a bitch.

Justin turned his attention back to Annie. She was still pressing her hand to her cheek, even as blood continued oozing and smears across her forehead and chin were drying into a dull maroon. She looked like a zombie, the loveliest zombie imaginable, a zombie worth getting your brain stem munched on so you could hold hands and trip together through the blighted landscape.

"You came," she said.

"I came."

"I was afraid you would and I was afraid you wouldn't."

"You don't have to be afraid anymore. I'm not going anywhere."

"He cut me."

"A scratch."

"He made me ugly."

"Impossible."

"I'm sorry."

"Don't be, not about anything."

"It's only what I deserve."

"No, you deserve only the best. Instead you're ending with me. But I'll try to take care of you from here on in."

"Okay, I'll let you try."

"It's a promise."

"I believe you, but only because I want to."

He leaned down and kissed her, and even with the fear that had soaked through his pores that night, and the blood, and the pain now from his stabbed hand, he kissed her, and it felt like a sunny day, like the first sunny day since his mother died.

He was staring at her still when Scott lumbered back through the door into the hallway.

"Gone," said Scott.

"How?" said Justin, without looking up.

"Window open, fire escape down. Son of a bitch is going to get away."

"Somehow," said Justin, looking at love's bloodied face, "I don't think so."

66.

RED BULL

"Who killed him?" said Justin's father in a hushed tone at their table in the Graterford Prison visitors' room.

"I don't know," lied Justin, his stitched and bandaged left hand lying heavily on the table.

"Who do the police think it was?"

"They would probably think it was me, since they tried to link me with every other killing that happened in the city in the past few weeks, but I was with that Detective Scott at the time Bickham was murdered, so I'm in the clear. They found his body in a parking lot, his neck snapped like a twig. Bickham apparently had an accomplice, and there is a thought that the accomplice turned on him for the money."

"The money you got from Frank."

"Yes."

"Money well spent, then. You can't say the malicious son of a bitch didn't deserve it."

"No," said Justin. "You can't say that."

"I've been thinking about it, over and over, and I still don't understand."

"Understand what, Dad?"

"What I did to make Bickham hate me so much."

"Hate you?"

"He had to hate me more than life itself to do what he did to me."

"To you?"

"Of course, yes, don't you see? He took every opportunity to ruin my chances of getting out of this hellhole. His hatred of me must have been so overwhelming, it was pathological."

"That's exactly the right word," said Justin.

"First he killed Timmy before Timmy could testify on my behalf. Then he had you beaten and warned to stop trying to help me. Sensing you wouldn't stop, he followed you. And after you found Janet Moss, he brutally killed her. That he tried to kill you and then went after Annie only proves it. A hate like that is like a wild animal. It just stalks and kills. Vernon Bickham was my very own Iago."

To Justin it was a shocking reference, and he savored it for a moment. Justin knew it was about as close to a confession as he would ever get from his father. But if it was a confession, it was purely Freudian, because Justin's father kept on as if he had given away nothing, as if Othello, who had been viciously hated by Iago, had not himself placed the pillow over Desdemona's mouth and smothered her to death.

"Now we must figure out what to do about my case," said Justin's father.

"What does your lawyer say?"

"Sarah? She's quite overcome by all that's happened. This has been more than she bargained for, I expect."

"I have no doubt of that."

"She wants to wait awhile, on everything. She thinks my motion has become hopeless. She is worried that we might only get one bite of the apple and thinks that now is not the time to take it."

"She's probably right."

"I've told her to withdraw my motion."

"Good. I'm glad, Dad. Strategically, I mean."

"Yes, of course. We must hold on to whatever ammunition we have. You keep bringing up the same things, they begin to ignore you, like that Mumia."

"Just like."

"In any event, she wasn't a good enough lawyer to pull it off. Patent law. I'm going to find someone new to help me out."

"Good idea."

"Someone with a criminal background who knows what the hell he's doing. Now tell me about Annie. How is she?"

"Shaken."

"I heard that animal cut her face. How bad is it?"

"Bad."

"It's a shame. She was always such a good-looking woman."

"Yes she was, if you like that sort of look."

"I feel for her."

"I'll make sure she knows."

"Take care of her for me, will you?"

"If you want me to. For you, I mean."

"She should give up on me, she should start dating someone her own age. It's time. She needs a life."

"I'll tell her."

Justin's father glanced around at the cruel banality of the visiting room. "I think if I stay too much longer, I'm going to go insane."

"Go?"

"You don't know what it's like to be caged for something you didn't do."

"You'd be surprised."

"But one thing keeps me going."

"Red Bull?"

"You, Justin."

"Me?"

"You cannot know how much it means to me to see how hard you worked for my freedom. Just the thought of it keeps me going."

"I'm glad, Dad."

"And look at us, after all these years of silence, talking now like the best of friends. The irony that you've become my new champion is almost too precious for words."

"It leaves me speechless too."

"See, the thing is, Justin, of all the people outside these walls, the only one I can count on not to forget about me is you."

"You're right about that."

"We're going to find the one responsible, you and me, together. Father and son. We're going to find who it was who killed your mother and we're going to make him pay for everything."

"That's exactly what I intend to do."

"While I'm in here, stewing, he's out there, Justin, eating shrimp and fucking lithe young girls."

"And all without inviting me. The nerve."

"But we're going to find him."

"The one-armed man."

"Exactly. You and me, Justin."

"Okay, Dad."

"Working together for a common cause."

"Like in a storybook."

"Yes."

"It's a funny thing about those storybooks, how the deepest wishes of the hero so often come true."

"Let's hope, let's only hope. I love you, son."

"I love you, too," said Justin, and when he said it the most peculiar thing happened. Despite everything he had been through, despite everything he now knew with utter certainty, when he said those four words, something thick and heavy lodged in his heart.

It was the truth, what he said, he did love his father, despite everything, maybe because of everything. And at the end of the visit, when they were allowed once more to touch, he gave his father a hug, and it was shockingly genuine. And there were tears, at least the tears of a son.

Something had come over him, some peace that was truer than anything he had tried to find in his battered old *Book of the Dead* or during his meditative purges. The emotion hadn't flowed out of him, like in those sessions in his upstairs room, it had flowed in, gushed in, and the gushing changed everything. He didn't feel hate anymore, or despondency, or despair, he didn't feel overwhelmed by his worthlessness or his guilt. What he felt instead was love. Love had flowed in and brought light to the darkness and resurrected his soul like the precious words of the book, only it was a gift given to the living, not the dead.

67.

GIN RIKKI

Mia Dalton was outside Graterford Prison with Detective Scott, waiting. The sun was shining, the birds were singing, the asphalt was hot, the air smelled of the burned oil of outdated cars. Mia sat on the hood of the unmarked police vehicle that had brought them to the lot, parked right next to a Harley-Davidson motorcycle with a cobalt-blue gas tank. Scott leaned against the side of the car, his reading glasses low on his nose, a folded newspaper in one hand and a pencil in the other.

"E-M-E-D-E-R," said Scott.

"Emetic?" said Mia.

"There's no C," he said, tapping the paper with the tip of his pencil.

"If you had any real brains, you'd be doing the crossword."

"If I had any real brains, I'd have your job."

"What's taking him so long?" she said.

"You can't rush family," said Scott. "I still don't know why, if you wanted to talk to the boy, we had to charge up here when they told us he was in for a visit. Wouldn't it be easier if you just called?"

"I've been calling. He doesn't answer and doesn't return my calls. I've even knocked on his door. Nothing."

"Maybe he doesn't want to talk to you."

"If I waited until someone wanted to talk to me, Detective, I'd be talking to the walls."

"There's a message in that, Mia." He tapped the paper in his hand. "Redeem."

"It took you long enough."

"I'm getting old."

"Not too old. I'm pulling you from your Missing Persons gig."

"No you're not."

"It's done already. You're working for me."

"But I don't want to work for you."

"Tell it to the commissioner."

"You know I will."

"You're too good to fade away at a desk. And I got your pay grade bumped up too, which will bump up your final pension."

"It's no fair you trying to bribe me."

"Is it working?"

"I didn't say it wasn't working, I just said it wasn't fair."

"You start tomorrow."

Mia Dalton had hoped it would allow her to sleep more soundly at night, learning the truth about Mackenzie Chase. When Detective Scott had called with the whole story about Vernon Bickham and his playacting as Birdie Grackle, she had felt a keen sense of relief. It didn't answer all the questions about the murder of Eleanor Chase, and it didn't yet solve the connection between the murder of Timmy Flynn and Rebecca Staim, a mystery that might never get solved, but it certainly made it clear that Mackenzie Chase was exactly where he should remain for the rest of his miserable life. Whatever she had done at that trial five years ago, she had done the exact right thing.

And yet still she tossed and turned with insomnious vigor

through the night as Rikki slept heavily and peacefully beside her.

Which meant her uncertainty was not focused on any one case, on any one defendant, but on the span of her career, or on the whole of her life. She somehow had slipped from a delicious certainty into an existential crisis without noticing. When the hell did that happen? And what would she do about it?

Detective Scott clucked his tongue and nodded toward a thin, bladelike figure leaving the prison's visitor entrance. In the calm, steady gait, Mia recognized Justin Chase.

When Justin reached Mia, still sitting on the hood of the car, he smiled at her. A smile was something she hadn't ever seen on Justin Chase before. He looked good in it.

"You guys still following me?" said Justin.

"We wanted to see how you were getting on," said Scott.

Justin lifted his bandaged hand. "I'm trying to meditate the pain away."

"And how's that working out?"

"Not well. The blade went right through."

"My advice is pills," said Scott, "and lots of them."

"How's your father?" said Mia.

"Angry, bewildered, more determined than ever to get out. But I do have to tell you, Ms. Dalton, in some strange way, my relationship with my father has never been richer. I guess I have you to thank."

"So you're still going to work to get him out of jail?"

Justin turned his gaze to the gray surface of the prison. "Ever since my mom died, I've been looking for something meaningful to do with my life."

"Bartending, wasn't it?" said Scott.

"For a while it sufficed, I suppose. But I've finally found something I want to dedicate my life to."

"Your father?" said Mia.

"That's right," said Justin. He turned to stare straight into Mia's eyes. "And making sure he never, ever steps foot out of that foul building."

Detective Scott laughed at that. "Now you're learning."

"You know, Justin," said Mia, "the best place to keep tabs on your father's case would be in the DA's office."

"I'm not a lawyer anymore."

"You were never a lawyer," said Mia. "But your legal education is impeccable and you have something that most of our lawyers don't have: you know what it is to be a victim. We spend much of our time dealing with the victims and their families, yet it's all too easy to forget what they're going through as we fight to build our cases. You never would."

"I don't know what to say."

"Don't say anything. Think about it. Take the bar exam, buy a suit, cut your hair."

"Cut my hair?"

"Do all that and I promise there will be a job waiting for you at the office."

"How's that Overmeyer girl?" said Scott.

"Not bad considering she's got a face full of stitches," said Justin.

"Give her my regards."

"Come over for tea sometime, Detective, and you can give them yourself."

"I just might."

Justin smiled before hopping onto the seat of his motorcycle and taking hold of his helmet, ready to ride like a hero into the setting sun.

"One last thing, Justin," said Mia. "I thought you should know that it was highly unlikely that your mother was having an affair with Austin Moss."

Justin turned his head and stared at her.

"When Austin Moss died, he was living with a man named Nick. They were more than roommates. His struggle was to be truthful to himself, and apparently, according to this Nick, your mother was a great help to him. Which sort of puts those letters of your mother in a different context. I thought you should know."

"Thank you," said Justin, his voice as cold and as distant as his gaze as he tried to figure it out. Without anything further, he put on his helmet, kicked the bike alive, pulled out of the lot.

"He didn't take it like I expected," said Mia.

"He's got to process it. He's got a load to process still."

"Like living with his father's mistress. Is that Oedipus laughing in the distance?"

"Life is full of surprises if you're open to them," said Scott.

"Well, here's one for you. From now on you're working full-time on the Rebecca Staim murder. Find the killer, and I don't care how far you have to go to do it. And then maybe when our Justin Chase finally shows up in his suit and buzz cut, you can work with him."

"That I'll look forward to," said Scott. "So, Mia, what surprises are in store for you?"

"Who knows," said Mia, thinking on it for a bit. Something about the way Justin Chase always seemed ready to reevaluate everything in his life made her want to do the same. "Maybe I'll run for my boss's job."

"Heaven help us all."

"Or maybe I'll just get married." Married? What the hell? Talk about surprises. Mia didn't know where that came from, and didn't even know what Rikki would think about it, but just saying it made her feel suddenly lighter, like she was rising from some depth. "Yeah, married. It's about time, don't you think?"

"I don't get paid to think," said Scott. "That's why I do the Jumble."

68.

SIDECAR

Derek holds on tight as Sidecar gallops around the circle. He does not have to grip so tight when Sidecar walks slowly. He can just sit like a king atop the saddle. But when Sidecar gallops and his head bobs and the saddle rises and falls like on a wild amusement ride and the great huffs of breath spurt from his huge nostrils, then Derek has to squeeze with his legs and lean forward while his fists grab the horse's mane. And he feels his own heartbeat, and the horse's heartbeat, and the horse's hooves thundering beneath him, and that is the best feeling ever, like he is rising right out of himself, becoming some new kind of creature formed of horse and man.

It is thrilling and frightening both, and he owes it all to Cody. Cody is the only one of his special friends who kept all his promises. Vern or Tree or Rodney or even Sammy D, none of them were as good to him as Cody. He can count on Cody to take care of the details, count on Cody to take care of him. And Cody, true to his word, has gotten Derek a horse. Derek loves Cody with a warmth that wraps around his heart like a snake, which is why what is happening makes Derek so sad.

When Derek pulls back on the leather straps, Sidecar slows out of the gallop, and bit by bit Derek feels himself fall from the sky and slip comfortably back into himself. At the edge of the circle stands Graham, in his tight black pants and funny cap.

Graham is tall and lean, and he smiles at Derek with his big horse smile and Derek smiles back. He likes Graham, not as much as he likes Cody, but Graham knows horses and Graham has a hardness in him that is comforting.

Sidecar makes his way around the circle to Graham, and Graham grabs the horse by the leather strap and rubs his nose. "You riding well, young Derek," says Graham.

"We went fast."

"I saw. You was making time, good time. You should be racing."

"I am too big to race."

"I can maybe set something up." Graham scratches the horse's jaw, and Sidecar whinnies. "He's not the fastest, but he's sturdy, and when he gets going, there's no stopping him. Sort of like you. I was just thinking—"

Graham turns his head and quiets as a red car rumbles down the dirt road to the riding circle, spitting dust behind it. Cody's car.

When Cody clambers out of the car, he is wearing dress pants with a shirt untucked, and his nose and eyes are red. From the powder, Derek knows. Cody is always nervous now, he drinks too much, even during the day, and he has begun to stuff the powder up his nose like Rodney. It is strange and sad how all Derek's friends seem to fall apart over time.

"You look good up there," says Cody with a slight slur.

"Yes, he does," said Graham.

"Do us a favor and leave us a bit, Graham," says Cody. "We have business to discuss."

"No problem, boss," says Graham, looking up and giving Derek a wink before he ambles off.

"We have a job," says Cody, looking back down the now-dusty road. "There's a girl who is missing."

"I did not do it," says Derek.

"I know that. There's a man in the neighborhood, and the parents are certain he knows where she is. But the police can't do anything about it. The girl's parents want us to ask him some questions."

"But he'll see me. It won't be tidy."

"We'll make sure to tidy it up after we ask." Cody turns so Derek can see his eyes, red and crazy. "He's a bad man, Derek. He's done it before. He needs to be stopped."

It is funny how Cody always tries to make sense of it for Derek, even though Derek does not care. It is as if Cody is really trying to make sense of it for Cody. Graham would not have to do that, Graham wouldn't care either. Graham is more like Derek.

"Okay," says Derek.

"And then I think we have to go."

"Go?"

"Leave Louisville. I got word that someone was down here asking questions about me. Some old cop from Philadelphia."

"Looking for me?"

"I think just me for now, but either way it's time."

"What about Sidecar?"

"We can't take him with us."

"But he is mine."

"I'll get you a new horse when we settle down again."

"I do not want—"

"We don't have a choice."

Derek stares at Cody for a moment, notices the redness of his nose, the fear in his eyes, the way he staggers slightly as he reaches up to take hold of the leather around Sidecar's jaw.

What Derek sees is what he so often sees in Cody now, the weakness pouring off him. Cody is not the same man anymore who taught him that trick with the penny and the quarter.

"Okay," says Derek.

"We just do this job and then we go."

"Okay. Let go of Sidecar."

"Sure," says Cody, letting go of the leather as Derek jiggles the straps.

Sidecar starts walking again around the circle with Derek sitting high in the saddle like a king. Derek turns and looks at Cody, who is rubbing his nose. He turns back and sees Graham smiling at him in the distance, encouraging him to go faster. Graham was born in Louisville, and he knows everyone, the rich with their horses, the workers in the paddocks, the bookies who take bets, and the gamblers who make them. And Graham is going to set up a race for him. More than anything, Derek wants to race, to see how fast he can go in a straight line, to merge into the horse and never have to stop.

Derek kicks Sidecar with his heels, and the horse begins to gallop again. Derek holds on tight as the saddle bounces and the hooves clop beneath him. His heart begins to race, merging with the heartbeat of his horse, and he feels again like he is something more, like he has burst through his limitations and is flying high, a force of nature, rising above the rest of the world, melting like a ray of light into the cloudless sky itself.

He is really going to miss Cody.

ACKNOWLEDGMENTS

I remember first seeing *The Tibetan Book of the Dead* in my father's bedroom. This was in the Age of Aquarius, when a psychology professor named Richard Alpert changed his name to Ram Dass and, along with his colleague Timothy Leary, touted *The Tibetan Book of the Dead* as a manual for life. My father was as straight an arrow as ever flew, but he was always willing to check out new ideas, and thus the book. I'm not sure what he made of it, but he did end up practicing his own form of meditation. Like Justin Chase, my father was always a seeker, who taught me to be more interested in the questions than the answers.

My father grew up in the Logan section of Philadelphia, two streets over from the home of David Goodis, a Philadelphia novelist who died in 1967. Though Goodis and my father grew up in the same neighborhood and are now buried in the same cemetery, I can't imagine two so different lives. While my father was living the suburban dream, Goodis followed a starker yet more literary path, writing *Dark Passage*, from which the Bogart movie was made, and then *Down There*, which was turned into the Truffaut film *Shoot the Piano Player*. After an unsuccessful marriage, and a failed stint in Hollywood, his career dimmed, his drinking picked up, and his writing turned ever darker. He ended his life holed up in his parents' house, banging away one seamy pulp noir masterpiece after another, books like *Night Squad* and the brutal and brilliant *Cassidy's Girl*. His memory has been kept alive by a coterie of admirers such as Lou Boxer, Deen Kogen, and Duane Swierczynski. Partly through their efforts, a Library of America volume of five of his noir novels has been released, edited by Robert Polito.

I bring up Goodis because one of his stories, "Professional Man," published in 1953, about an elevator operator who is also a hit man, was an inspiration for this novel; give it a read and you'll find the connection. Goodis's hero in that story, Freddy Lamb, would have been a hell of a bartender if he wasn't so busy killing. I haven't bartended since college and needed a barkeep's help with the book, not just with mixing the drinks but with the whole feel of what it's like behind the wood these days. Chris Myers, known online as Chris The Bartender, kindly agreed to read the manuscript and correct my many mistakes. He also gave me many terrific suggestions that found their way into the book. If you are of the noble class of barkeeps and something in the book feels right, thank Chris. And if anything feels dead wrong, blame my editor.

I am incredibly grateful to be part of Thomas & Mercer, working with Daphne Durham, Alan Turkus, Alison Dasho, Jacque Ben-Zekry, and the rest of the team. My work couldn't be in better hands. I want to thank the indefatigable David Downing, whose clear-eyed readings kept this book as tight as a spring. Wendy Sherman, my agent, has been incredibly supportive and loyal as my career moves in ever-shifting directions. And finally, as always, I offer unbounded love and gratitude to my children, Nora, Jack, and Michael, and to my wife, Pam Ellen. They are my joy and inspiration.

ABOUT THE AUTHOR

William Lashner is the *New York Times*–bestselling creator of Victor Carl, who has been praised by *Booklist* as one of mystery's "most compelling, most morally ambiguous characters." His crime novels include *Blood and Bone, A Killer's Kiss, Marked Man, Fatal Flaw, Hostile Witness,* and *The Accounting.* His novel *Kockroach,* published under the name Tyler Knox, was a *New York Times Book Review* Editors' Choice selection. Lashner is a former prosecutor with the Department of Justice and a graduate of the Iowa Writers' Workshop; his work has sold worldwide and been translated into more than a dozen languages.

COMING IN 2014

THE RETURN OF VICTOR CARL

You know what a bagman is. He's the scurvy errand boy for some fat-faced pol. A dark, malevolent figure in a shady fedora and long leather jacket, the bagman lugs his satchel full of black cash and dirty tricks through the city night, and when he whispers in your ear you shiver because he holds the shiv of his boss's clout at your throat.

I was a bareheaded lawyer, a credentialed member of the bar, lank and weedy and as threatening as a chipmunk; I was nothing like I imagined a bagman to be. Yet somehow I found myself running errands for a power-mad congressman and carrying a valise filled with illicit cash through the city streets. What had I become? You tell me.

But with bag in hand, was I wrong to believe I was finally heading toward the heights? Was I wrong to hope the raw game of politics could shower me with the riches I so richly deserved? Was I wrong to expect I'd be the barracuda in the cesspool?

Evidently.

BAGMEN

a Victor Carl novel by
William Lashner